From **TANSTAAFL Press**:

CorpGov Chronicle novels by Tom Gondolfi
An Eighty Percent Solution – CorpGov Chronicles: Book One
In a world where corporations suborn governments as a part of good business practice and unregistered humans can be killed without penalty, Tony Sammis, a midlevel corporate functionary, finds himself unwittingly a pawn in a guerilla war between a powerful cabal of business leaders and an elusive but deadly underground movement. His final solution to the biological terror unleashed mirrors Tony's own twisted sense of justice.

Thinking Outside the Box – CorpGov Chronicles: Book Two
Winning one war doesn't seem to be enough. Tony Sammis and the Green Action Militia are once again thrust into the center of a conflict that will change the lives of everyone in the solar system. This time they are allies with the fledgling CorpGov and even the United States government against the ravages of the corrupt Metropolitan Police Force. The GAM and their allies are fighting a losing war with few soldiers and even fewer weapons. Behind the scenes, a humble and unsuspected power block lurks with its own axe to grind.

Self-interest, romance, freedom, and a lust for power are stirred together in this chaotic soup of tension, intrigue, assassination, and war.

Also by Tom Gondolfi
Toy Wars
Flung to a remote world, a semi-sentient group of robotic mining factories arrive with their programming hashed. They can only create animated toys instead of normal mining and fighting machines. One of these factories, pushed to the edge of extinction by the fratricidal conflict, attempts a desperate gamble. Infusing one of its toys with the power of sentience begins the quest of a 2-meter tall, purple teddy bear and his pink, polka-dotted elephant companion. They must cross an alien world to find and enlist the aid of mortal enemies to end the genocide before Toy Wars claims their family—all while asking the immortal question, "Why am I?"

By Bruce Graw
Demon Holiday
Torval, Demon Third Class, Layer Four Hundred Twelve of the Eighth Circle of Hell, has been in the business of chastising sinners longer than he can remember. Delivering punishment is the only job he's ever known—the only job he's ever wanted. After Torval witnesses something unexpected, his demonic Overseer demands that he take time off to resolve this personal crisis. And so Torval, the demon, finds himself sent on vacation...to Earth, the proving ground of souls!

Demon Ascendant
Torval, Demon Third Class, Layer Four Hundred Twelve of the Eighth Circle of Hell, on *vacation* to Earth has managed to find another demon, has dated an angel and inadvertently explored some of the sins of humankind: greed, gluttony and lust. Through all this his biggest struggle involves deciding if he wants his holiday to end or to continue forever.

The Gremlin of Morningside Heights

Book Two of *The Fey of New York City*

Bruce H. Graw

TANSTAAFL PRESS

TANSTAAFL Press
891 PH 10
Castle Rock, WA 98611

Visit us at www.TANSTAAFLPress.com

The Gremlin of Morningside Heights

First printing—TANSTAAFL Press
Copyright © 2021 by Bruce Graw
Cover art: James O'Reilly – Orb Art Studio - www.orbartstudio.com

Printed in the USA
ISBN: 978-1-938124-65-5

Book layout by Hydra House Books

PART ONE

~ *Morningside Tunnel* ~

Morningside Tunnel – Sithlac's Tower

For the first time in his life, Sithlac found himself humming. Gremlins, as a rule, don't normally hum or whistle, or produce any sound that could be considered the least bit musical. When gathered into groups, they sometimes chant in time with drumbeats, or raise their voices with each other to drown out their rivals, but only in the broadest definition could this be considered anything akin to music.

Nonetheless, Sithlac hummed softly to himself as he rubbed some untarnish-oil onto his latest find, an open-ended silver cylinder about as long as his spindly forearm. Not the greatest loot he'd ever discovered, not by any means, but it should be worth at least two wood-squares at the market. He didn't really need them, of course, unless he wanted to add a fifth level to his home—a spiraling tower of metal rods, shiny discs and layered wooden stairs, all supported by an interlocking grid of fasteners and bolts collected over a lifetime of exploring the Outside. For that kind of upgrade, he'd need a great many wood-squares, just for the framework itself. Then reinforce-rods for support, and a flat-plane to rest upon...fasten-clamps and joiner-hooks to hold it all together...

He blinked and lowered his head slightly. *Add another layer...?* Such an idea hadn't occurred to him for quite some time. He started to shake it off, and yet...*why not?*

The thought wouldn't go away. He paused his humming for a moment, idly regarding the shiny treasure in his hands. He could see himself reflected in the flat edge he'd just finished polishing. A typical, average gremlin face stared back at him: a froglike visage sporting a wide, toothless mouth and two oversized, bulbous eyes that could move independently of each other. Two small flaps covered the almost invisible nostrils, and tiny cup-like appendages formed the ears. The head merged straight into his rotund body without any visible need of a neck. Although he appeared squat and overweight, his scrawny-looking limbs could easily support him on long journeys, and he could climb walls and jump great distances with ease.

So could most gremlins, of course. Sithlac had never considered himself anything special or unusual. True, as a hunter, he regularly undertook forays outside his Tunnel home, but many others did the same. After returning from his last mating, several seasons past, he thought himself content. Four levels to his home felt perfectly adequate, and he hadn't really thought of upgrading for at least as long, and probably longer. He hadn't seriously considered the possibility, until now.

Each gremlin's dwelling looked radically different from the next. With space limited by the Tunnel's shadowy confines, a gremlin received only a small allotment of actual groundspace on which to build. Thus, using whatever building materials they could scavenge, each raised his dwelling ever upward, toward the distant, dripping ceiling no tower had ever safely reached. The taller the structure, the more likely its collapse—the ultimate disaster for any gremlin, for his precious possessions would swiftly vanish into the hands of his greedy fellows, forcing him to start over with only the few items he could drag back to his territory. Theft in one's home was all but unknown—a gremlin's personal dwelling-space was inviolate—but any object that fell loose of its own accord was fair game.

The taller the structure—and thus the more treasures owned—the greater the status in gremlin society. Sithlac's four levels marked him as someone of noteworthy skill, but by no means the greatest. He could count ten five-level structures visible from his own pinnacle, with many more out of sight beyond the pale lamp-glow shining up from the commons. A single tower six levels high spiraled up just on the edge of his vision, one of only three to achieve such heights, but even these spectacular arrays of shiny loot paled in comparison to the majestic eight-story spire owned by Tirchoth the Grand, undisputed leader of the Morningside Tunnel.

Sithlac had studied Tirchoth's amazing handiwork on many occasions—what gremlin hadn't? A long brown rod, made of flexi-strong not-metal from the world of Men, skewered the center of the Grand Tower, rising almost to the ceiling itself. Tirchoth had chosen his groundspace well, directly beneath a steady water-drip, which slid down the rod all the way to the voluminous tin cup forming his personal cistern. Amazingly, the rod itself sported built-in loops of metal at regular intervals, providing a perfect location to anchor each of the tower's seven other levels. Where Tirchoth found such a thing, and how he managed to bring it back here, was the stuff of legend. When asked about it, he would only cackle and inflate his baggy throat in satisfaction.

Sithlac had nothing quite so spectacular going for him, but he'd done his work well, at least in his own estimation. During his earliest forays Outside, he discovered a number of notched wood-blocks that formed the foundation of his humble tower and also served to claim his borders quite nicely. He'd also been lucky enough to find an unusually curved metal implement with an enlarged, bowl-like tip, which now jutted partway out the side of his second level, diverting dripping water from above into a small, ground-level bucket sealed with melted candle wax. This provided a consistent, self-replenishing water supply, thus ensuring he never had to waste precious trinkets buying hydration at the market.

His tower's third and fourth levels stood firmly upon metal frames bound with tightly twisted bolts checked daily to ensure their stability. Upon these levels he hung his most prized possessions: a few shiny treasures taken from the land of Men. The way these precious objects glittered and gleamed never failed to impress the females during the spring festival, and ever since installing his fourth platform, Sithlac hadn't failed to find a mate.

Thus, he hadn't considered upgrading to a fifth level much at all, at least not until now. The idea definitely had merits, though. Several impressive shinies from his collection remained hidden out of sight, lacking a place to properly display them. Plus, his pride and joy, the interlocking double golden chain he found just a half-moonrise ago, would look spectacular wrapped around a fifth level overhead. His status would increase dramatically, not just from the height, but also by displaying this impressive treasure. What manner of mate might he attract this season, should he complete the structure by spring...?

Sithlac started humming again, returning to his polishing with renewed vigor. In order to complete a new level in time, he knew he'd have to improve his tower's stability first, and that required plenty of wood-blocks from the market. Thus, his next few forays wouldn't be for shinies, but tradeables he'd have no other use for. On market-day, the goblins and spriggans would bring their wares to the Tunnel foyer, and the frenzied swapping would begin. Sithlac knew he'd have to be there early, with as much trade-bait as he could carry, if he wanted to claim two hefty building-blocks for himself. With this metal cylinder, and a few other simple items not worthy of display, he felt certain he'd succeed.

A shuffling sound interrupted his work. Sithlac swiveled his left eye toward the new arrival, who stood silhouetted against the candle-glow outside. The hunter's right eye remained fixed on his metallic possession as he buffed its surface clean, a job he knew so well he could accomplish it almost without even trying. "What business does the visitor have, Sithlac wonders?" he said by way of greeting.

"Heard a strange noise, Bongcor did, and came to see," answered the gremlin outside, his bulbous eyes swiveling this way and that as he peered intently around the first level of Sithlac's home. "An odd treasure, to be sure, that makes such a curious sound."

"Not a treasure, oh no," answered Sithlac, inflating his throat-sac ever so slightly. "'Twas only I, echoing a song heard in my journeys this past night."

"A song, you say?" inquired Bongcor curiously. Though gremlins didn't make music, they knew of it well enough from their travels. More often than not, Men created the odd noises, often with strange implements or devices, and they were also known occasionally to sing, for what purpose only they knew. "The songs of Men are like nothing such," the visitor went on. "Different this was, oh yes, of that, I am sure. A story awaits—this I can tell most surely."

Sithlac sighed and set down his prize, which happened to be the cap from a mechanical pencil, though he had no way of knowing that. Bongcor, his nearest neighbor down the moonward slope, had only two levels to his home and seemed uninterested in building more. A poor hunter (if he even hunted at all), Bongcor owned very few shinies, most of them collected from other gremlins who let their possessions get away from them—a scavenger among scavengers, in other words. Nonetheless, despite his lowly status as a lesser gremlin—not the lowest rung of society, but very near the bottom—Bongcor had a way of learning things that other gremlins couldn't, and could be easily coaxed into revealing such secrets. If he had any cleverness about him, Bongcor would demand some sort of payment, but he hadn't quite figured that out yet. He did, however, often require a tale or two to loosen his tongue a bit.

"Very well, Sithlac will weave a story for you, most certainly I will," he told his eager neighbor. "Enter and sit, but first, I would know what news you heard. On the hunt I have been for most of this night, and the night before besides."

Bongcor vaulted over the low entrance-wall in a single easy leap. The visitor's fat, toadlike body looked even more obese than his host's, yet even he could jump quite easily. A gremlin's wiry leg muscles, partially concealed by the creature's thick-skinned flanks, could spring open like rubber bands snapping taut, allowing for prodigious jumps.

Should Bongcor choose to stand fully erect, which would be very uncomfortable indeed, he might just barely reach six inches in height, but most of the time he stayed hunched over, rocking slowly back and forth as he walked. Like others of his station, he wore only a simple dusty rag, wrapped about him like a shawl. His hands and feet, both bare, sported flaps of skin covering an array of tiny suckers for use in climbing. In a social setting, such as this one, he kept the flaps closed, holding up four thin fingers in greeting before wiggling them about, the gremlin way of saying "Thanks for letting me come inside your home."

Sithlac replied with a similar wave. With the formalities thus taken care of, Bongcor sat noisily down on one of the rusty bottle caps that served as sitting-stools. His left eye swung about to survey the rest of the messy, junk-filled interior, while the right focused on the shiny cylinder in Sithlac's hand. "A successful hunt it was, I see," he offered diplomatically. "So smooth and pristine, and from the looks of things, not too heavy besides."

"Of little value it is," replied Sithlac, holding up the object and turning it so his guest could see the opening in one end, thus revealing the cylinder's hollow nature. "Not worthy of display, but trade-bait most surely. Perhaps a spriggan will make a cap of it."

Bongcor snorted in laughter, obviously enjoying the amusing thought of one of the bouncy little creatures trying to keep such a small, thin lid upon its head. "Or a container, to carry tiny things," suggested the visiting gremlin. "Goblins are digging somewhere always, or so the stories say. It seems a waste for such a spotless gleamer, but I suppose it could move dirt quite well."

"Yes, I will hint at such," replied Sithlac, not bothering to mention that he'd already considered that, and several other options besides. He knew that Bongcor looked up to him, and Sithlac couldn't help but feel a bit flattered by the attention, but he really didn't consider his neighbor anything like a real friend. Gremlins understood the concept of friendship well enough, but only in the vaguest sense of the word—levels of tolerance and nothing more. In Bongcor's case, Sithlac usually tolerated his neighbor's presence only insofar as he provided a consistent source of information about the goings-on elsewhere in the Tunnel. Still, the overeager visitor did at least come by to chat quite often, and Sithlac had of late found himself unconsciously appreciating the companionship. He'd always told himself he didn't need such things, for like most gremlins he'd always preferred solitude, but that didn't seem to be the case quite so much anymore.

"So, to the news it is, then," Bongcor went on, his independently rotating eyes finally ceasing their wandering to focus fully on his host. "The Moon shone long past sundown, so the night-magic harvest proved quite worthy. Rations are to be increased, it seems."

"Already have I claimed mine, oh yes," explained Sithlac, although of course his supply had been substantially reduced thanks to his activities the previous evening. He figured he'd get to that particular story in short order, but not until he heard more from his guest.

Bongcor went on without delay. "Good, good, then this you knew already. The commons chatter spoke of another gremlin's failure to return from hunting. Know you of Erixus? He dwells beyond the waterfall, opposite the Great Tower."

"I have heard the name, of course," said Sithlac patiently. Of course he had—not quite a thousand gremlins lived in the Morningside Tunnel, after all. At some point in his life, he'd had occasion to meet each one, at one time or another. Only the rarest individual couldn't say the same, though some of those less bright might not remember every such encounter.

"It seems Erixus has not returned," went on Bongcor. "Three nights past he set forth, according to the exit logs. Still he remains Outside. He may as yet return, but few hunts last so long—you know as well as I his likely fate."

Sithlac nodded, pulling his eyes back into his head about halfway, a look that expressed his apprehension. Of late, once or twice with every turning of the Moon, a gremlin hunter would go missing. Such things had always happened in the past, but only rarely. Since last winter, though, instances had increased many times over. Rumor had it one of the Fallen had moved into the great structure of Man beyond the Tunnel, hunting gremlins and other Fey without remorse or pity. So far, no one had seen this terrible beast and returned to tell about it so the truth could not be known, but no one as yet could offer another explanation that made any sense.

Sithlac had taken extra care on his hunts ever since this pattern started to appear, as had they all. Unlike some of his fellows, he didn't carry a spear, but he did have a sharpened sliver of metal concealed within his weathered tunic. Furthermore, he made sure to collect his allotted ration of night-magic straightaway, just in case he encountered one of the Fallen, or some other unexpected danger. Of course, if such a monstrosity actually did confront him, he doubted he'd be able to harm it with a spell. The Fallen were supposedly resistant to magic or at the very least able to avoid such efforts with ease.

He almost let his eyes completely pull back into their sockets, thinking about such frightful things. With a quick snap of his head, Sithlac put those worries out of his mind. "Let us speak no more of that," he suggested firmly. "My forays are no longer quite so long, and I jump at every sound as it is."

"Yes, yes, of course," his guest went on. "Truly do I envy you, staying out so late, and collecting such fine rewards. Not even half a half-night could I last Outside, I fear."

"You could, if you so chose," pointed out Sithlac with a forceful nod. "The Men drop new treasures daily, and rarely search for them. Easy wealth and status await, and perhaps a mate besides, if you did well enough."

Bongcor's head bobbed up and down in agreement. "Often have I thought of attracting a mate," he remarked wistfully. "The seasons come and go, and I watch my neighbors hop away to the birthing-place, while I remain behind with only the infertile for company."

"Ambition is what you lack, not skill," offered Sithlac encouragingly. "Build well, you do, oh yes, and treasures aplenty you could find, were you but to try."

Bongcor sighed and deflated noticeably. "It is not ambition, but rather courage that I lack. The thought of meeting one of the Fallen is more than I can bear. I know not how you stand it, O great neighbor mine. I bow in awe before you."

He lowered his head and scraped his forearms across the floor. Sithlac allowed his thick throat to puff up with pride about halfway, then let the air noisily escape. "Worthy am I not of such unbecoming praise," he insisted, wondering if Bongcor really meant what he said, or was just buttering him up so as to coax a good story out of him. *Perhaps I can find out with but a simple query*, the gremlin host considered, a strange idea occurring to him just then. Without any heed to the ramifications, he put forth his offer immediately. "And you could become a good hunter, of this I am sure. Come with me on my next hunt, after nightfall just past market-day, and I will teach you things I know."

Bongcor's eyes grew wide and popped outward, all but straining against the rough skin of his narrow, angular face. "This you mean most surely?" he asked breathlessly.

"Always hunted alone, I have," replied Sithlac, "but perhaps two sets of eyes are best in these dangerous times, say I. What say you?"

He half expected Bongcor to refuse outright, or scramble for some excuse, but the normally timid gremlin surprised him with a quick response. "Agree do I, most heartily!" he blubbered with unconcealed excitement. "Three nights hence, oh yes! A spear have I prepared, made of strongest metal, that I dared not use alone. Sharpen it I will, and ready shall I be!"

"Good, good, your presence will be most welcome," agreed Sithlac, thinking perhaps that Bongcor might have his uses after all. Sithlac had little in the way of fighting experience, but his guest bore several scars, most likely from scrabbling with other lower-class gremlins for scraps of food or fallen treasures. In a true battle, he would likely prove his worth, if only he didn't break and run at the first sign of danger.

"Prepare myself I will, oh yes," went on Bongcor, "but now, I would hear your tale. What befell you this night just past, that you would make such odd sounds come from deep within your throat?"

"Listen, then," began Sithlac, settling back on his haunches as he spoke. "Two nights ago, I set forth to hunt, exiting through the Moonrise Gate. Once within the vast Tower of Men, I searched in dark places with little success, until the Moon at long last set. Weary, I sought out an old rat's nest well known from earlier forays. Having had no luck thus far, I slept the day away, jumping at each sound uttered by the Men outside the walls."

"Never have I roamed as much as you," admitted Bongcor, whose eyes had retracted halfway into his head by now. He shuffled his feet nervously, scratching at the dusty wooden floor. "Did you not fear to be found by Men?"

"Not in so secure a place, oh no," Sithlac explained. "No portals entered there, and well-sealed it was, indeed. There are many such places within Man's towers, places I will show you on our journey—hiding-holes where no Man searches, and few other dangers lurk."

"If you say it is safe, believe you I will," Bongcor agreed nervously. "Always returned to the Tunnel you have, thus far at least."

"That I have, most clearly. Now, with the setting of the Sun, the Men do not sleep readily. Restless they are, continuing to move about long after moonrise, and often well past half-night. A hunter learns to know their sounds, that one might freely move when they cease at last. Thus, upon the nearest Man's final settling, I crawled forth in silence, intent on exploring once more, only to hear a most amazing sound—a song unlike any other I have ever heard."

"And it is this that you repeat, this strange vibrating buzz from well within your throat?"

"I could not repeat it, oh no," Sithlac admitted. "Not like she who sang it. The music was not like that produced by Men. It drew with it strands of magic, but not just the power of the night—the very light of day itself echoed within those haunting strains, oh yes!"

"Day-magic, in the dark of night?" wondered Bongcor. "How is such a thing possible? What manner of creature could do such a thing? Not a Fallen, surely!"

"If a Fallen it had been, no chance would I have had," explained Sithlac. "The tones drew me forth like a wondrous jewel, glittering in the dark. A shiny treasure I could not take, oh no, but only lock within my memory. The humming you hear from me is but a pale shadow of its faded glory. I can still hear it, deep within my mind, oh yes. It echoes there, and I feel...I feel..."

"What?" insisted Bongcor eagerly. "Whatever do you feel?"

Sithlac blinked and rubbed his head with his spindly fingers. "I cannot explain. Defies words, it does, oh yes, oh yes. But so drawn to that music was I, that I approached its source without fear. A source that made no sense, there in that place of Men."

Bongcor leaned forward, clearly hanging on his host's every word. "What source, oh what, pray tell...?"

Sithlac's eyes drew downward, as though he knew his next words would not be believed. "A faerie it was," he answered slowly. "A female, barely half my size, high in the realm of Man! Who would think to see such a thing?"

Bongcor's eyes moved back and forth and he twitched several times, struggling to make sense of what he'd just heard. "No faerie would ever dwell within Man's walls!" he insisted. "Not of her own free will, oh no!"

"Broken was her wing," Sithlac went on. "Captured, well and true, she was. A prisoner, forlornly singing in the night, while her captor slept."

"Taking our night-magic!" gasped Bongcor. "Surely you slew her, did you not? Such an affront must not go unchallenged, oh no!"

Sithlac shook his head. "I should have, oh yes, this I know, and freely tell," admitted Sithlac with a sigh, "but no harm was she, wounded and a prisoner; and besides, had I done this deed, the Man would surely question the cause. You know the Rule, I trust?"

Bongcor cringed and nodded slowly. Seventh of the Twelve Rules of the Hunter: *Never give a Man a reason.* "Yes, I see the dilemma, oh yes. Slay her, and her captor knows not how it came to pass. Wonder and search, he would, and call to question all he knows. A wise decision, indeed."

"So it would seem, but my tale is not yet done. She could speak the darkling-tongue, though not well, not well at all; yet nonetheless she chose to treat with me. She asked for guidance, but of course, I offered none. She asked for aid in escaping her captor, and that I could not do, per the Seventh Rule. Yet when she asked a simple favor, I found I could not refuse. Her song captivated me beyond all words. She sang, and I carried her from a high place to the ground, in a way that satisfied the Rules. She gave the song, and I gave aid, and my share of night-magic besides, and regret it not at all."

Bongcor bobbed his head as he listened to his host's carefully chosen words. "Judge the bargain I cannot, without the song itself, oh no," he remarked, "but a bargain it was, most surely, and well met indeed. What of the theft of magic?"

"And to that it was ended," stated Sithlac, "for in desperation only did she take what is rightfully ours. Free to hide on her own, by being on the ground, she had no further need of it. The morning's light would be free to take, and that is all she needs."

"Ah, yes, of course, and a wiser bargain still. I worry, though, that faerie-song might've snared you in some foul tangle."

"Thought of that, oh yes, of course I did," insisted Sithlac. "This very morn, upon my return, I endured a purge. No spells are upon me now, not even of my own making."

"Good, good," agreed Bongcor. "I need not worry, then. Thus ends your tale, it seems?"

"Very nearly so. Upon our parting, I left the faerie upon the ground and resumed the hunt, though I feared I would have no luck this trip. Still, the song remained, lifting my spirits in a way no night-magic ever has. Explain it I cannot, but the more I hummed it to myself, the more determined I became. In the end I found this shiny gleamer, and several smaller treasures besides. Were it not for the song, quit in frustration long before, I would, of this I am quite sure."

"I wish I could hear this song myself, oh yes," said Bongcor hopefully, "and perhaps I will meet this faerie, upon our coming journey."

"I would think her gone by now, or perished," Sithlac replied with a sad shake of his head. "And now my tale is ended, oh yes. Away with you, I must insist, as I have more to shine, and many preparations to make, ere the market comes."

Bongcor's head weaved from side to side as he stood and then, in a single easy hop, he leaped over the inner wall, back into the narrow alley that led downhill to the commons. "A fantastic tale it was," he offered, bowing once again to his host by way of thanks. "Not so worried about visiting the Outside am I, in the company of one so wise. Farewell."

As his neighbor hopped away, Sithlac inclined his head ever so slightly. How strange that he should make such an unexpected offer of partnership—and to Bongcor, of all people! While it wasn't unprecedented for gremlins to team up on a hunt, such things were rare, and usually only happened for very specific reasons, upon approval from the Council. A few nights ago, such a thought would never have occurred to him, but now, the idea of having a traveling companion felt strangely appealing. Two pairs of eyes would have better chances of spotting danger approaching, and Bongcor's spear would be most welcome should they come under attack.

Yes, a good idea indeed, Sithlac told himself, turning his attention back to his work. Rolling the metal cylinder carefully in his hands, he went back to polishing his newfound treasure, humming to himself all the while.

Morningside Tunnel
– Sithlac's Tower

Two nights later, on the evening after market-day, Sithlac busily readied himself for his upcoming hunt in the same manner as he did on every other such occasion, trying not to concern himself too much with the radical idea that this time he wouldn't be alone. With practiced care, the determined gremlin moved back and forth through his tower, checking the fasteners to make sure nothing came loose, and ensuring none of his treasures could fall out if some errant water-drip should disturb them. With security assured, he then set about to checking them all again, just for safety's sake, and followed up by triple-checking after that.

Gremlins take great pride in their adherence to the Twelve Rules set forth long ago by their ancestors—the basic laws that govern their society. Of course, some Tunnels had slightly different variations on a few of the Rules, and occasionally a couple of extra ones were thrown in for good measure, but in general, staying true to the Rules kept everyone out of trouble. Greatest of them all, the First Rule stated that no gremlin could ever harm or steal from one another. Thus, Sithlac could safely leave his home for days at a time, without a need for doors or locks, and know that when he returned, his treasures would remain exactly as he had left them—as long as nothing accidentally fell out of an upper floor to land on neutral ground, of course. He always took great care to ensure nothing of the sort ever happened.

After his fourth or fifth pass through his tower—he lost count, actually—Sithlac nodded to himself and stepped into the alley. He knew everything would be safe, but he always worried nonetheless. Even after so many hunts, and so many nights spent Outside, he never really felt comfortable leaving his home. Everything he owned, everything he'd spent his life collecting, could be found within this rickety-looking (but surprisingly stable) structure. If something happened to it while he was gone, he'd have to start all over.

Sithlac wasn't old, having seen a mere twenty winters, with over half his life still before him. He'd started his collection on his tenth birthday, as was the custom, and earned his plot of groundspace by his thirteenth—a fairly young age to start construction, yet not a record by any means. Still, that meant seven years of hard work, long nights out hunting, and shrewd trading in the markets to earn the building-blocks for his spacious four-level tower. If he had to start from scratch…well, that's something he didn't really like to think about.

After a bit more pacing, he finally convinced himself that everything would be all right. With just a few extra backward glances, he forced his rotund body down the alley and turned the corner, whereupon he found Bongcor already waiting, spear clutched in two quivering hands. The lesser gremlin wore a ragged strip of cloth with a small bag fastened about his thick neck by a wide wooden strap. His eyes, pulled back almost all the way into his body, shifted to and fro, and he bobbed and weaved on his stubby legs in obvious nervousness.

Sithlac acknowledged him with a coughing grunt that served to say "hello" in darkling-speech. Bongcor returned the sound and leaned upon his spear, running a thin finger along its shiny haft. "Ready to go am I," he announced, "and worried, oh yes, yet curious about where our journey leads this night."

Sithlac grinned, which on a gremlin's froglike face made his head appear to split almost in half. "As you have informed me repeatedly, at every chance you get," he pointed out. "Never have I hunted and known my path erefore, so our destination is a mystery even to me. Through the Moonrise Gate we shall proceed, and from there, wherever the sounds and smells take us."

"Not so far, I hope," answered Bongcor, still bobbing up and down nervously. "But a single night is all I could possibly stand in the great Outside. If daylight comes, and trapped out there we are—"

"Then we shall shelter and find rest," interrupted Sithlac, firmly fixing both eyes on the would-be hunter at his side. "I know many hiding-holes, and if the Fallen lurk without, they would not move within the light, any more than we. Sleep we will, and rest, and come the night set forth once more for home. All will be well, this I know, oh yes."

"Such courage warms me through and through," Bongcor said quietly. "My awe of you increases still, and so my terror fades."

"Good, good," Sithlac replied, once more wondering if his companion spoke truly, or had some ulterior motive in mind. Compliments like that didn't come often in a society ruled by greed and envy, after all. "Then let us away, before your fears return. Once Outside, all will settle still, of this I am sure. Come, and speak no more of such."

With that Sithlac started briskly walking down the alleyway, but not without a parting glance back toward his tower, no longer quite as impressive-looking with all the shinies pulled inside. Bongcor fell in behind him, moving with a kind of half-walking, half-hopping gait, for, being slight of build compared to his fellow traveler, he had to move somewhat quicker to keep up.

In due course they came to the commons, not very crowded at this early hour, just before sunset in the world Outside. Perhaps a dozen gremlins shuffled about, or lounged upon broken chunks of wood no longer suitable for use in construction. A few hovered near one or another of the food-tents, trading small baubles for a meal or drink. In lieu of coin, gremlins barter small items and simple foodstuffs with tiny beads or bits of metal otherwise worthless for any other purpose.

Without a word, Sithlac moved over to the nearest tent and held up two spindly fingers, pointing them at a tall box bearing a telltale white-and-black label. The gremlin foodsmith, dressed in a long robe spattered with colorful streaks of green and yellow ichor, grunted in assent and withdrew two squirming termite grubs from the container. Sithlac then produced a bent staple from his backpack, which the seller accepted without comment. With several quick motions, almost too fast for the eye to see, he decapitated the grubs and cleaned away the claws and hairs. The staple vanished into the payment-box, and the carver cleaned his knife in silence as Sithlac and Bongcor carried their breakfast out into the commons.

They found a suitably sized wood-block and sat down nearby, not bothering to clean the surface before setting down their meals. Bongcor immediately started fishing in his bag for a bauble to use as payment, but Sithlac waved him off with a quick gesture.

"Pay for my own, I should," the smaller gremlin said in confusion.

His companion shook his head and bowed ever so slightly. "No, this is mine to buy. I have many such trinkets, oh yes. Two meals for each, but eat alone I do, most of the time. To buy for two is a rare occasion."

"Yet still I can pay," insisted Bongcor. "Smaller trinkets did I bring, just for this and other trades."

"Then save them you should, for need them you might. Range to goblin-lands we could, if the hunt goes well, and such trinkets they do love."

"Surely not so far," Bongcor replied worriedly, withdrawing his hands from his bag and taking a bite out of the grub. He proceeded to continue complaining about the possibility of traveling what would be at least two nights' journey away and then, once satisfied that such a thing would most likely not come to pass, he went back to fretting about the other dangers that might come up Outside.

Sithlac spent most of the meal chewing slowly on his grub and wondering whatever possessed him to buy lunch for his companion. Somehow it seemed right to do so, but he didn't know why. He'd never done such a thing before, and hadn't intended to when he arrived, but for some reason he wanted to do it. In fact, he liked it so much that he started humming to himself, and when they finally finished eating, he kept right on humming all the way to the Tunnel gate.

Morningside Tunnel –
Moonrise Sentry Post

The sentry, an older gremlin named Norbac, fixed his eyes narrowly upon the two travelers, naturally suspicious of the unusual pairing. After a few moments of careful study, Norbac ultimately concluded this wasn't some kind of disrespectful prank, at which point his head slowly wiggled from side to side curiously. As if to proclaim his befuddlement, both eyeballs switched targets repeatedly as the head changed angles. A gremlin's bulbous eyes can focus independently on different objects, affording unrestricted peripheral vision, among other things. In this case, the sentry now regarded the two supplicants with undisguised confusion.

"Heard me quite clearly, he did," commented Sithlac with a barely concealed snicker. "Yet unwilling to believe, he is."

"So it would seem," agreed Bongcor, not bothering to hide his amusement. If nothing else, the comical look on the gate-guard's face helped to relieve his tension. "So difficult it is to believe that two would go together, then?"

The sentry's head finally straightened as the little creature snapped itself back to the task at hand. The elderly gremlin shifted uncomfortably on his wooden chair, rubbing his spindly fingers on a leg that flexed unnaturally to one side: an old injury, perhaps incurred while hunting, that left Norbac suited only to tasks requiring little movement. Sithlac idly noted the sentry's swizzle-stick cane leaning against the wall nearby. At least with that he could make his way to and from his post, though the journey probably still took quite a while. Without at least some mobility, he'd have no way to earn trinkets for trade, and thus would eventually starve.

"Forgive me you must, oh yes," said Norbac after a long delay. "Three winters here have I, never to see such a pairing, oh no. Some trick it must be, or joke being played upon a poor old gremlin, yes? Or perhaps a debt being repaid, it is."

"None of these, oh no," stated Sithlac succinctly. "A free joining of two hunters, nothing more. To venture Outside together, we will, and share the bounty as equals."

Norbac's eyes swapped back and forth between the two gremlins a couple more times before he shook his head and turned one toward the parchment in his lap. The other eye remained fixed upon Sithlac while he dipped a small sliver of wood into a cup filled with dark liquid. "This one I know," he remarked, making a couple of marks on the paper with his improvised pen, "for he hunts often, perhaps more than most. Yet his companion I know not. What name have you, new supplicant?"

Sithlac's companion shifted uneasily, perhaps a bit dismayed to have his lack of experience so brusquely acknowledged. "Bongcor am I," he explained nervously. "I hunt most rarely, it is true, and the Sunset Gate I do prefer. My first visit here, it is, most truly."

Sithlac watched his fellow traveler with one eye, trying to discern if Bongcor was lying about using the other gate, or if he'd actually ever hunted at all. It had occurred to Sithlac yesterday, after his market visit, while he slowly trudged his way back to his home with two huge wood-blocks in tow, that perhaps Bongcor had never actually been on a hunt. That would explain his eagerness to accompany his fellow gremlin Outside, a place he feared to visit alone. However, Sithlac doubted his companion would ever admit such a thing, and eventually decided it didn't matter much at all, for the truth would be clearly visible as soon as they left the gate. If Bongcor had never been Outside, he'd be completely overwhelmed upon his first visit, just as Sithlac had on his first tentative foray as a youth.

He could still remember that first trip quite clearly. He'd been alone, of course, and set forth through the gate with nervousness and fear, trembling uncontrollably all the while. The evening sentry offered nothing in the way of support, in fact all but laughing at his fellow gremlin's difficulties. Upon reaching the exit, Sithlac emerged into a vast chamber, so big and empty he felt immediately lost and afraid. It took all his strength of will not to run squealing back into the safety of the Tunnel; yet, the thought of the sentry's cruel laughter at his heels stayed his hand. Even so, it was quite some time before he forced himself to move one way or another.

He almost wished he had a companion that day, but such a thing was unheard of. Young gremlins are left to fend for themselves, almost from the moment they're old enough to walk. Gremlins have little in the way of a family life, after all. Once mated, their parents travel far from their home tunnel to a distant birthing-place, where the father protects the mother until the child arrives. He then hunts for the "family" (if it could truly be called such) for a time, usually most of the spring and well into summer, until the baby is old enough to be left on its own for short periods. The father then bids both mother and child farewell and returns to the safety of his tower, while the mother raises the young gremlin in secret places no male ever visits. If the child is strong enough and survives, he is brought back to the Tunnel after a few winters and left to fend for himself. If still fertile, the mother then seeks a new mate; otherwise, she joins the infertile females in whatever tasks she can, performing menial work to earn trinkets for food and other necessities. On rare occasions, such a female might endear herself to a wealthy male, tending his home in a form of permanent employment, but such attachments rarely form any sort of emotional bond. Gremlin society affords little room for such things.

Alone in the great tunnel without any sort of school or tutoring, young gremlins must carve out a life for themselves in whatever way they can, without breaking any of the Twelve Rules or any other edicts set forth by their older fellows. If strong and clever enough, and perhaps with a little bit of luck, they might survive and prosper; otherwise, they either starve or—if so desperate they turn to crime—are permanently banished to the terrors of Outside. What they might do then, no one knew, and Sithlac hoped he never had to find out.

He considered himself fortunate enough to be a successful hunter, ranking somewhere in the top fifty or so gremlins in the Morningside Tunnel. If he'd given in to his fears and fled the Outside on his first visit, he might well have turned out much like Bongcor, who clearly had skill—he could gather information like no other, of course, and the spear he'd made would serve as a fine weapon. Only his timidity stood in the way of his success. For that reason, Sithlac looked upon his companion with a kind of measured pity. *I will help him*, he thought, humming softly to himself, not really knowing why, but imagining it as a challenge—one he felt determined to complete.

Sithlac watched Norbac with his right eye as the sentry jotted down notes on the parchment before him. Somehow, the little lines and scratches recorded the comings and goings of gremlins through the nearby gate, but in a way that had nothing to do with magic. Sithlac understood the concept of writing well enough, but had no idea how it worked, or how to read the markings. Nonetheless, other gremlins who did could gaze upon the paper and understand the message there, even in the complete absence of magic. A fascinating concept, to be sure, but beyond Sithlac's comprehension. He only knew that whenever he exited or returned, the sentry would make those little marks as a permanent record of his travels.

Still, this time he seemed to put a lot more etchings into the paper than usual. Sithlac waited patiently until finally Norbac fixed his gaze upon him once again. "It matters not to me," he remarked with obvious curiosity, "but why is it, I wonder, that two hunters work in unison? Others may ask, and an answer have I not."

"It is as I said," explained Sithlac calmly. "Travel together, we will, and share between us the bounty."

"That answers not at all," Norbac complained. "A reason you must surely have, oh yes, and this I would know."

Bongcor's eyes moved back and forth nervously, sinking slightly into his head. The sentry didn't fail to notice his apprehension, snapping first one eye and then the other upon him. "Fearful times these are," admitted the lesser gremlin, in response to this visual prompting. "Rumors swirl within, of the Fallen lurking without. Together we shall hunt, for greater safety."

Norbac nodded slightly and moved one eye back to his paper, where he resumed writing. "Explains for you, it does," he remarked, flipping the other eye back to Sithlac, "but not this one, oh no. What reason could you have, skillful hunter, for journeying with such a one?"

"Stronger he is than I," explained Sithlac. "You see the weapon that he bears. Keep watch he will, and defend, while I am free to hunt."

Norbac wrote some more. "A bargain you have made," he noted. "Makes sense, it does, oh yes, but such things are almost never done. Successful you should be, I do suggest. Leave your trinkets here and begone, if that is what you will."

"As you say," agreed Sithlac, reaching for his bag, but before he could pay the sentry's fee, Bongcor dropped two plastic beads into the waiting box nearby. Sinking slightly toward the ground, his left eye met Sithlac's right, which widened in surprise.

"Food was bought by you, it was," he pointed out meekly. "The exit price is mine to pay. Only right and fair it is."

Sithlac nodded, and his face widened into a smile. He found himself humming once more as they left the tunnel behind, a confused sentry sadly shaking his head as they departed.

Morningside Tunnel
– Moonrise Gate

The Moonrise Gate wasn't a physical barrier, but rather a sort of shadowy portal to the Outside, crafted long ago by powerful works of what the faeries called *dinathi-kai,* the night-magic. Unlike most such creations, the shadow-gates didn't fade over time, but remained in place, sustained by the turning of the Moon. There were many such gates, scattered here and there about the world, each of which led to tunnels of various sizes—caves, of a sort, that extended outside of what Men might think of as "reality."

If the old tales were to be believed, the tunnels had always been there, in one form or another—the gates simply permitted access to them, as long as one knew the way. Yet the cost of keeping the gates working was high, and the supply of night-magic limited, so each gremlin was allowed only a small ration daily. To exceed one's allotment fell under the same restriction as stealing from one's fellows—an unforgivable crime.

Thus, Sithlac had to guard his supply most carefully. He'd already claimed his ration for the day, plus what little he'd managed to save from the night before, but the conjuration he intended to use now would take nearly half of his stored power. Nonetheless, he had little choice, lest he unwittingly violate the Seventh Rule. While he rarely moved when Men were about, he might step into view of one by mistake, and under no circumstances could he allow his true form to become known.

Thus he paused, right at the gate's edge, watching Bongcor study the exit with both curiosity and trepidation. After leaving the sentry post, the path ahead stretched out into a long, sweeping corridor, one that slowly contracted toward a distant point. The closer the travelers moved toward that dark cavity at the end of the passageway, the farther it seemed to get. Now, with their destination only a few body-lengths away, the illusion became quite pronounced. The air itself seemed to stretch and curve toward that hovering black spot before them, which looked very much like a hungry maw sucking everything into itself.

Bongcor bobbed back and forth, his eyes alternating between the exit and his companion. He looked quite worried and nervous. Sithlac no longer had any doubt that this was in truth Bongcor's first hunt. He clearly had never seen a gate-point before—at least, not since his mother brought him here in infancy—and didn't know what to make of it.

It occurred to Sithlac then that his companion might not actually have a Shaping prepared, or even know how to use one. If so, that would mean the end of the hunt before it even began, for Sithlac couldn't possibly spare the magic for a second conjuring without all but draining his own reserves. He was about to ask when his fellow gremlin spoke first.

"Admit this to you I must," the cowering creature said in a low, frightened voice. "Never before have I been Outside."

"Yes, I did so surmise," answered Sithlac succinctly.

"Surprised, you are not," the lesser gremlin twittered nervously. "So obvious a failure am I, then?"

"If a failure you are," replied Sithlac firmly, "then here you would not be. Press on, and earn your courage you shall. Now come, it matters not what came before. Have you a Shaping?"

"Yes, oh yes," answered Bongcor, with an odd mixture of agitation and eagerness. "Planned and prepared for this long and hard, I have, yet never could begin. Eleven Shapings do I know. Upon which one would you have me call?"

Sithlac managed to keep his eyes steady, not betraying his surprise. Eleven was a considerable number to have in one's repertoire—he himself had only five, and had never heard of any gremlin with more than seven. For the most part he usually stuck with a rat or mouse, though sometimes, if his travels required frequent climbing, he might employ the lizard. The pigeon and squirrel had their uses as well, but he chose them only rarely. To have studied so much, and learned so many different forms, showed Bongcor clearly had a sharp and able mind. All at once Sithlac felt much less worried about his would-be apprentice's ability to function Outside.

"You have a rat disguise, you must, so choose that one. A Man might recoil or strike at us in fear, but when we flee, as well we must, he will not be so likely to chase us down."

Bongcor nodded in assent and called upon the night-magic, weaving the Shaping with surprising skill. He'd definitely practiced until he knew the form by heart, at least. Sithlac joined in with his own magic and within a few minutes, the spells were finished. Both gremlins sat back upon their haunches, rolling slightly back and forth as they recovered from the effort. Expending so much night-magic wasn't particularly difficult, but it did take its toll.

Although outwardly neither appeared different, both could now see the faintly shimmering distortion about themselves, confirming that the conjurations had taken hold. The Shaping wouldn't fool another of the Fey, but if a Man looked upon the two of them, he would see only a pair of ordinary rats.

At length Sithlac stood and shook himself a couple of times, making sure he'd fully recovered from the casting. He carefully reached out before himself and swirled his fingers about, keeping an eye on his companion, who watched intently. As his spindly limbs approached the black spot ahead, they seemed to stretch, becoming impossibly thin, as though the exit-hole had pulled them in somehow. With a quick motion, Sithlac yanked his arm back and wiggled his fingertips around, flexing and unfolding the sucker-flaps to show no harm had been done.

"Heard of the exit-gate, I have," admitted Bongcor, getting to his feet. "All of us have, of this I am sure, but I thought never to see it for myself."

"Harmless it is," Sithlac told him. "A faint pull you will feel, but harm you it will not, so long as you continue through. To stop and linger upon the locus is to court disaster."

"This, too, I do know quite well, oh yes," replied Bongcor nervously.

"Then gather your courage, and step forth," Sithlac insisted. "Follow behind you I will, of this you can be sure."

His companion twitched and shifted about worriedly. "I would follow you, oh yes, I would prefer, for I fear what lies ahead more than that which lies behind."

Sithlac inclined his head ever so slightly. "So be it, but know this: return to fetch you I will not, neither will I tarry." He placed an arm upon his companion's quivering shoulder, which steadied partially, but not completely. Then he spoke with a firm, gentle voice he'd never used before, or even known he possessed. "Now come, neighbor mine, for your new life awaits."

So saying, Sithlac stepped forward toward the exit. As he walked briskly ahead, his body appeared to stretch and contract into that mysterious black spot. For an instant he seemed to fall into it, the rest of him sucked away into that impossibly tiny hole, and then he was gone.

Columbia University – Adams Hall – 8th Floor Commons

For about fifteen seconds, Sithlac considered the very real possibility that Bongcor would chicken out, but then at last the exit wavered as the lesser gremlin pushed his way through. First his two arms arrived, extending out from thin filaments to form into fingertips, the suckered layers fully extended, as if seeking something to grab onto. Sithlac backed away as the rest of his companion slid into view, both eyes tightly shut and pulled all the way into his head. As he stepped forth, he blindly waved about, a comical sight that made Sithlac chuckle loudly.

"You may cease your waving, for arrived you have," he announced after a moment wherein he barely managed not to break down into open laughter. "Look, and see the greater world."

Bongcor's eyes slowly opened and withdrew from their sockets. The two gremlins stood on the floor of a vast chamber filled with massive, unidentifiable structures. To their left, a wall extended outward, into the shadowy darkness, toward a huge, barely visible wooden contraption rising high overhead. To the right, a monstrous green tower extended just as high, covered in some kind of fuzzy, thickly woven material. Nearby, a black rectangular object protruded from the wall, terminating in a thick line that snaked its way upward out of sight. Ahead, the view extended into shadow as far as the two gremlins could see, revealing a chamber larger than any open space Bongcor had ever seen or even imagined could exist.

The awed gremlin took all of this in without a word, his eyes darting this way and that, fixing on different objects and details before zipping on to the next. Here and there he would also glance toward Sithlac, and again back toward the black spot that marked the tunnel entrance, as if to prove that both were, in fact, still there. To his credit, though, the rookie hunter didn't attempt to flee, or even beg for reassurances from his fellow.

"It is frightening, oh yes," Sithlac remarked at length. "Remember my first visit I do clearly, as you most surely will forevermore. Yet the

Men are not about, and thus, there is no danger."

"This is a Man-place," Bongcor noted worriedly. "What if they were here, lurking about upon our arrival? What if they had seen us?"

"Then we could not have exited," explained Sithlac patiently. "The gate would block our passage were it so, for it, too, must obey the Rules."

"Yes, of course it must. Forgive me, for this I did not recall. Too long has it been since such things were explained to me. But what if a Man comes now?"

"Then hide we would," said Sithlac simply. "Now come, and let the learning begin."

He led his companion behind the massive reclining chair that occupied most of the room's corner, showing him how to slip underneath it, and once there, how he could move upward and disappear into the wood-slabs above. With this done, he then demonstrated the same technique with regard to a long sofa and several other plush chairs that occupied a great deal of the expansive chamber. To the little hunters, these ordinary pieces of human furniture towered overhead like enormous upholstered monoliths, each one taller than the greatest towers ever built by any gremlin. As he stood beneath them, Bongcor looked up with eyes pressed deep within his head, unable to stifle a shudder at the sight.

"The Men will come here sometimes," explained Sithlac, "even late into the night. They will focus their attention upon that great box upon the wall, which in such times will glow and flash with strange, unnatural images. Man-magic, it is, and not for us, but draw their attention it will. Yet even so, do not be tempted to move from your hiding-hole. The gate will not open while the Men are about, and should they spot you, no escape will there be."

"Do you suppose," asked Bongcor worriedly, "that the missing hunters met just such a fate?"

"Possible for one or two," came the answer, "but so many, it is not so likely. I know those hunters well, by name as well as deeds, and such mistakes they were unlikely to make. Yet even so, the ways of Man are strange and ever-changing. Thus, we must be vigilant."

"I will endeavor to fulfill my role," said Bongcor sternly. "Not so fearful am I, not with such as you to guide me."

"You are new and inexperienced," answered Sithlac, "but this night I consider such things an asset to our cause, oh yes. In your naivete, you may note some detail that always before have I taken for granted. Thus, ask questions, as many as you like, unless I raise my hands like this, in which case fall silent you must, for something lurks about. Remain quiet and still, above all things, until I signal otherwise."

Bongcor agreed at once, and they moved along, continuing their circuit of the room, which actually served as a common area in Adams Hall, a dormitory at Columbia University in New York City. Had the gremlins understood the concept of weekends, they would've known that students tended to occupy such areas more often on Friday and Saturday evenings, and to a lesser extent Sundays, but rarely during the week, such as now. Thus, the halls were mostly empty, although the sounds of Men could still be heard echoing here and there, from rooms and stairways deeper in the building. With each such noise Bongcor would stiffen and cast his eyes about nervously, but Sithlac merely pressed on until he reached one of the distant walls. There, he took up a position just beneath one of the gigantic reclining chairs and came to a halt.

"Into the open passages we must not go," explained the veteran hunter. "Even deep into the night, the Men will sometimes come, and they would see us most surely."

"Then where can we go?" inquired Bongcor. "All exits from this place are as this one, are they not?"

"For Men they are, but not for us," Sithlac went on. "We shall use a hunter's hole, like this one here."

With a pair of curving fingers, he reached out into what, to most, would look like empty air. A gremlin, however, if he focused both eyes just so, could spot the faint shimmering, like moonlight filtering through the lightest fog. With a few quick syllables, and a slight expenditure of night-magic, Sithlac took hold of the edge and lifted up and sideways, as though pushing aside a curtain. A dark hole in the air awaited beyond.

"Step through into safety," said the more experienced hunter. "The hole will not wait long."

Bongcor didn't object this time, or say anything at all, though his eyes did retreat somewhat into his head. He walked gingerly forward, into the opening, and stepped right through the wall itself, emerging into a cavity beyond. All was darkness, save the window-like opening into the room he'd just left, so he huddled there, emitting a faint moan, until Sithlac stepped into the area alongside him. His fellow gremlin let his arm drop, and the hole closed, leaving both explorers in pitch blackness.

Sithlac reached into his tunic and withdrew a metal stick with a rounded tip. A few more words of magic caused the end to light up in a faint, pale glow. Now surrounded by the glow-rod's faint but welcome illumination, Bongcor relaxed slightly as he found himself protected by walls on both sides. A narrow corridor extended in either direction between the high barriers of flaking drywall, supported by wooden slabs high above. Several large chunks of debris blocked his view either way, casting the area beyond into shadows thick with dust and cobwebs.

"Hunter's holes," explained Sithlac, "are the best way to move about in Man's domain. See them he cannot, nor can he reach us here. Yet quiet we must be, oh yes, for he can hear us still."

"And this is where you hunt?" inquired Bongcor, taking a few cautious steps. His feet, protected by the Shaping, left little rat-shaped prints in the dust below.

"Hunting within Man's walls is fruitless now," said Sithlac patiently, for he'd told his companion to ask as many questions as he wanted. "No shinies remain loose for us to claim. See some metal you might, but remove it you cannot. Only that which is forgotten can be taken, not any object with a purpose Man may know."

"I know the Ritual of Assayance by heart, oh yes," Bongcor explained. "Always I did dream of this, and plan, but never could I bring myself to go."

He sank about halfway toward the ground, and lowered his eyes deferentially.

Sithlac blinked and hummed softly to himself. He felt something, then, that he'd never really felt before, or even known he had the capability to feel; yet, if asked to explain it, he would have no words.

"Great hunter-neighbor," whispered Bongcor after a moment, "why is it you do this thing? Why bring me here to hunt? The tale you told the sentry served us well, but there was little truth about it. You and I both know I am of no value to you Outside, and there is nothing owed, or to be gained, by what you do for me this night."

"Wondered this myself I have," answered Sithlac at length. "It pleases me, and that is all, it seems. It seems strange and wrong to you, and, I would suspect, to any other of our kind, of this I know quite well, and yet, it is the truth of things."

"And again you make that humming noise," pointed out Bongcor. "The faerie-song may yet have a hold over you."

"The sound is pleasing as well, and that is all," Sithlac went on. "There is no spell behind it, this I know most surely."

"But acted strangely have you, oh yes, ever since you heard that music."

"If so, it is only because I have learned to like new things. This breaks no Rule of which I am aware. If you believe it wrong, return home you can, or hunt on your own you may. Free to go, you are. I ask no payment for anything you have seen or done this night. But if such is to be your choice, you must make it now, before we venture further."

Bongcor's eyes twitched and shifted about. He could see the faint shimmering of the hunter's hole nearby, and could find his way home if he wanted, yet he made no attempt to leave. "Stay with you I would," he went on, "and I ask no change of you. Still, upon our return, we may find our joint venture questioned."

"Yes, of course, but to that, we will keep to the tale we told the sentry. Now come, if you would follow, and stay close. There are many corridors in this place of Man, and lost you will become, of this I am sure. Yet if you listen, deep within, you will find you always know the way."

With that, Sithlac shuffled off through the space between the walls, and Bongcor fell in behind him, watching and learning as best he could.

Adams Hall – The Hub

The journey proceeded slowly. The two gremlins spent the better part of an hour sneaking quietly along inside the walls, moving between sections one after the other. They climbed over chunks of fallen debris, wriggled their way through narrow holes in wooden support beams, and meandered between clumps of cables tied together with shiny, interlocking white strings, occasionally pausing to clear off cobwebs and shake the dust from their round bodies. In quiet voices, Bongcor asked questions about the things he saw and felt, while Sithlac explained their surroundings as best he could. They had yet to actually do any real hunting, however.

As they moved along, strange mechanical sounds grew steadily louder ahead of them, causing Bongcor to grow more and more nervous. Of this Sithlac offered no explanation, except to say that the place ahead was called "the Hub," and represented the center of the great Man-tower in which they lived.

Finally, they came to a wall festooned with wires and cables, snaking their way up and down through gaps in the floor. A faint vibration could be felt on every surface. Sithlac reached out a hand and indicated a twisted mass of lines heading upward a short distance before they curved into an open gap. "Follow this we shall, and there the Hub awaits," he told his companion. "This is something I cannot well describe, but see it for yourself you must. Frightening it will be, oh yes, but dangerous it is not, of this I can attest."

"I am ready," replied Bongcor nervously, following along as Sithlac climbed nimbly up the twisted cables. The lesser gremlin pulled himself up, took two steps forward, and stopped in his tracks, his eyes extending out of his head as far as they possibly could. Then he stood there for the better part of a full minute, taking in the sight.

A great chasm stood before him, extending deep down as far as he could see, a gleaming metallic shaft unlike anything he'd ever imagined. Above, the same walls rose high into the sky, all clad in shiny metal and twisted wires. A great machine, gleaming and glinting in the glow of several artificial lights, hovered in the air, suspended by thick cables. The whole place smelled of oil and ozone.

Then, as Bongcor looked on in amazement, the entire central pylon began to move. Wheels turned, metal clanked, and the whole structure lifted upward, the cables pulling it somehow toward the distant ceiling far above. A second, smaller metal object slid past, going down at the same speed as the main part moved up. After a few moments, both came to a halt, and the sound of Man-voices echoed down from somewhere far above. The great structure bounced and shifted ever so slightly and then moved downward once again. The smaller piece of metal reversed its course as well, and both passed each other, somehow not quite touching, and the great machine rumbled down, down, down, until it became just a tiny square at the bottom of the hole.

Sithlac grinned. "Welcome to the Hub," he said as his companion settled back upon his haunches, his face the very picture of confusion.

"You were right," Bongcor managed after a few moments. "Defy description it does, indeed."

"This is so, oh yes," agreed Sithlac. "Climb upon it you can, and no harm will come to you. From above, the truth of it is clear: it is a room that moves. Up and down it goes, carrying Men here and there within their tower."

Bongcor just shook his head. "Powerful magic it is," he managed. "That Men are capable of such things, I did not so much as dream."

"This is but a taste of what Man-magic can create. When you are at last a hunter true, and seek for yourself a birthing-place, even more wonders will you see. Strange and wondrous they are, oh yes, but to each a purpose has. Things of Man always have a reason, always. Remember this you would be well to do."

"I shall, I shall," agreed Bongcor, watching in amazement as the elevator once again began to rise, answering some unknown summons from its masters. Creaking and moaning, it once again slid right by the two watching gremlins, passing close enough that they could feel the faint wind of its passing. Yet it never wavered from its track, intent upon its sole purpose, and after watching a bit longer, Bongcor noticeably deflated, realizing he was in no danger.

"No longer as afraid, you are, now that you know its ways," Sithlac pointed out. "Always has it functioned thus, for as long as I have visited this place. Up and down, up and down, and nothing more, yet to no schedule does it keep. Use it we shall, oh yes, but we must take care, for to slip and fall into the shaft will mean your doom."

"So I would imagine," agreed Bongcor with a lingering trace of worry in his voice. "How, then, are we to use such a thing?"

"Halt it may before us," explained the veteran hunter, "but perhaps now, perhaps some time from now, I cannot say; thus, we will not wait, but jump upon it as it passes by. Never as it rises, oh no, only upon its descent."

"Jump upon it?" Bongcor asked, looking even more worried now. "And then what?"

"Look about you, at this platform where we stand. At each stopping-point, another place like this awaits. When the Hub stops, jump off we will, but only when it stops."

"If it rises to the top, will we not be crushed?"

"A gap there is, wide enough for us, of this I know. Now worry not, and remember, it matters not where we stop. This is a tower of Man, and yet, it is not unlike our own towers, only upon a much grander scale. The tower has levels, just like ours. The entry-point to our Tunnel lies on the eighth such level, to which we shall return when the hunt is done. But for now, we go where the Hub takes us, and there the hunt will truly begin. Now, come, for it descends once more. Jump when I do, and linger not, lest you be left behind."

Bongcor nodded, gathering his courage once more as the great lift descended. Despite its nearness, Sithlac moved forward until he could almost touch the metal walls as they slid by. Bongcor watched, one eye fixed on the immense structure and the other on his companion. The instant the elevator went past, Sithlac jumped, and Bongcor followed right behind. Predictably, the more experienced gremlin landed on his feet, while the other bounced and rolled, clutching at the slick metallic surface with his sucker-flaps, eyes tightly shut the whole time.

"Well done," said Sithlac in a reassuring voice that managed to just barely avoid sounding sarcastic. "Now count the platforms as we drop, that we know which level we have reached. Usually, it goes all the way down, but not always."

Bongcor stood and glanced back the way he'd come. The feeling of descent was new to him, yet he knew at once what it had to mean. "The walls," he said in amazement. "It is as though they move, while we stand still; and yet, my gut tells me this is not the case."

"It takes some getting used to," agreed Sithlac. "When first I found this place, I avoided it most surely, until I overheard others talking about better hunting on the different levels. There are other ways to move up or down within the tower, but this is the best and fastest way, especially if the hunt has been good, and you must transport something large and heavy."

The elevator reached the ground floor, and Bongcor found that, indeed, there was another platform he could jump onto, but Sithlac didn't move. "Why do we not exit?" asked Bongcor curiously.

"Not good hunting here," explained his companion. "Wide open rooms and no dwelling-spaces to explore. Upper levels are better. The first level this is, so count as we rise, and be careful, for all levels look the same."

The elevator moved once more, lurching at first and then rising steadily. Both gremlins counted in silence as it moved upward, eventually passing the floor where they'd boarded, and finally coming to a halt on the twelfth level. At that Sithlac immediately hopped off, and Bongcor hurried along behind. They passed into the crawlspace beyond, leaving the Hub behind, and moved on in silence for a while.

Adams Hall – 12th Floor Crawlspaces

Even in the absence of moonlight, gremlins have an innate sense of what they call "night-depth"—in other words, how long it's been since sunset. By the time the two travelers stopped for a rest, both knew they'd been going for a while, perhaps one-fifth of the evening. They stayed within the walls, pausing to listen often, with Bongcor asking endless questions while Sithlac answered with infinite patience. However, each hunter's hole they found led only to rooms populated by Men who hadn't yet retired for the night.

After the sixth such attempt, Bongcor dusted himself off and shuffled over to a long-forgotten block of sawed-off two-by-four. He regarded the chunk of wood for a long moment, as though contemplating whether it might make good building material, before finally shrugging and plopping himself down for a seat. Sithlac also considered the huge wood-slab, going so far as to run a hand across its dusty surface from one end to the other, but decided he couldn't possibly carry such an enormous thing back to the Morningside Tunnel. So, without commenting on that, he joined his fellow gremlin on the makeshift bench.

"Apologies to you, great hunter," said Bongcor at length, "but I must rest a bit. Not used to such walking am I, oh no."

"Not unexpected," replied Sithlac, leaning his head sideways so as to suggest the incident meant nothing at all. "Even after so many hunts, I too must rest sometimes. A water-drop would be most welcome now, but such is not to be within the walls."

"There is some water to be had nearby, I hope?"

"Of course, and not so far from here, but two ways there are, the long and the short. If the next hole is open, the short we can take, otherwise stay within the walls we must, and a long time we will be, indeed."

"Then I hope there are no Men without, for I thirst most dearly," commented Bongcor, his long, slick tongue circling the outside of his mouth, extending not quite far enough to touch his eyes. "Can we not bring water for ourselves, within a container of some sort?"

"We could, oh yes, but a great weight it would be, and slow us down too much—and stash it we do not dare, lest it be gone upon our return."

Bongcor nodded. Gremlins needed about a dozen drops of water daily, more if they were on a hunt, as now. Although they could last many hours without quenching their thirst, they would begin drying out, causing their movements to become slow and jerky, and making them easy prey for anything dangerous that might come along. Sithlac, being used to long journeys, had survived dehydration on many occasions and knew his limits. Bongcor, of course, did not, and Sithlac had no intention of testing them this night.

After a few minutes, Sithlac stood and started to walk down the dusty corridor between the walls, following a line of plastic cable, but his companion didn't move. Instead, he shifted his left eye up and around, while his right stayed fixed on his leader. At the same time, the lesser gremlin crouched slightly, turning in a slow arc, the little flaps around his cup-like ears standing straight up. He finally stopped, peering into the gloom, his eyes retreating about halfway into his head.

"Being watched we are," he whispered in a low, hissing voice.

Sithlac nodded slowly. "Yes," he agreed quietly. "For quite some time, in fact."

"Knew of this you did, and told me not." Bongcor's voice stayed even, making it a statement, not an accusation.

"A test of your perception, nothing more, and passed you have," replied Sithlac, gradually raising his voice back to normal levels. "There is no danger here. This is a creature I know well." He made a quick wave with one hand at something unseen in the darkness overhead.

Bongcor partially inflated his chin in satisfaction at his minor success, but chose not to dwell on it. "What is it, then, that follows gremlins in the dark?"

"A goblin outcast, nothing more. He roams these walls unseen, without a voice or face, but goblin-sounds I know quite well. From what the other goblins say, his name is Yog, or something near, but if I call it out he answers not."

Bongcor nodded, accepting the explanation at face value. "Why is he outcast?"

"That I do not know, but it is true, oh yes. If we move too close to goblin-lands, he will follow us no longer."

"What does he want? Why follow gremlins, if not to do us harm?"

"That also I do not know. A game, perhaps, or he may hope we will leave something useful behind. Sometimes, if I stay beyond a single night, I will catch a meal, and if it is more than I can eat, I will find its remnants gone when next I pass that way. A goblin can last many nights without food, or so the stories tell, but eat they must, oh yes."

"A curious thing it is," remarked Bongcor, "that such a creature moves fearlessly within these walls, while the Fallen hunts our kind. Too small for prey, perhaps he is, or too quick."

"Very large the Fallen are, or so the stories say," explained Sithlac. "I wonder if one could even fit herein. If it only lurks out there, then safe in here we are, and so is Yog, for if we take a hole, he will not follow. Never have I heard his scuttling anywhere else but between the walls."

Bongcor nodded in understanding and got to his feet. "I wonder only one other thing and then will be silent once more."

"What is that?" inquired Sithlac as the pair started walking again, heading further down the narrow passage, following the cable's winding path.

"What crime so terrible could a goblin commit, that they would cast him out...?"

Adams Hall – 12th Floor
Dorm #1210 (Bathroom)

At the next hunter's hole, they finally had some luck. Sithlac's careful probing through the faintly shimmering veil showed only darkness beyond, with no sight or sound of Man whatsoever. He held the passage open while Bongcor stepped through, then snuffed his glow-rod and followed.

The two gremlins waited about ten seconds while their eyes adjusted. In between the walls, with no light at all, they had little choice but to create artificial moonlight in order to see. Here, though, in Man's domain, the darkness wasn't total. Once their pupils widened enough— so much that their eyes now looked almost completely black—they could see quite well.

They found themselves in a large open space like nothing Bongcor had yet seen. The floor consisted of row upon row of carefully placed square tiles, each about half again as wide as Sithlac was tall. An open door provided the only exit, while painted walls rose on opposite sides, and a shiny, exceptionally smooth white surface blocked access to the far side of the room. Directly above the two explorers, a silver pipe jutted outward and connected to a basin several feet above. The only structure within reach was another slick white object with a curved, oval-shaped body ending abruptly high overhead. Four featureless white cylinders surrounded the edifice like little statues.

"Come, it is time to drink," announced Sithlac, extending his sucker-flaps and starting up the side of the shiny white thing. Bongcor followed slowly and carefully, finding the going difficult, for his hands didn't want to stay attached to the slippery porcelain. However, once they moved out onto the sides, where he wasn't hanging unnaturally on the curved underside of the toilet, he made better progress. In due course both gremlins stood on the lid, looking down into a wide pool containing more water than Bongcor had ever seen in one place. He drew his tongue across his face, licking his nose in anticipation.

"Ssst," cautioned Sithlac. "Taste it first you must! Lakes like these are common in Man's lands, but sometimes they are poisoned."

Bongcor nodded, not bothering to ask why Men might foul their own water supply, but then, Men were strange and fickle creatures. Some of their creations made sense, like the elevator, but others had no discernible purpose, and still more seemed contrary to Man's own interests. Rather than inquire, when he already knew what the answer would be, Bongcor instead cautiously followed his companion as he lowered himself down the side of the bowl and sampled the water with the tip of his tongue, uttering a few quick syllables under his breath.

"Safe it is," explained Sithlac after a moment, "but test it yourself you should. You know the incantation, yes?"

"Of course," Bongcor answered, "though never before have I used it thus." He repeated Sithlac's efforts with the water, casting the spell with a drop held just inside his mouth, underneath his tongue. If there had been poison present, the liquid would've bubbled into a froth, but instead, it remained cool and quiescent. He slurped it down quickly, then followed with two more drops, quenching his thirst completely.

Sithlac climbed out of the bowl and back onto the lid, where he crouched for a few moments, watching his companion. After he finished drinking, Bongcor managed to make it out without falling, whereupon he sat back upon his haunches, gazing down into the vast lake before him.

"I know your thoughts," said the veteran hunter quietly. "You think to yourself, 'If only I had such wealth as this, never would I need to hunt again.'"

"You speak most truly," agreed Bongcor, "for just now I thought that very thing."

"In the Tunnel, we know only steady drips of water, which are consumed daily," explained his de facto mentor, "but in the Outside, such lakes as these are commonplace. Where water stands still, it sometimes fouls, so trust it not. Flowing water is not so often bad."

"Your experience is most helpful," said Bongcor deferentially. "To have learned this all yourself is greater still. Most guilty do I feel for taking such knowledge without giving anything in return. Still do I not understand why you help me so."

"And I still cannot answer, but this I do admit: I find this much more enjoyable than hunting alone. When goblins hunt for wood or scraps, they always travel in groups, or so I hear. Wondered why, I always have, and now at last I think I know."

Bongcor lowered his head and shuffled slightly. "There is a word for this," he intoned in a quiet voice. "A word not often used, and yet, it still lurks within the darkling-speech."

"Friendship," answered Sithlac just as quietly.

Bongcor cringed and sank even lower, as if the word had physically struck at him. "Goblins can be friends with each other," he hissed, "and spriggans, and sprites and faeries too, if the tales are true, but not so gremlins, of this I fear most greatly."

Sithlac nodded. "The Rules have not been breached," he stated firmly. "No bargain has been broken. No harm has been done to another. Nothing exists to stand in the way of gremlin friendship, should we both desire it."

They remained silent, mulling that over for a few more moments. "I think it is not a matter of desire," said Bongcor eventually. "I think we are already friends."

Sithlac nodded, the corners of his wide mouth ever so slightly turning upward. "I think you may very well be right. What this portends, I cannot say, but for now, we will hunt together, for a vast Man-cave awaits beyond this room. Come, my friend, and let us see what we can find."

They clambered down from the toilet seat, quietly making their way out into the empty hall, keeping their voices to themselves for a while.

Adams Hall – 12th Floor Dorm #1210

The gremlins explored the dormitory for the better part of two hours. To them, the apartment-like living quarters felt like a series of vast cathedral-sized open areas connected by a wide, L-shaped hallway. Within each chamber adjoining the halls, numerous towering pieces of furniture surrounded wide open spaces too dangerous to cross. Instead, the hunters kept to the walls, sneaking quietly through the shadows, seeking anything that might've fallen into the cracks.

After a while, a faint rasping sound began, eventually becoming loud enough to give Bongcor pause. "It is a Man-noise," explained Sithlac quietly. "Nothing to fear from it, and in fact, quite the contrary, for it proves our safety."

"How can this be?" inquired Bongcor. "The Man is close, yet we are in no danger?" He shuffled about nervously, his eyes flicking about as he watched the open spaces overhead for any sign of movement.

"The Man sleeps, and while he does, he makes this sound," explained Sithlac. "For as long as we hear it, we know he hears us not. Unless some loud noise disturbs him, he will likely sleep all night." In fact, he knew from experience that he could climb right up the wall next to an unconscious Man and he would not awaken, but Sithlac had no intention of mentioning that to his already nervous companion.

Instead, the explorers made their way out of the kitchen and into the living room, where Bongcor got a new surprise—here the floor no longer consisted of flat, smooth segments, but became a thick, furry mat of twisted, hairlike fibers. Sithlac chuckled several times as the lesser gremlin hopped to and fro, the tiny threads tickling his bare feet whenever they tried to find a safe spot to stand. Eventually he figured out the trick of it and learned to balance his weight on the thicker clusters, almost sliding through the carpet instead of walking.

When they passed beneath the couch, Bongcor's eyes stood up. "Something shiny, just ahead," he called out, waving his spear off to the side, very near the wall.

Sithlac nodded. He'd already spotted the flat disc-shape of a coin, but discounted it at once. "Good eyes, oh yes, but such a thing is not for us. You will see them often, here and there, but they have too much importance to Man. Take one we could, but into the Tunnel it cannot go."

Bongcor slumped. "A shame, for it is very shiny, and carved with great precision."

"And there are many more just like it," replied Sithlac. "I recall the first time I saw such discs and thought them valuable and unique. Then another, and another, all the same. Leave it be, and look further still."

He pointed with an extended arm beyond the dusty silver ring. There, just barely visible, caught between floorboard and carpet, something gleamed in the faint light. Bongcor crouched warily, listening, but heard only the ever-present sleep-noise far in the distance. He continued to brandish his spear nonetheless as Sithlac moved in for a closer look.

The veteran hunter recognized the shape at once and bounded forward eagerly. Clutching the inch-long object in one hand, he gave a tug and freed it from where it lay stuck within the fibers. The thick metal shone in the pale light as Sithlac inspected his prize—a paper clip.

"A *durg-tog'nortic*," he said, a wide smile filling his face. In the darkling-tongue, the name meant "flexible double metal-beam," as apt a description as any. Sithlac bobbed up and down in excitement. "A fine find so early in the hunt. This will fetch a great price at the market."

"Not so pretty, but a useful thing, oh yes," agreed Bongcor at once. "And not so heavy as to burden us."

"Have you seen such things before?" inquired Sithlac, for he knew them to be in high demand, and thus not likely to be encountered by non-hunters.

"A few, a few, after their twisting," came the answer, "but only once unbent. I watched it pulled and curved in a neighbor's roof, so as to hold a shiny."

Sithlac nodded. The *durg-tog'nortic*, often abbreviated *durgnort* (which loosely translates to "flexbar"), came in a variety of sizes and strengths, but almost always looked the same. He always imagined Men made these things for use in building small, temporary objects or structures. In their original shape, they were flat and easy to transport, but once moved to their destination, they could be easily bent or folded into a useful form. He had several small ones in his tower even now, acting as supports for various decorations. Unfortunately, once bent, they were all but impossible to return to their original portable flatness, but since he had no intention of moving them, he didn't mind at all.

"You will see these from time to time Outside," explained Sithlac, "usually atop the great structures overhead, or held in place by larger things. Of course, there they cannot be touched, lest the Seventh Rule be broken. In this dusty space below, where they lay forgotten, they are ours to take."

"And yet we cannot take the discs," asked Bongcor curiously. "These are less important, then?"

"So it would seem, for the sentries will refuse a disc, saying a Man might hunt for such, but not so the *durgnort*, oh no."

Bongcor ran a thin finger across the slick, perfectly even surface of the paper clip before fixing his left eye on his companion. "Friend hunter," he asked quietly, "forgive my curiosity, but pray tell me this: if these things are easily found above, as you say, what is to stop us from climbing there, and seizing all we can?"

"The Seventh Rule, oh yes," answered Sithlac, slipping the shiny treasure into his carry-bag, "but I see your meaning plain. If there is none to see, then who would know?"

"Yes, but be sure, I ask only in curiosity, not suggesting we pursue such things. Yet surely other hunters have thought such thoughts, you see?"

"And so have I, of course, in the desperation of a failing hunt," Sithlac agreed, "but upon such paths does lie our doom. The victim Man would grow suspicious, and in seeking a cause, perhaps find our hunter-holes, which cannot be allowed. But even without such things, we could not break the Rules without consequence. Such a secret cannot be kept, oh no, no matter how much you may try."

Bongcor nodded, accepting the explanation, and moved along the floorboard slowly, near where they'd found the paper clip. The carpet there had worked itself free, standing up from the ground so as to create a kind of loose flap. He tugged experimentally, and the section lifted up a bit, so he gave it more of a pull, causing it to rise up toward him.

Sithlac immediately moved around toward the opening, peering in with first one and then both his eyes. "More," he called out. "Pull harder! Something hides within!"

His companion dropped his spear and grabbed the loose carpet with both hands, putting all his strength into it. The entire section rose up, but didn't curl as Sithlac hoped. He got down on all fours and started to wriggle into the gap, toward the metallic shape just visible deep within the opening. On the other side, Bongcor began to wheeze and cough. "Hurry," he called out. "Not much longer can I hold!"

Sithlac immediately withdrew, but with a purpose. "Hold a moment longer," he insisted, grabbing the fallen spear. With a quick lunge, he shoved the long, thin nail into the gap, positioning it so the loose carpet would be held open, like an umbrella.

"There, you may relax," he said after a moment, holding the spear steady as Bongcor released his hold. "Come hither, and see what you might find, for you are smaller than I, and may reach what I cannot."

The lesser gremlin came around the back side, peering into the opening. At first he saw nothing, but as his eyes adjusted, he spotted the long-forgotten carpet tack just visible underneath. Eagerly, he crawled in, wriggling as far as he could while Sithlac held the spear steady. Reaching out as far as he could, and flattening himself as much as possible, Bongcor was just able to grab hold of the tip and pull it out. However, he didn't pause to congratulate himself, but instead kept on tunneling forward.

"What is it?" called out Sithlac, immediately aware that something else was going on, but unable to see from his angle.

"Two more there are," came the answer. "Reach them I can, if I cast out all breath. Hold on."

"Careful, for the weight may well crush you should this drop!"

Bongcor grunted in reply and flattened himself as much as possible, emptying his lungs and squeezing into the opening as far as he could. A moment later a second tack slid out from underneath the carpet. The smaller gremlin's limbs flailed about a few more times as he pulled himself in even further, before finally stopping. He sputtered once, gave an incomprehensible squeak, and lay still.

Sithlac let go of the spear and grabbed Bongcor by the ankles. Overhead, the heavy carpet shifted, but remained in place, supported for the moment by the spear. Sithlac pulled once, but his friend didn't budge. Bracing himself as best he could, the larger gremlin took hold and tugged with all his might. His companion popped free and slid backward swiftly, knocking the spear aside, and the heavy carpet settled down just to one side of the two hunters.

"Are you injured?" asked Sithlac worriedly, taking a few deep breaths after his sudden exertion.

Bongcor coughed a couple of times, sucking in some air to refill his lungs, before getting to his feet. "No, I think not," he replied, holding up his prize—the third carpet tack. "And I brought with me the treasure, oh yes!"

Sithlac smiled and clapped a hand on his companion's shoulder. "Then well and done it is! A score beyond that which I could have found alone. To find one such shiny would mark this hunt a success. Three is a great bounty indeed."

Bongcor nodded and inflated his throat-sac over halfway in satisfaction. "The wisdom of teamwork cannot be denied," he pointed out. "When the others learn of this—"

"Perhaps we should not tell," chuckled Sithlac, pressing his fingers down on his mouth as if to hold it shut. "Keep this to ourselves, we should, and the benefits are ours to reap, oh yes!"

"Word will travel fast indeed, when we return together with so much useful metal," pointed out Bongcor, sitting up and examining the heavy tack with appreciation. The thick, black object had a sharp tip and a flat end, making it ideal for hammering into blocks of wood or holding shiny treasures in place upon a wall.

"If we return separately," offered Sithlac, "perhaps we will not be noticed. Here, let me place these within your bag so the points do not cause damage."

He used a thin leather strap to bind all three nails together before pushing them into the sack with points facing up. Bongcor shifted the much heavier bag around on his shoulders until the heavy tacks settled into a comfortable position, the sharp tips facing outward. "Do we return now to divide our bounty?" asked the smaller gremlin, looking very pleased with himself.

"If you like," answered Sithlac, "although the night is but half over. Already we have had success beyond what I ever imagined, but who knows what other treasures we might find, ere the morning comes?"

"Agreed," replied Bongcor eagerly, and they pressed on.

Adams Hall – 12th Floor
Dorm #1210 (Living Room)

They explored the rest of the living room, but found little else of interest. On his own, Sithlac might've tried climbing higher to have a look at the tops of some of the furniture, but decided against it for now. Bongcor remained excited and enthusiastic, and Sithlac didn't want to spoil the mood. Plus, with the hunting already more than successful, he saw no reason to take any unnecessary risks.

For that same reason, he didn't bother trying to lead his friend down the corridor toward the sleeping Man. Bedrooms were the most likely places to produce takeable shinies, but the hunters would have to stay absolutely silent, lest the Man awaken. If he did, they'd be pinned in place until he fell asleep once more, or left the room, either of which could take some time. Sithlac had on more than one occasion found himself trapped behind a shelf or under the bed until well after dawn, forcing him to spend the day Outside—never a pleasant thing.

Instead, he headed back toward the nearest hunter's hole and let Bongcor find it this time, which he did quite readily. Sithlac could tell his new friend would make an excellent hunter, for he had all the right instincts. He looked forward to many more hunts with Bongcor at his side, for they definitely worked well together, and being with another had far more advantages than he ever would've imagined. Not only did he have someone to talk to, and to watch his back, but as a team they could get to treasures that would otherwise be out of reach.

Sithlac hummed quietly as the two explorers made their way through the hole and back into the walls, congratulating himself on his excellent decision to bring Bongcor along. In fact, this whole partnership was working so well, he thought of something else, something so radical he doubted it would be allowed, even though no Rules suggested otherwise.

"Fellow hunter," he offered after he'd considered some of the ramifications, "I have another idea for you to consider, since we work so well together."

Bongcor pressed his chin a bit at being called a hunter, which was to him a great compliment. "What is it, O much greater hunter?" he asked in return.

Sithlac laughed at that, pridefully puffing up his own throat-sac before letting it deflate just as quickly. "Not much greater for long, I fear, but even so, hear me out. In the Tunnel, always toward the sky do we build, but never far, lest our towers fall."

"So it is always done," agreed Bongcor, "but why bring this up, unless...?"

Sithlac shifted nervously, for what he was about to suggest went against everything he'd ever known, yet in light of the present situation, it made perfect sense. "What if, together we built our towers?" he offered cautiously, just barely stifling his enthusiasm. "With walls secured against each other, many more levels could ours rise, even perhaps to the very ceiling itself, where the water-drops form...and then they would be ours to claim, oh yes!"

"And rule the Tunnel, then we would," agreed Bongcor, instantly catching on. "Yet between our structures, there is the alley..."

"Yet not by rule or boundary is it there," Sithlac pointed out. "Only to divide our towers, and ensure no complaint from a neighbor. Our groundspace shares a common border, do you see? If we were in agreement to build together, with walls pressed firmly at the edges, then much more stable would they be, for they would lean upon each other, and rise all the higher in return."

"That they would indeed," agreed Bongcor, hopping back and forth in excitement as the idea swelled within his mind. "But would such a thing be allowed? Tirchoth, I am sure, would argue against our joint venture most assuredly, if a ninth level we did reach."

"The Rules say naught about such things," the more experienced gremlin insisted, twitching and shuffling around as he tried to contain his own enthusiasm about the proposed project. He knew quite well that no gremlin ever allowed his tower to touch another. In such cases only arguing and fighting would result, and in the end, one or the other building would be modified or torn down. Whenever such things happened, or in the case of any similar dispute, the Council of Nine would form, made up of those gremlins with the highest current status in the Tunnel. If together they were called to rule against a dual tower, they would be inherently biased against it, their judgment predictable and preordained. But if no dispute occurred...

"The Council might convene," Bongcor pointed out, echoing

Sithlac's own thoughts. "They would stand against us most assuredly."

"Yet the Nine would have no say, for we would call them not," urged Sithlac. "Do you see? They settle only complaints, nothing more. If we do not complain, they cannot judge against us."

"But they could bring complaint upon us, could they not?"

"Think carefully now, oh yes," Sithlac answered. "The Nine cannot convene upon their own behalf. The First Rule protects us—no gremlin can harm another. If we are doing no harm, and have no complaint, what grounds have they to convene? Only their own desires, and in that they do us harm without any cause save their own. With such a judgment, they would break the First Rule most assuredly."

Bongcor nodded and shifted about. The two gremlins fell into silence as they both considered the ramifications of their plan. Thus constrained, the Nine could not convene. The way seemed clear, and yet, if the Council passed judgment anyway, who would stand against them...? No gremlin could harm another, so how would justice be done?

"It worries me greatly, I will admit," said Bongcor, "but I would try, having little to lose; however, you have many shinies, and thus much more to risk. I bow to your decision."

"I am inclined to try, but if we do," Sithlac explained, "we must not falter. We could never argue, never fight, for any reason, lest they seize the opportunity to claim dispute. Understand this now we must, and never waver."

"I see no reason we should ever fight, once we begin to build," said Bongcor firmly.

"So say you now," Sithlac replied, not the least bit antagonistic, "but many seasons from now, can you be so sure?"

"Of the future, I cannot speak," Bongcor told him, "but if we do this not, would we ever see ourselves standing at the Tunnel's greatest heights? At least that we can achieve, oh yes, of this I am quite sure— quite sure, indeed."

Sithlac nodded in agreement, but with shoulders slumped enough to indicate a small amount of caution. "I too believe we could reach great heights together, but there are many details, far too many for a single night. We can work them out, I think, but first let us conclude this hunt. Another Man-place waits not too far ahead. Let us see what we can find and then return once more to home."

"Agreed," answered Bongcor, and on they went, each dreaming of a tall double-tower reaching toward the sky.

Adams Hall – 12th Floor Dorm #1213

The next hole led them to another dorm shaped exactly like the first, but with a much different arrangement of furniture. Sithlac let his charge take the lead for a while, and it didn't take Bongcor long to figure out the similarities in design. Why two Man-caves should be almost identical in form made little sense to creatures used to randomness and chaos in construction, but then, little about Man could be easily explained, after all.

They heard no snoring in this particular dwelling, so Sithlac showed his apprentice the room where its occupant usually slept, and the bed he used as well. The Man was absent for some reason, although they saw plenty of signs that he'd been there recently. Neither gremlin questioned their good fortune, instead enjoying the rare opportunity to root around unchallenged, even sampling some food scraps left behind on a cardboard surface in the occupant's living room. Bongcor had never tasted anything like the half-eaten chunk of leftover pizza, and didn't like it much, but at least it quieted the rumbling in his stomach.

Their unopposed explorations produced a few more small items of value, including a dark blue map tack, about six inches of waxed dental floss, and two bent staples. In addition, they spotted numerous other items that they couldn't take, including some more lost pocket change, a mechanical pencil, and a plastic fork. As Sithlac explained, the pencil was the sort of thing the Man might look for, making its disappearance something that might arouse suspicion, while the fork simply wouldn't fetch a price worthy of the difficulty involved in transporting it home. Unlike metal, the flimsy white material would break too easily to be of any practical use.

Even so, the extra treasures they collected made the hunt a very successful one indeed. With all their loot in tow, tied on or stuffed into bags as best they could, the two happy gremlins made their way back home about an hour before sunrise. As per their earlier agreement, Bongcor took the Moonrise Gate, bidding his mentor farewell and proceeding home alone. Sithlac, for his part, headed around to the far side of the Tunnel and entered through the Sunset Gate. The sentry there, having not consulted with his opposite number, had no idea Sithlac had left at all, much less traveled with a companion, so getting back in presented no difficulties whatsoever.

By the time he reached his tower, Sithlac figured his new friend would be fast asleep, but instead found Bongcor pacing back and forth, somehow managing to stay awake. The two proceeded to divide up the spoils, amid multiple deep yawns by both parties, until both felt satisfied by the results. Promising to discuss things further on the morrow, they took their leave and went to sleep in their own homes.

The next day, they met once more to discuss the details of their impending partnership. If gremlins had lawyers, they would've drawn up a contract at this point, but lacking any such thing, the two instead hashed out the agreement on their own. The alley between their towers was to be closed off by wood-blocks, which were to be equally anchored to the walls on either side. More blocks would then be stacked on top and the process repeated until both Bongcor's levels and the first two levels of Sithlac's dwelling were firmly joined together. At that point they reached the first potential sticking point in their arrangement because with one side so much lower, the higher levels couldn't be connected together right away.

After some debate they settled upon the fairest possible plan, given the circumstances. Bongcor would concentrate his profits from hunting on buying more wood-blocks at the market, using them to construct his third level, while Sithlac tore down his admittedly rickety fourth level and used its wood to reinforce the walls and flooring of the lower levels. Both gremlins agreed, Sithlac somewhat reluctantly, that his efforts weren't structurally sound enough to support the new dual tower they were contemplating. Bongcor, on the other hand, had done his work very well, taking great care in making a very stable foundation for his tower. Of course, lacking any appreciable drive to reach skyward (at least before now), he had no reason to be hasty, and could afford to move with greater deliberation.

In any event, once both structures were of equal size and stability, the two friends would jointly hunt for a while, putting their earnings equally toward building a fourth level to the dual tower. Sithlac estimated that by the time this happened, winter would be over and mating-time would arrive. At that point he'd decide whether to take a mate this year, or press on with the construction plan. He preferred mating, of course, but also appreciated the idea of having two or three more levels on the tower by the time the others on the Council returned from their birthing-places. He tried to imagine their surprise when they realized what had happened in their absence, and the thought made him grin and hum quite loudly.

There was one final matter to discuss, namely, what would happen should they ever reach their ultimate goal—building their tower high enough to earn the greatest status of all and become Tunnel leader. According to the Rules, the gremlin with the highest tower had supreme authority over the Council, although in practice this generally only meant he cast the tiebreaking vote in any dispute. Two gremlins had never before shared towers of exactly the same height—they would always try to outdo each other with flimsy spires and pennants, many of which didn't stay up for long. Eventually, one of the two competitors would add a new level, if they dared, or their tower would collapse or topple from the effort, thus ending the leadership duel.

In the case of Sithlac and Bongcor, though, their tower would be for all intents and purposes a single building. That meant they would either both be leader, or neither would, thus creating a real problem—the Rules simply didn't allow for such a situation to exist. To forestall any arguing or debate by the Council, the two partners agreed that should they ever actually reach this point, they'd take turns as leader by building a mobile roof-cap that could shift back and forth between sides at sunset each night.

Thus assured that they'd come up with a fair and equitable agreement, the two gremlins went back to their homes, very pleased with themselves and eager to get started.

Morningside Tunnel
– Sithlac's Tower

Somewhat disgustedly, Sithlac pushed against the wood-block until the corner lifted up just enough to slide his thick toes underneath. With a grimace he endured the brief pain of the heavy weight on his foot long enough to reach down and grab the edge, whereupon he heaved the heavy slab of wood upward. For a moment it balanced on a corner before finally rolling over and settling on the short side, up against the wall of his home.

He stepped back and regarded the block from this new angle before leaning into it and pressing firmly, swinging the flat side up against the tower wall. The slab settled into place well, but jutted out quite a bit beyond Bongcor's property line. That presented a problem because another wood-block would be needed to join the two buildings together, and a second just wouldn't fit. They would need either a thinner block or some means to cut the heavy wood to the right proportions.

Another gremlin hopped by, slowing and staring with one baleful eye at Sithlac's efforts. He seemed about to stop and ask for an explanation, but thought better of it and moved on, just barely able to squeeze past the wood in the narrow alleyway. All towers had some amount of space between them, but the structures weren't laid out in any kind of regular pattern, so the paths between buildings to the common areas and exit gates produced chaotic mazes of narrow streets often blocked by protrusions and piles of trash or cast-off construction materials. While it was generally accepted that a gremlin could freely walk between structures if enough space existed between the walls to allow it, one absolutely never climbed on somebody else's tower without permission.

The space between Sithlac and Bongcor's towers, being relatively wide and straight, acted something like a well-traveled thoroughfare. That was about to change, as soon as the first wood-blocks went into place. Word would travel quickly, and Sithlac had no intention of looking foolish by having to tear down anything once he got started.

That meant the initial connections between their buildings would have to be done right the first time.

He walked around and studied the situation for a few more minutes. Wood-blocks were usually bought at the market, carried there by goblin traders from whatever mysterious source they had for such things. Sithlac had no idea where they got the wood and really didn't care. For whatever reason, though, goblins offered these construction materials in only small, medium, and large sizes, with rarely any variation. This one was the largest kind, and medium ones just wouldn't do. They were too thin, and he had no way to fasten so many together.

Just eyeballing the alley, Sithlac could tell he needed no less than six large blocks, assuming he could figure out how to thin them down enough to fit in the opening. The blocks, rectangular in shape, would be too long to fit lengthwise without knocking down one of the walls first—something he and his friend had already rejected. This had to be done without tearing down anything they'd already built or they might as well not bother.

Additionally, Sithlac recognized another problem he hadn't anticipated when they first came up with their idea. While the veteran hunter's home sat on a relatively flat section of land, Bongcor had to contend with the moonward slope, a drop of about ten percent in elevation from one side to the other. He'd done well with his foundation, managing to level it out as best he could, but the structure still leaned slightly to the side. That meant if the two buildings were to be connected, the blocks used at higher levels would have to be wider than those at ground level.

Sithlac still hadn't figured out a solution to either issue when Bongcor arrived, having finally finished his morning meal. The smaller gremlin eagerly bounded up the alley, ready to get started with their joint project. "A fine day it is for construction, friend neighbor," he called out. "What needs have we to begin?"

Sithlac hopped up on top of the block and waved his arm. "This I do know: six blocks will we require, but narrow at bottom they must be, and wider at top—a perplexing issue, oh yes."

Bongcor circled the rectangular slab of wood, which, lying on its side, stood half again his own height. "Yes, yes, too wide it is, indeed, and not nearly long enough; and once attached, guard it we must lest it be thought as debris and hauled away."

Sithlac frowned. With all his thoughts of how to arrange the blocks, it hadn't even occurred to him that other gremlins might think the blocks weren't actually part of anything, and were therefore free to take. The truth of things most likely wouldn't become apparent until they reached the second level, which meant the construction materials would have to be guarded day and night until that time.

"A quandary we are in," he sighed at last. "We need at least four more blocks, beyond the five already bought, but where to keep them I do not know. Plus twice again as many fasteners, to ensure our work is undisturbed."

Bongcor paced about. "This means more hunting, I am sure," he complained. "If only there were larger blocks! Ask the goblins come market-day, perhaps? They may have larger blocks they would bring, if we asked in advance for such."

"Delays us three more nights before the market, it does," he answered, "and still another five thereafter, for the wood to come. But if a larger block we need...hmm..."

He shut his eyes and hunkered down, lost in thought. "What is it?" his friend asked after a moment. "What new plan do you have, I wonder?"

"On our hunt just finished," Sithlac replied after a moment, "we encountered a very large wood-block, did we not?"

Bongcor nodded. "Oh yes, we surely did! I remember it well, but too large it was to carry."

"Alone, indeed, what you say is true, but you have seen the goblins carrying larger things, working as a group. If the two of us together lifted, one per side, could we move it hither?"

"This I do not know," Bongcor replied eagerly, "but try we should, oh yes!"

Sithlac grinned. "Then try we shall this very night!"

Adams Hall – 12th Floor Crawlspace

They found the piece of wood exactly where they left it, still with Sithlac's hand-tracings visible across its dusty surface. Many years before, a small fire on the twelfth floor of Adams Hall resulted in quite a bit of smoke and water damage. During the resulting renovations, some construction materials were left behind, most of which by now had been carried off by opportunistic gremlins. This piece of partially cut two-by-four must've fallen down between sections of drywall at some point, and the lazy construction worker who dropped it just left it there, rather than go to the trouble of retrieving something he intended to throw out anyway.

Sithlac and Bongcor studied the long-forgotten treasure for a few moments, each wondering whether or not it could actually be lifted, much less carried all the way down four stories and halfway across the building all the way to the Moonrise Gate. They answered that almost immediately by trying to lift the slab together, one on either side. To their mutual surprise, they were able to get it off the ground and move it a few steps.

"Carry it we can, or so it seems," said Bongcor hopefully. "But will it fit?"

"If not, we are done before we begin," Sithlac answered. "Bring it over here. If through this gap it goes, we are halfway home."

They took hold again and lugged the heavy piece of wood over to the gap between wall-frames. With some care, they were able to just fit the beam through the opening, along the narrow side. Shuffling along with short half-steps, they got all the way into the next section of wall before setting down their burden once again.

"A long time will this take," gasped Sithlac between deep breaths, "but succeed, I think we can."

"The others will be quite surprised, to see us carry such a treasure," pointed out Bongcor, grinning at the very thought of two gremlins hauling something so large through the Tunnel gate. "I wonder, perhaps, if Tirchoth received as much attention as we shall surely see."

"Perhaps he did, though none can truly say," replied Sithlac. Like most gremlins, he'd seen the long brown fishing rod that rose eight levels high in the center of their leader's tower, providing most of the support for his amazing spire. Nobody had any idea where it came from, or could remember seeing him lugging such a huge burden through the gates—a mystery that most likely would remain unsolved until he finally passed away, whereupon his tower would be dismantled and auctioned off to the rest of the community. Only then would other gremlins have a chance to directly examine the structure and divine its secrets, whereupon the rod, no doubt, would fetch an amazing price.

"Let us move this cautiously," said Bongcor after a moment. "If it drops upon our feet, we will be gravely injured."

"We will lift together, and when we tire, speak so at once, that we may also lower it together."

"Agreed. Shall we go again?"

"Yes, now lift."

Together they hauled the wood-slab about fifteen steps. They probably could've gone a few more, but both gremlins paused, peering upward into the shadows. "Cease," whispered Sithlac, and they set their burden down carefully, ears perked up as they listened.

"The goblin?" Bongcor asked quietly.

Sithlac nodded. The faint scuttling sounded once more, somewhere overhead, and a few tracings of dust fluttered down into the artificial moonlight. He retrieved the lamp from his right shoulder and waved it back and forth, stopping as he caught sight of two small reflections high above. "There," he said quietly. "Goblin-eyes, they are. A rare glimpse of Yog, oh yes, for most times he stays far away."

Bongcor followed the pointing finger and spotted the tiny glows, which vanished for an instant as their owner blinked. The distant shadow then disappeared, and they clearly heard the faint skittering of tiny claws on wood, neither retreating nor closing the distance. A moment later the eyes reappeared a short distance away, and a new sound filtered down from above—the high-pitched sputtering of a goblin-laugh.

"Two gremlins, hee-hee, working together!" twittered Yog, and his shadowy form writhed and jumped with each jovial giggle. "Never before have I seen such a thing! And they try to carry such a burden through the walls! What fun!" He clapped his hands together with glee.

"Only together can we do this thing," called out Sithlac. "Mock us not, goblin outcast!"

Yog stopped laughing and his eyes disappeared once more. For a few seconds the gremlin pair thought he might run away, but instead, he did the opposite. Yog's shadow detached from the plank overhead as he scuttled downward swiftly, using his claws to keep a grip on the cobweb-shrouded drywall. At his approach, Bongcor drew his eyes halfway into his head and crouched behind Sithlac, gripping his spear firmly. His fellow gremlin stood his ground, barely moving at all, figuring he had little to fear from a lone goblin.

Yog got almost close enough to touch before suddenly leaping away and landing in the middle of the wood-slab. Ochre-green in color, he sported a very thin body from which two gnarled arms and legs protruded, all covered in scraps of cloth and dusty cobwebs. His head looked too small for his torso, especially considering the enormous ears that almost wrapped around the back of his head. He carried no visible weapons and only a small bag about his waist, from which a single spider leg protruded.

"Hunters come, hunters go, here in the walls of Man," Yog pronounced, extending himself to his full height, about half that of either gremlin. Standing on the piece of wood, he could look them both right in the eyes. "Yet they are always alone, until this evening past. Then I saw a most amazing sight—two gremlins hunting side by side. An anomaly, or so I thought, and now I must know more."

"No explanation are you due," answered Sithlac calmly, showing no aggression whatsoever, merely stating the facts. "We owe no debt, and thus, have no reason to explain ourselves to such."

"Apologies, great hunter," replied Yog, deferentially inclining his head. "I am merely curious, that is all. Curious that you would work together as goblins do, without some hint of desperation."

"We do not copy goblin ways," insisted Bongcor, obviously a bit irritated at the insinuation. "This we do of our own accord."

Sithlac's left eye swung about to face his companion, and he waved him back with the hand on that side, out of sight of Yog. Meanwhile, he kept his right eye fixed on the goblin, and pointed in his direction with an accusing finger. "No concern of yours is our mission here. Away with you, that we might complete our task, unless you have some help to give."

Yog cocked his head sideways, almost at a right angle to his body. Goblin joints are extremely flexible, and their skin can stretch a considerable amount, giving them the ability to squeeze into very tight places, and navigate through tiny holes no gremlin could ever reach. Though small, they also have surprising strength, and working together can carry very heavy loads a great distance. Unlike gremlins, however, goblins usually don't have much of a sense of individuality. This one appeared to be the exception.

"If help I give, great hunters," he offered after a moment, "what help can you give in return?"

Sithlac and Bongcor exchanged glances. They hadn't intended to do any serious hunting, so neither brought much in the way of supplies. Sithlac, as usual, spoke for the pair. "What does a goblin want that a gremlin can provide?"

"Food," answered Yog immediately. "Always in search of food am I, and spiders are not very filling." He chuckled to himself, pulling a thin arachnid leg from his pouch and sliding it between his sharp front teeth, as though it were a toothpick.

"We brought none this night," answered Sithlac. "Not long here did we expect to be."

"No problem at all." Yog scuttled along the piece of wood, grinning. "Expected as much did I, but I can wait. Simply bring some with you on your next hunt. It has been some time since I dined upon a fat, juicy grub." He licked his thin, narrow lips in anticipation.

Bongcor looked at him in confusion, bobbing up and down a few times as his eyes swiveled back and forth between Yog and Sithlac. "Such a bargain makes no sense," the lesser gremlin finally sputtered. "You give us a thing, we give you a thing, that is how agreements are. That is the essence of the Third Rule."

"Rules, pah!" scoffed Yog. "Your gremlin-laws mean naught to such as I. Agreements are not always about things of now. They can include the promise of things to come."

Bongcor just stared at him in complete befuddlement, but Sithlac nodded slowly. "I have heard of such bargains before," he explained, "although they made little sense to me. Promises are only words, with nothing to maintain them. There are deeds and there are things, and precious little else."

Yog moved closer to him, staring into Sithlac's enormous eye. "Truly believe that, you do not," he hissed. "There is a concept called *trust*, of which you are well aware."

"I have heard the word, oh yes," answered Sithlac, "and understand its meaning, but gremlins have no use for it."

"That is not always true," the goblin replied, pointing a pair of claws at the nearby gremlins in turn, "for the two of you are friends, is that not so?"

Sithlac settled back on his haunches. He considered denying it, but saw no need, for the goblin had obviously been watching them long enough to figure that out. In fact, he'd probably heard most of their conversations the previous night. With their enormous ears, goblins had excellent hearing, after all.

"Be that as it may," Sithlac answered noncommittally, "what has that to do with anything?"

"Friends trust each other," replied Yog with a quick shrug. "They must, for it is the very essence of friendship. We goblins learned this long ago. We bond together, as you have surely seen, and in groups accomplish far more than we ever could alone. This is all made possible because of trust."

Sithlac sighed and rolled his eyes about. "I fail to see how goblin ways explain why such as you would make such a lopsided bargain with two gremlins you know not at all."

"I don't know this one, that is true," said Yog, pointing Bongcor's way, "but you I know quite well. I know all those who hunt within these walls. I watch you come and go, collecting your shiny prizes in the dark. Perfect little thieves, you are."

Bongcor bristled again at the insult, but Sithlac waved him back once more. He was about to say something, but Yog went on. "And then you changed, great hunter. You did something no hunter ever did— you began to hum to yourself. Never before have I heard music from a gremlin. And then, not long after, you brought an apprentice along, and became a friend to him. You are different than before, but still the same. Something has awakened, something new, and with that, I see you can be trusted."

Sithlac shook his head and considered Yog's words. He wanted to argue, but could find no fault in the goblin's conclusion. He had, in fact, felt quite different ever since his encounter with the faerie, humming pleasantly to himself ever since. Her song...something about it must've changed him, in a way that didn't involve magic. Yet Bongcor hadn't encountered her, and he also seemed different, which made little sense.

"So," Yog went on, smiling a toothy grin after making his point, "here is the agreement. Bring to me a fat grub, still wriggling and alive, when next you hunt, and in return, I will help you carry this block to your Tunnel, and show you the best way there as well."

Sithlac cast an eye upon Bongcor, who shrugged. "I see no reason not to agree," he explained, "for with his aid this will be far less difficult, and a grub will cost us little."

"Very well, then," Sithlac replied, "let it be so."

And thus the deal was struck.

Adams Hall – Crawlspaces

Yog proved as good as his word. He showed the gremlins how to heft the long wood-block up onto their shoulders, thus sharing the burden between themselves. Then, as they made their way through the shadowy corridors between the walls, he helped further by walking between them, supporting the plank in the middle as best he could.

As Sithlac expected, the goblin made no attempt to guide them down several levels using the elevator. Such an attempt would've been too complicated, and one slip would send their prize plunging into the dark chasm beneath the Hub. Instead, Yog brought them to a place where the plank might slide downward through a wide slot in the floor, in between an enormous batch of cables as big around as a gremlin's belly. Of course they had to release the wood, but instead of falling with a loud clatter, it instead slid easily down to rest in the cable-cluster below. They then repeated this thrice more until the plank had reached the proper level. After that they had only to carry it a short distance to the hunter's hole, where they paused before the final crossing to the Moonrise Gate.

A simple enough process, and yet it took the trio a little over two hours to complete the task. Gremlins aren't built for heavy lifting, and stopped for frequent breaks. Furthermore, they had to pause for every sound passing by on the other sides of the walls, for if Men heard even a hint of their efforts, they might decide to investigate. Sithlac and Bongcor also failed to bring enough water with them, not expecting the process to take so long, and had to scurry off to refill their containers halfway through their efforts.

Through all of this Yog never complained, instead taking the opportunity to scout around and patrol whenever the gremlins took one of their breaks. Finally, when they reached the hunter's hole, he scuttled away and didn't return. "This is as far as I go this night," he called out from the darkness overhead. "Return here upon the morrow with my reward, and I shall be eagerly waiting."

His last words faded into the distance. Sithlac and Bongcor sucked on a water-drop as they followed the sound, glad for the chance to rest, for they both knew they would now face the hardest part of their journey. Without the goblin helping to share the load, they'd need to go all the way across the outer room and enter the gate without stopping. If a Man chose that moment to approach from one of the halls, it would spell disaster.

Once fully rested, Sithlac stood and paced about, worriedly considering the crossing to come. More than once he tested the hole, and found it accessible, meaning no Men lurked beyond. With a few deep-throated chants, he renewed the fortification spell that strengthened his arms and back, and also ensured the shaping hadn't faded. Nearby, Bongcor did the same, but without standing, keeping his eyes almost completely shut.

"A long journey it will be, across the open floor," the lesser gremlin remarked after a while. His voice echoed faintly around the room, almost sounding unnatural in the near darkness.

"We will succeed, oh yes, in that we will most surely," answered Sithlac, "but that is not my greater fear. Once beyond the gate, we must carry our burden through the streets, to its destination, and install it straightaway. In this we must not falter."

"Will the sentry challenge us?" asked Bongcor worriedly.

"Quite possibly, but we should press on as soon as possible. Once we do, we will stop no more until we reach the alley. Are you prepared?"

"I am, but there is one thing left to do. Saved this spell I have, and all my ration will it take. When I finish, we must wait no more."

"What spell—" began Sithlac, but stopped at once as his companion began to chant. The lesser gremlin stood, putting his hands on the wooden plank, and, keeping his eyes tightly shut, directed the unfamiliar incantation into their burden.

For several long seconds he cast and then, with a kind of wheezing gasp, he stopped. "Let us go at once," he suggested urgently, lifting up the wooden slab as though it weighed nothing. Sithlac, eyes wide with astonishment, repeated the gesture and found the plank light as a feather.

Shaking his head in wonder, he opened up the hunter's hole and hurried through.

Morningside Tunnel – Interior

The best part of the whole evening, at least in Sithlac's eyes, came about a minute later as the two hunters strode brazenly past the goggle-eyed sentry, holding aloft an enormous wood-block as though they did so every night. Norbac, who at any other time would've asked to see and log their treasures, just sat there with his huge mouth dangling wide open, unable to even gurgle a single guttural syllable as Sithlac and Bongcor cruised on by.

The deburdening spell, a difficult and magic-intensive incantation by any measure, didn't last long. Before the two hunters got halfway to their homes, the weight started to return, reaching its full strength before they made it to the moonward commons. Unwilling to stop lest other gremlins question their ownership of such a fine treasure, Sithlac urged Bongcor to hurry on. Both were staggering by the time they reached the alley, dropping the plank just within Sithlac's groundspace before the two exhausted gremlins all but collapsed from the effort.

As they sipped on a refreshing water-drop, many curious gremlins stopped to marvel at the enormous wooden plank, the largest one they'd ever seen in the Tunnel. Despite needing more rest, Sithlac hurried into his home and retrieved several metal fasteners, including the carpet tacks they'd recovered some nights before. With Bongcor's help they pushed the plank into position, completely blocking the alley, and Sithlac commenced to hammering it into place. This brought more than a few murmurs of complaint from passersby, for most were used to using the formerly empty alley as a shortcut to and from the commons.

Sithlac didn't respond, instead collecting more wood-blocks from within his home. Bongcor, by now recovered from his efforts, assisted as well, and soon they'd completely blocked the space between their towers with slabs of wood a full level high, all of them firmly attached to both homes equally well. Passing gremlins muttered and complained, for the most part, but could do nothing about it, for of course Sithlac and Bongcor had every right to fill their allotted groundspace as they pleased. The former alley existed only as a convenience, after all.

Both were busy attaching another piece from their wood stockpile to the second level of their joint structure when the focus of the constant murmuring shifted noticeably. Sithlac glanced to the side with one eye, not stopping his hammering, and saw something shiny approaching. Bongcor saw it too, and immediately dropped his tools, bounding away to disappear inside his second level, a single eye just barely visible in the window.

Sithlac knew full well what this meant, but didn't waver. His right eye focused in on a squat, grossly overweight gremlin wearing overlapping plates of metal like a suit of armor. The clunky outfit wouldn't do a thing in combat, except weigh the wearer down, instead functioning only as a ceremonial badge of office. Only someone as wealthy as Tirchoth the Grand would march through the streets of the Morningside Tunnel wearing so many valuable shinies as though they were clothing.

"You there!" the Tunnel-master called out, waving a pearl-topped, golden stick pin around as though it were a staff. "What madness do you pursue? Cease this ludicrous activity at once!"

Sithlac, undaunted, continued his hammering until the carpet tack settled firmly in place. Only then did he set down his tools and focus both eyes on Tirchoth. "There is no madness here, O greatest among us. A fair and just bargain it is, between two agreeing neighbors, nothing more."

"Bah! No division do I see!" yelled out Tirchoth, banging the tip of his staff on the lowest wooden plank. "Where is the border between your groundspace? I see it not!"

"It is there, upon the ground, as it has always been," replied Sithlac, pointing at the clearly obvious scratching on the bedrock below. "It need not carry to our structures at all, and no such Rule exists to suggest such, as well you should know, Great One."

"Do you dare mock me?" demanded Tirchoth angrily. He stormed about, waving his staff all about in frustration, causing the nearby onlookers to retreat. More than a few, however, chuckled faintly at his difficulties.

"Not mockery as such," replied Sithlac calmly, "merely a statement of fact. Nothing in the Rules prevents what we do here so you seek to stop our lawful efforts with empty threats and feckless bluster. Begone, for we have work to do." With that, he waved a hand dismissively and resumed hammering, turning both eyes away from Tirchoth.

The crowd's mild chuckling turned to open laughter. The Tunnel-master, fuming, spun on his heels to depart. "Not the last of this have you heard, fool of a hunter," he hissed, storming away, his worthless metal armor clanking noisily in his wake.

The crowd gradually dispersed, many among them still snickering at the spectacle of their ostentatious leader being taken down a peg. Bongcor emerged a moment later, eyes darting about warily, and picked up his tools. "Was that wise, to anger him so, friend neighbor?" he asked worriedly.

"Perhaps, and perhaps not," said Sithlac with a shrug. "He would always oppose what we do here, no matter my response, but word of this encounter will no doubt spread. Perhaps, by standing up to him, we might gain an ally where otherwise we would not. Now come, let us continue. If we finish the second level soon, we can sleep the day away."

"And a worthy goal it is, oh yes," Bongcor agreed, and the two gremlins resumed their work.

Morningside Tunnel – Sithlac/ Bongcor Dual Tower

As hoped, the industrious duo had enough energy in them to complete their task before retiring. When finished, they had effectively filled in the former alleyway with a series of strategically placed wood slabs forming a kind of bridge. The structure wasn't solid, but hollow inside, although that hardly mattered for now. They expected to fill it eventually, whereupon it would support and brace the towers on either side, with a ledge all around the edges where decorative shinies could be hung. For now, though, the connector served its purpose, keeping other gremlins off the property while Sithlac and Bongcor took a much-needed rest.

Upon rising that afternoon, they placed their remaining four wood-slabs, using the last of Sithlac's store of carpet tacks and other fasteners in the process. Now they had the framework of their joint third level, but the lack of building material left the project stalled for now. After some eager discussions of how to proceed from there, they purchased a meal, along with something extra for their new ally. Then, anxious to continue, they headed out of the Tunnel just after moonrise, sharing the duty of lugging along a large sack that occasionally twitched in their grip.

Bongcor set the wriggling bag down as they finally neared their destination. "Friend hunter, do you suppose the goblin will truly come this night?"

"What is there to fear?" replied Sithlac with a casual shrug. "His enthusiasm was plain to see, oh yes. Why such doubts?"

"A goblin he is," answered Bongcor matter-of-factly. "Not the most reliable of creatures are they, as well you should know."

"And yet they are true to their bargains," pointed out Sithlac. "At market-day, and again in their own burrows, they do not break their word. Besides, this one has nothing better to do. He will come."

Bongcor nodded as he stepped over a coil of twisted wire that curled its way between two holes in the wall. Ahead, he saw the edge of the hunter's hole where they had left the goblin the night before. Of Yog, there was no sign. The lesser gremlin let out a long puff of breath and carefully set down his squirming burden, making sure the sack remained sealed as he rested.

"In just a few nights' hunting, you have learned much," Sithlac informed him. "Much more than I learned in my first season alone."

"To this I owe you all, oh yes," Bongcor replied, slurping a single drop from the waterskin at his side, "and it is a debt I cannot easily repay."

Sithlac acknowledged that by puffing up his throat a bit and then went on. "Yet there are some things that cannot be taught. On your senses you must often rely. Use them now, and reveal that which you can learn from them."

"A test," stated Bongcor.

"Just so, and in all silence, now."

The lesser gremlin nodded, peering out into the gloom. The pale light emitted by the glow-rod in Sithlac's open hand cast shadows all about. Bongcor stood, stepped forward, and took the shining stick, holding it overhead. His eyes twisted this way and that, one moving up and down while the other roamed side to side. He turned slowly, keeping as quiet as he could. A faint, distant clank echoed through the walls, but by now he'd learned to recognize the sound made by the faraway Hub, which, for now, interested him not at all.

After about fifteen seconds, Bongcor's right eye stopped moving, peering into the darkness overhead. The other eye swiveled around to face the same direction. "The goblin," he whispered in a low voice. "He is here."

Sithlac nodded. "Your senses serve you well, friend hunter. He is here, indeed."

"Then why does he not show himself?"

"He sleeps, of course," chuckled the more experienced gremlin, raising his voice quite noticeably. "Yog! We come! Awaken, for your meal awaits!"

The two gremlins heard nothing for a few moments and then a few scratchings echoed down from above, followed by a faint trickle of dust. Several seconds later, Yog dropped down onto the enormous wooden plank, rubbing at his eyes and yawning. "About time," he grumbled, shading his eyes from the glowing rock in Sithlac's hand. "Making me wait here all day, with nothing but the thought of food to sustain me!"

"After nightfall, we did agree," pointed out Sithlac. "Gremlins travel not by day, as you should surely know."

"Yes, yes, of course," scoffed Yog with a dismissive wave of his hand. "Even though the Sun's light cannot penetrate here, you still cling to your pointless traditions. Whatever. I have assisted you as per our bargain so I beseech you, keep me waiting no longer!"

Sithlac opened the bag and withdrew a wriggling grub, handing it out toward the wide-eyed, hungry-looking goblin. "As we agreed, your reward awaits."

Yog hopped forward and snatched the squirming creature out of Sithlac's hands, needlessly bounding back in an instant as though terrified of retaliation. Without releasing his grip on his prize, the goblin scrambled up the nearby wall to a protruding ledge just overhead. There, he produced a knife from somewhere unseen and sliced the grub into several pieces. Without a word of thanks, he began noisily devouring his meal without a thought toward politeness or courtesy.

"Did you know he had a blade?" asked Bongcor quietly, keeping one eye focused on Yog while the other faced his friend. "In what secret place did it lurk?"

"I knew not," Sithlac replied. "Perhaps he is more than he appears. Although, just now, he merely appears hungry."

Yog paused momentarily in his hungry chomping. "I said I haven't had a grub in quite some time, don't forget," he called out. "Not since leaving my home, in fact. So good, so good indeed! And to think you eat so well all the time. No wonder you're both so enormously fat." He snickered to himself for a moment, before noisily slurping on another chunk of insect flesh.

"Such gratitude," remarked Bongcor, rocking his head from side to side. "We offer aid, and he delivers naught but derision."

"While you speak as though I cannot hear," Yog responded. "Besides, our deal is done. What other aid are you referring to? Do you have another proposal? Because if so, I'm all ears." He laughed again, waggling his oversized lobes in their direction.

"We do bring another proposal, it is true," pointed out Sithlac, "but one not so easy to define. We await the conclusion of your meal."

"Wait no longer," came the reply. Yog picked up the last of his grub and sucked it down, tossing the remnants of rubbery skin aside. After wiping his hands and face on his tattered rags, he bounded down off the ledge and back to the floor, his belly noticeably swollen. Regarding the gremlins with curiosity and a slightly suspicious glare, he scratched a claw between his sharp front teeth and scowled. "Get on with it, then. What do you need now, and what would you offer me?"

"Before I tell," said Sithlac, his eyes shifting up and down as he tried to figure out where on Yog's skinny body he might've stashed his knife, "there is a thing that I would know. You are outcast from your own people, is that not so?"

"That is true," answered Yog. "What of it?"

"Why would they cast you out?" inquired Sithlac. "What crime would such as you commit that demands a rejection by your own kind?"

Yog glanced away, cowering slightly, as though the question caused him physical pain. For a moment both gremlins thought perhaps he wouldn't answer. Ever since Bongcor wondered that very thing during their first hunt together, Sithlac had been curious about Yog's past. However, he'd already decided that the answer hardly mattered. Mostly he just wanted to find out if the goblin would explain himself or not, or if he'd spin some outrageous lie.

Yog hesitated still further, rubbing his swollen stomach idly before backing up and settling on his haunches. "I shouldn't tell you," he finally replied. "Such things are not your business. Yet, I should not be speaking to you at all, should I? I really should keep to myself, like the wizened little hermit I am. I just can't do that anymore, though. It's too lonely. But then, that's the point, I guess."

Sithlac and Bongcor exchanged single-eyed glances, but said nothing, waiting for Yog to continue. He finally did, after another long pause. "I got old," explained the goblin with a weary sigh. "Most of us don't see more than thirty summers, but I just kept right on going. I guess I'm too stubborn to die or something, but you see, there's this rule we have. It's just as stupid as some of your gremlin rules, but it's there, and rules are all we have sometimes, I think, so there you are. When a goblin hits fifty, you see, that's the limit. That's all you get. So on my fiftieth birthday, they declared me dead."

"Dead?" asked Bongcor curiously. "Yet you appear quite definitely alive, oh yes."

"Yes, you'd think the fact that I can still walk and talk would mean something, but not to goblin-kind, I'm afraid. Do you know what happens when goblins die, hmm? Do you?"

"I have never seen such a thing," replied Sithlac, "but when gremlins die, our bodies are returned to the night, and our possessions bid upon in a great auction."

"Sounds like fun," Yog commented with a protracted roll of his beady eyes, "but you see, we goblins don't keep private property or possessions like you do. What we own is part of the community, and that includes our bodies. So when we die, our corpses are devoured by our friends and family, just like any other food."

Bongcor looked noticeably horrified, shying away slightly and retracting both eyes partway into their sockets, but Sithlac managed to conceal his disgust. The idea of consuming another gremlin turned his stomach, but he forced himself to remember that goblins were different and had their own ways of doing things. "So terrible a fate, it seems," he remarked diplomatically, "for someone still alive."

Yog pointed a clawed finger right at him. "Exactly so!" he all but shouted. "And that's what makes what I did so terrible, at least to my people, anyway. You see, I wouldn't accept that fate. I didn't fancy being eaten alive, you see, so I did what I had to do—I left! I took what little I could carry and high-tailed it right out of there. If I ever go back—or if they ever catch me—you can guess what'll happen. Only this time I won't be an honorable meal for my family—I'll be dismembered alive and thrown to the criminals and beggars. Oh, and just in case you're wondering, it'd be the same if I went to some other goblin enclave. They'd find out my age easily enough, and that'd be the end of me."

"So terrible a tale," replied Bongcor. "How is it, then, that you persist? What keeps you going, having lost all you know?"

"Mmm, that's the question, isn't it?" Yog paced back and forth for a moment. "Like I said, I'm stubborn to the core. I just can't lie down and die like that. I want a better death than getting munched on by my kin. There's also part of me that just wants to stick it to them, to show them all that being fifty isn't the end of everything—and even better, if someone shows a rule's too stupid to keep using, they should get rid of it. I'm living proof of that—my fifty-first winter is coming up. I've survived almost a year out here already, and that means I could've still been productive back home, couldn't I? I might last another five more years at this rate, and I could've still contributed. Maybe somehow I can prove them wrong, and that'll change things. Who knows? In the meantime, though, I've got to survive, and so, here I am, making deals with gremlins, of all things! Speaking of that, I answered your stupid question, so will you please get on with it? I'm not getting any younger, you know."

Sithlac nodded and bobbed up and down for a moment. He hadn't expected such a long and detailed answer, but Yog's tale certainly explained a lot. Sithlac really knew very little about goblin society, but he did know they were very regimented, living by the letter of their rules with even more dedication than gremlins. In fact, from what he'd heard, he would've expected most goblins to accept their fate rather than flee as Yog had. Perhaps there was more to this story, but then, this didn't seem like the time to press further. Instead, Sithlac proceeded with his pitch, as he and Bongcor had already discussed earlier in the day.

"As you noted once before, the two of us have become friends," explained Sithlac, while Bongcor inclined his head slightly. "In our Tunnel, we are neighbors, and now, we seek to link our towers, that we may climb ever higher than before. To do this, a great many wood-blocks do we need, oh yes, and much more besides."

"What does that matter to me?" demanded Yog. "Simply purchase what you need at market-day. Surely a hunter as great as you possesses trading materials aplenty."

"There will be no market-day for us, oh no," explained Sithlac. "The Council will block our efforts at every turn, for they would see us fail. Thus we must acquire our materials through the hunt. That is why we need your aid, you see. A goblin can enter places we cannot, can spot that which we would never find."

"Wait, you want me to hunt for you?" Yog asked, aghast. "You want me to drag things through this place, so you can—"

"You need move nothing, oh no," Sithlac insisted. "Simply find for us a source of raw materials; that is all we ask. Enough that we can raise our tower as high as it can go, and that is all."

Yog's eyes narrowed to little slits, almost too small to see. "I see what you get out of it," he hissed, "but what's in it for me?"

Sithlac grinned. "A fat grub, each night, at the rising of the Moon," he answered. "This much we can provide, as well you know. You need hunt for food no longer, nor will you ever starve."

"So let me see if I understand this correctly," the goblin all but growled. "You're offering me a...a *job?* You're...*hiring* me?"

"As you say, and so we are," Sithlac agreed. "And as proof, we offer this, our first payment upon the deal." He gestured with one hand, and Bongcor pushed the bag across the floor—a bag that wasn't completely empty after all.

Yog looked inside, to find another fat, juicy grub within. He pulled the squirming creature out, eyes wide with wonder. He hesitated but a moment before blurting out his answer. "A bargain it is, indeed," he insisted eagerly. "Very well, gremlins, I accept your terms. You have yourselves a scout!"

Morningside Tunnel Commons – Market-Day

Sithlac moved cautiously through the busy street, glancing about with both eyes repeatedly, even as Bongcor shuffled along close behind, clutching a great sack filled with shinies for trade. Their final efforts the previous night scored a red pushpin and two bent staples, along with a few strands of dusty thread, but little else. Upon returning home in weariness, the two gremlins slept as long as they dared, rising late and hastening to collect what they could for trade, hoping their fears of being ostracized from the market would prove unfounded.

Sithlac entered the commons cautiously, as though he might be apprehended at any moment, or at least challenged by one of Council's enforcers—a worry he knew had little basis in reality, but stuck with him nonetheless. Noting his superior's apprehension, Bongcor stayed close to the ground, one eye fixed on the bag of treasures, though theft of such things was all but unheard of. He swung his other eye around to regard the various nearby stalls, packed with wares and surrounded by jabbering traders of all kinds, unsure of what to do, but determined to keep as close as possible to his friend.

"A busy place this day, oh yes," said Sithlac, studying the normally wide-open area with one sweeping eye. "Many more than I have seen of late, which might bode well for us, though not so many wood-blocks as I would expect. Come, the goblins usually bring such things only as far as they must."

Having not seen any indication of challenge, Sithlac raised himself a bit and pushed forward through the crowd. Gremlins of all ages and social levels moved freely about, pushing past each other and frequently arguing as they sought pathways through the chaotic sea of bodies. Some dragged sacks full of tradeables, while others lugged their purchases along, always by themselves, never accepting or requesting help of any kind. Sithlac, having already experienced a better way, had to stifle the urge to shake his head in bewilderment. Even the sight of a trio of goblins, trotting in from the Sunset Gate with a fresh wood-slab for trade, its bulk shouldered easily by the three of them, didn't register at all on the individualistic gremlins passing by. Sithlac paused as he studied the wood, nodding at its shape and strength, and followed along behind.

"Ah, I see you noticed our fine quality building-block!" called out another goblin, this one dressed in the bright blue tunic of a trademaster. "See the precision of its angled cuts! Why, such a thing would be perfect for the corner of a new level, wouldn't you agree? Step right up and let's talk business!"

Sithlac approached, with Bongcor lingering a short distance behind. "I do indeed seek such slabs, for just that very purpose," he agreed readily. "I bring many shinies for trade, enough to purchase several, should you have more."

The goblin shuffled aside as his workers deposited the wood-block on the ground nearby and paused to catch their breaths. He studied Sithlac for a few moments through narrowed eyes before finally hopping on top of the cut plank to regard him from a position overhead. "That's funny," remarked the goblin eventually, "but you don't look like you've brought very much at all, O eager one, unless that shawl of yours hides something special."

"My neighbor holds what I offer," announced Sithlac, pointing at Bongcor, who ambled forward with the bag clutched in both hands. "There is more, as well, should our dealing proceed most successfully."

The goblin frowned, his demeanor suddenly shifting from one of a hopeful salesman to that of a nervous backroom dealer. "You are Sithlac and Bongcor," he noted in a hushed voice.

"That is so," agreed the hunter. "What know you of us?"

The goblin glanced around worriedly, scratching at his chin, and his fellows nearby seemed to cower up against the wall, acting as though ready to bolt. After a few moments' thought, the trader came to a decision. "You have nothing that I want," he insisted. "Begone, that others might approach and make their offers."

"But we have not yet presented—" began Bongcor, reaching into the bag, but he never got to finish the statement.

"I said you have nothing!" barked the goblin. "Go, that I might find other worthy customers! I wish you luck, brave gremlins, but there can be no trade between us. Go!"

Bongcor started to protest again, but Sithlac held up a hand, silencing him instantly. The two moved off, along the edge of the crowd, until they sidled into an unused space along the edge of a nearby alley. "It is as we feared most surely," said the lead hunter. "The warning has been passed not to trade with us."

"Your words ring true, sadly enough," agreed Bongcor, "yet they cannot refuse us if they know not who we are. Perhaps we should not travel together."

"If we do not," noted Sithlac, "spies for the Council might claim one of us made a deal on behalf of the other, and initiate a dispute. No, all works upon our tower must be done in concert, lest we invite their wrath."

Bongcor nodded slowly. "Again, wise counsel, but perhaps we might disguise our teamwork better. I can stay close by, yet speak not at all, as though but another interested customer."

"Agreed," said Sithlac, taking the bag and hefting it over his shoulder. The two proceeded back out into the commons, Bongcor doing his best to stay close without looking like he followed in his friend's wake. They meandered through the chaos for a few minutes, occasionally pausing to rise up on their haunches and peer about, looking over the wares of nearby sellers. Most were goblins, of course, though a few gremlins had set up small booths of their own. Sithlac spotted no significant sources of wood, though, so he moved slowly onward, crossing the commons toward the spriggan side, adjacent to the cistern. As he headed toward the gaily decorated booths, covered in bright cloth so as to attract the eye, he caught sight of a pair of elves and came up short.

"What is it?" inquired Bongcor, rising up slightly to peer through the maze. "Are those indeed elves I see?"

"They are," agreed Sithlac, studying the two closely. He'd seen elves before, of course—tall and thin, with bodies similar in shape to those of Men (but only a fraction of their size), they wore bright green uniforms made of cured hides and carefully carved insect shells. Their narrow heads, topped with shocks of black hair, turned slowly from side to side, regarding the great crowd nearby with obvious disdain. Though market-day was open to all, Sithlac seldom encountered elves who cared to make such a journey, for their travels would be long and arduous—the nearest kingdoms being located quite some distance away.

"What brings such as they?" inquired Bongcor, regarding the two elves warily. They stood before a small booth draped in light green cloth, their wares out of sight and thus a mystery. "No elf has come hither in at least two seasons."

Sithlac nodded, not bothering to ask how his companion would know such a detail. "I doubt they carry much in the way of wood, so what do they have to trade, I wonder? I think we should find out."

So saying, he approached the booth with bag in hand. Bongcor, trying not to look too obvious, swung wide and then slipped up from a slightly different direction, so that each drew the attention of a different elf. "I seek fasteners and seals," claimed Sithlac. "Can such things be found within? If so, I humbly request an audience with your master."

"As do I," added Bongcor quickly, "if I may, at least, and you don't mind, that is."

The two guards nodded. Both gremlins had already noted the twin blades at their sides, but the elves didn't make to draw them. Such items would almost never be unsheathed within the confines of the Tunnel—they were there for show, and for defense during the long trip home. Without a word, the two gremlins found themselves waved inside.

They slipped within and found themselves surrounded by stacks and stacks of long metal fasteners, ranging in length from that of a forearm to about half their own height. At one end of each gleaming pole, the tip tapered to a fine point, while opposite, the metal widened into a flat surface suitable for hammering. Sithlac's eyes went wide, for he'd never seen an array of nails quite like this—enough to build a tower to the sky, should he so choose, if he could but afford such a vast collection of treasures.

Before he could so much as reach out to touch any of the amazingly powerful-looking fasteners, another elf stepped out from between a fold in the cloth draped all about the booth. Unlike the guards outside, this one wore no armor, only a thin, green robe decorated about the seams in gold trim. His hair bore streaks of gray, and his eyes were somewhat sunken, attesting to a greater age.

"Greetings, fortunate ones," said the proprietor. "I am Ruvian, and as you can see, we've come upon quite a cache of these nails your kind find so useful. Alas, we of the Birchspears now face war, and while these will serve us not at all as weapons, they might trade for such. Do you bring anything today that might be used to slay our enemies?"

Sithlac cringed slightly. He knew quite well that the Council had declared the Morningside Tunnel neutral in all wars that might take place within the Great Wide Park—something that happened with annoying frequency, for the kingdoms there seemed incapable of settling even minor disputes by any other means. To provide weapons to one combatant might appear as choosing sides to some. Yet if such a deal followed all other established Rules, with a fair transaction for both parties, Sithlac figured he could safely argue otherwise—after all, the opposition, too, could take advantage of the same opportunity, should they but choose to do so.

So, with that in mind, he nodded slowly, lifting up one of the nails with something very near to reverence. "I would have as many of these as I could buy," he admitted readily, pushing his sack closer so that it fell open. "Here within this bag I bring many shinies. Some might work as weapons, as you can see, and others, perhaps, as armor for your warriors."

Ruvian smiled and bent down, poking through the bag briefly. "I do see some items of use," he commented, "but while I have given you my name, you have yet to confer the same honor upon me."

"I apologize most surely," offered Sithlac, crouching toward the floor by way of apology. "I am known as Sithlac, the hunter."

At the sound of that name, Ruvian loosed his hold on the bag, shaking his head. "Ah, well, regrettably we can't do business then," he sighed. "I apologize, and it's truly a shame, for I could use a couple of those pins, and some of those metal bits can be shaped into shields, exactly as you suggested. Pity."

"I understand not at all," sighed Sithlac, though of course he knew exactly what this meant. "For what reason am I turned away?"

"This other one here must be Bongcor, correct?" the elf went on. "Well met, gremlins, but surely you must be aware your own Council has directed those of us at market to deal with you two not at all, lest we be banished from this place. As I said, a true pity, for I would surely love this item here, and this one." He lifted out the pushpin the two hunters had found the previous evening, as well as the longest and straightest of their carpet tacks. "Not to mention this." He withdrew a tarnished key ring, rolling it back and forth in his hands. "This would make an outstanding frame for a very sturdy shield, indeed. Were it within my power, I would offer you this for these three items."

With that he reached down and separated eight short, thick nails from the rest, pushing them across the floor toward Sithlac, who cast a single greedy eye upon them. Such a trade was far better than he could hope for—yet to hear the elf tell it, no such deal could possibly be made. "I would agree most readily to your terms," he noted succinctly, "yet see not how it matters, seeing as you dare not violate the Council's edict."

Ruvian nodded slowly. "You are, of course, correct. I cannot possibly engage in trade with such as you, nor shall I attempt to do so. You will leave now, carrying only what you brought with you, and I shall keep what's mine. However, upon the close of business, should you happen to find yourself outside the Sunset Gate, alongside the first descending pipe past the transit-hole, with those items in hand, perhaps you might find a cache of nails awaiting you. Such a discovery would be, of course, a mere coincidence—a fortunate happenstance well within the bounds of luck for hunters of your obvious skill."

Sithlac bobbed his head up and down eagerly. "Yes, of course, and so it shall," he agreed at once. "It is indeed a shame, clever elf, that we could not come to terms this day, oh yes indeed. I wish you luck in your quest to aid your tribe. Farewell."

At that he turned and scuttled out of the booth, doing his best to look disappointed as he dragged the sack along behind him. Bongcor, too, kept himself low to the ground and the two moved into an eddy in the crowd, shaking slightly, each with one wide eye fixed upon the other while otherwise surveying their surroundings.

"Another failure," complained Sithlac boldly. "Let us continue to search, for we might yet find someone who might deal with us."

"A shame the elves would not bargain," offered Bongcor, just in case someone nearby might be listening in. "Nonetheless, the quest goes on."

They proceeded on into the spriggan section of the market, where they found, as usual, the little creatures had done their best to top each other for the most garish of displays. Spriggans, which stood only slightly taller than a goblin, resembled short, stocky elves, but with bald heads and long, brightly dyed beards, usually colored to match the pure pastel colors of their outfits. Although at any given moment the gremlins could see at least two or three dozen spriggans, not a single one's chosen color matched that of any other. Sithlac had on occasion wondered what purpose the various hues might mean—perhaps wealth, or social status, or a measure of personal power—but never bothered to ask. The way spriggans loved to tell jokes and play tricks, he figured he wouldn't get a straight answer, anyway. Yet despite their jocular nature, the little creatures were fair bargainers, often giving more than expected for a shiny thing they found interesting—even something no goblin or elf would give a second glance.

Sithlac and Bongcor tried several booths, hoping to secure a small wood-block or two, or perhaps more fasteners, but the traders always exchanged names first—a regular custom at the market—and upon learning the identities of their customers, sent them away at once. After a few rounds of this, Bongcor began to grow disenchanted, his body flattening out as he walked, but Sithlac pressed on. As the trading-day neared its end, and they passed near a small, gaily-colored booth near the back corner of the commons, a pink-clad spriggan arm reached out and waved them inside.

Seeing no reason to do otherwise, Sithlac scuttled into the small, confined space with Bongcor on his heels. They found themselves confronted by a pair of young spriggans: a female dressed in bright pink and a male in a dark lavender tunic. Both sported beards reaching halfway to the floor, and tall conical caps with golden tassels at the top. "I am Keena," said the lady trader, "and this is my mate, Pineel. You must be the infamous Sithlac and Bongcor."

"Our names precede us, it seems," agreed Sithlac. "Yet you speak to us nonetheless, so perhaps our day might not end in abject failure."

"Perhaps it might not, at that," said Pineel. "We care little for your Council's declaration against you, which to us seems quite capricious. The penalty they threaten means little to us—you see, this is to be our last visit to this Tunnel, for we are mated now, and shall soon undertake the Great Journey."

"The what?" asked Sithlac curiously.

"I have heard of this," put in Bongcor. "A spriggan pair, mated of two clans, might spark dispute should they settle with one over the other. Thus they travel far, to find a new home elsewhere, if they can."

At that, the two lovers held each other close for a moment, smiling. "It is as you say," Keena agreed, "and a long and dangerous trip it shall be, indeed. Thus we have spent the day seeking treasures that might help us on our trip. What do you bring, gremlins, that we might buy with the last of our worthy fasteners?"

As she spoke, the other pushed out a small bag containing a collection of short, twisted screws of various lengths. Sithlac frowned slightly, recognizing these as useful, but much more difficult to work with than nails. While the others might be driven with a simple pounding-spell, the method for manipulating screws took a great deal more effort. Still, seeing as they'd had virtually no success finding someone to trade with today, he felt he couldn't really complain.

Bongcor took the initiative and showed off the shinies in their bag. Pineel and Keena sifted through the items, discarding most right away, but openly discussing the merits of others one after the other. They ultimately selected a thick coil of purple thread, a long chain of metal bits linked together, a piece of soft rubbery material that seemed malleable (but that Sithlac had yet to find a use for), and the shiny metal cap he'd been working with the morning he first spoke to Bongcor about becoming a hunter. With almost no hesitation, both gremlins agreed instantly to the trade.

"That's all we have, then," said Keena. "Come, love, let's take what we have and go. Our journey begins on the morrow. Thank you, gremlins, and good luck to you."

"And to you," agreed Sithlac, pushing the six screws into his bag and departing straightaway.

Adams Hall – Interior

As soon as the market closed, Sithlac and Bongcor took the key ring, pushpin, and carpet tack out the Sunset Gate, making sure the sentry there saw nothing other than a large bag containing what might simply be travel supplies. This particular gate exited not into a common area, but directly into a crawlspace at the junction of two sections of wall. Overhead, a large pipe branched off in both directions, to the right suddenly bending and dropping into the floor. To this the two gremlins made their way in haste, slipping past the pipe into the dark area beyond.

Here they found the contingent of elves waiting patiently. With barely a word, the illicit swap was made and both sides took leave of the other, the travelers hastening off into the darkness as if they might be challenged at any moment. Sithlac and Bongcor, flushed with success, took the long way around to the Moonrise Gate, so as not to alert the Sunset sentry to their unusual activities. Someone paying close attention to their movements might make the connection, considered Sithlac, but even if they did, something taking place outside the Tunnel would be extremely difficult to adjudicate. By the time anyone figured out the elves might be involved as well, they'd be long gone, anyway.

Though grateful to have collected a nice stash of fasteners, the gremlins knew the lack of building-wood limited any further construction for the moment. After returning to the Tunnel, the pair made their way back to their joint structure and stashed the nails. Next they ventured forth once more, this time bringing several water-skins along, stuffed inside their carry-bags. Normally Sithlac would insist on leaving such bulky items behind, instead foraging as they went, but he didn't expect to undertake a full-fledged hunt this trip, only meet up with Yog for advice and ideas.

However, to Sithlac's great disappointment, they didn't find their would-be guide at the first hunter's hole, leaving the two gremlins at a loss. After perhaps fifteen minutes of waiting, they gave up and moved in the direction of the Hub, before the more experienced traveler let out a low hiss, keeping his eyes quite deliberately forward.

"What is it, friend hunter?" asked Bongcor worriedly, struggling to detect whatever might've disturbed his mentor. "What comes?"

"Something follows, that is all I know," replied Sithlac. "Not a goblin-sound, oh no, but being followed we surely are. Look not, but increase our pace, oh yes. To the Hub we must make haste."

They raced onward, but the faint sounds behind them neither faded out nor increased in volume. At length Bongcor picked them out from the noises he and Sithlac were making as they scurried through the walls. "Another gremlin, perhaps?" he asked softly. "Making for the Hub, same as we?"

"Possible it is," agreed his companion, "but let us tarry not. When we reach the cavern, we must not wait, but rather climb. If another gremlin it is, he will not follow, unless he aims to seek us out."

Bongcor nodded in agreement and the two hurried on. As soon as they stepped into the hollow shaft, they started making their way up the walls. This proved more difficult than normal, for the bare metal was slick and sometimes their suckers didn't hold quite right. Still, there were plenty of handholds to use, so they made slow but steady progress. After a couple of minutes they reached a kind of hollow depression in the wall and took refuge there, keeping their backs to a cluster of wires held together by a single interlocking string. From this perch they could look down at the landing below and see who or what might emerge, if anyone did at all.

They waited several more minutes and started to wonder if perhaps their mysterious pursuer had given up, when at last they heard the noticeable sound of footsteps approaching. Just then the Hub activated and started down, forcing the gremlins to retreat, lest they be struck as it moved past. The moment the elevator passed by, they peered down below to see another gremlin face looking up at them. As the two bulbous eyes widened in recognition, the froglike mouth opening into a toothless grin.

"Departed you have not," said the new arrival. "A good thing it is, for we must speak, where no others can hear."

"Then come, for there is space for you here, and our words will not carry," called out Sithlac, trying to keep his voice as even as he could.

The other gremlin, noticeably older and thinner, started up the shaft without the slightest hint of worry or concern. He had a lithe, athletic look to him, not grossly overweight like so many others of his wealth and status, but then, unlike the rest of the Council, he still hunted regularly, not content to sit on his laurels. This was Gurtok, owner of one of the few six-level towers in the Morningside Tunnel, and currently ranked Third of the Nine. Neither Sithlac nor Bongcor failed to recognize him, but what business he could have here, in secret and outside the Tunnel, they could not guess.

In due course Gurtok reached the alcove and squeezed inside, having little trouble getting comfortable in the shallow space. "You know my name and rank, I trust?" he inquired casually as he settled in.

"Of course," agreed Sithlac, "and you ours, as well?"

"You at least I know, but this other not at all," replied the Third. "At least, not until the day just past, when our great leader called us to Council and demanded action against you both."

"So the Council convened, as we thought it must," stated Sithlac with a calmness that surprised him, "and now you come to deliver the news."

Nearby, Bongcor shuddered and shifted nervously about. They had both entertained various thoughts about what might happen should the Council choose to act, and now, it seemed, they would learn their fate. Still, it seemed terribly odd that this news would be delivered in secret, and by Gurtok the Third, of all people. Sithlac would've expected any proclamations would be pronounced directly by the First, and in a public forum.

"It is so, but only in a way," answered Gurtok, who seemed a bit amused by the reactions from the two lesser gremlins. "Tirchoth's ire was as grand as his tower, and yet, he swayed the Council not at all. The First Rule stands firm, as I believe he knew it must, and our votes were unanimous, as of course he knew they would be. Yet, agreed with him some did, in secret and in silence. The result of this you saw today."

"At the market," answered Sithlac succinctly.

"Just so," Gurtok replied with a nod. "The Rules protect you, as I assume you know quite well, for as long as you break them not. Yet there are other ways the Grand can assert his will. Two spriggans aided you, and have been expelled. Word will travel swiftly, oh yes, and no more violators will there be. Closed to you the market is, for as long as you persist in your new goal."

"We expected this," Sithlac answered, "and yet, we will indeed persist, oh yes, of that you can be sure."

Gurtok nodded ever so slightly. Leaning forward, he let his eyes survey the shaft, up and down and side to side for a careful moment.

Then he withdrew into the alcove and let his eyes pull almost completely into their sockets before speaking once again. "Good," he said softly, almost too quietly to be heard over the Hub's ambient mechanical noises. "Although it would not do to be heard speaking thus, I say again: good! Continue upon your path, if you so choose, and know that I, for one, will not oppose you."

"Yet you would be surpassed," Bongcor put in, managing to speak despite his obvious nervousness. "If we succeed, you would lose your rank."

"It matters not to me," replied Gurtok. "The others of the Nine no longer hunt, for they no longer have the need, and in this they have forgotten who they are. I am a hunter, now and always. I do not hunt for riches or for wealth or status. I hunt because it is what I was born to do, as I suppose you are, as well."

"It is so," agreed Sithlac, "but even so, you will one day hunt no longer."

"Until then I will venture forth as best I can," declared Gurtok, "but these others are naught but fools, and of them, Tirchoth is the grandest fool of all. He would stop you, and end your plan, despite the simple brilliance of it, just to keep his power. He realizes not that your way is something new, something greater that could change our Tunnel for the better. I say to you, continue as you can, and I will cheer in private. Yet you must not falter, oh no! Tirchoth will be watching you, watching always, and you must not give him a reason, not at all. Not even for a moment. This I do so warn."

"We understand," agreed Sithlac. "We will be wary."

"Good," Gurtok replied, grinning once more, and standing slightly as the Hub hummed into action nearby. The immense elevator started down, reaching their position and passing swiftly. "Now I must hunt. Farewell and good luck to you, fellow hunters!"

The Hub went by, and as it cleared the alcove Gurtok leaped away. The other two gremlins leaned over, watching him recede into the distance, until he gave a final wave of salute and hopped off, disappearing into the dark recesses below.

Adams Hall – Up Top

"Is he gone?"

Sithlac and Bongcor all but jumped out of their skins at the unexpected voice from overhead. Bongcor fumbled with his spear for a moment, recovered quickly, and poked it forcefully upward, even as four independent eyes swung that way to lock on their target. Just out of reach, not flinching at all, Yog grinned down at them, chuckling to himself.

"Ha! You should see the looks on your faces!" the goblin snickered. "Ah, and here I thought you two could always tell when I was around. Not so good with a piece of noisy machinery next to your heads, eh?"

"No, most assuredly not," agreed Sithlac, trying not to look too embarrassed about being caught by surprise so easily. "For how long have you watched us?"

"Long enough to hear your good fortune, such as it is," Yog replied, "but still, I don't quite trust that one. I'm going to follow him, just to see if he's really up to something."

The goblin moved to skitter by, hot on Gurtok's heels, but Sithlac stopped him with a gesture. "A good plan, oh yes, and we do approve, but have you any other news, ere you depart?"

Yog nodded briefly. "Nothing direct, but I know of one who might help you. As I cannot bargain on your behalf, you must seek her out yourself. Go to the highest point in this Tower of Man, above the very Hub itself, where she even now awaits. I will join you when I can. Good luck!"

With a quick wave, Yog hurried down the shaft, ignoring Sithlac's further calls to halt. Obviously, the goblin didn't want to lose track of Gurtok, but a final glance revealed an almost evil-looking glint in his eye. Clearly he enjoyed giving the gremlins only a tantalizing sliver of information, as though playing a trick on them.

"What means he, do you suppose?" inquired Bongcor curiously, once Yog vanished into the shadows below. "What female dwells atop this place, who would speak with such as us?"

"Not a goblin, surely," offered Sithlac, "and no gremlin female would be seen outside her tunnel, save at mating-time. Another faerie, do we dare suppose?"

"Within this tower, most surely not," the lesser gremlin supposed, "unless a prisoner of Man she is; and then, how can she be safely reached?"

"I know that not, but even so, no Man goes above the Hub," his mentor explained. "There is a place there, this I know, but many seasons have come and gone since I visited last. Empty it was of any shinies, so a bad place to hunt, oh yes; but I marked it well, as a potential place of refuge, in time of danger. Not yet have I had the need to return, ere now. Come, let us travel there, and see what awaits us."

Bongcor nodded in assent and the two gremlins headed up to the next platform. Climbing further would only wear them out, so they instead waited for the Hub to pass once again, and jumped on top as usual. After a few trips up and down that didn't get them any closer to their goal, the elevator finally got called to the second level from the top, which Sithlac deemed close enough. From there they made their way carefully up to the top floor and then into a gap between the rails. Meandering around among the thick metal cables, irregular metal structures, and twisted wires, they soon found themselves in a dark, hollow area. Sithlac once again produced his glow-rod and started searching around carefully.

Bongcor waited patiently while his older friend poked around until he located a tiny gap between two slabs of wood. Flattening himself as best he could, Sithlac squeezed through and emerged into a much larger chamber, which resembled an unfinished room. Enormous unpainted wooden planks created a framework all around, topped by a slightly angled roof made of some kind of slick black substance. Lines of immense wood slabs divided the floor into numerous long, rectangular sections filled with a fuzzy pink fibrous material that looked soft and yielding, but somehow repellent, as though inherently treacherous. Both gremlins avoided the fiberglass insulation instinctively and pulled themselves up onto one of the rails, looking around at their unfamiliar, distressingly open surroundings with obvious worry.

"I like this place not at all," muttered Bongcor, keeping his body low and spear at the ready. "There is nowhere to hide, save this unnatural fur, and I care not to enter it."

"Dangerous it is not, oh no, but terribly uncomfortable," Sithlac explained. "The fibers cause a most distressing itch. If attacked we are, into it we must go, but only for as long as we must."

Bongcor nodded but said nothing more. Both gremlins shuffled along one of the rails, looking for some sign of the mysterious female they were supposed to meet, but found nothing but dust and the occasional ancient animal dropping. Clearly mice or some other small rodent had lived here once, but were now long gone. The air felt cold and dry, as though the walls were thinner here, letting some of the chilly winter air penetrate from Outside. Perhaps that's why the Men never bothered completing their work on this part of the tower.

At length Sithlac came to a halt. Bongcor, too, paused, sniffing the air and drawing himself up to his full height. As he did, a faint howl came down to them from the rafters overhead, causing both gremlins to tense up. "Ready your spear," the stronger hunter whispered, "but blindly use it not."

Bongcor nodded, but hissed in warning almost at once. "Something comes," he murmured, trembling, his voice thick with fear.

The howling sounded again, and this time they felt the air move around them. A chilly breeze swept across both gremlins, causing them to shudder involuntarily. A faint female laugh followed, echoing around the chamber, giving no clue to its origins.

"Sithlac and Bongcor we are, come to speak with you," called out Sithlac, trying to sound confident. "Sent by Yog the goblin this very night, oh yes."

The voice laughed again, and the wind repeated itself, coming from a different direction this time. A shadow detached itself from the rest, darting swiftly across the room, lodging in between two beams where the ceiling met the farther wall. "Two winters here, with none to see," a thin, reedy female voice replied, her words a high-pitched singsong, "and now, three times today it be! Help a goblin once, it seems, and friend to all within it means."

The laugh sounded again, and the shadow flew another direction, disappearing into the floor somewhere on the other side of the room. Sithlac let his eyes emerge from his sockets partially and rose to half-height, visibly relaxing. "No danger here, I think," he whispered quietly. "I know not what creature this may be, but this I feel most surely."

"A zephyr it is, of that I have no doubt," replied Bongcor, "and no more dangerous than you say, oh yes; but remember, even a goblin frail can hide a knife."

Sithlac let a single eye shift over to regard his companion, who kept both eyes fixed straight ahead at the distant shadows. "A zephyr, truly? How can you be sure?"

"Stories have I heard," explained Bongcor in a quiet voice, "of winds Outside that shriek and howl, and ride within the storms, but indoors almost never to be found."

The shadow flitted back and forth a couple of times, drawing Sithlac's full attention once again. The words came swiftly, sharp and clear within the moaning winds—a strange, warbling chant not at all like darkling-speech, yet nonetheless perfectly understandable. "Zephyr, yes, that is what I be," the song whispered in their minds, "but Outside not will you find me. Ithess, that is how I'm known; it's how the winter's snow is blown. Now come, pray tell, what brings you here, two gremlins shivering in fear? There's no real reason to be wary, unless you think I'm truly scary!"

She cackled at that, darted straight at them, and at the last second zipped upward to merge with the shadows overhead. Sithlac caught a brief glimpse of something indistinct, like a ghost, filled with swirling sawdust and twisting cobwebs, winding its way around a small figure about the size of his fist. Before he could focus on that, she flitted out of sight again, the cold wind of her passing wafting across his face without any actual physical contact. Her voice, light and feathery, swept over him like a breeze teasing his ears, as pleasant and mellifluous as that of the faerie he'd heard sing some days ago, even without magic to enhance the effect.

He had to shake himself to break out of his fascinated stupor. Reminding himself why he was here, Sithlac offered, "But two humble gremlins we are, seeking assistance in locating building-blocks for our homes. Hither we were led by Yog the goblin, who told us—"

"I would give aid, that's what he said," Ithess called out, sailing forth from her hiding spot to loop around the room, not dashing anymore but instead drifting in a wide, lazy circle. "How'd he get that in his head? Alone up here I like to be, and quiet peace is what I'd see. Unless of course you've what I want—but that, you'd never deign to hunt."

Sithlac stared at her as she passed overhead, unsure of what to say. Her faint, whispering voice and odd manner of speaking left him somewhat befuddled. Besides, he knew very little of zephyrs. They were wind-spirits, distant kin to all Fey according to the ancient tales, but with very little in common with gremlins. What one might want that he could provide, he had no idea; but more than that, he couldn't understand how one would come to be here, atop a tower of Man, instead of dwelling Outside, in the wide open sky such creatures were supposed to call home. He wanted to ask, but feared reprisal, or that she might simply leave, and how could he ever hope to find her again?

As he hesitated, Bongcor stepped forward, lowering his spear and opening his arms wide. "Our ignorance shames us," he intoned deferentially, "but it is a bargain that we seek. Tell us, how may we assist? Are you trapped here, that we might free you?"

She laughed again, spinning faster around the room. The wind whipped up a swirling storm of dust and debris, causing both gremlins to duck down and huddle within their shawls, shivering. "Trapped not, save by my own hand, the finest prison in the land! Seek a purpose, that's my goal, some great quest to make me whole. Gremlin needs are not for me, so go in peace and leave me be!"

"You mean to say," replied Bongcor evenly, "that bored you are, and that is all? Is that why you dwell here, and not beneath the open sky?"

"Not quite, oh no, not quite at all; you need not know what made me fall! Now off with you, lest patience sail, and with my wrath I shall not fail!"

Bongcor shuddered and started to speak, but she emitted a loud, unearthly howl that made him cower, shut his eyes, and draw them all the way into his head. Despite the terrifying noise, Sithlac stood unmoved, facing the tiny female creature he could now see hovering in the center of her own personal whirlwind. "Help you in any way I can, I will, oh yes," he called out, speaking the words instinctively, without thinking. "For this I ask no further reward."

Ithess suddenly came to a complete halt. The wind died out and all the debris drifted down, like a fine, dusty drizzle. Tiny wings fluttering in almost complete silence, she slowly regarded Sithlac, who remained completely still. She hovered in front of him for several long seconds, saying nothing, surrounded in a halo of sawdust and loose fibers. He could see, now, that she resembled a miniature faerie—thin and frail, with wide, catlike eyes, two curling antennae jutting out between fluttering golden hair, and white butterfly-like wings larger than herself. He could've fit her in his palm with ease, if he cared to try and grab her, but instead remained totally motionless as though paralyzed.

"Something different, I can tell," she whistled after a moment, quietly drifting around Sithlac's head. "Much more than just a gremlin's shell! A song you've learned, I know not where, but now it seems that you can care. A thing you have that gremlins lack—a friend who'll always have your back. And now you say you'll help me clear, with no reward to keep you near? Any other I would doubt, but you, I think, I will try out."

"Very well," agreed Sithlac, a bit flattered by her words, and hoping he understood her singsong prose clearly enough. "What must I do?"

"Nothing now, that would be wrong," Ithess told him, almost whispering the words in his ear, "but listen to your brand-new song. Should you find what I do seek, then call and I'll come take a peek. Until then, here is what I know: to the Forlorn Tunnel you must go."

"The Forlorn Tunnel," Sithlac replied, his eyes widening. "Not there, most surely...?"

The tiny figure nodded. "What you seek does lie within," she told him, flying upward and gradually merging with the shadows there, "so travel there you must begin. Off you go, I must insist; a longer stay you must resist. Now or then, I care no whit—good luck, gremlins, you'll need it!"

With a final laugh, the last of her flowing form merged into the darkness, her voice fading like a distant whistle carried off by the wind. Bongcor stood slowly, letting his eyes emerge once again from his sockets, whereupon he realized he still had a death-grip on his spear. He released his hold with a brief downward glance of embarrassment.

"I suppose we should go, then," remarked Sithlac, and so they did.

PART TWO

~ The Forlorn Tunnel ~

Adams Hall – Above the Hub

"The Forlorn Tunnel," said Bongcor quietly, once the two gremlins finished squeezing their way back out of the dusty attic. "Are we to venture there most truly? I fear what courage I still possess may take flight ere I reach such a place."

"And mine soon after," agreed Sithlac, "if the legends hold but a sliver of the truth. Wait here we shall, for Yog's return, and while we wait, share what we know."

Bongcor nodded, keeping hold of his spear as he inclined his head ever so slightly and began a brief incantation. The glow-rod in Sithlac's hand brightened somewhat, and the air grew noticeably warmer, a welcome change from the zephyr's chilly environs. Both gremlins loosened their shawls and relaxed as Bongcor launched into a brief story.

"A youngling I still was, struggling to earn a place, doing what I could to earn a grub, as you well know," the lesser gremlin explained, letting his throat puff up slightly, clearly enjoying the opportunity to show off his knowledge. "Among the many things I tried, though not as well as some, was to spin a tale at feeding-time. Of the legends I did learn, and oft repeat, came that of the Forlorn Tunnel, a terrible tale of wrath and destruction unlike any other I had known before. Listen well as I repeat it now, as well I can recall.

"Once, long ago, another tunnel dwelt within these walls of Man; brother to our own it was, and trade between the two was strong. Two gates they had, just like ours—one that faced our own, the other toward the Great Wide Park, where the elves and trolls dwell, and others not so pleasant, I am sure.

"In those days this other tunnel, its name now long forgotten, prospered fine and true, oh yes—filled with wonders from Outside, not just from the Men, but also from the Park beyond. Then one day, for reasons no one knows, trouble came to call. A war began within the Park, between two factions now long gone, and both sides sought to court our kind as allies for the fight. Some gremlins were for, and others against, as can be well imagined, exposing a dilemma deep and wide as the very Hub itself, it seems. Argued well and true, their Council did, but no agreement could they find; and when neutrality at last their First declared, then the fracture came. Even so some joined the fight, and were cast out, causing yet more strife. Others, staying within the Rules, expanded their towers: the mantle of First they did desire, to send their people into war. To strive for this they had the right, of course, but push too far they did, taking aid from Outside in their desperation. Thus the towers grew ever higher and higher, until finally they could stand no longer. They crashed down, in a great cascade, wreaking terrible havoc; and worse still, spawned by this disaster came the fire, some say by accident, others by unnatural materials brought to boost the tower-growth.

"Yet the worst was yet to come. The flowing smoke escaped the tunnel, drawing the ire of Man, who tore open the structure all about, seeking its source. Thus exposed their nearer entrance was, and it was blocked, but then came the death-blow at the last. The tunnel's water, it seems, came not from rain or sky, as does ours, but from Man's place itself—and in his blind fury, Man ended the flow for good. The surviving gremlins fled, some to us and others far away, so only the Forlorn Tunnel remains, broken and empty and dry, where only the ghosts and shadows dwell this day."

Bongcor settled back on his haunches and withdrew one of his water-skins, sucking a drop from it as he collected himself, rocking slightly from side to side and blinking rapidly. Sithlac nodded and drew his eyes partway into his head. "A tale well told," he remarked after a while. "Heard it before have I, in many variations, but with most details the same. Deserted it is, and haunted, perhaps, as you do suggest. A possible lair of the Fallen, so say my fellow hunters, and thus avoided at all costs. Recall you what I said, upon your first visit to the Hub?"

"So many things were said," replied Bongcor with uncertainty. "A place of many wonders, it is, and you said much. A thing of Man that rises up and down, never to the side; yet its destination never truly known."

"All of that and more, but one thing to be sure: we could stop at any time, yet the lowest level not at all, for the hunting there is never good."

Bongcor nodded in understanding. "And more, it seems, I do perceive."

"Yes, as you surmise, the Forlorn Tunnel lies there, as well." Sithlac shuddered slightly, partly from the idea of what was to come, but also because the extra warmth from the glow-rod had by now faded away. He pulled his ragged cloak tightly about himself and stood. "If the truth within the tales is sound, the Forlorn Tunnel straddles Man's tower and the Great Wide Park. I do know where the former entrance likely lies, but not the latter. We must descend and enter, this very night, I fear, ere our goals become known, and the Council act to stop us."

"As they surely would," agreed Bongcor. He, too, stood, taking hold of his spear with both hands, holding it forth in a vain attempt to look courageous. The fear showed easily on his face, but he pushed it aside as best he could. "I am ready, friend hunter."

"As am I," agreed Sithlac, raising his voice and turning his eyes toward the dark space near the cubbyhole's far side. "What of you, goblin? Will you join us, as well?"

Yog's head emerged from the shadows overhead. "Aha, you heard me that time!" He dropped into view, almost bouncing as he scuttled over to join them. "Good, I thought you were losing your touch. Sure, I'll come. Sounds like fun. I've never been on the ground floor before—it's shadow territory, or so I'm told."

Bongcor's eyes went wide and then sank into his head as he stepped momentarily away, almost cowering behind his friend. Sithlac, too, looked momentarily worried, but steadied himself. "Let us hope not," he intoned firmly, "although if so, we stand ready to call forth the light. No shade dare approach in high brightness."

"Of course, of course," agreed Yog. "They're not really a threat unless we get taken by surprise, or something else goes wrong. We should have no trouble as long as we don't plow into one of their nests. Anyhow, I'm more worried about the Fallen, truth be told. Luckily, I'm faster than both of you, so if we run into one I'm not in any real danger. Ha-ha!"

The two gremlins exchanged worried glances. Although the goblin spoke in jest, they both knew he'd told the truth just then. An encounter with one of the Fallen could have but one result: they would flee or die. Yog, being quickest, would have the best chance of escaping.

"Perhaps so," offered Sithlac after a moment, "but let us speak no more of such things. Difficult enough will this be, of that I am sure. Now come, we must descend as far as the Hub will take us this night."

Adams Hall – The Hub

They didn't have to wait long, for the elevator arrived at the top level about a minute later, answering a summons from an unseen Man. The Hub immediately dropped all the way to the ground floor, right where they wanted to be, as if it knew all along where they were going and wanted to get them there as quickly as possible.

The three unlikely companions hopped off and waited until the lift passed overhead again before descending downward to the bottom of the elevator shaft itself. Here they worked their way back into the walls and followed a thick, twisting line of cables as it meandered through narrow passages for a while before splitting a dozen different ways: some into holes too small to navigate, others upward toward higher levels, and one into a protrusion on the nearest drywall plank. Now they hesitated, Bongcor fidgeting worriedly as he waved the glow-rod back and forth, while Yog just eyed Sithlac impatiently.

The larger gremlin uttered a quick incantation and took hold of the edges of a hunter's hole that now shimmered in the air. "Tarry not we must upon passing through," he explained curtly. "A wide expanse must we cross, and into another hole we must go. If comes a Man, then upon our disguises we must rely."

Both his eyes fixed on the goblin, who shrugged briefly. "They shouldn't be able to notice me, as long as I stay still," he explained. "It's not invisibility, like a faerie in the forest, but it's sort of similar. It's more like I'm just not there at all. Plus you two will be a nice distraction, anyway. What do they see when they look at you?"

"At the moment, rats," explained Sithlac.

"Yeah, I figured it was some kind of small animal like that, from the things I've seen and heard. Nice spell, that one. Not sure a rat is the best choice here because a Man will probably try and kill you if he can... unless you meet a female, then she'll likely run."

"Change our forms we could, at the cost of our reserves, oh yes," pointed out Bongcor. "Perhaps a squirrel or a shrew?"

"Nah, don't bother," Yog answered with a shrug. "No matter what you look like, you'll have to run away if they see you. It's not like you want to get caught any more than you want to get whacked over the head. Just remember, when you run, I won't be following so I'll catch up to you later when I can."

"Very well," agreed Sithlac. "Now come, stay close, and do as I do."

They agreed, and after taking a few deep breaths, Sithlac opened up the hole. He passed through quickly, waiting only a moment as the others followed, then rushed across the open space beyond. They'd emerged into a foyer, actually near one of the dormitory exits, but at this late hour no students were about. Racing across the slick white tiles at their feet, they slipped into a shadowy area underneath a water fountain, near a small puddle where the occasional drop of water fell from a slow leak high above. As Sithlac opened up the next hunter's hole, the other two quenched their thirst as quickly as they could.

They found the area beyond the hole much different than their usual travel-spaces. Instead of narrow passages lined with beams and drywall, festooned with wires and cables, this much wider passage featured a dizzying array of pipes, some metal and others plastic, all snaking off in various directions throughout the building. The air felt cold and damp, and instead of the usual silence, they could all hear a faint humming interspersed with the occasional knock or ping, or the drip of water somewhere in the distance. Cobwebs hung everywhere, tattered and torn, fluttering ever so slightly as the air moved in faint, barely noticeable swirls. The dusty floor below them sported a mesh of footprints and drag marks, so jumbled as to reveal nothing about what could have made them.

"I like this place not at all," said Bongcor nervously, glancing back with longing at the shuttered hunter's hole behind him. "Much farther is our goal, pray tell?"

"As far as I have ever come, this is," admitted Sithlac. "Once I thought to hunt within, but turned back from this very spot. The prints upon the floor have changed not at all, oh yes, yet still seem fresh."

Yog shifted about, studying the dust carefully. "Some of these are goblin-prints," he noted, pointing out a couple of clearly obvious spots along the edge of the drag marks. "Gremlin, too, but these are old. And something big. Very big, and dragging something. I'm not sure what to make of it, but it's not a Man, that's for sure. Not in these tight quarters."

"The Fallen, perhaps, if such as they leave prints behind," offered

Bongcor. "Let us make haste, if we should indeed persist."

Sithlac turned to his friend, sensing the reluctance in his voice. "We need not go, if we so choose," he pointed out. "Our mission is but self-imposed. Turn back we could, oh yes, and then in safety dwell hereafter."

He let the moment hang in the air. Yog glanced back and forth at the two gremlins with an expression of disbelief. "Are you two really going to quit—" he began, only to be cut off by a quick wave of Sithlac's hand.

"To safety we could indeed retreat," sighed Bongcor after a moment, worriedly twisting his spear in his hands, "and that would be the end of it. Never again would we return, and into obscurity would we fade. No, great hunter, we must not falter. Our plan is worth the risk, I think."

"Then onward we shall go," agreed Sithlac with a nod. "My thoughts aligned with yours, it seems, but not so certain was I, until that moment hence. Now look most carefully as we go, for it is a gate that we do seek. Closed it was, or so say the tales, but open again it must be, for so many tracks to exist upon the ground."

They moved forward slowly, into the maze of pipes, dodging the occasional thick spiderweb or cluster of dead insects. Twice they passed the desiccated corpses of mice, covered in dust, clearly long dead. Here and there they found one pipe or another coated in a thin sheen of moisture, but never so much that it leaked like the water fountain outside. A few small bugs scattered at their approach, but other than the occasional distant sound, nothing really seemed dangerous. Relaxing a bit, Sithlac even fell into his hunting ways, moving to examine glints shining in the faint glow-light, but none of these turned up anything useful. Bongcor, in the meantime, remained vigilant, always on edge but still determined to move forward.

For about ten minutes they wandered aimlessly to and fro, searching for some sign of a gate-point, until finally Yog started chuckling to himself. "Ah, I see what they're up to," he snickered quietly, his face and hands so close to the ground as to be almost crawling. "Very clever, indeed."

"What is it?" inquired Sithlac, looking around for something the goblin might've spotted, but coming up empty.

"Ha! And you call yourselves hunters!" He giggled again, hopping back and forth and pointing at the ground. "You only search for things, though. Inanimate things, that never move. Not other creatures, as I so often do. Here, look at this. See the drag marks, here and here? And the partial footprints? They all look the same. Here, here, and here." He moved back and forth, pointing at several different spots. "Don't you get it? Come on, at least try!"

"I know not what you might mean," Sithlac answered, clearly at a loss.

"Yet I think I know," Bongcor put in. "They are meant to deceive, oh yes! To make us think a great number of feet trod here, where none at all have been in quite some time."

"Yes, that's it exactly!" chuckled Yog. "Oh, don't get me wrong, a couple of these prints are probably real. But whoever made them is carrying around something that's creating the others. A big stick, perhaps, with fake feet on it, pushed into the dust, and dragged behind to make these marks. Ha! A classic tracker's ploy, when you want to hide your numbers. Nicely done."

Sithlac nodded. "Right you very well may be," he admitted, "and yet, this helps us not at all, save to ease our nerves."

"Ah, but it does, it does," Yog went on. "See, now that I know whoever this is dragged something along, we know which way it's going. Here, and here...notice the way the dust is pushed aside? We only have to follow the route it took to find whoever made it. I'm betting it leads straight to the gate."

Sithlac kept right on nodding. "And if right you are, indeed," he explained, "then live there someone does, oh yes. Not a shade, or ghost, but someone real."

He turned both eyes back toward Bongcor, about to ask if he still wanted to continue, but his companion didn't hesitate this time. Holding his spear at the ready, the lesser gremlin returned his gaze with steely confidence. "Then find him we shall," he said firmly, and that brought an end to all remaining doubt.

Adams Hall – Ground Floor Crawlspace

With its secrets now exposed, the trail proved easy to follow, so easy that Yog had little trouble skipping past a couple of false paths designed to throw them off the track. About ten minutes later, after many twists and turns among the pipes, the little group reached a spot where the trail appeared to continue along its way, but Yog paused and crouched down slightly. The gremlins, suddenly alert, readied themselves for any approaching danger, but nothing moved and neither of them heard any new sounds.

"Something's not right here," Yog remarked in a quiet voice, shifting from side to side as he examined the faint grooves along the dusty ground. "I thought it doubled back, but it's more like something else joined in right here."

Sithlac and Bongcor studied the tracks for a moment, their eyes shifting to and fro from the floor to the shadows all around. Finally Bongcor pointed at a faint tracing heading off into a nearby alcove, where a pipe extended out from the wall before joining another. "Something from this side came, I think," he commented, holding his glow-rod over the area.

"Close, real close," the goblin replied. "It didn't come from there... it left this trail and went that way, smoothing out the dust behind itself. I bet if we kept going, the trail would make a loop so anyone following just goes round and round. Clever critter, whatever it is."

"Once more you prove your worth, friend Yog," put in Bongcor. "A fine, fat grub you have earned this night, most surely."

"Ooh, I can't wait!" hissed the goblin, rubbing his protruding belly anxiously. "I'm gonna turn into a giant fat blob if I keep this up! Now where's that gate? I want to finally see what a gremlin tunnel looks like, even if it's a haunted one."

"Never have you seen a tunnel?" inquired Sithlac as they cautiously moved into the alcove, searching carefully in all directions. "Do not all goblins come to market, at least some time in your lives?"

"Depends on your job, really," said Yog, hopping up onto the pipe and poking around in the shadows there, without success. "See, when we goblins mature, we get assigned a job, something we've proven good at in the past. I was pretty good at hunting bugs, so they made me do that for a while—as part of a team, of course. We had a quota, you see, and if we didn't make it, we all went hungry. That's pretty powerful motivation to get good at your job, I can tell you."

"Yet by yourselves you were, yes?" inquired Bongcor. "So eat before all others, I should think."

"Oh, no, that wouldn't do," Yog explained. "To betray your clan that way? Ugh! We would sooner starve. Some did, I'm told, but not among my team. We were way too good for that. Plus, I learned another trick. After we were done for the day, I could go out hunting on my own, if I still hungered, as long as we'd met our quota. That, at least, wasn't against the rules. So, as you might imagine, I got pretty self-sufficient after that. How do you think I've survived so long out here alone, hmm?"

"An impressive feat, I do agree," agreed Sithlac, before turning his attention back to the matter at hand. "Searched well and true, we have, up and down and all around, but nothing can we find. A dead end, it seems, so where to now?"

"I'm pretty sure I read those tracks correctly," Yog replied, hopping back down and studying the trail once more. "See, right here, these thin tracings...something got dragged along right here, spreading the dust out perfectly. That's no coincidence. So why hide your tracks if you're just going to a dead end?"

"The legend says the Men came here, whereupon the gate was blocked," offered Bongcor. "What if this wall itself can move?"

So saying, he tapped his glow-rod on the surface just ahead, below the pipe. The resulting bang sounded muffled and deep, clearly indicating a solid section. Then he moved slowly to one side, toward the corner that marked the alcove's end. As he walked, he kept on tapping, until just as he reached the angled edges, the noise abruptly changed. Instead of a thick, solid sound, it made a noticeably hollow echo.

"Aha!" Yog leaned closer, grabbing Bongcor's arm and pulling the light close to the wall. With a single claw he indicated a faint line rising up from the floor level, stopping just over Sithlac's head, and turning left to join with the corner itself. "Good thinking, my friend! Never would've noticed that in this dim light."

Bongcor puffed up his throat about three-quarters of the way, showing his pride, as Sithlac nodded appreciatively. "A true hunter you have indeed become," he remarked, inclining his head slightly toward his smaller companion. "A shame you did not start far sooner! Surpassed me by now you would, most surely! Now, how to move this wall, I wonder?"

"Leave that to me." Yog hopped about for a moment, studying the secret entrance carefully, before finally pointing to two barely visible notches along the corner. Without a word he grabbed hold of these and pulled, resulting in a very faint click from each. He tugged unsuccessfully for a few seconds before grinning with understanding and pushing instead, all while holding the notches carefully. The hidden door slid easily inward without a sound.

"See, it's like a latch," Yog explained, pointing at the two pressure plates he'd clicked open with his fingertips. "It's hinged on the inside. Come on, get that light in there! I want to see!"

Bongcor moved the glow-rod into the dusty space beyond, revealing a kind of hallway running from side to side. The pipe they'd followed to the alcove passed through the wall overhead and split in a T-shape, following the narrow passage into the distance. To the right, in the shadows behind the pipe and the farther wall, an immense metal structure loomed, with a shadowy entrance visible just on the edge of the light. Before that, just beneath the split in the pipe, the air swirled ever so slightly, as if spiraling into a fine point. Tracks lined the dust at their feet, no longer hidden or concealed, heading directly toward what they all recognized as an open Tunnel-gate.

"So that's what it looks like, eh?" Yog asked as they approached, studying the aperture carefully. "They never let us bug-hunters get anywhere near one. That sort of thing was only for the traders. Anyway, how's it work?"

Sithlac explained for a moment, while Bongcor studied the tracks more carefully. After a bit of study, he asked, "What manner of creature makes a track such as this? No claws or toes can I see, not one."

"Not sure," Yog answered, "but they're wearing shoes, I can tell you that. Not too many of us darklings bother, unless you often venture Outside in harsh weather. These are small, at least—probably elves, I'd bet. They love playing dress-up, you know. Trying to look like Men, all the time. They even have a word for it—they call it 'fashion,' if you can believe that! Ha-ha!"

"I know not what that means," Sithlac replied, as Bongcor nodded in agreement. "A ritual of some kind, no doubt."

"Who knows? Elves are kind of weird that way. Anyhow, it makes sense. They mostly live Outside, so if the Forlorn Tunnel really has another gate that goes out there, they could use it as a shortcut to get into this part of the tower. Why they would, I have no idea, but like I said...they're pretty weird."

"If up to no good they are," wondered Bongcor, "would they defend this place, should we persist? A secret this has been for quite some time, it seems."

"A true concern it is, oh yes," Sithlac agreed. "How many elves, would you suppose, and how recently did they pass?"

"That I can't tell you for sure," Yog answered. "Could be one, could be many. These tracks—they're all about the same size, and the dust is pretty well spread around, at least right here. This one looks like the most recent, but even that is probably a few days old. Could be a hunting party, or a trading group coming in the back door. No way to be sure. They do all converge right here at the gate, though, except this one." He moved over a bit, toward the enormous box-like metal structure up against the wall a short distance away. "It's like it separates from the rest, see? He comes over here, looks in that opening there...back and forth a few times, see? Not very curious, I suppose, since he didn't go in, or at least he didn't leave any evidence behind. Odd...the floor inside is completely clean. No dust at all. What's that all about, I wonder?"

"On another day, I might investigate," said Sithlac, "but hunting we are not, save for the Forlorn Tunnel...and that awaits us here. I will proceed, and step aside at once. Follow close, and be prepared, in case some danger lurks within."

The others nodded in agreement. Bongcor readied his spear, but kept the point facing upward, so as to not inadvertently injure one of the others after passing through the gate. Yog, though apparently unarmed, kept his hand at his side, where his hidden knife awaited. Sithlac bobbed his head up and down nervously for a moment, swallowed, and then stepped through.

The others followed, ready for anything.

The Forlorn Tunnel – Entrance

Sithlac arrived in darkness, and since he wasn't carrying the glow-rod, he could do nothing more than step aside as planned, feeling around for anything that might halt his progress. The tunnel entrances back home were always brightly lit, so he found himself at a loss. What if the Fallen could see in the dark? He'd be helpless, unable to defend himself or even find the exit now that he'd moved a few steps away.

He hadn't really thought about the Fallen as a threat, at least not since meeting Yog. The mystery of the disappearing hunters had moved into the back of his mind, as though no longer important, except as a reason to remain wary when exploring. Yog had survived quite well on his own, for some time now, without ever seeing one of the Fallen or noticing any evidence of their presence. Furthermore, Sithlac truly doubted he'd find such a monstrous, evil creature in this place. The elf-tracks, if that's what they were, meant the Forlorn Tunnel was probably safe (unless, of course, the elves themselves proved hostile).

In truth, Sithlac knew very little about the Fallen. They were bogeymen, in a way—horror stories told to young gremlins, still new to the world, as a way to remind them that dangerous beasts were out there, ready to kill and devour the unwary. Long ago, the legends said, some Fey became corrupted by magic, driven mad by a thirst for power, swelling into fearsome beasts that destroyed every living creature they encountered—save for Man, whom they couldn't affect directly. Instead (the stories claimed), if so inclined, a truly dangerous Fallen might attempt to influence a Man—corrupt him in some way, like a dark voice whispering in his soul, turning him to evil. Such creatures were sometimes referred to by a special name—*demons*.

Sithlac had no idea if demons really existed—in fact, he didn't even know if the Fallen themselves were real. Certainly no gremlin he knew had ever encountered one. Yet before today he'd never met a zephyr, either, so if they were real, so too might be the Fallen. He shuddered slightly in the darkness, worrying in the scant few moments he remained alone, that such a monster might be lurking somewhere near—and then, to his great relief, Bongcor stepped through the gate, bearing the comforting light of the glow-rod in his hand.

Yog followed immediately after, and the trio found themselves in an empty passage. Like the gates back home, this one occupied the end of a protrusion in the Tunnel's otherwise dome-like shape. Ahead, the area opened outward, presumably into the main body of the Tunnel, but their faint light didn't reach that far. A few scraps of broken wood lay about them on the ground, but other than a few tufts of sawdust, the ground was otherwise clean. They could see no footprints to indicate how many others might have passed this way.

For a moment they remained silent, listening, all three understanding the need for quiet. In the Morningside Tunnel, the sounds of gremlins always filled the air. That's one thing Sithlac always liked about going hunting: his departure offered an escape from the ever-present cacophony produced at all times by his fellows. An empty, quiet tunnel felt strange and unnatural and *wrong*.

As they listened, though, a few sounds came. First, they heard a distant rustling, like something skittering about, quite possibly an insect that somehow found its way inside. Then, a faint hissing sound, farther away, rising and falling in a regular pattern, followed by a clearly audible drip of water from another direction. They waited a bit longer, and the water-sound repeated. After that, a few more faint sounds came: a buzzing overhead, back and forth; a tapping, rising and falling, disappearing completely for a while, then back again; and something far away that may or may not have been a voice, talking quietly, the words unintelligible at this distance.

"Well, here we are," said Yog, keeping his voice down, but not quite whispering. "I somehow suspected it'd be brighter."

"As did I," agreed Sithlac. "Always, in our home, we had what light we needed, drawn from our Tunnel's daily supply of magic, replenished thus by those whose task this was. Never did I think to see a home so dark as this."

"Not so dark, I think," offered Bongcor, moving slowly ahead. "See, a wall awaits, so as to block our view. Beyond, from here, I do spy some light."

The others moved slowly forward. Sure enough, as the passage opened out, a crudely built structure made of broken wood-blocks cut off their view of the rest of the Tunnel interior. The wall had no connectors or fasteners, but consisted solely of slabs stacked up to a level above their heads. To the left, a large stone blocked their path, while to the right they found an aperture just big enough to squeeze through. Before they could consider taking a step toward it, though, a light flickered beyond, and they clearly heard footsteps approaching.

"Who comes?" called out a female voice, with a distinct air of disapproval. "That better not be you, Jozan! You're not supposed to be back until—"

The three travelers froze as an elvish figure stepped out from the gap, halting in mid-word as she beheld the newcomers. She stood about the same height as Bongcor, dressed in a light green tunic and breeches, with gray boots and a folded brown cap topped with a stylish red tassel. Although human-like in appearance, she looked noticeably thinner than the typical female Man, with more angular features and wider eyes. She had dark skin, and even darker brown hair that curled and twisted all around her face, held at bay by a thin band encircling her forehead. Across her waist she wore two belts, each bearing a prominent scabbard, and from these, after but a moment's hesitation, she drew two blades so quickly the motion seemed all but invisible to the naked eye.

"Who are you?" she demanded instantly, scowling at the intruders. "What is your business here?"

"Sithlac, I am, a hunter of the Morningside Tunnel," came the immediate reply, "and Bongcor, my hunter friend; plus Yog, our guide, whose advice led us here this night. We seek only that which is not claimed, for our own use, and mean no harm to you."

"Hunters don't come here," insisted the elf. "No gremlin ever comes here. This place is cursed, don't you know that? Now be off, or you'll feel the sting of my blades—and you can tell the rest of your thieving kind that they're not welcome, either."

Sithlac hesitated, not sure what to do. He had no doubt this elf knew how to fight—the way she held her twin swords was proof enough of that. He'd never met an elven warrior, though he knew they existed, of course. All the elves he'd ever spoken to were traders, and while they did always bring a couple of armed escorts along, they never brandished their weapons in the market. Although outnumbered three to one, she didn't seem the least bit worried, even with Bongcor nervously pointing his spear in her direction. That meant she either felt sure she could win any battle, or had reinforcements behind her that Sithlac couldn't see.

With that in mind, he ruled out trying to fight his way past her. He didn't want to leave, though—not after coming so far, and especially not after being told to come here by Ithess the zephyr, who clearly knew about this place and knew it had what he needed. So, with that in mind, he decided to try something else.

"We come here not as thieves," he said firmly, "but as students of this place. Heard of it we have, from our own kind—and others, too, oh yes! A place of gremlins it once was, so every right we have to come."

"Don't pull that crap on me," insisted the elf, frowning as she pointed one of her weapons in Sithlac's direction. "I know how your laws work. It's yours until you leave it, right? So your kind left here long ago, and that's where your claims ended. You don't get to cruise back in here, Axos knows how many years later, and say it's yours again!"

"No such claim do I make, oh no," Sithlac explained patiently, "merely that I have the right to step within. What right claim you, O unknown elf, to deny me passage, save that of force?"

She nodded slowly, narrowing her eyes as she regarded Sithlac carefully. "That should be enough, but I can tell you're not going to go away easily, are you? I could probably slice both of you open from head to toe in ten seconds or less, but then what would I do about your little friend, hmm? The minute I step out of this doorway, he'd put a knife in my back for sure."

Sithlac started to reply, glancing toward where he'd last seen Yog, only to realize the goblin wasn't there. In fact, as he twisted his eyes about, he couldn't see their diminutive companion anywhere. No wonder the elf was worried! "No need for violence do I perceive," Sithlac mentioned casually. "Our journey here has been long, indeed. We seek to rest and search this place, not to drive you out, or lay any claim upon your home, oh no. Nor would we tell our fellows what we find, for they would come and pick it clean most surely."

"Now *that* I can believe," she replied with a nod, relaxing just a bit and lowering her twin swords. "Okay, here's the deal, then. You three can come and have a look around, but I'd better not have any more gremlins coming here after you leave, got that? They start showing up and we'll just close that gate right up straightaway."

Sithlac nodded, although inwardly he wondered if the elves really did have that power. After all, wouldn't they just open and close it only when they needed it, if they had the ability to do so? Still he kept that thought to himself. "Accept we do your terms," he said, motioning to his companions to lower their weapons (assuming Yog was still close enough to see him). "By what name are you known, elf-guard?"

She abandoned her combat stance and slipped her weapons back into her sheaths. "You haven't earned the right to know my full name," she pointed out, "but you may call me Lyza, which in the tongue of my people means 'bird-sighted.' In other words, I've got really good eyesight, so don't any of you try anything!"

"You sure are the suspicious type," remarked Yog, suddenly dropping down between the two gremlins, as though falling from the sky. Somehow he'd managed to scramble up onto the wall up ahead during the conversation, without anyone noticing—although Lyza herself didn't seem the least bit surprised, or at least did a good job hiding it. "Are all elves as trusting as you, I wonder?" Yog went on. "If so, this should be a lot of fun, that's for sure."

"Most would've just run you through without a thought," said Lyza, crossing her arms and glaring at the goblin contemptuously. "I probably still should. Never trust a goblin, that's what my daddy always said. What in Gaia's golden firelight is a goblin doing traveling with gremlins, anyway? Never seen anything like that before."

"They hired me," said Yog with a shrug, as if such a thing were an ordinary occurrence. "Didn't see that coming, either, but it's working out pretty well. You guys got any grubs in this place? All this guiding around has made me pretty hungry."

"And promise him a grub I did, 'tis true," explained Sithlac. "Not this very night, perhaps, but a fine meal to him I owe most truly."

Lyza rolled her eyes. "Not even here two minutes and you're already begging for food. Figures! That's what I get for being nice! Fine, it's not like we're going to run out anytime soon, and besides, I'm getting hungry myself. Right this way!"

Forlorn Tunnel – Interior

The Morningside Tunnel's lighting came from hundreds of dangling glow-globes, their magic refreshed daily from the *dinathi-kai* collected by caretakers stationed on the periphery. The same network of globes still existed in the Forlorn Tunnel, but the gremlin lightsmiths were long gone. Nonetheless, a few of the hovering spheres still emitted enough faint light to provide a dim, shadowy view of the Tunnel's cavern-like interior.

What had once been a thriving gremlin city had fallen into complete ruin. A few rickety towers still stood, broken shells of their former selves, remaining upright only by leaning upon each other. Most of the structures had collapsed into piles of debris covered in bits and pieces of shattered wood, rusting metal, and cracked plastic. Only the vaguest semblance of the town's original layout remained: partially cleared paths between adjacent lots, the mostly empty area that must've once been the commons, and a shoddily built cistern into which a single drop of water fell every half-minute or so. Some of the wooden parts showed signs of fire damage, but not nearly as much as expected, considering the nature of the disaster that supposedly befell this place.

"Not much to look at, is it?" asked Lyza, breaking the silence. Sithlac realized, then, that he'd been staring openly, wide-mouthed, for quite a while. Hearing legends and stories was one thing, but to actually look upon the results of such a catastrophe left him momentarily speechless. "Yeah, it's pretty terrible," the elf went on, "but it's not like I live here permanently or anything. Just a waystation, really, when I'm not out and about. Come on, food's over here."

She headed toward the cistern, which adjoined the open commons, a square area covered in thin, flat stones. A path had been made through the debris along what once must've been the main avenue through town. Some of the pieces of rubble were quite large, but nonetheless had clearly been lifted or pushed aside to clear the way. This, combined with the work done to repair and preserve the cistern, suggested that at least some effort had once been made to make this place habitable. Certainly a lone elf-girl couldn't have moved such large blocks of stone and wood on her own.

"Sorry about the low lighting," Lyza remarked as the little party meandered through the ruins. "There's a few of us elves who come and go through here from time to time, so we always keep a few of the globes burning. We don't have enough *kai* to light them all, though. If you want, you can shine up the nearest ones while you're poking around. They work on anything, not just night-magic, in case you were wondering."

"Truly?" asked Bongcor curiously. Since arriving in the dead city, his eyes hadn't stopped roaming in all directions, but now he fixed his gaze on Lyza. "All tools of gremlin make use of *dinathi-kai* alone, or so I always thought."

"Maybe where you're from, but not here," she explained. "This Tunnel touches both realms, you see. One entrance into Man's place, another to Outside. Anyway, don't worry, I know how picky you gremlins are about your magic. You're outside your Tunnel's influence now—you can collect as much *kai* as you want, and whatever kind you want. Nobody's going to track your quotas or any of that crap, or get mad if you use a little day-magic. There's plenty of that to go around."

"Day-magic," muttered Bongcor, shuddering a bit. "A most distasteful thought, and yet, never before have I had a chance to test its worth."

"Different it is, and nothing more," explained Sithlac, for he himself had tried it out during his few journeys Outside. "Always changing, never stable, yet ofttimes more powerful than the *kai* we know. Try it you should, upon the morrow, should we then remain. Yet now, more queries do I have. Tell me, elf, if you do know, how it is that such as this should come to be?"

He indicated the cistern just ahead, and the completely clear stones upon the commons. She nodded, smiling. "I thought you might notice that. Yeah, I wondered the same thing when I first found this place. After you gremlins left, it was pretty much deserted, but not completely. Seems someone else moved in, and he's still here. In fact, he's the one who keeps me coming back, for the most part."

So saying, she reached down, picked up a loose pebble, and flung it into the broken remnants of a tower a short distance away. The rock bounced off what looked at first like a pile of dusty cloth covered in a thick layer of shaggy gray moss. As the stone clattered away, the mound stirred, causing both gremlins to worriedly step away, Bongcor bringing up his spear reflexively. Yog, for his part, bounded backward in surprise and disappeared behind the cistern.

"Dinnertime already?" growled a deep, resounding voice as the fur-covered mass stood up, stretching and yawning. Easily twice Sithlac's height, the gray-skinned creature turned, revealing a wide, craggy face topped with two horns that twisted and curved their way around two tiny, almost invisible ears. A pair of long tusks protruded from a wide mouth filled with enormous, flat teeth jutting out at various angles, as though pushed in place at random. As the monstrosity took a step toward the group, two thick, ropy arms unfolded, revealing a pair of comically oversized hands so long and wide they almost brushed the ground.

"A troll," muttered Sithlac, his eyes flicking this way and that as he contemplated possible escape routes. "A troll dwells here, within a gremlin-tunnel? I thought no troll would ever enter such a place!"

"Aw, but I like it here," rumbled the troll in an exaggerated, petulant voice. "Big and dark and warm, all the time, all day long! Who speaks such nonsense to a poor, harmless troll? Ah, 'tis a gremlin pair, come back home at last!"

"Not our home, oh no," replied Sithlac, still wary but sensing no immediate danger from the enormous brute, who could probably crush his skull with a single squeeze from one meaty paw. Trolls were powerful creatures, but slow and easily avoided in the open. This one didn't seem remotely hostile, fortunately. "But visitors we are, nothing more," Sithlac went on, relaxing despite himself. Although he knew he should remain wary, he somehow felt quite at ease.

"Hungry, too, no doubt," the gray-skinned colossus went on, still making no move to approach. "Well, you two sit right down and let ol' Meathead go to work. I got just the thing to feed the lot of you. Lyza, gonna use the last of them orange-roots, got that?"

The elf nodded, smiling. "Figured you would. I'll look for more next time I'm out. Oh, there's a goblin here, too, in case you missed that."

"Ah, wonderin' what that other smell might be. Hey goblin, you like some cock-a-roach, or maybe fresh wriggly-worm?"

"Whatever's handy, I guess," Yog's voice called out from somewhere nearby. He seemed some distance away, and higher up, quite possibly on one of the still-standing tower-frames beyond the commons area. "I'm not picky, as long as it's not me on the menu."

"Ha! Like I'd eat me a goblin! Too stringy by a stretch, that's for sure! Anyways, I'm gonna get me to cookin' now. You all just make yerselves at home."

So saying, the troll moved out and around the building, toward a series of low-walled, crudely built boxes nearby. Just visible among them stood a large, metallic bowl resting on a flat, silvery plate. As the gremlins watched, he began collecting bits of vegetable matter, mostly mushrooms, from containers nearby, casually tossing his selections into the bowl. This done, he visited the larger boxes one by one, peering inside and poking around, occasionally inspecting an insect or worm before adding it to the menu. Finally, he moved to the cistern, scooping up some water into a plastic bottle cap. After adding the liquid to the mix, he bent down and began chanting in a low voice. The metal surface underneath slowly glowed red as it heated up, causing wafts of steam to rise up from the bowl. Satisfied with this, the troll began stirring the makeshift cauldron, keeping up the slow, rhythmic chant all the while.

Sithlac and Bongcor watched all this in silence, not really sure what this all could mean. For most of their lives, they'd never eaten anything other than termite grubs, save the rare leftover scraps scavenged in Man's tower, or on the few rare occasions Sithlac went Outside and had to hunt for worms. Furthermore, neither had ever even so much as contemplated heating up their food like a Man would. As the dumbfounded gremlins stared in confusion, Lyza chuckled quietly to herself, with Yog joining in as he returned to the group, fading into view from the shadows.

"You have to forgive them," the goblin explained, offering no apology or explanation for his disappearance. "They've never had a real meal before. This is gonna be good. How'd you get a troll to cook for you, anyway? I thought they hated elves."

"Not all of them do, it seems," replied Lyza with a shrug. "Meathead was here when I found the open gate, and like you did just now, I thought the worst upon seeing him—but he's not really dangerous at all. He moved in here when your kind left, and sort of set up shop, taking care of the grubs and other things your people left behind. Good thing, too, or the termites would've overrun the place soon enough. Anyway, he grows a couple kinds of mushrooms, back there in the back corner, and keeps a few dozen kinds of bugs and worms around for variety. Every time I come and visit, I always bring some herbs or roots to add to his collection, and he whips up some new recipe to celebrate. I've been here what, a hundred times or so, and never had the same meal twice. Say what you want about Meathead there, but he's quite the accomplished meal-maker."

By now an enticing aroma had started filling the air, an odor quite unlike anything the gremlins had ever smelled before, but nevertheless quite appealing. "If tastes as good as it smells, it does," offered Bongcor diplomatically, "a most amazing meal awaits."

"I'm sure you'll love it," agreed Lyza, flashing him a quick smile. "I know I always do. Anyway, it'll take a little while before he's done. While we wait, tell me why you're really here. You're not just explorers, I know that much. Gremlins wouldn't come here just out of curiosity, and you have to expect this place has been picked clean of anything useful, so you must want something else."

"Engaged in a project we are, Bongcor and I," explained Sithlac, seeing no reason to hide their true mission, especially not in light of this unexpected hospitality. "To raise our towers together, as high as can be done, and thus share the rank of First among our people."

"Ah, yes, you gremlins are always building up and up, aren't you? Such a strange little society—but then, so is ours, in its own way. But you say you're doing it together? Connecting your towers, is that right? I didn't think that was allowed."

"No Rules exist to forbid this task," offered Bongcor eagerly. "At least, none that do exist in truth; yet there are those who seek to block our path. No more can we acquire our building-blocks on market-day, and none exist in easy reach to take. Thus it is that we came here, though before we stepped within we knew this not at all."

Lyza nodded, waving a hand at the vast array of fallen timbers and leftover building material all around them. "So you're here for this, I take it? Not a bad idea, I guess. The goblins already carried off the best of it, but there's still plenty of decent pieces still around. You can take what you want, I guess, as long as you don't touch the stuff we've built. You say you didn't know what was here before you came, though? What do you mean by that?"

"Not for such did we knowingly come," Sithlac answered. "Admit we must, oh yes, that never thought of this would we, without advice from another source—the zephyr known as Ithess. Her words alone did bring us hither."

Lyza wound her fingers through her curly hair, scowling slightly.

"Really? Ithess told you to come here? Why would she—hmm, well, that's very strange, but then, who knows what she's really all about? I certainly don't, and I've tried to get it out of her on more than one occasion."

"You have been there, to see her, then?" asked Yog curiously. "To the top of the great tower, above the Hub itself? I wouldn't think to find an elf in such a place."

She shook her head vigorously. "Oh, no, I'd never go up there! Into the very lair of Men? No chance! No, she makes her way down here every now and then, when she gets bored flying around scaring all you darklings. Anyway, she hits me up for news, just like everybody else does, I suppose. How she knows when I'm here, I've no idea, but she always does. I'm surprised she's not here now, although I guess she could be, and we'd likely never know."

The others glanced around, wondering if Ithess might choose that moment to put in an appearance, but she didn't. "You are a news-bearer, then?" inquired Bongcor after a short pause, seeming more than a little interested. "A traveling tale-spinner?"

"That's one way to put it, I suppose," Lyza replied with a shrug. "I bounce around from kingdom to kingdom, swapping stories, mostly just to keep myself busy, but not because it's my job or anything. I just like to travel, meet people, and see what's going on in the world. I've been as far as Battery Park, you know. The view of the waterfront is just incredible."

"I know not where that is," said Sithlac. "Only as far as the Great Wide Park have I ever gone before."

"And never have I left our Tunnel, until a few days past," put in Bongcor, both eyes fixed on her, clearly intrigued.

"Well, I have," commented Yog somewhat pridefully, "but I've never heard of such a place. Where is this Battery Park? That's a weird name, too. It's a Man-word, isn't it? Or at least as close to their garbage-talk as we could ever say."

"In a way, it is. You live in the Morningside Tunnel, right?" asked Lyza. Seeing their nods, she continued, "Well, that's a Man's word, too. Haven't you ever wondered how different it sounds than the rest of the darkling-tongue? There's several more like that, too, if you think about it. No Fey can speak the tongue of Man, yet their words find their way into our language—how does that happen, do you suppose? None can say. Anyhow, be that as it may, what do you mean by the Great Wide Park, exactly? Do you mean Central Park?"

"Not so sure am I," Sithlac answered. "It is the birthing-place, oh yes! For three mating-seasons past, I've traveled there, through the holes and secret paths below, to spawn a child and then return. A great journey, many days indeed, east and south it is."

Lyza considered that for a moment. "Is it on a really steep slope? Possibly with a great wall on one side, and stone stairs used by Men to pass within? Long and wide, but narrow to the east, filled with great trees, rising toward the sky, and ivy on the bricks? Then, far below, a great plateau filled with Men, coming and going, taking no notice of us at all?"

"As you describe it, so it is," agreed Sithlac. "Elves at either end, and trolls here and there within, in the hollows and beneath the stones, but leaving the high walls alone, where among the cracks we gremlins might mate in safety."

Lyza nodded. "That's not Central Park, then, but Morningside Park—the same name used for your Tunnel. Not a coincidence, I'm sure. Your city's founders probably emigrated there from the very same park, somewhere in the distant past. That's probably also how you and your fellows keep coming back there in mating season—you know the way, instinctively, like when birds fly off to migrate, and always go to the same place every time."

Sithlac nodded slowly, considering her words. He didn't know anything about how birds migrated, but he could definitely recall somehow knowing the way to the well-hidden hunter-holes and other passages that led, eventually, to the park where he'd taken all his mates. He always chalked this up to the faint recollection of his journey as a child, when his mother carried him back to the Tunnel three years after his birth, but even that seemed unlikely at best. He had no actual memories of that time at all—his earliest conscious thoughts were of himself and the other children squabbling over scraps in the market. Of his time in infancy, he had no memory whatsoever.

"Anyway," went on Lyza, "you know how far that is, right? Well, imagine going all the way to the south end of Morningside Park—about three times as far as just getting to it in the first place—then another journey like that one, and that'll put you in Central Park, which is— and I'm not exaggerating here—at least a hundred times bigger than Morningside. Then picture yourself going all the way to the end of *that*, then another three times *that* distance, and that would put you in Battery

Park, at the very tip of Manhattan. That's as far as I've traveled—pretty impressive, huh?"

"A great journey, to be sure," agreed Sithlac, bobbing his head in amazement. "Far too long for such as I. Half my lifetime it would take, oh yes, of that I can be sure."

"Not if you know the elven ways," said Lyza with a grin. "There are portals, here and there, where lines of power cross—nexus-points, they're called, and very hard to find."

"Heard of these have I," put in Bongcor, apparently eager to show off his knowledge. "Upon a certain time they do depend. The proper shining of the Moon, perhaps, or when a shadow strikes a special spot."

Lyza nodded, looking somewhat impressed. "I'm surprised you know that much—you're very well-informed, for a gremlin. Anyway, you've got the right idea, but it's not just that—you have to know how to direct the nexus to send you to the right place. Even if you happened to randomly stumble onto one, and thought it was one of your hunter-holes or a tunnel-gate, you'd wind up sending yourself to some random exit-point, only Axos knows where. Not terribly far, most likely—maybe just a block or two, but far enough that you'd be lost, most likely. Especially for someone like you, who's never been out of your tower and has no idea what the world is really like."

"Like to know, I would," admitted Bongcor at once. "Always afraid was I to travel hither, and now I see much more there is to learn. Perhaps, when our task here is at last complete, I will journey forth and see the world of which you speak."

"Good, that's what I like to hear—another fellow explorer joining the ranks!" Lyza laughed and clapped him on the shoulder. "We'll see about that when the time comes, but for now, it looks like our food's ready. Let's eat!"

Forlorn Tunnel – Commons

Meathead approached bearing a large plastic bottle cap from which wisps of white steam floated out and up, bringing a tantalizing aroma unlike anything the three visitors had ever smelled before. Even Yog, though visibly nervous and ready to bolt, remained in place as the huge, furry creature approached, not quite getting within arm's length. The troll set down his burden, then passed out small bowls made from carefully carved plastic beads. Without a word, he used the flattened end of a tarnished chunk of metal to scoop out a serving to each of his guests. Once they each had their meal, he took two steps back and sat, his great weight causing the floor-tiles to jump ever so slightly. Then he took a drink of soup right from the cap, licked his lips, and grinned.

"Hope you like," he said in a rumbling, deep voice, pointing a thick finger at Yog. "I put an extra worm in there, just for you."

"Thanks, I guess," agreed the goblin nervously. He took a cautious sip from the steaming broth, nodding appreciatively. Using one claw, he poked around in the orange-colored liquid until he found a chunk of meat, which he devoured in a single bite. "Not bad," he commented, comically licking his chops. "Not an earthworm, but...well, something I've had before, just so much better. Whatever you put in here, it's really great!"

He began to slurp down the soup with great haste, as though it might be taken from him at any moment. Nearby, Sithlac and Bongcor exchanged glances, a bit nervous about this meal, for it was unlike anything they'd ever tried before. Still, the troll hadn't hesitated to eat his own concoction, and Lyza didn't seem the least bit concerned, sipping slowly at her portion and watching her guests with barely concealed amusement.

Sithlac decided to throw all caution to the wind. In the wild, he would've used a purification chant, but here, such a thing might be perceived as an insult. Instead he took a sip, and found the soup quite enjoyable. He could definitely taste the worm-meat flavor, but quite a bit more besides. He took another sip, and another, and in a few moments found himself ready for seconds.

Bongcor, too, quickly devoured his portion. "Never before have I known such as this," he remarked in between swallows. "That such tastes should be, and I not know, proves my life before now but a tragic waste. You eat such each and every night?"

Lyza nodded. "Like I said, this is part of why I come by this place so often. Good job, Meaty—you've won yourself a fan."

The troll inclined his head and smiled. "'Tis what I do, milady, and all I do, so I figure, might as well get good at it."

"And good you are, indeed," offered Sithlac. "Henceforth, I fear, a simple grub will likely seem a bland and tasteless thing. I would come here often, should I have the chance, and payment of some kind seems right and fair. What type of fee would such as you expect?"

"Oh, you don't gotta pay me nothin'," responded Meathead with a shrug. "I gots everything I needs right here. Always lookin' for more spices and such, though, so you come across stuff like that, bring 'em right on in."

"He'll take about anything you could think of eating, really," offered Lyza. "I'm Outside a lot, so I'm always collecting herbs, seeds, mushrooms, and that sort of thing. You've got a poison-finding spell, right? Just use that to make sure it's okay, and trust me, Meathead will figure out a way to make a meal of it."

"I would not know where to start," said Sithlac. "The world Outside is filled from sky to ground with endless plants, and I go there rarely, if at all."

She nodded, thinking about that for a moment. "Hmm. Well, yeah, I guess you gremlins don't get out much. I keep forgetting—I'm used to being out in the open, not inside the walls. Let's try another angle. You guys wander around in the caves of Man pretty much at will, don't you? Surely you've seen the sort of things they eat, right?"

"And sample them as well, should we have a chance," agreed Bongcor, remembering a time not so long ago when he experienced a few bites of stale pizza on his first hunt. "Not so interesting as this, oh no, not so much at all."

"Well, there you go," Lyza concluded. "When you're out there making the rounds, if you find anything you think might work, bring it by. You never know what might happen."

"A new and worthy thing to hunt," agreed Sithlac at once. "It shall be done, oh yes, ere we come this way again, which we will most surely do. This place is filled with just the sort of things we need to raise our tower high. Visit here we will, perhaps each and every night, until we reach our goal."

Lyza nodded, narrowing her eyes as she considered the ramifications. "Well, I don't think either of us will mind if you haul off some of this worthless junk, as long as you leave our stuff alone," she explained patiently. "There's a few other elves who come by every so often, too, and I'm sure you'll be able to figure out where they like to stay. Any of the rest of it, though, feel free to take what you want, although you're going to have a tough time carrying most of it."

"Ideas for that I have," pointed out Sithlac, "but it is not the weight or size I fear, but the danger faced when crossing to the Hub."

Yog bobbed his head up and down at that. "Yeah, getting across that gap's no big deal right now, but doing it while lugging one of these beams? Good luck with that. Then you have to get it up on top of the Hub—not gonna be easy, I'm telling you."

"Find a way we shall," said Sithlac optimistically. "Perhaps another way there is, that we have not yet found. A nexus-point, perhaps, of which you earlier spoke...?"

Lyza shook her head. "Sorry, not inside the tower, I'm afraid. The things Man builds always suppress the orderly flow of magic. Nobody really knows how or why, they just do. Outside, if you're in tune with the Weave, you can feel the lines of power all around. Wherever they hit concrete or metal, they just come apart. Anyway, using a nexus is sort of like sliding really fast along the more powerful lines, from one intersection to another. Since they don't go through the walls, neither can you."

"If Man's work disrupts the *kai*," inquired Bongcor curiously, "then how do such a thing as tunnel-gates persist? Ours lies within Man's very tower, with walls upon all sides."

Lyza shrugged. "I've no idea. You darklings use shadow-magic, for the most part, which is different from the Weave. Maybe it has to do with that." She looked momentarily worried, as if she'd said something wrong. "Sorry, I don't mean to sound elitist or anything, just saying it's different, that's all."

"Offended I was not, oh no," said Sithlac diplomatically, letting his eyes retreat into their sockets just a bit. "It is the truth you tell. The other

Fey are not like us; there is no shame in this. Perhaps long ago we were, but now we're not, and this is not so wrong."

Lyza got up and refilled her bowl, offering some to the others. They agreed readily and sipped eagerly away at their seconds as she sat back down. "You know, you don't sound like any gremlin I've ever met before," said the elf. "And I'm not talking about your voice, either. I mean, you're just...different. I don't know how to put it without sounding like I'm insulting your people, but I can't help it. You actually seem like you value other people's opinions, which is just not normal for a gremlin."

Sithlac nodded, and his eyes retreated a little bit further. "There is some truth to this," he agreed. "I have learned to think quite differently of late."

"And all the better for it, I submit," offered Bongcor. "A friend to me he has become, and I to him, and this is something new to gremlin-kind. There are those who doubt our way, but together we shall prove its worth."

"You're friends, sure, anybody can see that," agreed Lyza. "And you hired a goblin outcast as a guide, which is just about unheard of."

"Outcast, you say," Yog put in, scowling momentarily. "So, you know about that, hmm? You do get around, don't you?"

"I have my sources," she admitted with a smirk, then turned her attention back to Sithlac. "Still, there's something about you I can't quite put my finger on. You talked to Ithess, and she agreed to help you, which is also quite unusual. How often do you use day-magic?"

"Only rarely, if at all," explained Sithlac. "During mating-runs, perhaps, but lately not so much. What importance does this have?"

"Just wondering something. See, friendship is one of those things you don't really encounter much in darklings. You gremlins don't even really have a sense of family—you're usually just all about yourselves. Nothing wrong with that, if it works for you, but I just can't see how any of you would really develop a true friendship—maybe a business partnership, or something like that, but not the real thing."

"Oh, trust me, it's real," claimed Yog. "You haven't been around them long enough, but this isn't some kind of trick or ploy. I've seen that sort of thing before, plenty of times, and this isn't it. They're definitely friends, you can count on that."

"I believe you," Lyza went on. "In fact, I'm quite sure of it. So, how do gremlins suddenly develop the capacity for friendship? Was it always there, or did something happen to change you?"

"Wondered this myself, I have," admitted Sithlac, shuffling his feet nervously. "Not so long ago, such a thing as this would never be, and then..."

He paused, wondering how much of this he should reveal. "And then what?" Lyza inquired curiously.

"Yeah, what?" asked Meathead, taking another gulp of his soup.

Sithlac glanced his way momentarily, and realized he'd almost forgotten the troll was even there at all. How quickly he'd become used to the presence of such a creature—something he never would've imagined just a short while ago. In fact, having this conversation at all should seem wondrous and strange, but instead, it felt quite natural and completely normal. Did that mean these two, the elf and troll, were now his friends as well? If so, how could he have changed so dramatically in just a turning of the Moon?

"I heard a song," Sithlac explained at length, letting out his breath in a long, protracted sigh. "A faerie-song, within the halls of Man. A prisoner she was, of the Man in whose cave she dwelled. Her voice...like nothing I had heard before. I gave her aid, when I should not, and that is when the change began. The song is gone, and yet, I am no longer what I was, of this you can be sure."

"A faerie, eh?" rumbled the troll. "No faeries hereabouts, not for many years. They all left, I heard, 'cept that one, and she lives way far away."

"Really? A faerie?" Lyza looked at him doubtfully. "You sure it wasn't an elf? We look similar, you know, but we're a bit taller, not that you'd really notice when we're by ourselves. Oh, and they've got wings, of course...let's not forget that little detail."

"A broken wing she had, oh yes," Sithlac went on. "And in the song she wove a faerie-tale, which I think no elf could hope to do."

Lyza nodded, giving a brief shrug. "Well, I doubt any elf could affect you quite that strongly, anyway. When we use magic, it's very temporary. Even so, Meathead's got a point. There's only one faerie still around these parts—at least until recently, that is. Did she happen to tell you her name?"

"She did, oh yes, but I recall it not. In our language she did try to speak, and poorly so; and yet..." He paused, trying to remember the meeting, which now seemed very long ago. He followed the voice, and came upon the faerie, and she said...she said...what?

He found himself humming softly, which caused the elf's long eyebrows to go up. Sithlac withdrew his eyes and shut them, picturing the faerie in his mind. The song...so sweet upon his ears, swirling about him, as if to lift him up...her voice, so melodious and powerful, bringing with it her fears, and pain, and doubts...and deep within, so very faint, a tiny spark of hope.

"Tilly," Sithlac finally managed, almost gasping the word, blinking rapidly as he forced himself to focus once more upon the present. "Longer was the name, oh yes, but that much I do know."

"Tillianita," Lyza answered, nodding. "So, you did meet her! There's no way you'd know that name, unless you really spoke to her. Another piece to the story, then...who would've thought I'd hear it from a gremlin!"

"Of what story do you speak?" inquired Bongcor curiously.

"I'll tell you the whole thing," said an eager Lyza, "but first, you have to tell me this: what happened after you helped her escape?"

"Not much more to tell, there is," Sithlac explained. "A broken wing, she had, as I did say; and to the floor I helped her climb. There I left her, still entrapped within Man's cave, but free to move about. I took my leave, and hummed her song, yet nothing more of her did I ever learn. The cave in which she dwelt is empty now, its master gone with all his things, and nothing more to find. When the seasons turn, another Man will come, as they always do, but for now the cave lies empty."

Lyza clapped her hands excitedly. "That confirms it! Oh, this is great! Wait until you hear this! You might want to get some more soup because this might take a bit."

"Very well," agreed Sithlac, needing no further prompting to have some of the wonderful broth, which he'd decided he liked very much. "By all means, spin your tale."

"Okay, here goes." Lyza took a deep breath. "So, here's the thing. That faerie, Tillianita, was the last of her kind pretty much anywhere in Manhattan, at least as far as I've ever been, at least—and I'm pretty sure I've been to every park and greenspace you can take a portal to. Then, just about half a moon ago, what happens? She disappears for a few days, without a word, then shows up back in Central Park *with a mate!* Another faerie, just like that! At first I didn't believe it—I figured it was just a rumor, one of those tall tales the spriggans tell after getting drunk on honey-mead. I kept hearing various travelers going on and on about it, though, so on my way back here I popped into Central Park for a better look. I never saw the guy, but I did talk to the elves who live over by the zoo, and they confirmed it. They'd seen both faeries flying together, with Tillianita showing the male around the place."

"From whence did such a faerie come, then?" inquired Sithlac. "If she has been the only one for so very long, how could another come to be?"

"Well, that's the best part," Lyza went on, clearly enjoying the chance to tell this story, especially considering Sithlac's role in it, however small. "I thought maybe one had come from some great distance away, perhaps brought by a bird or zephyr, but that doesn't seem to be the case at all. The rumor is—and get this—he used to be a Man!"

Yog gasped and almost dropped his bowl, while Sithlac and Bongcor's eyes popped almost completely out of their sockets. "A Man...?" Bongcor stammered. "A Man, transformed into a faerie-form? But can it be truly so...?"

"She transformed a Man?" gushed Yog. "Faeries have that kind of power? Who knew? Wow, good thing there's only one! Well, two, now, I guess, but still..."

Sithlac's eyes settled back and he nodded, all at once understanding the connection. "The Man who held her captive," he stated firmly. "That is why he went away—he went to be with her! The power of her voice, it seems, is not to be denied."

"Yeah, I had the same idea," agreed Lyza readily. "He captured her, somehow, and took her back to his home—and then she turned the tables, and wound up capturing *him!* But, see, here's the thing you may not realize—magic can't affect a Man, unless he truly wants it to. That's one of the few completely immutable rules about magic. So she couldn't just cast a spell on him at random. He truly wanted to become a faerie, or it wouldn't have worked at all. He must've fallen completely in love with her, totally on his own, without magic making it happen. Can you imagine?"

"A faerie and a Man," sighed Sithlac. "He met her, and he changed, oh yes—it seems, perhaps, that I am not quite as alone as I did once believe."

"Yes, but I don't think she really changed either of you," Lyza pointed out. "Not like that, I mean. Not directly—you changed *yourselves.* After all, these other two—" she pointed briefly at Bongcor and Yog—"they never met her, did they? Yet you're all friends with each other, right? So that means you always had the ability to feel this way, you just didn't allow it until now."

"Nonetheless, it is she who put me on this path," Sithlac noted. "Not magic, as you say, but another power just the same. Should we ever meet again, I would give her thanks for this most surely, for a gift it truly is."

"That it is," agreed Lyza. "That it is indeed."

Forlorn Tunnel – Interior

For most of his life, Sithlac had always been alone. Oh, he spoke to other gremlins from time to time, but never for very long. Usually when he had any kind of extended chat, it had something to do with business: agreeing to a mutually beneficial trade, for example, or arranging a purchase at the market. The only time he ever really interacted with another for a long period was as part of the mating process, which, as it turned out, never really led to much in the way of conversation.

Back home, on mating-day, prospective females paraded through the streets, while males like himself tried to catch their eye by flaunting their wealth and bragging about their towers. If a female approached, she would be invited inside, where she could inspect the merchandise and decide whether the male was up to her standards. Some meaningless words would be exchanged and then, if she accepted his proposal to mate, he'd close up shop and depart immediately for the long journey to the birthing-place. Conversation was kept to a minimum, as no emotional attachment was expected or desired. The phenomenon of love, while known, was something to be avoided at all costs. As a result, sometimes a day or more would pass without a word being spoken between the new partners, who generally treated the whole thing as a kind of mutually agreed-upon business relationship. Eventually, when the child was old enough, the male would simply leave, ending the coupling in relative silence.

So to say Sithlac wasn't used to making small talk would be a tremendous understatement. Fortunately, he and Bongcor had enjoyed a few decent conversations that gave him a bit of recent training in that area, but not nearly enough. He expected, when he sat down to a meal with the elf, that they'd speak for as long as it took to eat and that would be that. Instead, Lyza kept right on chatting, telling stories about her journeys Outside and the elves and other creatures that lived there. Sithlac listened politely, and to his surprise, found himself enjoying the chance to socialize a lot more than he would've expected. Bongcor, for his part, looked absolutely enthralled.

In between anecdotes, Lyza kept the visitors involved by asking them questions and getting them to tell tales of their own. In this way she found out more about Sithlac and Bongcor's efforts to link their towers together, as well as Yog's experiences trying to survive on his own after getting cast out from his tribe.

During the course of these inquiries, Sithlac and Bongcor finally learned the location of Yog's original home—a nest located underneath a drainage tunnel just outside the tower walls. A short distance away, in a large, fenced-off area, the Men would deposit cast-off boxes and junk on a daily basis, and goblins would raid the place nightly. That's where they came up with their seemingly endless supply of wood-blocks and other construction materials. When Bongcor suggested they visit the place themselves, Yog just grinned and explained that his people made a habit of fighting off anyone who challenged their "ownership" of this treasure trove and wouldn't hesitate to do away with a couple of nosy gremlins trying to muscle in on their territory.

Even after this exchange, Lyza kept right on talking, obviously enjoying the chance to communicate with a few non-elven travelers. Meathead occasionally joined in with a comment or two, but mostly kept to himself, handing out a little bit more soup before finally polishing off the rest himself. After that, he washed out the plastic bottle cap with water from the cistern and shuffled off to check on the various insects and other creatures he kept in boxes near his makeshift home. Sithlac watched him go with one of his eyes, wondering, not for the first time, just how he could possibly accept the presence of a troll so casually, as if normal and commonplace. He'd never met a troll before today, and all he'd heard suggested they were vicious brutes, prone to fighting, attacking first and talking later. Meathead seemed quite the opposite, something Sithlac definitely appreciated, given the situation. Plus, he certainly made excellent soup.

Lyza was about to launch into another story about some far-off corner of the mysterious "Manhattan" she kept referring to, when she suddenly stopped cold, shaking her head and rubbing her temples. "Oh, no, I'm boring you, aren't I?" she gasped. "I'm so sorry! I just let myself get out of control! I don't get too much of a chance to talk to gremlins or goblins, so I'm just—well, sorry, anyway!"

"It's fine, don't worry about it," offered Yog. "It reminded me a lot of being back around my cousins, and I've missed that. I hadn't realized how much, until now."

Lyza smiled at that. "Well, you know what, you should just move in here," she offered without hesitation. "Why wander around in that dusty tower all the time, anyway? We've got plenty of space and you'd have food whenever you wanted."

Yog's eyes went wide. "You—you'd do that?" he stammered. "You'd—accept me? An outcast? Just like that?"

"Sure, why not? I can already tell you'd be a lot of fun to have around. Plus you know the tower really well, right? If you get bored, you could go around and collect the news for me. You know, from the gremlins, and Ithess, and a couple other places I can't really get to myself. Not that I'd ask anything in payment, though—it's strictly voluntary, of course."

Yog nodded eagerly. "I'd be happy to. Thank you so much! No more holing up in dark corners for me! Hey, gremlins, you need me from now on, this is where you can come look! Gonna go find me a place to build a home—seeya!"

With that he scurried off. Lyza just chuckled to herself. "Yeah, this should be interesting, that's for sure. Can't wait to tell the others there's a goblin living here. They'll be furious, of course, but who cares? None of us really has a claim to this place anyway. If anyone does, it's you two. So what now? You going to shop around a bit?"

"Look, perhaps, we shall," agreed Sithlac, "but take nothing large for now. First, another passage we must find."

"Legends tell of two exits from this place," Bongcor continued. "To Man's tower one does go, to Outside the other. Another exit might there be, or are there only these?"

"Just those two," Lyza answered. "On opposite sides, as you might've guessed. The other one drops you out on the edge of the stairs to Morningside Park, all the way across the street—quite a ways from your tower. I've been in more than my share of goblin-tunnels in my travels, you know, and this is the only one that has entrances so far apart. That's part of what makes it so unusual."

"Other than its emptiness," Sithlac wondered, "what other ways do make it so?"

Lyza shrugged. "Well, right now it's got that one steady drop of water, see?" She pointed at the ceiling, where high above, near a very faint glow-globe, a new drop dangled, not quite ready to fall. "When we got here, it didn't even have that. The Men cut off the water supply by sealing up the pipes above us. Well, Meathead figured out where they did it and opened up one of the leaks just a bit—not enough to alert the Men, but enough to give us what we need."

"The troll did this?" inquired Bongcor curiously. "But however did he know? Even I know not the source of water for my Tunnel. It is there, and there, and falls ever steadily, but how or why I could tell you not at all."

"Yet some goblins in your Tunnel have to know, right?" Lyza pointed out. "In case something goes wrong, so they can try and fix it, right?"

Sithlac and Bongcor exchanged baffled glances, indicating they had no idea. Lyza, seeing this, rolled her eyes and continued. "Well, *you* may not know, but somebody probably does. Anyway, Meathead told me when he first got here, there were two gremlins still hanging around, trying to figure out how to restart the water. Meaty agreed to help, and they showed him where to go—they needed his strength, you see. After he got the water dripping again, they went off to try to find their fellows with the news, but never made it back."

"Perhaps they will return, one day," offered Sithlac, "though more water, I suspect, they would need, to fill a place like this."

"No doubt," Lyza agreed. "Anyway, I was trying to explain why this is unusual. See, most Tunnels get their water from natural sources—a creek, or rainfall, or whatever. This one depends completely on those leaky pipes I was telling you about. Even though there's an exit halfway across campus, the water comes from Adams Hall—Man's tower, I mean. Sorry, you probably don't know its real name, do you? That's what the Men call it."

"How is it you know the names Men speak?" inquired Sithlac curiously. "Not at all the first time have you said such things."

"I have my ways," Lyza answered with a grin. "The point is, the water comes in from somewhere overhead—one of the pipes. And Meathead went up there once before, right? Well, trolls are too big for gremlin hunter-holes, so there must be another way up there. When you're ready to leave, I'll have him show you the way. Maybe you can find another path home from there."

Forlorn Tunnel – Ruins

They continued chatting for a while longer, having no need to be in any particular hurry. Perhaps half the night had passed by now, with plenty of time remaining to travel back to the Morningside Tunnel, if the gremlins chose to do so. Sithlac saw no need for that, however. This place, however broken and damaged it might be, felt perfectly safe—he already trusted Lyza and Meathead implicitly, having no idea why; and furthermore, no Fallen ever came here, of that he had no doubt.

Eventually, he did manage to withdraw from the conversation and go for a walk around the immense interior of the Forlorn Tunnel. Back home, from the edge just adjoining one exit corner, he could just barely make out Tirchoth the Grand's eight-level tower, almost exactly at the Tunnel's midpoint. That gave him a pretty good idea of just how big the dome-like cavern really was. Here, he had no idea. Certainly it looked and felt much larger than his home, but he couldn't really be sure. The darker conditions, and the need to constantly dodge large chunks of debris, could've given the place an illusion of greater size.

As he moved away, Sithlac could still hear Bongcor talking with Lyza for quite some time. The sound carried quite well, with no buildings or gremlin-sounds to break it up. Bongcor seemed rather infatuated with the elf-girl, or at least her amazing stories—tales of distant kingdoms, politics and wars, trolls and ogres and all other manner of Fey who somehow still survived in a world otherwise completely dominated by Man. Bongcor, who until a few moonrises ago had never left his home, seemed all but hypnotized by Lyza's words. Sithlac puffed up his throat a bit as he moved out of earshot, a bit proud of himself for helping his friend come out of his shell.

As he wandered, Sithlac spotted more than a few slabs of wood that might prove extremely useful in his construction work. Many were damaged, but not so much as to be rendered useless. Most were too big to carry by himself, but working with Yog and Bongcor, he should be able to lift them well enough. Perhaps he could even convince Meathead to help—what would the other gremlins think, to see a troll hauling wood for a gremlin? He chortled at the thought, and again at the reaction Tirchoth would surely have at such an affront. Not that Sithlac would ever try it—if Meathead actually entered the Morningside Tunnel, the Council, fearing some kind of attack, might well take up arms against him, which could have only one result. He'd never risk subjecting his new friend to such a thing.

After a while Sithlac reached the far side of the tunnel and started making his way back, mentally mapping the locations of useful wood-blocks as he went. Unfortunately, at least at first glance, he didn't find any kind of fasteners—no staples, bolts, nails, clips, or anything like that. Apparently the place had been picked clean of such things, which made sense considering only the largest slabs of wood remained. As Lyza pointed out earlier, the gremlins probably took most of the portable stuff when they left, all those many seasons ago, and opportunistic goblins swept through soon after.

This, of course, meant Sithlac's problem had only half a solution, at least so far. Thanks to Yog's help and Ithess's advice, he'd found a viable supply of building material, but nothing to fasten it with. Lacking nails or some other method to hold the wood together, the pieces would topple or fall away, allowing his fellow gremlins to make off with the unattended prizes when he and Bongcor weren't around. That meant Sithlac had no reason to carry away any of these wood-blocks tonight— more hunting would be needed first. With the night only half over, perhaps now would be a good time to start.

He moved back over toward the others. As he approached, he paused, eyes moving back and forth as Lyza's voice became audible. Instead of speaking normally, as she'd done before, she now sang softly, in a slow, purposeful voice. Not only that, but strange notes of music attended her words, produced by some kind of stringed instrument held with two hands. Meathead sat nearby, eyes closed, his mouth slightly open, while Yog observed from atop one of the nearby mounds of debris. Bongcor, for his part, just stood there, eyes fixed on her, leaning upon his spear as though enraptured.

Sithlac hesitated, wondering if this might be some sort of spell. With a quick incantation he tested the air, and felt no flow of magic at all. He let himself listen, and discovered Lyza was, in fact, simply telling a story, and in the elven tale-spinning tradition, she did so to music.

...and in his despair, so great, the Man did grieve for his people, and begged the One to guide his hand. But the One did not answer, for the Man's heart was impure, and yet he admitted this to himself not at all. And thus, toward this darkness came another, one of the Fallen: a demon most foul—Ethayen the Black, Corruptor of Souls, who whispered hateful lies and poisoned promises; and when the Man at last succumbed, Ethayen passed to him a terrible power: that he might see and recognize the Fey, wherever they did hide.

To the Man, instead of true Fey forms, he saw naught but evil, twisted beings, which at first he sought only to destroy. But soon, with the Corruptor's subtle guidance, the Man thought to capture them, and take their magic for himself; for no Man, since the Great Bargain, could hope to wield Fey magic on his own. To aid this foul task, he found other Men, others just as easily corrupted, and passed to them this gift as well, thus endangering all Feykind.

And perhaps, had they kept their secret task better hidden, they might well have succeeded; yet they were seen, some say by zephyrs, others the spriggans or faerie: it matters not the means. Yet soon the plot leaked to the elves and then to Prince Isoni, the Bolt-rider, one of the great heroes of old. Knowing he could not harm the Men, for no Fey can, the prince sought out Ethayen instead, tracking him through long, dark corridors deep within the earth. Many adventures he had, and some are stories unto themselves, but in the end he came upon the Black One's lair and called him out.

The battle was the stuff of legends: a war like nothing seen before or since. The Prince of Lightning brought his own allies, and so did the Corruptor—truly a battle for the ages: one that could have had but one result, else our world today would exist no longer. In the end, with his champions struck down, the Fallen One tried to escape into the shadows, but Isoni called forth the greatest of thunderclaps, driving Ethayen out into the open at last. Weakened but not defeated, in desperation the Corruptor charged, and fought hand-to-hand, tooth and claw, and in the end struck the prince a mortal blow—but with his last breath Isoni struck down the Evil One, ending his corruption at last.

Outside, the Men were freed from the Black One's grasp, but the gift given them could not be undone; and so the danger had not fully abated. Even so, though the Fey could harm these Men not at all, they could instead expose them for their true purpose. In those days, in the world of Men, to attempt to practice magic was a great affront, a crime with only one punishment: and so, thus revealed, these evil Men were put to death by their own kind—a just and fitting end, and a message to all others never to try such a thing again.

"So that's the sort of thing the Fallen are all about," Lyza concluded, her voice returning to its normal, lilting tones as she stopped strumming her instrument. "There are lots of names for them—demons, imps, devils, and so on—but they're subtle. They almost never get directly involved, unless cornered. They hide in the shadows, tricking you, corrupting your mind. Maybe that's what happened to those other gremlins—I don't know. I suppose it's possible. But you probably wouldn't ever see the Fallen directly, I know that much, so you can stop worrying about one of them attacking you out there."

Bongcor nodded slowly as she spoke, his eyes never leaving her, not even to glance Sithlac's way. "So such a thing does not live here, most surely?" he asked slowly, his words slurring a bit, as though coming out of a trance.

"Well," she went on, "I've been traveling around the world for many years, and I've never seen or heard of one around these parts, so I wouldn't worry about it. Oh, hey, Sithlac, you're back already! Sorry, I didn't mean to get so long-winded, but he asked about the Fallen and wanted to hear a tale spun the old-fashioned way, so..."

"A pleasing melody, to be sure," Sithlac told her, lowering his body slightly in a show of respect. "No magic, oh no, but entrancing nonetheless. I would hear such tales again, but not tonight, I fear, for we need hunt once more."

"A hunt?" inquired Bongcor, one eye shifting to face his mentor, the other not moving from Lyza. "What need is there for that, with such worthy treasures all about?"

"No bolts or clips remain," explained Sithlac with a shrug. "Cleaned out of such this is, it seems, so venture forth we must. Come, the night awaits."

Bongcor nodded, hanging his head ever so slightly. He obviously wanted to linger here, and Sithlac as well, but they had a mission, after all. "I come, of course, friend hunter," said Bongcor somewhat sullenly, "but return I would to this place upon the morrow. Will you remain, O elf, to tell us tales aplenty?"

"I hadn't intended to leave for a few more days," Lyza replied with an affable smile. "A goblin came through yesterday, name of Jozan, from the Dark Oak enclave—ever heard of it?"

"I have," Yog put in from his perch high above. "Bunch of rat-tailed liars, the lot of 'em, but they've got stuff we need. I don't know any Jozan, though, but that's not surprising. Possibly a youngling, looking to make a name for himself. Was he a trader?"

"No, not exactly—he's looking for some kind of food item—not sure what, he didn't tell me. He was going to hunt around inside for it, while the Men sleep. I told him he could pass, but only if he agreed to bring me a few things I can trade when I go back out. I'm going to hang around until he gets back, which should be no later than tomorrow, I'm hoping."

"Good," Bongcor replied eagerly. "Then I shall return at first opportunity. Come, great hunter, let us be off!"

Forlorn Tunnel – Interior Gate

The two gremlins made their way to the exit, Bongcor almost literally dragging his feet, saying goodbye to the others several times until finally Sithlac had to hurry him along with a good-intentioned shove. Overhead, atop the crude wall near the gate, Yog just shook his head and chuckled at the sight. Bongcor kept one eye facing back over his shoulder as he shuffled along, until finally Lyza appeared in the gap and gave him a final wave, flashing a smile in the process. The gremlin waved back, turned his attention forward, and emitted a happy sigh.

Only with the greatest of difficulty did Sithlac avoid commenting right then and there. Instead, he used a quick incantation to reactivate the glow-rod and pushed his way through the waiting gate. Bongcor emerged a moment later, and before his elder could say a single word, the younger gremlin sighed again, quite loudly this time.

"Is she not amazing?" gushed Bongcor. "Such a voice, and such tales she tells! Entranced was I most surely, as though carried forth to the places she speaks of, such wonders I could never before imagine. I would go there, someday—not now, oh no, of course not now, but I would go, if such a thing were possible."

Sithlac shook his head, not to answer negatively, but merely to suggest caution. "Young you are, and as yet new to this greater world you've now discovered," he explained patiently. "The dangers and pitfalls are many, as even such as you must know."

"Of that I have no doubt," agreed Bongcor at once, "and yet, I would still try, just to be with—I mean, just to see these wonders."

Sithlac nodded, and put a hand on his younger friend's shoulder. "She is indeed compelling, of that I must agree; and she means us no harm, this much I can tell. Yet she is not our kind, oh no, so take care your infatuation does not lead you astray."

Bongcor just stared at him. For a moment he looked about to speak, but kept silent, clearly battling his emotions. Finally he could meet his mentor's gaze no longer and turned away, drawing his eyes half back into their sockets. "I..." he began at last, struggling to find the words. "I...am not sure what this is that I feel," he offered quietly. "I think, perhaps you may be right, as per the norm. Tell me, O much wiser one, is this what taking a mate feels like? A female thus catching your eye, singing to you, her voice working its way into your mind, driving you to think of naught else but her, until you take her out and—"

"Much like that it is indeed," interjected Sithlac, "but without the song, of course, for what gremlin female sings? Yet again, it seems, the songs of other Fey bring more mysteries to the fore. What is it, I wonder, that affects us so? You see, now, what I faced when I heard the faerie song not so very long ago."

"You felt this way about such a one?" Bongcor inquired, leaning forward a bit as though eager to hear the answer. "I confess, when I first heard you tell your tale, I had my doubts—but now, I feel that way no longer. A lure, it is, most surely, and yet, there is no malice afoot. I wonder, though, would all gremlins react this way? If such a song could enrapture us so well, what would happen if she sang thus upon the commons?"

Sithlac shook his head and grinned. "Perhaps that is why no elven tale-spinners are allowed within our Tunnel," he offered. "Now come, let us speak no more of this for now. A hunt awaits, don't forget. We need fasteners aplenty, if we are to use the wood-blocks here for any purpose save simple stacking."

Bongcor nodded eagerly, obviously glad to change the subject. "Where, then, can we find such a supply, in this place?" he asked, looking around in the shadowy, dusty space around them. The pipe overhead, splitting just at the edge of the wall, stretched off into the distance without any sign of ending. On the other side of the gate, on the edge of the shadowy area, the mysterious metal structure loomed, a dark hole beckoning. "Perhaps in there?"

"The footsteps in the dust," Sithlac reminded him. "They approached but did not enter. What lies within, I wonder?"

"Let us find out," said Bongcor, moving over to the immense object, which was unlike anything either had ever seen. The vaguely rectangular building stood many times their size, expanding outward to a kind of flange halfway up, then returning to its normal dimensions high overhead. At various points along the sides the two gremlins could see what looked like tiny windows set at regular intervals. The edges all along the top and bottom, and the railing across the middle, were all arrow-straight, so much so that the two observers knew, without speaking their thoughts aloud, that this could only be some mysterious creation of Man.

Along the nearer edge, directly in the middle and at ground level, a dark opening awaited, more than wide enough for a gremlin to enter. Bongcor moved up close, spear in hand, and peered inside, while Sithlac held the glow-rod close enough to shine within. Unlike the ground beneath their feet, the metal surface inside showed no evidence of dust, and appeared at first glance empty. However, in the faint light, far ahead, a few shapes could be seen within the shadows. The faintest smell of food wafted forth, quite stale and unappealing.

Sithlac was about to step forward, but before he could move, his younger charge took the initiative and slipped inside, keeping the spear cautiously pointed ahead. The moment he crossed the threshold, the entire structure shifted ever so slightly, and before either gremlin could so much as twitch, an enormous metal door clanged down across the entrance, sealing Bongcor within.

Adams Hall – Ground Floor Crawlspace

Sithlac instantly dropped the glow-rod and threw his weight against the wall ahead, but it didn't budge. "Bongcor!" he called out worriedly. "Can you hear—?"

The reply was faint, but audible. "I am unharmed," he called out, "but all is dark, save a red glow ahead. Hold, I will bring light." A pause followed, during which he must've created a glow for himself, but Sithlac saw not the faintest glimmer along the seams of Bongcor's prison. "I am trapped, I fear," his faint voice went on. "Perhaps another exit can be found. I will search."

"As will I, from this side," replied Sithlac, immediately moving to do just that. Making his way quickly around the metal structure, he found no more entrances, and couldn't quite fit between the wall and the panel itself. However, while surveying the problem, he took note of the small windows overhead. Encouraged by that, he unfurled his sucker-pads and began to climb, only to find his hopes dashed as he discovered the openings completely sealed by double rows of thick iron bars.

From the wall near the top of the structure, he could look down inside, where Bongcor's shadowy form could easily be seen, wandering to and fro with glow-rod in hand. The lesser gremlin paused to examine a faintly flashing red light along the smaller wall opposite the former entrance, but found nothing of interest and continued searching. He discovered a few small objects, including a couple of chunks of moldy food, as well as at least one useful-looking nail, but none of these had anything to do with escaping.

At length he noticed Sithlac's light overhead and scurried up to meet his friend. "No other exits are there, it seems," Bongcor hissed, his normally cheerful voice now deep and thick with fear. "Truly trapped am I within this place."

"What of the door itself?" asked Sithlac. The light within didn't shine that far, so he couldn't tell much about it, other than its obvious size and weight.

"A Man-thing it is, most surely," Bongcor managed, trembling all over. "The glowing redness below, as well. They are things of Man. If they come, I will be found. What can I do? I must escape!" He began to shake all over, eyes sinking deep within his head.

"Worry not, friend hunter," said Sithlac reassuringly, trying to sound strong, when in fact, he felt quite the opposite. "If a trap this is, as I suspect it must be, then for another it must be. Man knows not of us, lest you forget. What form have you?"

"The rat, of course," muttered Bongcor. "What would a Man do, upon capturing a rat?"

"I know not, for never have I seen or heard of such a thing. Can you take another form? Do you have the strength?"

"Perhaps, if I could calm myself," stammered Bongcor. His friend's reassuring words and demeanor were having an effect, as he started to fight back his fear. "All my energy would it take, but yes, a simpler form. A bird, perhaps..."

"You cannot fly," pointed out Sithlac, "which a Man might find suspect; and furthermore, what cause would a bird have to be within Man's walls?"

"Of course, yes, you do speak wisely," answered Bongcor, his eyes once more emerging from his head. He took a few deep breaths, and his trembling slowed to a faint murmur, though his skin did continue twitching here and there. "It is said that Men keep cats, sometimes...is this not so?"

"I have heard of this," agreed Sithlac, "though not within these walls have I seen such things. Outside, within the Great Wide Park, Men sometimes bring such creatures, for what purpose I do not know."

"They hunt mice, and rats as well, or so the stories say. I can take the form of a small cat, and perhaps, a Man might show me mercy."

"A good plan it is," said Sithlac approvingly, "but you must focus yourself, for if you fail the casting, your true form will be exposed, and all is lost."

Bongcor nodded, glancing at his flesh, which continued to quiver here and there. "I will meditate, as best I can," he agreed. "You must take my spear, for no cat would carry such a thing, and it would serve me not at all against a Man." So saying, he pushed the weapon through the gap in the metal grating, and Sithlac took it almost reverently.

"Calm yourself as best you can," the elder gremlin said, reaching through to put a hand on his friend's shoulder. "I will return at once to the Forlorn Tunnel and seek aid. Perhaps the others will know a way to free you, ere a Man comes."

"Thank you, friend hunter," Bongcor replied, slowly making his way down the wall toward the distant floor. "If something happens...if your efforts are in vain, know this: these last few nights have been the best of my short life. I would trade them not at all."

"And me as well," insisted Sithlac. "But fear not, I will save you from these Men, if a way exists. This I do so swear." Then he, too, hurried back down off the massive cage, heading back toward the Tunnel-gate.

Forlorn Tunnel – Commons

"Wait, he's *where*?" Lyza stared at Sithlac in disbelief. "You're saying there's some kind of trap out there? Right outside the portal? Really?"

"I do speak truly, oh yes," said the gremlin urgently. "Come, at once! You may know some way to release Bongcor that I do not."

Sithlac hurried back the way he'd come, watching over his shoulder to ensure the elven woman followed. She did, but not before calling out loudly for the others as well. By the time Sithlac reached the gate itself, Lyza followed right on his heels. She stopped in her tracks the moment she popped out of the tunnel, staring in surprise and awe at the metal structure towering nearby.

"You must believe me," she managed after a moment. "I've never seen that before, and I've been out here lots of times. Meathead and I would come through every so often to smooth out the tracks in the dust."

"Yes, so we did surmise," agreed Sithlac, "but we—"

"Wait, you figured that out? How?" demanded Lyza.

"To be honest," Sithlac went on, "it was truly Yog who—"

"Somebody call me?" The goblin popped out of the Tunnel-gate as if on cue. "Okay, what's this all about? Bongcor went in there and got himself captured, huh?" Yog scampered over to the side of the enormous cage, studying it carefully. "Okay, yeah, this door thing must've been set to shut when anyone went inside. Nice trick."

Lyza shook her head. "You figured out the tracks, huh? Okay, guess I'm not as clever as I thought. I'll have to come up with something else."

"Nah, you were great—I'm just better, that's all." Chuckling to himself, Yog knelt down in front of the cage, surveying the area carefully. "You know," he went on after a moment, "when we first got here, there were tracks leading over to this, and they came to an end right at this doorway. I thought maybe someone looked inside, then decided not to go in...but what if they did? They could've been captured, too."

"What kind of prints?" demanded Lyza at once.

"Clawed, like mine," Yog answered. "Goblin-feet, I'm sure."

Lyza shut her eyes and rubbed her temple. "Jozan," she muttered, almost to herself. "He would've investigated, too. That means he's not coming back. They captured him, just like your friend."

"But Jozan is not inside," pointed out Sithlac. "Bongcor would have seen him, this I know, even were he dead within. The door, besides, was open."

"The Men came, and took him away," Yog explained. "They could just pick this thing up if they wanted, and bring it back once they dealt with Jozan. In fact, see here, and here?" He pointed at a kind of furrow in the dust, and an area where some of it had been pushed up into a thick line. "They set it down, and it slid just so, see? The dust got shoved aside. So they caught somebody, then brought it back to catch another."

"But why?" Lyza inquired, shaking her head. "For what purpose would Men go after Fey? How do they even know we're here?"

"They may not," Yog pointed out. "Men will trap and kill anything they think is a pest. I remember skirting some poisoned rat traps during my forays. What do they see when they look at a goblin? Nothing, that's what, as long as we stay put. If Jozan just sat motionless in a corner, they might've thought their trap got triggered accidentally."

"Then why didn't he come back and tell us what's going on?" Lyza countered. "He would've come right back here, once they let him out."

"Maybe he thought he wouldn't be brought back here," suggested Yog. "He made a break for it, wherever he was, so now he could be anywhere. Maybe he'll show up here again and you can ask him. Anyway, it doesn't matter. We've got to get this thing open somehow. Got any ideas?"

Sithlac shook his head in the negative, not sure what he could say. The other two spat out their comments so quickly he never got a chance to provide any input. Now that he had a moment, he couldn't think of a thing to add. Just as he hesitated, though, the portal shimmered and Meathead stepped out, all but knocking the others aside with his sudden emergence. "Who dares trap my friends?" the immense troll demanded angrily, flexing his massive fists.

"Men, we think," said Lyza, pointing at the towering structure nearby. "Where else would something like that come from?"

Sithlac bounded over to the sealed door. "When Bongcor entered," he explained quickly, "this panel here fell down. Can you move it, friend troll?"

"Let's find out!" Meathead pounded a fist into an open palm and stepped forward. After trying in vain to get a grip on the slick metal surface, he resorted to pushing with all his might. The thick, ropy muscles in his forearms bulged and popped, but the wall didn't budge in the slightest. "Guess not," the troll muttered after a moment, lowering his head in failure.

"What about up here?" Yog called out. The others looked up to find the goblin sitting on the roof of the cage, pointing at the barred window nearby. "These are too narrow for even me to fit through, but could you bend them, you think?"

Meathead stepped back and looked up at the distant grating. "Probably," he replied, "but I ain't gettin' up there easy, that's for sure. Trolls, not so good at climbin', y'see." To illustrate, he tried hopping up along the edge of the cage, but just slid right back down again at once. He couldn't even make progress while pushing up against the edge where the structure met the nearby wall.

"The pipe," suggested Lyza, but even that didn't work. Meathead could get up onto the first section, where the split was, but couldn't ascend any higher. Even if he could've, he still would've had to make a significant jump across to the cage itself, and if he missed, he'd have a considerable fall to the ground. None of the others had the strength to lift him up, either.

"To the Tunnel we must go," Sithlac decided. "Enough wood-blocks could be stacked—"

"Yes, of course!" Lyza agreed at once. "It'll take a while, but we could build a ramp, or something much like one. Let's get started."

Sithlac nodded in agreement, and turned to head back to the Tunnel-gate, but just as quickly halted. Yog, scrambling down the side of the cage, stopped at once and cocked his head. "What?" he wondered aloud, causing the others to halt as well. "You're thinking about something, aren't you?"

"A task," Sithlac replied after a moment. "That is what she wanted, oh yes, and perhaps in this she can find it, for she is small enough to fit within, and find what we cannot."

"What are you blathering about now?" Yog asked and then lifted up a single clawed finger as he figured it out on his own. "Ithess, of course! She can get in there, can't she? And who knows how much power those winds of hers might have? Maybe she can lift the door!"

"Great idea, both of you!" agreed Lyza. "Can you fetch her, Yog, while we attempt to build the ramp?"

"Sure thing!" the goblin agreed immediately. "You all get started, and I'll be back before you know it!"

Adams Hall – Ground Floor Crawlspace

Constructing a ramp high enough to reach the bars proved surprisingly time-consuming. They had no fasteners, so their only option was to stack slabs of wood one at a time into a big pile. Sithlac and Lyza, working together, could carry smaller blocks (not really caring if they were damaged or not) while Meathead just hefted up the first one he came to and threw it over his immense shoulders. After a while they had quite a collection scattered around the edge of the enormous cage, but not enough raw volume to make something the troll could possibly climb onto.

At this point Sithlac directed Meathead to lay the largest woodblock on the ground next to the structure and then start piling more on top, working from biggest to smallest until they formed a kind of crude scaffolding. The stack didn't appear to be very stable, so they went back inside to collect a few smaller but thicker blocks, which worked as stabilizers. Now Meathead could climb up onto the wood and reach the wide flange that bisected the cage horizontally, but even then he still couldn't quite jump far enough to reach the windows high overhead.

Sithlac wondered if he should suggest he and Lyza climb up there and get on hands and knees, so the troll could use them as stepping-stones, but before he could suggest that dangerous idea, Yog reappeared. Instead of coming in through the nearby secret door, he instead came scuttling down the wall from some hidden aperture high overhead. Before anyone could ask if he'd been successful, a gust of cool wind jetted past, sending some of the loose dust along the floor to whirl about in little swirls.

"I'm here, it's true, and not too late," the zephyr whistled, sweeping past Sithlac toward the cage nearby. "I hope we didn't make you wait. What's this, a thing of Man in here? Nothing good from this, I fear!"

Sithlac nodded, trying to focus on the tiny creature as she zoomed around the cage. "Bongcor, my friend, is trapped within," he called out. "Perhaps inside, a way can be found to release him?"

"So your goblin friend did speak," answered Ithess. "Now wait here while I take a peek."

With a flourish, she swept just past Sithlac's head, causing him to withdraw his eyes and duck while she flashed by, disappearing quickly through the bars in one of the windows overhead. These served as air vents, of a sort, though of course the gremlin had no way of knowing that.

"Thanks, Yog," Lyza said a short distance away, nodding at the goblin, who Sithlac only now noticed looked quite exhausted. "That didn't take you as long as I thought it would."

"Got lucky," Yog replied between heavy breaths. "Nobody outside, and the Hub went right on up. Helped that Ithess knew a quicker way back down, too." He glanced over at Sithlac, grinning and pointing overhead with one clawed finger. "Got a lot better way to get your wood up top, so long as we can haul it up from here."

"About that later we will talk, oh yes," said the gremlin, "but for now, we must complete our task here, in case Ithess fails. Come, Lyza, let us climb up, and perhaps—"

At that moment the zephyr returned, swooping back down out of the cage to hover in front of the others. Sithlac could see her quite clearly now: a tiny faerie-like shape surrounded by a thin cloud of dust and mist. She looked more than a little bit agitated. "To help break Bongcor free, I doubt," she sang in her high-pitched, lilting voice. "There's no way I can let him out. As a kitten he does hide, a perfect form to take inside. Nothing more do we dare try—the Men come now and we must fly!"

As if to punctuate those words, the ground trembled ever so slightly. They all felt it—the immediately recognizable vibration of an approaching giant's footfalls. Yog immediately darted for the Tunnel-gate, but stopped without entering, even as Meathead came up alongside. Lyza also retreated, and Ithess moved away, but Sithlac instead moved directly over to the closed door on the side of the cage. "What are you doing?" the elf demanded. "Quick, before they show themselves, or the gate will close!"

"Bongcor!" Sithlac called out as loudly as he could. "Friend hunter, you must trust in your disguise! Stay hidden, and I will find you!"

"You must not try!" a faint voice replied. "You must hide! I am lost, but you must not be lost as well! Go, friend mentor, and remember me...!"

"I will not give up!" called out Sithlac, backing away as the others yelled at him frantically. "I will find you, this I do so swear...!"

Then, as the floor vibrated even more sharply, the ceiling started to move. Light flooded inside, causing everyone to wince. Nearby, the Tunnel-gate shimmered and winked out.

"Now we're screwed!" cursed Yog. "They won't see me, but the rest of you—get out of here, now!"

"No! Stay close! Don't stray at all!" Ithess shouted, even as she began to circle around them, gradually picking up speed. "I'll keep us safe behind this wall! Speak not, and keep as still as stone, or else the lot of us they'll own!"

Sithlac obeyed, freezing in place, as did they all. The light grew brighter as high above, a pair of gigantic hands removed a panel overhead. A moment later a massive, pudgy face poked inside, with another, bearded Man watching from behind. "Aha, yep, this one's been tripped, all right," the overweight one said, although of course none of the Fey could understand him. "Let's see what we got, shall we?"

Reaching down, he used one finger to pop the folding handle up out of the top of the cage, took hold, and lifted the whole thing up into the air. Somehow, he took no notice of any of the tiny creatures below, or the small stack of wood nearby. Both Men instead peered inside the cage through the vents along the top edge. "Aww, look, it's a li'l kitten!" said the bearded one, tapping a couple of fingers on the bars. "How cute! How you s'pose it got in the walls, anyways?"

"Who knows, maybe one-a them college kids tried keepin' it as a pet and it got through some crack? Whatever, not for me to know or care."

"Well, what now, Jimmy? You think we oughta ask around? I hate to think we's takin' someone's poor li'l kitty."

The other one shrugged. "Hey, c'mon, Freddy-boy, it's like I said, ain't for us to say, amirite? Mr. Spencer, he says, anytime one-a these special cages trips, you gotta bring it to him no matter what. How we gonna open it, anyways? He's the only one wit' the key, right? Now come on, let's go. Sooner we get this li'l guy delivered, sooner we get paid."

"Yeah, sure, sounds good," agreed Freddy, sounding a little bit disappointed as he lowered the access panel back into place. "Such a shame, though. He really is kinda cute..."

With that, the access panel slammed down, plunging the crawlspace below once more into darkness.

PART THREE

~ Morningside Park ~

Adams Hall – Ground Floor Crawlspace

Sithlac just stared as the immense container lifted away, disappearing from view when the gigantic Men shut the access panel, plunging the crawlspace into near darkness. He felt paralyzed, not just from fear at the terrifying human presence, but also from the shock of losing Bongcor.

Gone...just like that! My friend, gone forever...lost, captured by Men, the one enemy from which there could be no escape, no chance of rescue...

"They're gone," a voice said from nearby. Yog, the goblin, scurrying back toward the reopened gateway. "Come on, let's get out of here, in case they come back."

"No need, they've left...we're safe once more," sang Ithess, her frantic whirling having come to an end without Sithlac noticing. She sounded exhausted, the words delivered slowly, between breathless pauses, but no less melodic. "They've taken...what they came here for. A trap they set... and set it well...their true goals...only time will tell."

"Thank you for your help," said Lyza, holding two hands open, palms up, in the direction of the hovering zephyr. "I'm not sure what you did, but they would've seen us for sure without that spell."

"The air, if asked...will oft reveal..." she gasped, settling gently into Lyza's waiting hands. "But if needed, too, it can conceal..."

She fell to her knees, panting, and grew silent. Sithlac, too, dropped prone, supported only by leaning on Bongcor's spear. He let himself deflate with a soft hiss, his eyes withdrawing almost completely into his head. The rest of the world all but faded out.

Gone...he's gone...Bongcor...my friend, gone...!

"Sithlac? You okay, buddy?" Yog moved away from the Tunnel-gate, which he hadn't yet entered, and approached the fallen gremlin cautiously. "We're safe, all right? Now we know what they're up to, you know? We know what to look for. Just stay out of big metal boxes from now on."

"Leave 'im alone," muttered Meathead, a sad look on his enormous, tusked face. "Can't you see he's hurtin'? He just lost his best bud."

"Yeah, well…" Yog's reply caught in his throat. The goblin paced back and forth for a few moments, struggling to come up with something to say. "There's nothing we can do, though," he finally spat, trying to sound harsh, but mostly failing. "He's gone, and that's that. Gotta move on, you know? No way we can chase after those Men, and they could be anywhere. I just don't get why they'd put out traps, after all this time. Never seen that before. What's that all about?"

"They were after us," Lyza replied sadly. "Fey, I mean. Special cages, they said. They weren't after normal vermin, like rats. I've seen that sort of thing before. This was designed on purpose, to ensnare one of us."

"Well, that's just…wait, what?" Yog stared at her. "Special cages? They *said* that? You mean you can understand Man-speak?"

"It's a useful thing to know, if you travel as much as I do," sighed Lyza, frowning. "Not an easy trick to learn, and half of what they say is gibberish, but that part I caught clearly. There was a name, too. Someone called 'Spencer.' That's where they took Bongcor…to a human named Spencer. They were getting paid for it."

"So this Spencer has put out a bounty on us," growled Yog. "That's disgusting! I didn't have a lot of faith in the Great Bargain before this, you know, and there went the last of it. What chance do we Fey have if the Men start coming after us? Maybe I should go back to my clan…"

Lyza frowned and glared at him. "You know what that would mean."

Yog glared back. "Better that than to be taken away and—"

Meathead hissed and took a step toward him, pointing an oversized finger at the quiescent Sithlac, who still hadn't moved or spoken. Yog at once realized what he'd been saying and cowered, his ears flattening against his head. "Oh, sorry, Sithlac, I didn't mean—oh, I'm sorry, that's not what I—oh, maybe I should just shut up now." He moved back toward the gate, but didn't enter, just sort of faded into the shadows nearby.

"Your fears are noted," answered Lyza after a few moments of consideration, "but if I understood their conversation correctly, those two Men believed they had captured naught but an ordinary kitten. They knew they had a special cage, as they called it, but didn't know its true purpose. So this Spencer they referred to is aware of our existence, but the others are not. What does that suggest to you?"

"That story you told earlier," Yog answered quietly. "The one about the Fallen giving Men the power to see us."

"Yes. Just so." Lyza nodded, almost to herself. "Some Men can see our true forms, it is said, and now it seems those legends are true. What purpose they could have for our kind, I have no idea, but it can't be good. I must find out more." She suddenly stood up straight, grim-faced and determined. "I will go after them. I've tracked things much smaller and stealthier, you know. Two giants should be easy. I'll come back when I can. While I'm gone—"

"I will join you."

Sithlac surprised them all, even himself, with his sudden response. His body reinflated aggressively, and he rose suddenly to his full height, clutching Bongcor's spear in both hands, as though challenging anyone who dared to argue. "I will join you," he repeated, "for an oath I have sworn, oh yes, and will forget it not."

Lyza, taking care not to disturb the still-resting zephyr in her palm, reached out to place a calming hand on Sithlac's shoulder. "I admire your loyalty, more than you can possibly know," she told him, "but where I go now, you cannot follow. I promise, I will return with news as soon as I can. In the meantime, you have a duty to your people. Tell them what has happened here, that they may avoid such traps in the future."

"I...I must help..." Sithlac answered, noticeably wavering. He began to collapse, unable to remain standing up straight for so long. He all but withered before the others, leaning on the spear for support. "I must... must follow. I must join, must find..."

At that, Ithess rose to her feet. Her tiny wings, shimmering in the faint light, flapped gently and she lifted into the air, hovering before him. "Your friend, you want to help, it's true," she sang quietly, "just now there's nothing you can do. Go home, tell your kin, and wait...I'll find you when we know his fate."

"Ithess?" Lyza looked surprised. "Are you...are you offering to help in this? You know I—well, we—we're going to have to go Outside."

The little zephyr nodded, faint motes of dust spinning around her in a kind of shimmering halo. "This is what I've waited for," she sighed, her musical voice assuming a melancholy tone, with the faintest hint of hope. "A reason to emerge once more. Though they will surely call it wrong, the winds again must hear my song."

"Then let's go," Lyza told her. "The longer we wait, the farther away they get. Come on. Sorry, Sithlac, but I swear, I'll get word back to you somehow. If there's a way to rescue Bongcor, we'll find it."

Adams Hall – The Hub

"You gonna be okay, Sithlac?" asked Yog as they stepped off the Hub into the nearby crawlspace. "I mean, I sorta know what you're feeling, I think, but…"

His voice trailed off as the gremlin shut his eyes for a moment, sighing. "I know not what will become of me," Sithlac answered, shuffling blindly along in the corridors he knew so well. "I feel as though I may never hunt again."

"Yeah, it's tough, losing a friend," answered the goblin. "It's happened to me lots of times, you know. I outlived lots of my buddies. Never gets easy, trust me. But you…you've never had to go through this, I bet. It's gonna be a lot harder for you, I know, but you can't stop hunting. Take a few days off if you want. You deserve that, at least. Just don't give up. Bongcor…he wouldn't have wanted that."

"Bongcor…" Sithlac opened a single eye part way, just enough to see as he worked his way through a tangle of wires snaking their way along in the dusty passage. "This…pain…I feel. It is the same for you? And always it is so?"

"Yeah, pretty much," agreed Yog.

Sithlac nodded slowly. "Then now I understand, oh yes," he remarked sadly. "I know now why gremlins work alone, and friendship is so rare: to spare ourselves this awful trial, when something goes awry."

Yog said nothing for a while, scuttling along behind his much larger companion as they crept slowly through the walls. They traveled for several minutes in silence, each alone with his thoughts, until at last Sithlac came to the hunter's hole that led out into the open hallway, and thence to the Tunnel-gate. Here they stopped, for both knew the goblin dared come no further.

"I know you feel terrible now," said Yog at length, "but trust me, you're better for having had a friend. Mourn for a while, if that's what it takes, but start thinking about all the good times you had together, and you'll see what I mean. You two made each other's life better, and that's the honest truth. Anyway, I'm leaving now, but I'm still willing to help out if you want to keep building. When you're ready, you'll know where to find me. Good luck...my friend."

Sithlac's eyes involuntarily retreated into their sockets at that, and before he could get them back out again, Yog had disappeared. The sound of his claws skittering over drywall echoed down from somewhere high above. Sithlac struggled to find a response, and failed; but after a few seconds it didn't matter. The goblin was gone.

Morningside Tunnel – Interior

The gateway opened as usual and Sithlac stepped into the entrance hall, blinking at the sudden light. He passed by the sentry with barely a word to explain himself and headed straight for his home. The partly built dual tower remained as before, with nothing missing, although someone had splattered something on the joint wall section, as though in protest over the loss of the common alleyway. Sithlac barely noticed the sticky mess as he went inside, shutting the door behind him and quickly covering the lone window with a stained leather scrap that served as a crude curtain. He wanted to be alone.

What was he to do? Bongcor's capture came as a grim shock, setting off a cascade of painful, gut-wrenching feelings through his body—terrible emotions he'd never known before, or even imagined could be possible. He felt certain, now, that this is why gremlins so steadfastly avoided such cruel niceties as friendship and love. What good did it do, to become so attached to another, only to feel so torn apart when they're taken away?

Guilt, sadness, remorse—those unfamiliar, overwhelming emotions had kept him occupied all the way back to the Tunnel, but now that he was here, reality started to poke its way into Sithlac's addled mind. What would happen to their dual tower now? He couldn't continue the work without Bongcor. While the Rules didn't stop them from working together, they did keep him from trespassing on his neighbor's territory in his absence. That meant that despite the unique tower design, Sithlac could now only work on one side of it. Furthermore, once the truth about Bongcor's fate became known, the auctioneers would come...and in tearing down one tower, they would almost certainly destroy both.

Sithlac shook his head in defeat, deflating completely and withdrawing his eyes all the way into their sockets. *Now our true folly is laid bare*, he thought morosely. *No wonder such things are never tried! A joint project only lasts so long as the pairing remains intact. The loss of one means the loss of all.*

A disaster, in every way...

"Sithlac?" The voice came from outside, through the covered window. "You have returned, or so the sentry said. If within you surely are, an audience I do request."

"Then enter, if you must, but a poor companion I will be, I fear," Sithlac replied, not even sure why he bothered answering. He didn't even know for sure who was speaking, and pointed a single weary eye toward the entrance in a pitiful pretense of half-feigned curiosity.

A moment later the wan, narrow face of Gurtok pushed its way through the makeshift curtain. "Ah, you did return, I see," the Third said amiably. "Alone, it seems, and not so pleased, oh no, or so the tales are told."

"Only just returned I have," remarked Sithlac as the older gremlin pushed his way inside, "yet my condition you already know. Am I watched so closely by the others as you do yourself?"

"I know not what others do, of course," answered his guest, taking a seat on a nearby bottle cap, "and spying is not a thing I try that often; yet still, I wished to know when you returned, and a filled water-skin sent the sentry's way worked quite well as payment, oh yes, it did indeed. Now speak, and tell me what occurred that leaves you so forlorn."

Sithlac hesitated before replying, focusing both eyes on Gurtok carefully. After last they met, above the Hub, the older gremlin had kept a low profile, making sure none of the others in the Morningside Tunnel knew of that encounter. Now, he'd boldly walked right into Sithlac's house, right in the middle of town—something bound to draw attention. Another day, with his emotions less clouded, Sithlac might've kept his concerns to himself, but now he felt no need to be so subtle.

"I will tell you, oh yes, I surely will," he offered somewhat reluctantly, "but first, explain to me why you come, that I might know your true purpose; for I find your boldness lacking of all sense and logic."

Gurtok hissed and pulled his head away, obviously insulted by Sithlac's words and forceful tone. "I come to you in concern only for your cause," the elder gremlin replied gruffly. "Alone among the Council, I do approve of your efforts here. If you care not for my attention, I can go elsewhere." He stood, as though making to leave, but paused for Sithlac's response, which didn't come immediately, but only after a few tense heartbeats had passed.

"Very well, stay if you would, and I will tell you of my trial," said Sithlac with a heavy heart. "Disrespect I did not mean to give, and your forgiveness I do beg most humbly."

"And it is yours to have," replied Gurtok, once again taking his seat, all his ire immediately forgotten. "As to your fears, I tell you this: to the Council I have openly admitted my approval. Thus it is that I need no longer seek you out in secret."

"And you received no penalty for this?" wondered Sithlac.

Gurtok grinned. "Such a thing was indeed discussed," he explained, "but to my position I have ascended, not only by building structures, but also...other things. Debts and favors, which need no further explanation at this time, but suffice to say, they were enough. And now, I ask again, pray tell, what has brought you down so low?"

Sithlac nodded. He had indeed intended to tell this story to the rest of the Council, eventually, so at least explaining it to Gurtok would get it out in the open. Besides, at least the Third might at least give him a fair response. He hated to think what it would be like when he told this story to Tirchoth the Grand. The very idea almost made him shudder.

Pushing that out of his mind, Sithlac began his tale, keeping many of the details to himself, not just to keep the story simple, but also to avoid giving away anything that might cause problems in the future. In particular, he didn't mention the Forlorn Tunnel, the other Fey he'd met, or anything about officially hiring a goblin. He couldn't possibly leave Yog out of the story, of course, but instead discussed him only as though he were an opportunistic guide, eager to offer his assistance in exchange for a meal.

"The goblin's words led us to a secret place," Sithlac explained carefully. "A place where what we sought could be found: loose wood and other things with which to build, yet quite some distance away from our homes. Together, with some hard times, we could bring these parts back here, but the way would be long and difficult. So we set out to find another path, some way to avoid the obstacles we most surely faced. It was then that disaster struck."

"And what disaster might this be?" wondered Gurtok, almost immediately taking note of Sithlac's crestfallen expression. "Bongcor...he did not...was it the Fallen?" Gurtok gulped hard at the very word.

"No, the Fallen it was not," insisted Sithlac, trembling at the memory. "A trap, instead, one set by Men. Bongcor stepped within, and found himself entombed. We could not...I could not..." He shut his eyes, withdrawing them completely within his head once more.

"Bongcor was...captured by Men? Is that the truth of which you speak? This cannot be…" Gurtok looked away, aghast. As the reality of Sithlac's words settled in, he began to babble openly, as though to himself. "The Great Bargain, broken…and Bongcor…no, not just Bongcor, oh no! All those of late who disappeared…into the hands of Men! Not the Fallen, as we were led to believe…but Men! I thought no worse could things become…!"

"At least we know the truth at last," Sithlac said sadly. "Our foe thus stands revealed, and the traps they lay can now be dodged."

"And to that we have you to thank, great hunter," Gurtok replied. "The Council must know of this at once. Come, at once, for tell them you must, without delay."

"Believe me, they will not," answered Sithlac. "What cause have they to believe such as I? The tower you sit within is something they despise, and so am I. They will hear my words, lay the blame at my feet, and cast me out."

Gurtok nodded slowly, narrowing his eyes. One of them slowly rotated around the room, as if taking in his surroundings, before withdrawing partway into its socket. "There is truth in what you say. Tirchoth has spoken against you most harshly, and thought to banish you, but others stayed his hand. Instead, they called for patience. Tales are told that joined towers such as yours have been tried before, and failed."

"Tried before…?" Sithlac cocked his head. "Never before have I heard of such a thing."

"Old stories, from long before our time, of course," said Gurtok, "but Urgnoct the Second, as you surely know, has an ear for such old tales. He said the two of you were like rotting poles upon which a great load balances. Sooner or later, one pole must break, to send the whole thing crashing down. Thus it is with you just now: without Bongcor to fulfill his half, all is surely lost."

Sithlac nodded. "Such is my conclusion, as well," he replied sadly. "At some point, I must tell the Council what I just told you. They will hear, and perhaps even believe, the danger from the Men; but I am done. Of that there can be no doubt. All I—all *we* built together—will soon be gone."

Gurtok stood up and began to pace about, obviously agitated. "This must not be," he hissed, almost to himself. "This cannot be allowed. But what to do…?"

Sithlac almost retreated into his deflated self again, but instead opened a single wary eye, watching his guest in no small amount of confusion. After a time, he finally gave voice to his concerns. "What bothers you so, Third among us?" he inquired in a low voice, almost afraid to ask the question. "Why would such as you be so concerned about a rival like myself? Truth to tell, your actions make very little sense at all. Why not leave me to my fate?"

Gurtok stopped pacing and looked directly at his host with both eyes fully extended. He held the gaze for several seconds, then pulled away. With a quick bound he whipped open the leather curtain and peered outside. Assured that no one was out there listening in, he then moved very close to Sithlac and spoke in a low, hesitant voice.

"You have told the truth to me, when you could have kept it to yourself," said the older gremlin. "I would think of us, not so much as friends, oh no, but as allies of a sort. Is this not so?"

"It is, most surely," agreed Sithlac without hesitation, although inwardly he could only hope that he wasn't making a grave error in agreeing. Something inside him suggested otherwise—a feeling he didn't quite comprehend—so he went along with it.

"Then I tell you this, a thing I've never told another," went on Gurtok, keeping his voice as quiet as possible. "I despise Tirchoth the Grand, with all there is of me. I would see him defeated and destroyed. I would see myself rise above him, if I could, of course; and yet, I know I have it not within myself to accomplish such a goal, despite a lifetime on the try. Thus, I would see another rise, and aid him if I could. Until some days ago I thought to never see such a thing, until at last I saw a tower paired. Then I knew at once it could be done."

"But why?" Sithlac couldn't help but ask. "Why do you hate him so?"

"Because he *cheats*," hissed Gurtok angrily. "He breaks the Rules. He always does and always has. The rod you see, upon which his tower rests—a forgotten treasure it was not. Stole it from the Men, he did, oh yes! And sought it out they tried, for many days, and into ruin we were very nearly brought."

Sithlac gritted his teeth together, echoing Gurtok's repeated hissing as he spoke those words. "But if what you say is true, he is a danger to us all. How can he be left in place? Why has there been no challenge?"

"There has, oh yes, there has," Gurtok answered. "The Seventh Rule is not the only one he flaunts."

"The First...?" Sithlac began, but a slow nod provided the only answer he needed. He gulped several times and turned away. The First Rule, never to harm another gremlin...to think that Tirchoth would break it, the greatest Rule, just to stay in power...!

Clearly there were many things Sithlac didn't know about what it meant to be among the Council. He remembered how easily he and Bongcor had treated the idea of building a few more levels, as if they could just ascend to the upper echelons without a care in the world! Yet Gurtok had already hinted about having something beyond mere structures at his beck and call, deals and favors that made him feel safe enough to openly express an opposing view among the Council. Until now, Sithlac had never had any interest in such politics, but now that he'd started to scratch the surface, he realized he had no business getting involved in such things.

"This is too much for such as I," he admitted, flopping down onto the bottle cap his visitor had been using as a seat just a few moments before. "I know not what to do, nor what to say. If I tell my tale, as you heard it now, I will surely lose my house."

"Much more than that, I fear," agreed Gurtok, "for Tirchoth will seize upon this as evidence of your betrayal of the Rules, and cast you out. Come the morrow, you will be exiled most surely, never to return."

"Of this I must sadly agree," Sithlac sighed, "but what else can I do? If I keep the truth about Man's traps to myself, other hunters will meet Bongcor's fate, and that I could not stand. If his loss is to have any meaning, the truth must be told—oh yes, it surely must!"

At that, Gurtok spun round and focused both eyes firmly on his host. "Oh yes, oh yes, but not by you!" he exclaimed. "Let me be the one to tell the tale! I will mention you not at all, nor Bongcor's name, but merely say I escaped a trap somehow. Then the others will be warned, at least, and you can return once more to hunt."

"And all the credit you will have," pointed out Sithlac, but before Gurtok could complain, he hurried on. "Yet, fear not—on that I care not at all, oh yes! If the rest are safe, it matters not. Although, for me, I am still bound. Without Bongcor, I cannot build, and when the truth comes out, it is all for naught."

"Do you think he can be found?" asked Gurtok directly, still staring at him with both eyes firmly locked on his.

Sithlac hesitated. "I do not know," he answered after a moment. "He was taken by Men. To retrieve him...the chances seem low indeed."

"Better than if you face the Council," pointed out Gurtok. "All this does is buy you time, I do admit, and yet, it is all I have to offer. When the morrow comes, I will tell the Council what I know. That you told me this they will suspect, and they will come to ask, and by then you must be gone. I will delay their wrath as best I can."

"That is all that I can ask," agreed Sithlac. "And with that my task within is done. I will depart once more, and find Bongcor if I can. Only then will I return."

Gurtok nodded eagerly. "Then together you can build your tower high indeed, that we might see the end of Tirchoth at last!"

Upper East Side – 2nd Avenue South

The pickup truck bearing the double helix logo slowed, cutting swiftly into the right lane without its driver bothering to signal. Ignoring the honk of displeasure from the trailing motorist, Jimmy chuckled to himself as he swung into the parking garage and screeched to a halt in front of an entrance gate bearing the same stylized logo as their company vehicle. As Freddy made a *tut-tut* sound from the passenger seat, Jimmy swiped his employee identification card, patted his hand impatiently on the steering wheel until the gate lifted away, and hammered the accelerator as soon as he had an opening.

"I swear, one of these days you're gonna hit somethin'," his companion complained. "Maybe then I'll be the one who gets to drive."

"Not likely, Freddy-boy," laughed the bearded man as he darted into the first parking space he came to in the employee area. "You know you don't got the heart to drive in the city, and don't bother denyin' it, now!"

"You keep drivin' like that and maybe I just might find me some," insisted the overweight passenger, unbuckling his belt and huffing with difficulty as he extracted himself from the narrow compartment. By the time he managed to carefully step down to the ground outside, wincing at the pain in his ankles, the much more nimble driver had already shut his door, moved around back, and unbuckled the locked cage from its restraints.

Jimmy glanced inside before lifting the container, only to find the kitten inside backed up into a corner and looking up at him in sheer terror. "Ride's over, li'l kitty," said the grinning Man with a clipped laugh. "Time to show you your new home, and for us to get paid. Let's go."

Freddy shambled up alongside, tugging at his pants to try to look presentable. Despite the cool air he found himself sweating, so he took off his jacket and tossed it in the cab of the pickup, wiping the sleeve on his brow before shutting the door again. Then he turned to join his fellow animal specialist as he headed deeper into the building.

Jimmy spent most of the short journey spouting baby-talk to the kitten, causing Freddy to roll his eyes in annoyance. "No sense gettin' too attached, y'know," he pointed out as they neared the security door. "You ain't gonna see that li'l critter again, that's for sure."

"Yeah, I know, but see, these guys are strays, y'know?" said Jimmy, waving goodbye through the bars before standing up straight at the entrance. "They got no chance at a real life with good homes, right? So this way they can at least do somethin' important."

"Whatever helps you sleep at night, bud," said the other, shrugging as he pulled the door open and held it for his companion. Freddy followed closely behind as they flashed their badges at the security man, who nodded and allowed them to pass without a word.

They moved a short distance down the hall to arrive at a spacious receptionist's desk shaped like a huge half-circle. A pretty young woman with impossibly huge glasses sat in an office chair before them, her seat set exceptionally low, affording both men the perfect angle to observe the unbuttoned top of her blouse. She took no apparent notice of them as she talked on the phone in a crisp, professional voice, and they didn't mind waiting at all, standing there patiently and enjoying the view.

At length she finished her brief conversation and set the phone on its cradle, jotting something down on a notepad before turning to regard them through those enormous lenses of hers. "You two again?" she said, one corner of her pretty mouth turned up in a mocking smile. "Don't you have weekends off like most reasonable people?"

"Not when there's bonus bucks in it for us," replied Jimmy with a smile. "It's time and a half, y'know. Besides, you're here too, don't forget."

She didn't react to that, keeping her eyes fixed on the large container nearby. "And what is it this time, another rat? Or maybe a squirrel?"

"Kitten," said Jimmy, setting the cage in an open spot on the desk. "Have a look—he's pretty cute, y'know."

"No thanks," the secretary replied with a dismissive wave. "Cats and I don't get along—just keep it away. I saw you coming and buzzed Alison for you, so she'll be here any second."

"Aw, but I like talking to you better, Kasey," complained Jimmy, leaning in closer and smiling as though trying to put on the charm. In response she simply shook her head, rolling her eyes and turning away, dismissing him without a word.

"Oh, c'mon, leave the poor girl alone," Freddy insisted, picking up the cage and dragging his companion over in the direction of the nearby seats. "They don't take kindly to that sorta thing anymore, y'know."

Jimmy sighed and waved a quick goodbye as he let himself be pulled away. "Ah, I miss the good ol' days, when a guy could hit on a pretty girl and she'd be flattered, not slap you with a harassment claim! Times change, I guess. You're right, of course, but I just can't help myself—she looks so darn cute in them big ol' glasses."

"Maybe so, but—oops, never mind, Miss Loomis is here already." He pointed in the direction of the nearby hall, where a crisply dressed businesswoman approached, her black hair tied back so intricately that not a single lock escaped. She, too, looked reasonably attractive, with sharp features and a trim, lithe appearance, but her face bore a stern, no-nonsense expression: blue eyes narrow and focused, her mouth set in a tight line, as though to say she was someone not to be trifled with.

"So, you've got another catch," said Alison Loomis, stopping a short distance away from the two animal handlers. "Let's see it."

In complete contrast to his happy-go-lucky attitude with regard to Kasey, Jimmy approached Alison with tentative reserve, holding out the cage with more than just a trace of nervousness. "We, um, got it from Adams Hall at Columbia," he commented in a careful tone, never once even considering treating her as he would the secretary. Under such treatment, Kasey might utter the occasional word of complaint or roll her eyes at him—whereas Alison would surely have him fired.

"Hmm, so soon after the last one," the woman remarked, peering in through the bars. Her eyes immediately went up as she saw the cowering creature within. "What is it, some kind of bullfrog? What's something like that doing at the university—escaped from a biology lab, you think?"

Freddy and Jimmy exchanged worried glances. For a moment neither could quite summon up the right response, for they both knew they had a cat in the box, not a frog. Without saying a word to each other, they knew if they questioned her or pointed out her error, they could be in for trouble—yet just the same, this might be some kind of test.

"Well, um, I'm not sure," mumbled Freddy after a moment, not really coming up with anything else to say in the heat of the moment.

"Yeah, we don't really ask questions, we just bring what's in the boxes," replied Jimmy quickly, nodding eagerly.

Alison flashed curious looks in both their directions. "You know, I was sure the last trap you brought in was empty, even though the trigger had obviously been set off," she remarked, "but Mr. Spencer seemed satisfied, and you know, he said something very much like that at the time."

"Well, he was right," agreed Jimmy, his beard bouncing up and down in time with his rapid nodding. "You see all kinds of weird critters out there in the city. We learned a long time ago not to ask questions, ain't that right, Freddy-boy?"

"Damn right," agreed the overweight man swiftly, a little thread of sweat meandering its way down the side of his pudgy face. He made no effort to wipe it away, instead standing straight and immobile like a military trainee standing at attention.

Alison smiled briefly and turned back to the cage, but once again her eyes went wide. "Okay, that's weird," she remarked, as though muttering to herself as she peered in closer. "I swear that thing looked just like a big frog, but it's a cat, isn't it? A little one, too. Hmm, must've been the way the light was hitting its fur or something." She blinked and shook her head. "You know, ever since I took this promotion, I've been seeing all kinds of funny stuff just like this. You two ever have that happen?"

"What do you mean?" asked Jimmy, a bit caught off guard by the question. Until about two weeks ago, they'd always brought their deliveries directly to Elias Spencer, the head of the testing lab, but then Alison started putting in appearances instead, having recently achieved the title of assistant lab director. At first they thought they wouldn't mind so much, what with her being relatively easy on the eyes, but she quickly proved to be a no-nonsense sort who accepted nothing less than complete professionalism from all company employees. To have her ask what sounded like a personal question took both of them by surprise.

"Well, I just mean, um, well..." Alison trailed off, still staring at the cowering kitten in the cage. "It's like what I said about the empty cage before—I keep catching myself thinking I'm seeing one thing and finding out it's something else. Maybe this place is getting to me. Tell you what, I'll do the next pickup run and you two can do my job, all right?"

They glanced at each other again, completely at a loss for words, until at last she stood up straight and smiled at both of them. "Of course I'm just joking," she told them with a weak little chuckle. "I'm sure we're all best at what we do, isn't that right?"

"Um, yes ma'am," agreed Jimmy readily.

"Yeah, yeah, definitely," put in Freddy, the line of sweat by now having reached the first of his two chins, where it tickled him so much he had to lean his head sideways and wipe it on his collar. Luckily, she didn't seem to notice.

"Okay then," said Alison, brushing them off quickly in order to cover up her mild embarrassment, "in that case, get yourselves down to primary testing—I heard there's some cleanup work waiting for you. I'll see to it your bonuses are properly logged for this catch. Oh, if you want some extra weekend hours, check back here tomorrow morning—there should be at least three new traps ready to go out."

"Sure thing, Miss Loomis," agreed Jimmy, turning to head for the elevator, his fellow worker scuttling along close behind. "Have a nice day."

"You too," she called out, but her eyes were back on the creature in the cage, so she only barely noticed their departure. She narrowed her azure eyes almost to slits, studying the kitten carefully, trying to find anything out of the ordinary, but couldn't. In the end, she shook her head, sighed, muttered something about possibly going crazy, and headed off toward the testing lab with the cage held tightly by the handle.

Not far away, alone in his office, Elias Spencer watched Alison closely on his monitor, nodding slowly in his chair. As she disappeared out of the camera view, he flexed his fingers together, his wide mouth gradually turning up into a smile.

"I think she's ready," he said quietly, almost to himself.

Morningside Tunnel
– Sithlac's Tower

After Gurtok left, Sithlac considered retiring for the rest of the day. His ordeal and the long journey back home left him somewhat weary, and normally he slept until nightfall, but not this time. He kept imagining what would happen if the Council didn't wait, but summoned him at once. He would go, of course; to do otherwise would bring their immediate wrath down upon him. Then he would tell his tale, and they would pronounce judgment and sentence immediately.

Banishment wasn't just a formality among gremlins. There were certain rituals involved—dark castings invoked in only the most extreme circumstances—that would cut Sithlac off from Tunnel-gates forever. The entry points would no longer open for him—not just the Morningside Tunnel, but all such gateways, anywhere in the world. That would mean no access to the Forlorn Tunnel, either. He could still use hunter's holes, of course, and thus would not be completely helpless, but for the rest of his life he would be forced to wander aimlessly, banished from his people for all time.

He shuddered a bit at the thought. He didn't mind being Outside for short periods, during a hunt, but to be stuck there forever...he couldn't even imagine what that would be like. Of course, Yog had been in a similar situation and somehow adapted, but he was a goblin. They were used to moving around all the time—it was part of their daily routine. Sithlac's home and tower were part of himself. To lose them would be akin to having an arm or leg cut off, or to have his friend—

Bongcor. Sithlac shut his eyes, and tried to think of something else. Every time his friend's name or face appeared in his mind, he felt that horrible sadness, wrenching at his gut. *If I hadn't led him Outside…*

No! I did nothing wrong. The choice was his to make. The fault is in those who captured him. Men…Men who set traps for Fey…they took my friend…!

Sithlac stood, frowning, the sucker-flaps on his fingers waving about angrily. *How dare they!* Men stood apart from the Fey—they always had.

Gremlins and all others avoided Men and left them to their own devices, as defined long ago in the Great Bargain. If the ancient tales were true, a great war nearly destroyed the world, halted only by the final, ultimate truce: Men would no longer perceive the Fey in their true forms, and were free to seek their own path, cut off from magical influence. The Fey, meanwhile, attended to their own pursuits, each in their own domains, and stayed out of Man's way at all costs. So it was decided many ages ago, and as far as Sithlac knew, nothing had changed.

But what if it had? The elf-girl, Lyza, certainly seemed convinced that the Men who took Bongcor did so in a deliberate attempt to capture a Fey creature. That itself was a violation of the Great Bargain. If the old rules were breaking down, what did that mean? What would happen to gremlins if Men were free to seek them out? The fate of the Forlorn Tunnel served as a grim reminder of what Men could do if left unchecked, and in that case, at least, they didn't even realize the Tunnel was there. If they *did* know...if they had ways to root out and destroy Tunnel entrances...why, it would be the end of gremlins altogether!

Sithlac opened his eyes, suddenly feeling very cold. He hadn't intended to let his mind go down that path, but it had, and now, suddenly, Bongcor's disappearance took on a new and darker meaning. This was now much bigger than a simple kidnapping. Sithlac simply *had* to find out what was going on. He would rescue Bongcor, of course, if he could—but if not, at the very least he had to find out why his friend was taken.

That meant no more waiting. If he hesitated, and the Council came, his efforts would be in vain. So, filled with sudden purpose, Sithlac sprang into action, hurrying around his house collecting what he thought he needed. Waterskins, a large pack, several bits of dried food he could use as rations, various tools, Bongcor's spear...soon he had quite a pile in front of him, and far more than he could reasonably carry.

When he hunted, Sithlac always traveled light. He never expected to be gone more than a half day, and if it did happen, he survived by scavenging. He'd really been on long journeys only three times before— when he went Outside to mate. During those expeditions, he and the female shared the burden of carrying supplies, mostly food and water, until they reached their destination. Then they worked together to fill their chosen nest with local materials—sticks, leaves, and a few bagfuls of loose earth. Food and water, once again, were acquired via foraging.

This time, Sithlac intended to be gone for several days, perhaps more, on a long journey to an uncertain destination—assuming he could even find Bongcor at all. Other than restocking his water supply in the Forlorn Tunnel, he expected to be in Man's buildings for quite some time. He had to be prepared for anything. He couldn't carry all these supplies, though, or he'd quickly become exhausted. Some of these things would have to be left behind.

In the end he settled on two skins, a single large pouch, a hooded collar, and Bongcor's spear. A small knife, useful as a cutting tool or a secondary weapon, hung at his side on a thin piece of twine wrapped twice about his waist. The pouch contained a light hammering tool, two staples, a map tack, four crystal baubles for use in trading, and a chip of silvered glass. The rest would have to remain.

With his choices made, Sithlac waited no longer. He exited without his usual worried back-and-forth searching, mostly because he'd done that before leaving the previous time and been quite thorough, but also because every minute wasted felt like too much of a risk. If Gurtok knew he'd returned from his hunt, others on the Council might as well. They could be on their way right now, for all he knew. Besides, the longer he waited, the harder it might be to find Bongcor.

In his mind, Sithlac saw the Men walking away with the cage. Bongcor's face, visible through the barred windows, pleaded with him as he disappeared into the distance…*find me, my friend…save me…!*

"I will find you, oh yes, of that you can be sure," Sithlac whispered aloud, hurrying away from his home without looking back.

Upper East Side – Research Lab (Animal Storage)

Huddled in the darkest corner of the cage, Bongcor nervously wrung his hands together, his eyes flicking back and forth at the barred vents high above. As the container moved, swinging gently to and fro with its unseen bearer's stride, he caught glimpses of things outside: doors, wooden structures, strange lights, metal towers, and—with terrifying frequency—the hulking forms of Men.

I am their prisoner, he thought, his thick skin literally quivering in fear. *They have brought me here, for some unknown purpose, and soon I shall learn my fate. I must be strong, and hide my true self as I can, for that is what Sithlac would do...*

He shuddered again as the Man carrying him came to a halt near another, and they commenced jabbering away in their guttural, incomprehensible tongue. The legs of the other, wrapped in thick white cloth, stood just barely visible outside one of the vents. His voice sounded deep, rumbling away like distant thunder, while the one overhead had a much higher pitch—this suggested his bearer must be a female, though he couldn't be sure. When she peered inside earlier, before taking his cage away, he saw naught but her eyes, narrow and stern, lined with some strange foreign substance that made the eyelids a dark, unnatural color.

I am not a gremlin now, he insisted to himself, struggling to regain control of his senses. *They see naught but my disguise. I must act as a kitten would, lest I give my true nature away.*

The conversation concluded outside and the woman moved on, swinging his cage once more. Bongcor felt his stomach lurch at the unnatural motion. This time, though, she didn't carry him far, instead hefting up the container to bring it to rest on an unseen, but very solid, surface. The vents on the far side grew dark as something covered them, and he heard odd rattling sounds outside before suddenly the exit doors slid open.

The gremlin momentarily felt a surge of hope, only to find that feeling dashed as he realized only another cage awaited. The space beyond initially looked like the open outdoors, with tufts of grass and a tree branch stretching across the way, but beyond that the illusion ended at a pane of glass. Further on, he saw only a wide gap before a featureless white wall.

Suddenly the female Man appeared, bending over to peer inside through the open doors. The enormous face looked terrifying, especially the way she smiled at him. "Come on, little guy," she said, waving a hand toward herself, but of course Bongcor couldn't understand the words. "Come on out—there's some food in here for you."

She pointed at the corner nearest her, where a small clump of green leaves lay in a pile. Bongcor's right eye swiveled for a closer look, following her finger automatically, but he kept his head fixed in place and didn't move, afraid of what might happen if he went in there.

The woman's smile gradually faded into a frown. "Hmm, okay, guess we'll have to do this the hard way," she complained, moving back out of sight. Bongcor shivered again, fully aware she wanted him to move, but unwilling to do so. He imagined a captured cat, trapped in a situation like this, would be just as reticent, and stayed put, fighting back the urge to run.

The woman's enormous shape flashed through the other nearby vents as she did something outside, and Bongcor realized then that at least one other Man was out there, further away, perhaps observing her actions. She muttered something else, perhaps to him, and then he saw her hand appear, clutching some kind of long stick. She moved closer, a bit more carefully now, and inserted the tip through the bars high above. "Come on, little one," she urged. "Move it, or I'll have to use this."

The tip of the bar drew near, and Bongcor shuddered, one eye fixed on it while the other considered the open doors once more. He hesitated, flattening himself as the stick got almost close enough to touch his skin, but still he didn't move.

"Okay, you asked for it," said the woman, flicking a switch he couldn't see, and suddenly a crackling spark of electricity popped out of the tip just alongside Bongcor's left flank. All rational thought left him and he broke, dashing forward through the doors, racing toward the imagined opening beyond, only to slam full-speed into the transparent wall. Stunned, he flopped backward, reeling from the impact, dropping to all fours and gasping loudly.

Behind him, the doors slammed shut as the rod withdrew. "There, that wasn't so hard, was it?" asked the woman, her face reappearing through the window pane. Bongcor brought one eye up to look at her, his vision swimming, while the other moved sideways to take in his surroundings. He found himself inside a large box, the floor lined with turf and sod, with a stick, some leaves, and a small pool of water to remind himself of the Outside. The walls to either side, which he couldn't see before, were also panes of glass, and through these he could see other cages beyond his own. The one to the right lay empty, but to his left he saw a ragged goblin looking back at him, its clawed hands pressed up against the window as he shook his head sadly.

The woman outside smiled and moved away, making a few more clattering noises in the distance. As Bongcor struggled to his feet, the goblin plopped down onto his haunches and gave a sad little wave. "Hey there," he called out, the voice muffled but still audible. "My name's Jozan, and I guess we're gonna be neighbors..."

Adams Hall – Eighth Floor

Sithlac half expected to discover Yog waiting for him as he returned to the dusty interior of Man's tower, but instead found himself alone. Reminding himself that the goblin expected him to take a few days to recover, Sithlac shrugged that off as normal and hurried on, angling straight for the Hub, down to ground level and then through the narrow spaces that led to the Forlorn Tunnel. He had no idea how he was going to track down Bongcor's kidnappers, but figured the ruined refuge would be the best place to start.

Upon arrival, he entered at once and immediately heard the sound of multiple voices speaking in the distance. By the time he reached the low wall that served as a partial doorway into the rest of the tunnel, the voices had stopped. "Who's there?" a deep troll-voice called out.

"It is I, Sithlac the gremlin," he hollered in reply, stepping out into the half-light to find all the others gathered around the common area. Lyza had returned, apparently, along with the barely visible form of Ithess swooping overhead in a gentle arc. The troll was there as well, hunched over while stirring something in his cooking-pot, barely glancing Sithlac's way, as if his arrival had been expected.

Yog hopped down from his perch on a leaning timber and bounded over. "Back so soon!" he said eagerly. "Glad to see it. Good timing, too. I thought you were gonna stay home a bit longer, though. What happened? You didn't get banished, did you?"

"Not officially, oh no," Sithlac replied as he made his way over to the assembled group. "I told my tale to Gurtok the Third, my only ally on the Council, and he agreed I should depart in haste. If before the Council I am called, and pronounced guilty of leading Bongcor to his fate, I would be banished, oh yes—banished most surely—never again to enter a tunnel, even this one, and how could I rescue Bongcor then?"

"So you left, in order to keep your options open," commented Yog. "Good thinking. You know you can't go back, then. At least not until we find him."

"Yes, yes, such a thing is clearly so," agreed Sithlac at once, brushing the idea away with a wave of his hand, in a false pretense of being unconcerned about such things. "Thus it is I have returned here, to begin my search apace," he added hastily, turning his attention to Lyza, with a brief glance at the orbiting zephyr overhead. "I see you have returned. What news do you bring, I wonder, that I may begin my quest?"

Lyza sighed and took a deep breath. "It's sort of a good news, bad news thing," she offered. "First off, yes, we were able to follow the Men. I couldn't find a trail right away, of course—they were walking on those stupid rock slab things the humans make. There's a word for this stuff, but I can't remember it. You know what I mean, though. The perfectly flat, annoyingly smooth blocks that cover up the earth and make tracking impossible. Luckily for me I thought to bring a zephyr along." She grinned and pointed a finger at the tiny creature above.

"The Men are many, spread around," sang Ithess, "but two among them can be found. 'Tis not the face I recall well, but things they wear—and how they smell." A tinkling laughter followed, and she gave a little mid-air dance, clearly proud of herself.

"Yeah, that's how we got started on the right path," Lyza explained, "but of course, compared to a little zephyr, Men are gigantic and very, very fast. We couldn't possibly catch them, only follow along, far behind. Luckily they didn't go into any buildings, but stayed outside. Ithess was like an arrow, pointing the way, but still, they were going to be long gone before we caught up. Luckily I had the opportunity to use a tree-step, which is risky, I know, with lots of humans around—but it took me almost right to them."

"A tree-step?" Yog inquired curiously. "What sort of magic is that?"

Lyza grinned. "An old elven travel trick. You step into one tree, and out from another. The trees have to agree, of course, and they have to be on the same ley-line—well, I won't explain the details, but it works, if you know the right places to tread. I had to leave Ithess behind, but she understood. She was tired out by this point, anyway."

"Hard work it is, to hurry so," she pointed out from overhead, "without the winds to help you go. It's been too long, since my sad fall—I fear they'll never heed my call. Perhaps one day they'll see me through, but not today, and this I knew."

"Anyhow," went on Lyza, as though eager to get the suddenly sad-sounding Ithess off that particular subject, "I had to climb up a bit, and when I popped out the other side, I could see the two Men talking to themselves next to one of those big metal monsters they use to move around in. I'm sure you know what I'm talking about. They all have this kind of oval, curvy shape to them, but this one had a big, blocky back end, with an open space for carrying things. The not-creature had a big label on it with some huge letters in Man-writing, along with a sort of twisty looking object—I don't read Man, unfortunately, so I have no idea what it said. I started to climb down from my branch, hoping to overhear what they were talking about, and find out where they were going, but that's where my luck ran out. As I watched, one of the Men flung down one of those white stick things they burn in their mouths and stamped it out with his foot. I think that's what caused them to delay—so he could do that stick-burning ritual, whatever it means—I've seen Men do that before, but I don't really know why. It's disgusting, though, just like they—well, never mind about that. Anyway, they immediately got in the metal monster and moved off. Following them from there was impossible, obviously—I like to think of myself as pretty fearless, but if you think I'm getting anywhere near one of those horrible beasts, you've got another think coming."

"That's it?" asked Yog curiously. "They didn't go anywhere you could see?"

"Well, I watched a bit longer," Lyza admitted, "but to no avail. The monster rolled on into the distance until it disappeared into a mass of them. Have you ever seen some of the gatherings of these things? There are so many—it's terrifying, and hypnotizing, and awe-inspiring all at the same time. They flow on, never-ending, like a great river of metal monstrosities, all the while making the most obnoxious noises! And the smell—well, anyway, you're better off keeping away as much as you can."

"Then it is over, before it begins," sighed Sithlac, who until this point hadn't uttered so much as a word since Lyza started speaking. "The path is lost, and Bongcor is gone, swept into the depths of Man's vast city."

"You'd think so, wouldn't you?" said Lyza, one corner of her mouth turning up into a smile. "Well, I said this was a good news, bad news sort of thing. That was the bad news. Here's the good news' side: I used a little elven magic to capture the view of that particular metal-beast. At least we know what it looks like. Here, I'll show you."

Reaching into a pouch at her side, she withdrew a small, shiny disc of a translucent, amber color. For a moment she rolled the bauble around in her fingers, smiling, and then chanted a few unrecognizable words.

The elven language, with its many vowels and chiming syllables, had deep roots in day-magic, and to hear it spoken thus was to risk enchantment. Sithlac knew this, but felt it worth the risk to see what Lyza was up to.

She didn't disappoint. In a few moments she completed her spell, holding the disc flat within her palm as it flared with multicolored light. Above, an image appeared, coalescing out of the very air itself. Parts of it slowly expanded into being, as though a sea of flowers sprouted, opening one after the other, each petal part of the picture, until the flowers faded and only the image itself remained.

Hovering in the air stood a frozen view of a pickup truck, viewed from slightly overhead, with two delivery men nearby, in the process of motion. The light green vehicle had a large, prominent logo featuring a double helix design and three very large words in block letters. None of those present could read the label, obviously, but the idea was clear: this uniquely marked vehicle would lead them to wherever they took Bongcor. They had only to find it again, and follow it somehow.

Lyza, humming to herself as she maintained her spell, managed to keep the image going for almost thirty seconds before finally gasping and losing concentration. The picture sputtered and winked out. She took a few deep breaths, returned the disc to its pouch, and waved a hand at the now empty air. "So there it is," she told them, once she'd recovered from the effort of reproducing that image. "That's how we find Bongcor. We go wherever they went in that thing."

"So simple it seems," remarked Sithlac, "but so difficult in truth. How, pray tell, can we find it again? If we do, how do we follow? If this river of metal-beasts is as terrifying as you say, none of us can enter such a thing and live."

"If only we could read their writing," sighed Yog. "You can't, you said that already—do you know anyone who can? Ithess? Meaty?"

"Can't even read my own tribe's stuff," the troll answered with a shrug. "Don't got no need for readin' where I come from."

"Writing's made for those who build," the zephyr said dismissively, "and—though I do admit they're skilled—to write, a zephyr has no need, and so, of reading, takes no heed."

"There are some of us gremlins who know the art," Sithlac commented, "but only to record things of interest to us. None of our kind can read Man's words. Yet it seems, at least this time, we must find a way."

"I know some elves who can do it, at least a little," Lyza explained, "but only with the aid of strong magic, and in times of direst need. I can't see how we could convince them this is one of those times. Maybe the threat of Men hunting us...but that could backfire, too. Such a thing might escalate quickly. No, we need to find some other way to do it—someone else who can read Man's writings, and who just might be inclined to help us because of who and what they are."

"What are you blathering about now?" wondered Yog, turning to face her with an accusing glare. "You obviously have somebody in mind—who is it?"

"Not just yet." Lyza smiled, in the sort of way one smiles when they know a secret and want to see who else, if anyone, also knows. "Sithlac? Any guesses? Come on, think about it for a minute and you'll figure it out."

Sithlac stared at her with both eyes open. For another few seconds he had no idea who she could be talking about. Then he thought about Bongcor, missing, lost, depending on him...and the faintest of melodies tickled his memory. Something he'd been humming to himself, on the very day he first opened himself up to the idea of having a friend. He began to hum that song again, very softly, thinking only he could hear it; but then, to his surprise, the orbiting zephyr overhead joined in. The music swelled, flowing over the assembled group, and then as one, all of them, even Yog, knew exactly what Lyza intended.

"The faerie," Sithlac stated simply, speaking for them all. "The faerie who was once a Man."

"Exactly!" agreed Lyza. "If anyone can read Man's writing, he's the one. And best of all, he's one of us now, so he should be willing to help out."

"Indeed," Sithlac replied, nodding. "Now all we have to do is find him."

Upper East Side – Research Lab (Animal Storage)

Bongcor's eyes swiveled about nervously, taking in his surroundings and watching to see if there were any Men outside. For the moment he ignored the goblin staring through the glass nearby. Some distance away, the two humans stood talking to each other near an immense door. They paid him no mind at all, as if he no longer existed. After a moment of blathering on and waving their hands, the Men left, letting the door slam shut with a loud bang.

Bongcor moved slowly about the cage, testing the walls. He'd encountered glass before, or trinkets made from it, during his time scavenging in the Morningside Tunnel. Since joining Sithlac on his hunts, he'd learned the stuff could occupy great amounts of space, acting as walls to keep a Man's cave sealed in from the Outside. Yet never had he thought it possible to use the mysterious clear substance as a kind of prison.

He tapped on it curiously, hearing a hollow sound in response, then drew his fingers slowly along the surface. The glass felt perfectly smooth, without any blemishes or imperfections. He unfolded his sucker-flaps and tested them, discovering that he could climb if he so wished, but since he knew a kitten couldn't possibly accomplish such a feat, he didn't attempt to do so.

Next he explored the cage a bit more, finding the sod and branch real enough, if a bit dried out. A thin film of water rested in a plastic cup near one corner, near a clump of lettuce and collard greens. He almost dismissed the food as unacceptable, but realized then that he'd likely have little choice. Gremlins preferred to eat insects or grubs, but are omnivorous and can eat vegetables if necessary. For the moment he had no interest, and turned away, approaching the goblin at last.

"Bongcor is my name, and I bid you greeting," said the gremlin, keeping his voice low as though he might be overheard. "I have heard your name before, oh yes. You are Jozan of the Dark Oak tribe, is that not so?"

"Yes, that's me," replied the little creature. "How do you know that? I can't remember the last time I spoke to a gremlin."

"I followed in your tracks, it seems, though I knew it not until now," sighed Bongcor, deflating noticeably at the admission. "Alongside my fellow hunter, Sithlac, this very day we sought out the Forlorn Tunnel and met those who dwelt within. Upon our exit, I fell prey to Men's grim trap."

Jozan nodded slowly. "That's what we get for being curious, huh? Well, we're neighbors now, like it or not. I've only been here for a single sunset, but it's been longer for some of the others."

At that he raised a skinny arm to point behind himself, toward other glass-walled cages visible further along the shelves. The nearest contained nothing but a large stone, but a bit further Bongcor spotted an elf peering at him sadly. There might've been more further down, but he couldn't see much more from this angle.

"For what purpose do Men capture us?" asked Bongcor worriedly. "Are they aware of our true forms, or do they think us naught but vermin?"

"That's how your defenses work, but not mine," explained Jozan. "When they look at me, they're supposed to see nothing—and I can tell, when they come by, that's how it works for most. There's this one Man, though—a male, with big bushy eyebrows—who comes by sometimes and looks right at me. Sometimes he talks, but I can't understand a damn thing. He knows I'm here, though. He can see me, when the others can't. He's the only one I'm really worried about because how can he possibly do that?"

"Perhaps your spell has failed," said Bongcor nervously, quickly testing his own defenses. The cat disguise remained active, as far as he could tell. "If you have no access to *kai*..."

"Ah, but I do," said Jozan, pointing up toward a line of windows on the wall high above. "The Sun and Moon appear within those squares, at certain times of the day or night," he explained. "When that happens, you can drink your fill and restore your spells."

"So the Men, it seems, know not how we work our magic, else they would surely hide us from its source," remarked Bongcor. "Should they think to do so, our true forms would be revealed in time."

"Or else they want us to keep using it for some reason," noted Jozan. "That's what the elf down there thinks, anyway. His name is Telan, and he's from someplace called Riverside Park, where there's something like six tribes of elves constantly battling for territory. He's been here four moonrises so far, and he thinks the Men have figured out what we are, and are trying to get us to show them how to use magic. The first thing he told me when I got here was not to use it for any reason, not even to try to escape, or we might be doing just what the Men want."

"So these clear walls, I dare not break them?" inquired Bongcor doubtfully. "With enough *dinathi-kai,* a crack might form…"

"No, that's the worst thing you could do," insisted Jozan. "Even if you get to that window up there, they'll find you before you can get out. Telan said there was another elf with him named Sellyn who was some kind of sorceress back in his tribe—he was a bodyguard of hers, or something, and they were attacked by some enemy, and took refuge in what turned out to be one of those big traps. You can ask him the whole story if you get moved close enough—they do shuffle these cages around sometimes. Anyway, soon as they got here, and the Sun came through the window, she drew in a whole bunch of *lana-kai* and broke open the doors to her cage. The Men came in just moments later—no idea how they knew, but they did. They had nets and after they captured her, she got put in a different cage and taken away. No idea where. So they must be watching us somehow, that's for sure."

"Yet how can they?" Bongcor asked, glancing back and forth through the glass-walled cages. "There are no Men here to see what we might do."

"Well, we can be sure they are, one way or another," Jozan explained, "because we've got Stony there in the next cage over. Dovok is his name, but you won't be getting any introductions anytime soon, unless those hidden eyes look away for a while."

The gremlin peered past his neighbor, into the adjoining enclosure, where he saw more natural turf and a large stone. "Who is Dovok? I see no one at all."

Jozan sniffed at that. "So you don't know trolls, then. Okay, I guess maybe you never met one, hmm? They turn to stone when Men see them. So as long as he's a rock, we know they're watching."

"Trolls turn to stone," muttered Bongcor. "I knew that not at all, but I see now what you mean. If that is the way of it, then we are being spied upon most surely."

"Yep," agreed Jozan, "so don't do anything you wouldn't want your momma seeing."

Bongcor nodded, ignoring the weak attempt at humor. He deflated still further and settled down limply into the stiff grass. "Then escaping is a hopeless task," he muttered grimly. "My friend, I feel, will seek me out, this much I know, but how is he to free me from this place? I would not have him join me in captivity, and yet, rescue is the only hope I have."

Jozan stared at him. "So your friend, this Sithlac you mentioned— he saw you get caught in the trap?"

"He did indeed, and called Lyza the elf, Yog the goblin, and Meathead the troll to assist. Even the winds of Ithess the zephyr could not free me from the cage, and the Men came soon after."

The goblin nodded, scratching at his chin. "I know all of those names except Yog," he noted. "Nobody saw me get taken. In fact, all of us here except you were caught without witnesses. You're the only one who might expect some kind of rescue, although how they'll find us in this Man-place, I have no idea."

"If they come," said Bongcor, moving back over to test the transparent walls for weaknesses, "we must be ready. I will work on breaking through, but not so that the Men will know. Perhaps a little progress will make things easier should they arrive."

"I like the way you think," agreed Jozan, "and I know it's not really likely they'll ever show up, but you know what? This is more hope than any of us have had since we got here, so I think I'll join you."

"Then we shall work together," Bongcor replied, "for of late I've learned the thing called teamwork can be very effective indeed."

Forlorn Tunnel – Ruins

"Aha, here, found some," said Lyza, rooting around in a half-collapsed tower a short distance from the commons. She emerged a moment later carrying a wrinkled, ragged sheet of woven cloth, badly frayed around the edges and stained with soot and ash. "This should do, at least for now. Meaty, if you don't mind, can you hold this up? Here, take the corners, and open it out so it's as flat as possible."

"Sure thing, babe, though I ain't real sure what this is all about," agreed the troll somewhat reluctantly. He did as she asked, shaking out the fabric a few times before holding it up like a homemaker about to fold a freshly laundered bedsheet.

"You'll see," the elf replied with a smile. "Hang on, and hold your noses, it's going to need some dusting. Hang on."

Without waiting for further instructions, Ithess flew down and began to race back and forth along the cloth, whipping up the wind as she did so. This caused a veritable cloud of ash and dust to fill the air, causing everyone else to shut their eyes and hold their breaths. Yog, the slowest to react, let off a trio of sneezes before catching himself. A moment later, the cloth now mostly clean, Ithess spun rapidly in place, forming a brief whirlwind that sucked all the debris away, into an expanding cloud settling halfway across the tunnel, well away from the assembled group.

Meathead opened one baleful eye. "Done now?" he wondered, still holding the sheet out in front of him as best he could.

"That's just part one," said Lyza. "Thanks for the help so far, big guy. Now, here's the thing. I've never met a faerie, despite all my travels, because they're pretty rare. Like I told you before, the one I knew about was by herself until this Man came along—and keep in mind, I'm not even completely sure that's what happened, but it's the best theory any of us have. Anyway, I digress. The thing is, if the stories are true, she lives in Central Park. Well, I tried to explain earlier what that means and where that is, but before we head off to go there, I think it's only fair I should do a better job of it. Ithess, if you please?"

"I may be small, but I've flown far, so now I'll show you where we are," she sang, hovering for a moment in front of the sheet, "and then you'll see, without a doubt, how far we'll go, and if you're out."

With that the little zephyr set to work, humming loudly to herself as she darted back and forth across what now served as her artist's canvas. With each pass, lines and symbols appeared, some black or gray and others in bright colors. At first it all seemed random, without purpose, but soon a prominent shape appeared: an oblong, wedge-like region, flanked by blue areas above and below, and a very long, rectangular green section near the middle. Above and to the side of this, a much narrower, thin green area soon faded into view, and above that, very near the blue, a smaller yellow square came into being. Ithess continued to fly around for a while, speckling the area around these things with more details in various colors, before finally finishing by adding a tiny black dot within the square.

"Not the best I've done, my dear," she sang, her voice sounding a bit forced, as though the effort tired her out somewhat, "but it's been a while, I fear. From high above, it's what you'd see...if you could only fly like me."

It so happened that Sithlac had never seen a map, nor ever imagined the existence of such things. Gremlins keep their knowledge of geography and architecture inside their heads, with an almost flawless ability to remember exactly how to get where they've been without need of assistance from anything other than memory. Whereas a human resident of the city, looking upon Ithess's impromptu painting, would immediately recognize the area around Central Park, Harlem, and Morningside Heights, none of the onlookers save Lyza had any earthly idea what they were looking at.

"I don't get it," said Yog after a moment, his head twisting frantically from side to side as he tried to make sense of what he was seeing. "Sorry, Ithess, it looks great, don't get me wrong, but what the heck is it?"

"It's a map, silly," said Lyza as the exhausted zephyr landed softly on her shoulder, obviously in need of rest. "You've never seen one? Okay, fine, I suppose I should've expected that. It's a drawing of what the city looks like from far above."

"Still not getting it," Yog complained.

"Me neither," muttered Meathead, shifting around uncomfortably. "How long I gotta hold up my arms, anyway? I'm gettin' tired."

"Just a couple more minutes, I promise," Lyza told him. "Don't let it go—the image only lasts as long as it doesn't hit the ground. Zephyrs can only paint in the air, you see. Anyway, I'll explain as quickly as I can, but first, Sithlac, what do you think? You're the one who needs to understand this, more than anybody else here."

"Certain of the image, I am not," he answered honestly, "but I do stand in awe of your abilities, Ithess, for such a treasure I could never create."

She smiled and bowed slightly, still trying to catch her breath, but didn't otherwise reply. Lyza, also smiling for her, moved over to point at the map, in particular at the little yellow box near the top of the image. "I'm sure you've looked outside the windows of this tower at some time or other, right? You've seen this area, where the Men live, with all the flowers and trees in the big courtyard, and the buildings all around?"

"From high above, I have," agreed Sithlac, "but only once in daylight. Trapped I was, as the Men within moved near, so with little else to do, I watched. I knew not what it was I saw, but remember it well, oh yes. A vast expanse of land, to be sure."

"They call this place 'Columbia,' whatever that means," Lyza explained, "and by that I mean this whole collection of buildings, all surrounding that great courtyard you saw. That's what this square is on this map. Try and imagine it: that whole area, all of it, is just this little square. You know how if you climb up really high and things way below you look smaller? Well, imagine you flew so high that all of Columbia looked just like this little square. Can you possibly picture that in your head?"

"I believe I can," agreed Sithlac after a moment, one eye locked on the map while the other remained fixed on Lyza.

"Yeah, I guess so," Yog said with a shrug. "Like, if you're on top of the Hub, and look down into the chasm—the bottom looks like a tiny little square."

Lyza shrugged back. "I've never seen that thing—it's way too unnatural for me—but I've heard of it, so I suppose you must be right. Anyway, see this dot here? The last thing Ithess put on the map? That's where we are right now. The tunnel we're in, the floors, the walls, the Hub, the whole Tower, all of it...this little dot. You see?"

"Okay, I get it, I get it," Yog said with a frustrated roll of his eyes. "What's your point?"

"I'm getting there, be patient." She then pointed at the thin strip of green below the box that was Columbia University. "This, Sithlac, is what you call the Great Wide Park but the humans call Morningside Park. It's a long, narrow stretch of woods on a steep hillside overlooking some of their recreational facilities. This is where you go to mate, as I understand things, and Meathead, this here—" she moved her finger to the far left side of the green strip, where a small, purple area could just barely be seen—"this is where your people live. The other side, opposite that, is another clan of trolls, and in between, that's all elf-lands—the Four Angry Kingdoms, as I like to call them."

"I know of them, oh yes," Sithlac put in, "for their territory is clearly marked upon the trees and stones, but in the mating-time, we keep well away. They do not like the walls, oh no, or so I have been told."

He referred to the towering stone walls that lined the upper section of the park, separating it from the road level high above. "Yeah, there's a treaty about that," Lyza explained, "but mostly it's just fear of being seen by Man. Those walls screw up elven magic pretty badly, which is probably why you gremlins take to it so readily. Each of us Fey have our places in the world, right? Anyway, let me move on. Sorry, Meaty, just another moment, okay? Now, Sithlac, you know how long a journey it is to get to this spot right here, where your nesting grounds are, right? Now, look over here."

She moved her finger across the park, all the way to the lower left corner, then across a couple of blocks of blackened city structures, to the nearest corner of the much wider green rectangle. "Imagine how far it would be to go here, all right? Through all the Kingdoms, then through Rock Troll territory, then across almost two blocks of human lands...anyway, all that would just get you to the very edge of what is known as Central Park—which is this whole area." She indicated the entire, enormous rectangle, which positively dwarfed Morningside Park, and which easily could've held a dozen Columbia Universities. With her point made, she looked directly at the gremlin before her, ignoring the others for the moment. "You see what I'm getting at, don't you? Yes, I can tell you do."

Sithlac's eyes pulled mostly back into his head as he gave a very slight, very grim nod of his head. "This is the task that faces us, then," he sighed loudly. "I see now why you showed it as you did."

"What? You do?" Yog shook his head. "I still don't get it. So we've got to go a long way, so what? You're going to use one of those nexus things, right? So, what's the problem?"

"Yeah, I'll get us there, not quite as easily as you might imagine, but I'll do it," Lyza replied, "but think about it, would you? What's the hardest thing about this? Not the traveling—something else entirely."

"Not the journey, oh no," Sithlac answered, collapsing a little as he settled back onto the ground. "Not the journey, but the *search*."

Yog frowned. "I still don't—oh, wait." He brightened for a moment, but then realized what he was saying, and his expression turned sour. "Oh...oh, yeah...now I see."

Even Meathead understood. Slowly letting his arms drop to their sides, he let the impromptu map collapse onto the ground, whereupon the image fragmented into a shower of colorful dust. He shook his head, causing the mat of fur to swish around, and let out a heavy sigh. Then he shut his eyes and succinctly explained the problem, as only he could.

"How we gonna find a tiny li'l faerie in a place that danged big?"

Upper East Side – Helixtech Labs (Alison Loomis's Office)

Alison paused a moment as she approached her office, for the door stood open and she knew she'd closed and locked it upon leaving, per company policy. She glanced around, but the other two doors further on remained closed, as the vast majority of the lab staff didn't work on Saturdays—so she knew someone had to be in there waiting for her. Furthermore, she knew exactly who that person would most likely be.

When she came to work for Helixtech Research Incorporated just over two years ago, she heard the name Elias Spencer mentioned occasionally, usually with great respect and admiration—he was pretty much in charge of everything in the research department, after all, but more than that, he had a certain mystique about him: a legendary figure who bought a failing pharmaceutical company and in half a decade turned it into one of the top-notch facilities of its kind anywhere in the world. Alison didn't expect to ever actually be working on the same floor as him, much less down the hall, yet here she was, and now she knew, somehow, that he'd be the one waiting in her office.

She nervously reached up and checked her hair, finding it still firmly in place in her typically professional manner. There was no sense in wasting time checking a mirror, though, or anything else so pedestrian. Elias Spencer had an eye for detail, and probably heard her coming as her pumps clacked away on the pristine tile floors, so he'd be well aware of any further delays.

Steeling herself, Alison advanced and tried her best to look nonchalant as she stepped through the open doorway. Elias awaited her, standing patiently in front of her desk, holding a stapled cluster of papers in his hands as he perused the contents. At her arrival he glanced up and smiled, looking devilishly handsome despite his nearly fifty years of age: a cleft chin, solid muscles, piercing blue eyes staring out from tightly knitted brows, his brown hair impeccably trimmed, whitening only slightly along the barest edge of the block-cut sideburns exactly halfway down his ears. As always, Alison's heart skipped a beat at the sight of him—as far as she was concerned, no more eligible bachelor existed anywhere in the city; yet she wouldn't dare, either professionally or otherwise, ever give the slightest hint she ever had such thoughts.

"Miss Loomis," said Elias pleasantly, folding the cover page back onto the report and setting it gently down on her desk. "Another well-thought-out proposal, indeed—I'll get my staff right on it."

"Thank you, Mr. Spencer," she said with a friendly nod. "I really think it'll improve the morale a bit up on the second floor. The protesters are getting a lot of air time lately."

"Yes, and of course they've got the right to do so, but as you say in the report, that doesn't make our jobs any easier. Still, that's not why I've come to talk to you today."

She nodded again. "I didn't expect so. Is there some new project I can help you with?"

"In a way," said Elias, returning her smile. "Are you aware, Miss Loomis, that you're the sixth person to hold your current position in this lab within the last year?"

"Yes, of course," she replied instantly. "They told me that when I did the internal interview—they said this is one of the toughest jobs to fill in the entire company. They didn't really say why, though, and I have to admit, I haven't seen any real reason for that so far. There's no long hours, the work's not difficult, and the only real hassles I get are from dealing with the occasional weird animal coming in from outside."

Mr. Spencer listened politely, not saying anything, and Alison almost continued on with more to say about that particular issue, but let her words die out. For a few moments the office went silent, until finally Elias spoke again. "Regarding that particular matter," he said carefully, "what is it you find so unusual?"

"What do you mean?" asked Alison, a bit confused by the question. "They're mostly just strays and wild animals our field operatives catch."

"Well, you said they were weird," he pressed, "so I'll ask again, what is it you find so unusual about them?"

Alison shrugged. "Well, first of all, that I have to handle processing them myself," she said plainly. "Not that I'm complaining, mind you—I don't mind the job—it just seems like something one of the handlers might be better suited for, or perhaps an intern. That's not all, though—sorry, sir, you did ask, so I'll come right out and say it. Some of the animals are—well, they look like something else and then it's like they change."

Mr. Spencer didn't appear confused or dismayed by that statement, not even bothering to raise one of his bushy eyebrows. Instead, he narrowed his eyes very slightly and said, "Change in what way? Please be specific, Miss Loomis."

"Um, of course," she replied, realizing now that this had to be some kind of test—more than likely, she'd been monitored on each occasion, so he must've seen her reaction on internal camera footage. *Honesty is the best policy*, she told herself before opening up completely. "Well, sir, I'll start with the one that came in today," she offered quickly. "When I first saw it, I thought it was a big frog, but it turned out to be a kitten. The time before that, I thought they brought me an empty cage, but when I dumped it into the enclosure, I thought for a second I saw—well, you're going to think I'm crazy, but it looked like a little hairless mouse or something. When I went to look again, well, it was gone."

Elias nodded. "Anything else?"

"Most are just normal animals," she continued, "but there was one I thought had to be a joke—a big rock, with some moss clinging to it. For an instant I thought it moved, but I knew it had to be a trick of the light. Then there's the glowing moth, and the gray squirrel that kept changing shades, and the chipmunk I thought was a little person wearing an outfit made of sticks and leaves...oh, I'm sorry, sir, you must think I'm crazy!"

"Not at all, Miss Loomis," he replied. "I'm just happy to hear you discuss so openly what to you certainly sounds that way."

"Well," she replied, catching her breath and absently tugging on her neatly tailored business suit, "this must be what they meant when they said this job was hard to fill, isn't it? Well, I suppose that means I've cracked under the pressure after all. Should I just get my things and go, then? Maybe there's another position I can apply for up in HR..."

Elias lifted up a hand, palm out. "No, no, there's no reason for that, please. Actually, the job is hard to fill for another reason entirely. Please, Miss Loomis, follow me, if you would. Come along, there's something I want to show you."

She nodded, collecting herself, for she honestly thought for a second there that she'd be fired on the spot. "Yes, of course, sir, and thanks."

"You may not want to thank me yet," he told her, heading out into the hall and moving swiftly toward the main animal storage area, where she'd just recently placed the company's latest acquisition. "In a moment," he commented smoothly, "I'm going to walk you through a selection of our newest specimens, and I want you to tell me, as you look into each enclosure, the first thing that comes to mind."

"Like a Rorschach test?" she asked nervously.

"In a way," he replied. "Yes, I suppose that's a very good way to put it, actually. Don't think as you look, just say what you see. As you do so, I won't reply or make any indication I've heard you, but rest assured, I'm listening carefully. At the end, we'll go through into the examination room beyond, where I'll evaluate your performance and we can decide where to go from here."

Alison nodded, biting her lip and flexing her fingers. Her palms felt suddenly very cold in the faint air conditioning, and she realized she hadn't felt this nervous in quite a while. To her, it no longer felt as though she might be fired, but rather that she might be on the edge of some kind of promotion, if she could only make it through the strange audition to come.

He turned a corner and passed through the swinging doors to the storage space, where a collection of glass-walled cages lined the shelves on either side. The first two pairs were empty, but Mr. Spencer stopped immediately thereafter, pointing at the enclosure on his left. Alison glanced that way and saw, for an instant, a hunched-over froglike figure with two chameleon-like eyes, one fixed on her and the other on her boss.

"Bullfrog," she said at once, glancing up at him to see his reaction, of which he gave none. When she looked back down at the cage, she now saw an ordinary gray-and-white kitten, its whiskers twitching against the glass. She shuddered a bit, now a bit concerned about what might be happening here, but forced herself to press on nonetheless.

The next cage looked empty, except for a shape in one corner, a small hairless thing with big ears, that faded into nothing as she peered inside. "Invisible mouse," she stated plainly.

Mr. Spencer gave no indication that he'd even heard her as he pointed at the next cage. "Empty," she said honestly.

He continued on. "Moving rock," she responded.

They moved slowly down the line. In about half the cages, she saw something initially that either changed as she watched, or didn't look the same if she blinked or glanced away even for a moment. The other enclosures held nothing visible, or what looked to her like normal mammals or rodents of one kind or another. She answered with the honest truth each time, limiting her responses to just one or two words, and each time he didn't even acknowledge her except to continue on to the next cage.

In due time they reached the end and Mr. Spencer opened the waiting door to the examination room, a dead end with no other exits. The chamber beyond had walls lined with countertops and shelves, with a metal table in the center. Alison knew full well the sort of things that happened here, and while she never participated in such activities herself, the idea didn't really bother her at all. These animals, if that's what they truly were, did a great service by being here, something she'd always comforted herself with whenever she took the time to question her morals—which, these days, almost never happened anymore.

The door clicked shut and Mr. Spencer turned to regard her with an appraising air. "So, you gave your honest responses in each case, is that correct?"

"Yes, of course, sir," she answered with a quick nod.

"I could see the uncertainty on your face, as plain as day," said Elias, "and yet you never hesitated. That's exactly what I was hoping for. You've passed this phase of the process, Miss Loomis. It seems you may be the person I need after all."

"I...I might?" she asked curiously. "The person you need for what?"

"Miss Loomis," he replied calmly, "did you ever wonder how it is that this company has produced so many revolutionary new products in such a short time?"

"Of course, sir, but I thought maybe it had something to do with you being a genius and all," she replied, smiling while trying to keep her knees from buckling beneath her.

He grinned at that. "I already said you're what I'm looking for," he told her. "There's no need to butter me up, although I must say, I do enjoy hearing such praise on occasion. Nonetheless, my own accomplishments aside, there's far more to it than that. The things we develop here are made possible because of the unusual creatures we use in our experiments. This is more than a mere animal testing laboratory, Miss Loomis—surely you must realize that by now."

"Yes, I guess I've wondered about that before," she admitted, "but again, I thought maybe it was just—"

"Only one person in thousands can do what you just did, Miss Loomis," he interrupted smoothly. "Perhaps one in millions, in fact."

"Do what, sir?" she asked, puzzled.

"Pierce the veil of their magic," he responded evenly. "Just to do so for a brief moment is beyond the capabilities of most."

"Did...did you just say magic?" She gulped and glanced from side to side, now suddenly aware that she'd been trapped in a little room, the only exit door shut tightly behind him. "You aren't serious, are you...?"

"I've never been more serious," he replied, sensing her discomfort at once and stepping aside. "I don't mean to frighten you, but please hear me out. In the event you wish to leave, you may depart at your leisure and I'll make no move to intercede. I ask only that you listen to my explanation in full before making up your mind."

She nodded slowly, relaxing a bit at the sight of a clear path to freedom. "I'm sorry, sir, but...well, I have only the greatest respect for you, but to hear you talk about magic..."

"I know, it sounds incredible, and I'm asking a lot of you here," said Elias quickly, "but consider the fact that before humans understood technology, we thought of things like comets and lightning bolts as things caused by magic. Even today, if you were to visit primitive people in remote locations and show them a cell phone, they'd consider it magic. So, if it helps, don't think of it that way, but rather as something different, beyond our understanding, that we just can't explain with the kind of science you're familiar with."

"Okay, fair enough," agreed Alison, still trying to make sense of what she'd just been put through. "Well, then, if I'm getting this right," she went on, piecing things together in her head one bit at a time, "then you're saying that when I look at those things out there, and see something different for an instant, that's magic?"

"We think it's more like a defense mechanism," explained Elias carefully. "A kind of shield, I suppose is a better way to think of it. For some, when you look at them, you see an illusion that tricks your mind into imagining something familiar to you—a rat, perhaps, or a bird or kitten. For others you see nothing because they appear invisible to human eyes. Others actually physically transform—the rocks, in particular. Are you familiar with what is commonly referred to as quantum observation?"

"The observer effect?" asked Alison. "Sort of—it's been a while, but yeah, it's one of those weird things about quantum physics. Basically, it's the idea that at the quantum level some particles exist in any of several states until they're observed, at which point they become fixed in a static form."

"Exactly so," said Mr. Spencer, nodding approvingly at her greatly simplified, but basically accurate, answer. "The stone creatures are much like this. They exist in their natural, living form until observed by humans. The moment they're seen, they become like rocks in every way. In our experiments we've found this happens even if they're being watched remotely via camera. Yet if we take our eyes off of them for a while, in time they revert and move around. We can use various instruments to test and monitor them, but any attempt to directly observe—even remotely—turns them to stone for the duration."

Alison nodded slowly. "This is the magic you're referring to, then."

"Yes." Elias sighed loudly. "I realize this sounds unbelievable to you, Miss Loomis, but I'm a scientist, and I wouldn't make such statements if I couldn't back them up with proven, reliable data. Still, it's one thing to read reports and see spreadsheets and tabulations, and quite another to observe it personally. Furthermore, I doubt very much you'd accept hard data, considering how many times you've considered fleeing this room in the last couple of minutes."

She gave a sheepish grin, lowering her head in embarrassment. "Yeah, I suppose you're right about that," she admitted.

"Then allow me to make one final attempt to persuade you," he went on. "You might consider this the final test, if you will."

With that, he reached into the inside pocket of his lab coat and brought out what looked like a cylindrical metal water bottle, perhaps six inches high and topped with a crystal stopper. After a couple of seconds, Alison realized the container had been crafted of wrought iron, its surface marred with raised glyphs and intricate tracings. The lid, cut into hundreds of tiny facets, glinted and flashed in the dull fluorescent lighting. "What's that for?" she asked nervously, unable to avoid glancing over at the exit one more time.

"Do you know what a genie is, Miss Loomis?" he asked patiently, holding the flask in his left hand at just below eye level.

"Um, well, I've seen the movies," she replied, "but somehow I don't think that's the whole story, is it? Don't tell me, let me guess—you're going to rub that thing, and some big blue guy's gonna pop out and grant me three wishes?"

He smiled. "Hollywood has an excellent way of corrupting old legends, doesn't it?" he noted succinctly. "Genies have their roots in Arab mythology, it's true, but the proper term for them is *djinn*—they are a type of Fey, what we might consider supernatural creatures, and while they don't exactly grant wishes, they do have certain other abilities—one of those being to pierce the veils other Fey use to hide themselves."

Alison gulped as he uttered those words, starting to realize that she'd inadvertently stepped into a much greater world than she ever knew existed. The idea at once shocked and terrified her, but also captured her interest immediately—she felt as one drawn like a moth to the flame. "W-what does that mean, exactly?" she heard herself asking.

"A djinn can only grant this boon to those who have the spark within themselves to do so, if they but had the training," Elias went on. "That's what the first part of this was all about, Miss Loomis. You've proven to me you can see through the illusions, and the djinn can open your mind the rest of the way. There's one last detail, though—one factor that's most important of all. You must accept this gift of your own free will."

"My own free will?" she asked worriedly. "Is this like—am I selling my soul to the Devil, or something? Is that what's going on?"

"A Fey cannot directly affect a human being with magic," explained Mr. Spencer. "We haven't been able to figure out exactly why that is, but again, it's reminiscent of quantum entanglement. By making the choice, you allow yourself to be subjected to Fey magic, for good or ill. I'm asking you to trust me, Miss Loomis, when I say this particular invocation won't alter you or your mind, but merely open yourself to a new world that until now you never knew existed."

She swallowed heavily again. "What if I say no?"

He shook his head sadly. "Then I will have lost a promising new assistant, which will disappoint me greatly," he told her, "but you'll be allowed to leave, should you so choose. Of course, your current position at the company will be terminated, but as you noted earlier, you can always reapply for another with a visit to HR—and you can count on a glowing recommendation letter from me personally, should you choose this option."

"Well, thank you for that, at least," she replied in a quiet voice.

"Of course," he went on, "you are aware you're still covered by the nondisclosure agreement you signed when you took this position, so you'll be expected not to discuss what took place here with anyone."

"Oh, don't worry, nobody would believe a word of it," she replied with a quick shake of her head, "but I don't think that'll be an issue. When I came to work here, Mr. Spencer, I thought this was the greatest opportunity I'd ever have. I was wrong then because you've just topped it—I can't wait to see what's next. Bring out the genie—let's do this!"

Smiling at her exuberance, he removed the crystalline stopper. As she watched, fascinated, a swirling cloud of gray-blue smoke floated out, pulsing with a faint white glow. As the creature assembled, little sparks and tiny bolts of lightning flared within the miniature storm. Alison's eyes, already wide with amazement, grew bigger still as two red points of light appeared, focusing on her with grim intensity.

"Say what you must, Miss Loomis," said Elias. "You can phrase it as a wish, if you like—I promise not to laugh."

"I wish I could see them," she all but whispered. "I want to see everything!"

The miniature cloud flared as a tiny blast of lightning arced across the gap, striking her in the middle of the forehead. For an instant she thought she heard a faint voice say, "Your wish is granted," but couldn't be sure. She staggered backward, reeling, catching herself against the wall before she lost her balance. Blinking, she brought the room back into focus, whereupon she found Mr. Spencer standing over her, the cloud gone and stopper back on the bottle. "D-did it work?" she muttered, collecting herself as she got back to her feet.

"See for yourself," he replied, opening the nearby door, waving a hand in the direction of the enclosures beyond.

Alison walked tentatively through, first cautiously and then with mounting excitement. In a few cages she saw only normal animals, but the others—now she saw them as they truly were: tiny elves dressed in woodland costumes; a troll folded up into its stone form; a once-invisible goblin trying to remain still; and a froglike gremlin peering up at the two of them with independently mobile eyes.

"They're amazing," she gasped at last. "What are they, exactly?"

"All of this and more will come in time," said Mr. Spencer. "Go home and get a good night's rest, Miss Loomis, for tomorrow brings a bright new day. I know it's a bit much to ask you to come in on your day off, but—"

"I can't wait," she replied eagerly, gazing once more at the unbelievable little creatures in their cages, the idea of an extra workday never once causing her the slightest pause. "I'm not sure how I'm going to get to sleep tonight, but I'll do my best. See you first thing in the morning, Mr. Spencer!"

"I'll be waiting," he replied with a smile, "and please, from now on, call me Elias."

Forlorn Tunnel – Commons

The five would-be rescuers spent perhaps an hour discussing their situation, beginning with the need to locate one or another of the faeries. Lyza, it seemed, could use elven travel-magic to get past the lands of Men and into Central Park, but this operated only between very specific points. Once at their destination, she might try other tricks, like the tree-step spell she used in the failed attempt to track down Bongcor, but these were limited and risky. The trees might not approve, or so she explained, and even if they did, the step was very taxing. Like Sithlac's limited ration of night-magic, she too had her limits.

Ithess, who could fly, had the ability to get an overhead view, but her small size prevented her from seeing too far, or moving very quickly. Plus, although she definitely intended to come along on the journey, she appeared nervous and hesitant, almost afraid. Sithlac wanted to ask why, but decided not to, mostly for fear of scaring her off. She'd already proved her worth on more than one occasion, and he didn't want to lose her before the journey had even begun.

While Ithess appeared reluctant, Yog couldn't wait to get started. He bounced around eagerly while the others discussed the travel plans, clearly excited by the prospect of action. When asked why he was so excited, he replied, "When you're my age, you just don't expect to ever get a chance to see anything new!" Nobody could argue with that, although Lyza had to shoo him away several times while she helped Meathead pick out supplies for the trip.

Sithlac was surprised to hear the troll intended to come along, for he seemed quite at home here in the Forlorn Tunnel, but apparently Meathead never even considered staying behind. "You all are gonna need food, right? Well, two things I'm good at is carryin' stuff and cookin' it, so you're stuck with me," he explained, in his usual straightforward manner. Lyza, too, seemed surprised that he chose to come along, but certainly wasn't complaining.

The elf-girl, too, seemed intent on participating, and in fact had pretty much taken the leadership role—not directly, of course, but as a matter of expediency. She had the travel-magic, and knew the way, so who better to lead? Sithlac supposed he should feel slighted, for this was his mission, after all; yet he felt no animosity or jealousy whatsoever. Lyza was the logical choice, and he was fine with that, at least for now.

Pretending to look once more through his own supplies, Sithlac watched carefully with his left eye as Lyza helped Meathead load cooking gear into a large rucksack. Bongcor was *his* friend, not theirs—the others barely knew the younger gremlin at all, though Yog, at least, had the benefit of having met him a few days before. Yet despite this, all four of the others were going to drop everything and travel far away to help find someone they only just recently met. Something about that seemed very wrong and unnatural, even though Sithlac supposed they all had their own reasons for coming. After a few moments he realized why he felt this way—no gremlin would ever do what they were doing. In fact, he himself wouldn't have contemplated something like this even a mere moonrise ago.

The faerie song, he reminded himself. *Since I heard it, I have not been the same, and yet, I would go back to my old self not at all.* Although friendship had its down sides—its anxious moments, worries and fears— he saw now what it could do. All his new companions were going out of their way to help a friend, something no normal gremlin would ever contemplate. In that, Sithlac felt sure, the others of his kind were missing out on something wonderful.

If they only knew, he thought to himself. *If they could only see...could I tell them? Were I to show them, would they understand?* Perhaps so, or perhaps not, but bringing Bongcor home would be a good first step. If gremlins could work together, instead of alone, who knows what they might accomplish?

Lyza interrupted his unusual thoughts with a quick, rousing shout. "Time to go!" she called, even as Meathead hefted up his backpack, easily shouldering an amount of gear far in excess of Sithlac's weight. The troll struggled for a moment, sliding some nearly hidden straps around his immense shoulders, before getting everything in position. To polish things off he tugged two small strings about his waist and tied them together, stabilizing the whole load. As he moved, with a slow, lumbering gait, the huge bag on his back shifted slowly from side to side, making only a couple of soft clanks before going silent.

Yog hurried ahead, darting back and forth in the ruins excitedly, as the journey began. Sithlac looked around for Ithess, wondering if the little zephyr might've chosen to stay behind after all, but soon noticed the barely visible creature sitting idly on Lyza's shoulder. As they slowly made their way across the Forlorn Tunnel, Ithess began to sing softly, but not in words, only faint notes that drifted away, swallowed up into the shadowy places all around. Though somewhat unsteady at first, the tune quickly shifted into a decidedly hopeful melody. Sithlac, soon catching the rhythm of it, began to hum along, with Meathead's tromping footsteps adding a slow and steady beat.

They moved on like that for several minutes, gradually making their way through the ancient, dusty tunnel, through broken sections Sithlac hadn't yet bothered to explore. Yog, apparently happy to take point, soon took note of their unusual music. "That's real nice, you all planning to start a band?" he joked as they neared the farther edge of the tunnel. "If you think I'm gonna sing along, better think again. Trust me, none of you want that!"

"I think it sounds nice," Lyza put in, "and I'll sing along, once I find the words, but don't get too involved just now. We've got to navigate the wall first."

"Wall?" asked Yog. "What wall?"

"When we get Outside," she responded. "You'll see. It's just beyond the gate. I doubt you'll have any problems, but Meaty and I will take a while."

"Yeah, I don't like that wall much," the troll agreed. "Got some stuff in the bag to help out, but it's tough goin'."

"We could take the stairs, if you want to risk it," offered Lyza.

"Not in the daylight." The troll sighed loudly. "You all got your ways of hidin' from the Men. It ain't so pleasant for us trolls. Why you think I like it here so much? Ain't no Man gonna see me in here, but out there…" He put out a hand to steady himself on the tunnel wall, which the group had just now reached. "And I ain't got no choice, neither. So if it happens, just wait round, I'll come back when I can."

As Meathead finished speaking, they reached the exit passage, whereupon the troll started moving the cobbled-together barricade out of the way so he could get by. The passage beyond was dark, so Lyza sang a few words of light-magic, setting off a glow-globe dangling from the ceiling overhead. The slight swirl at the end of the passage, some distance ahead, signaled the presence of the exit gate. Ithess, sensing the shift in mood, let her song die out and Sithlac, too, stopped humming to himself. Before he could ask the obvious question, Yog did it for him.

"Okay, I don't know much about trolls, so fill me in," the goblin stated. "What happens to you guys that's so awful bad?"

Lyza put her hand on Meathead's arm, which caused him to slump slightly, shutting his eyes. Seeing that he didn't intend to answer, she decided to do it for him. "Each of us escape the eye of Man in our own way," she explained. "Elves and faeries are invisible, at least in our own element. You goblins just don't get noticed, as long as you stay still, and gremlins take the form of some other natural creature. Zephyrs, of course, are so small, a Man can barely tell they're there, but even if they do look close, they see only a tiny insect. But trolls...well, they got the short haft of the spear, I'm afraid. You see, they turn to stone."

"They do what now?" demanded Yog. "Turn to stone? You mean forever? Why, that's ridiculous!"

"Not forever, no," Lyza explained, "but it can last a while. As long as the Men persist, they're stuck like that and then for some time after. I've never seen it myself, but I'm told it can last hours, even days. They're aware of time passing, too, so you can imagine how bad it can be, if they get stuck somewhere the humans are watching. Why do you think trolls like dark places, under bridges and such? They're less likely to be seen."

"Then why live outside at all?" Yog went on. "Just stay underground, all the time! It's not so bad—the rest of us darklings do it, why not trolls?"

"We ain't darklings, that's the thing," sighed Meathead. "I wish we were, but we ain't. We're forest-folk, like the elves and faeries. We gotta have fresh air, and eat outdoors food, and all that stuff. The only reason I stay here is cause the air's so good, and Lyza brings me good stuff to eat. That's why I'm comin' with ya all, y'know. She's been helpin' me so long—it's time for me to do the same."

"Oh, Meaty, you don't have to feel obligated like that!" Lyza insisted, slapping him on the arm with a smile. "I appreciate it, of course, but you can stay if—"

"Now, now, don't try talkin' me outta this!" he insisted, giving her a playful shove that almost sent her sprawling. "I ain't been outta here in far too long anyways, so I'm comin' and that's that. It's just, y'know, if I get stoned, don't leave me, y'know? I'll come back, it just might take awhile, okay?"

"I won't leave you," she agreed at once. "The rest of us might scout around or something, but I'll stick around, I promise. Now come on, let's not think about that, let's worry about the wall. Okay, everybody, here's the deal, okay? We step through this exit, and we're on top of a wall, so don't run or jump off to the side, just move forward a bit. It'll be daylight, but of course it won't open if there's Men around, so we'll have time to look for cover. Too bad it's not summer or there'd be ivy, but we should still be able to get into the shadows before anyone happens by. Just remember, go straight until you recover from the transit, then go for a hiding spot, got it? Once we're all together, we'll figure out how to get down. Oh, and one more thing—it's winter, don't forget, so it's cold out there. Put up whatever heating magic you have and then we're off."

Sithlac nodded, and although he'd never been Outside during winter, he knew it would be cold. Luckily, one of the few spells he knew was a frost-ward, which he'd used on several occasions before, when the spaces between walls grew too chilly. He spent about a minute chanting the spell, annoyed at himself for letting his supply of night-magic get so low, but of course he had no chance to replenish his supplies back home. If he'd gone to collect his daily ration, he risked having his request denied and his personal supply drained—if the Council had sanctioned him— or worse, they might've tried to apprehend him there. No, he'd done the right thing by leaving quickly, but that left him nearly out of magic.

Satisfied that the spell had worked, and also that he still had his rat disguise in place, Sithlac took a few deep breaths and relaxed, looking around at the others. Upon hearing Lyza's words, Ithess rose up off her shoulder and proceeded to dance about in the air, emitting a few faint notes as she cast her own anti-cold spell. Lyza, too, crafted a ward with song, quickly and with little difficulty, it seemed. Yog, for his part, now wore a heavy coat made of colorful bits of yarn woven together—where he got that, Sithlac had no idea. Meathead, unlike the others, did nothing at all, apparently content to put up with the cold exactly as he was.

"All right, looks like we're good," Lyza noted, giving a quick thumbs-up. "I'll go through first, and the rest of you follow, each a few seconds behind. Go straight, then look for a hiding spot, and don't wait too long. See you on the wall!"

Forlorn Tunnel – Exterior Gate

Sithlac expected to immediately follow Lyza through the exit, but Yog pushed past him with barely a pause, disappearing into the vortex right on the elf's heels. "The li'l guy's really enjoyin' this," mumbled Meathead, giving a couple of deep chuckles that sounded like distant drumbeats. "I hope it's as fun as he seems to think. Go on, now, and hurry off, I'll be right behind ya."

"So be it," agreed Sithlac, narrowing his eyes and stepping through. Like most gremlins, he generally avoided sunlight, though in the mating season it could hardly be avoided. Upon arrival beyond the portal, he winced even further and hurried forward, afraid to be stepped on by the trailing troll. Initially blinded, he recovered some of his vision after a few moments and glanced about, both eyes swiveling in different directions as he took in his surroundings.

He stood upon a narrow stretch of rough-hewn stone, covered in thin strands of dead ivy mingled with a few clumps of half-melted snow. To his left, a great fence of steel posts rose overhead, toward the cloud-speckled sky. Through the wide gaps between each of the sharply angled poles, he saw Man's towers rising in the distance, partly obscured by the scraggly tufts of winter-browned bushes. A wide expanse of sidewalk followed, with several great metal-beasts barely visible on either side, fortunately quiescent and not on the move. Beyond these, a two-lane roadway separated the parked cars from distant towers, but all seemed quiet at the moment.

To Sithlac's right, the stone platform ended at a steep drop-off, with a ledge just barely visible a great distance below. He knew now why Lyza had cautioned against moving too far to one side. A slip and he would surely fall, either to suffer great injury landing on the ledge, or bounce off and tumble out of sight beyond. He couldn't quite see the ground from here, only the many trees rising up from the shadows, but he knew from experience how long a fall it would be. He'd stood upon that ledge before, not this exact spot but somewhere similar, while foraging for his mate. He'd never climbed up to this level, though—the Men walked along this way quite often, as he knew well. Fortunately, none was about at the moment, perhaps due to the cold weather, but that could change at any time.

"We must not tarry here," he warned, seeing Yog frozen in place just ahead. The goblin seemed mesmerized, slowly turning to take in the view, his toothy mouth hanging open in awe. Lyza, just past him, nodded in agreement as she, too, cautiously surveyed the scene. The air felt cold, as expected, but Sithlac's anti-chill enchantment held firm, especially with the sun warming his skin. *At least it isn't windy,* he thought to himself, and indeed the air felt unusually still, which he didn't mind at all—not only did it make things more comfortable, it meant none of them was likely to be blown off the precipice by an errant gust.

Ithess, her tiny wings sparkling in the sunlight, flew back from a quick foray along the wall's edge. "The spike's still there, as you dared hope," she sang quietly. "I think it's safe to use your rope. It's not too bad a jump, you know. You'll land quite nicely in the snow!"

The zephyr laughed, darting away as Lyza made a half-hearted slap in her direction. Grinning, Lyza hurried ahead, toward a much taller, wider post marking a dividing point in the massive steel fence. Here she hesitated, looking at something on the ground, and Sithlac hurried forward to investigate just as Meathead made his appearance. The troll winced at the sunlight, covering his eyes, and stumbled momentarily, but caught himself and hunkered down, glancing to and fro worriedly.

"This way," Lyza called out, running her hands over a small piece of metal embedded in a crack in the stone by her feet. "Come on, be quick now! I need those ropes, so we can get down to the ledge before any Men show up."

Sithlac got a better view and saw at once what she intended. The spike had a curve to it, almost forming a loop, so that a rope could easily be tied in place. Meathead stumbled forward, still having trouble seeing, but followed her voice to the right spot. He started to take off the rucksack, but she stopped him with a gesture. "Yog, if you please, grab the rope out of there—left side, at the top."

"Um, what? Oh, right, sure thing." The goblin came out of his trance immediately and rushed over to help, scrambling up on the troll's back without hesitation and fishing inside the backpack. "Look at me, I'm climbing on a troll! Ah, if my clan could only see me now."

He found the coil of thread quickly and tossed it down to the waiting elf, who hurriedly tied it in a clove hitch and tested it with a quick yank of her hand. "All right, come quickly now, unless you want some passing human to spot us," she called out, tossing the coil over the side. Then, with barely any delay at all, she stepped off the side and slid downward, not stopping until she reached the ledge far below.

"Oh, this is gonna suck right here," mumbled Meathead, taking the rope in his enormous paws and following along behind. He moved much slower, for he didn't have any gloves and the rope would've burned his hands if he moved too quickly. Instead, he held on with his back toward the ground and walked downward slowly. As Sithlac followed, using his natural wall-climbing ability rather than relying on the thread, he couldn't help but notice the troll's eyes were tightly shut.

Yog, too, made his own way down, his claws easily finding purchase on the rough stone surface, naturally avoiding the dead strands of ivy that seemed everywhere. Sithlac could recall seeing the plants growing along the walls in the early spring, but it didn't seem quite as thick as this. The stuff must really take over in the warmer months, perhaps so much that the wall itself would be hard to spot with all the greenery.

Despite Meathead's misgivings, he reached the ledge below without incident and stood there for a moment, catching his breath. "Not so bad, was it?" Lyza said with a chuckle, slapping him on the back of his leg. "Just think, we're already a third of the way down."

The troll just groaned and shook his head. Sithlac was about to ask whether or not he should go back up and untie the rope when it suddenly just flopped down at his feet of its own accord. He glanced up, curious as to the reason, and saw Ithess fluttering down from the upper level. "Just in time, I do dare say—a pair of Men just passed our way," she pointed out, causing Meathead to involuntarily press himself up against the wall. "No need to fret, no need to fear, they have no way to know we're here," the zephyr added hastily.

"Whew, I was gettin' worried," Meathead said with an obvious tone of relief. "If I go stony hangin' onto that rope, well, y'know what that'll mean."

"You'd probably survive," Lyza reassured him. "See? There's snow down there. Of course, that'll make traveling a bit harder than expected, but nothing we can't handle. It's mostly melted anyhow. Have a look around, everybody, and see if you can find something else to tie the rope onto. Last time I used this little protrusion, but I don't that'll be enough to hold Meaty here."

They each started moving along the ledge, doing as she asked. "If I may be so bold," Yog put in curiously, "I can see how you'd get down, but how do you get your rope back if you're by yourself?"

"Slipknot," she answered with a casual wave of her hand. "It's a special knot that...well, tell you what, I'll show you later."

"You and your secret elven ways," scoffed the goblin. "I suppose you'll tell me you've got a special knot that gets you up this wall by yourself, too?"

"Nope, I have to take the stairs." She pointed off to the left, where a large stone staircase could just be seen poking out of the wall in the distance. Multi-leveled, and with its own human-height metal handrail on either side, the stairs descended from the street level almost directly toward them, down to a square platform before turning away, toward the forest level far below. The thick trees all around, though bereft of leaves, still obscured most of the view, but a couple of humans could be seen in the distance, climbing up from the park beyond, their hairless bodies covered in thick winter clothing.

Sithlac scuttled back from the edge, worried about the Men, but Lyza caught sight of his wary stance and shook her head. "They can't possibly see us from there, even if they looked right at us," she pointed out, keeping her voice low. "Too much cover, and besides, they've got hoods on. Just the same, we should make haste. I don't know how far that turn-to-stone thing works for trolls, so let's not test it, all right?"

"Agreed," said Sithlac, "but just the same, is it not worrisome that Men will be so close? I like being near them not at all."

"Look, you better get used to it," she insisted. "I know you're used to moving around at night, but the rest of us aren't, and besides, there are Men about at all times out here. We'll stick to the shadows and they won't see us, okay? With Ithess flying overhead, we'll know if any of them come toward us. Besides which, at least in here, they mostly stick to the pavement."

"Pavement...?"

"You know, the paths made out of flat stones. You'll see when you watch for a while. They don't like walking on the bare ground for some reason, especially in winter, which is where we'll be. Aha, I can see Meathead waving. Looks like he found something."

They moved on to join the troll, who'd located a thick protrusion within the irregular wall segments wide enough to wrap the rope around.

With some effort he and Lyza passed the thread about the jutting stone and she tied another one of her mystical knots, this one much different from the last, but apparently strong enough to do the job. This time, she let Meathead go first, and he repeated his earlier slow-rappel down the surface, all the way to the ground far below. Then Lyza and the others followed, and Ithess repeated her earlier efforts to send the rope down to join them.

They arrived in a small patch of bare ground, surrounded by tufts of vegetation turned brown by the cold. A few clumps of snow lay in uneven piles all around, obviously the remnants of some recent winter weather, but mostly melted by the scattered sunlight streaming through the trees. The travelers set off at once, heading away from the staircase, dodging the snow as best they could and keeping to the early afternoon shadows.

The ground sloped toward the center of the park, but the quintet stayed near the wall with Ithess fluttering several feet overhead, keeping watch. From their vantage point, they could see a concrete walkway some distance downhill, running parallel to the wall. Occasionally a lone human would stride past, or possibly several chattering in a group, and at those times everyone would stop and take cover. None of the Men so much as looked their way, however, and as Lyza suggested earlier, they all stayed on the path.

At first, Sithlac was nervous and worried, jumping at every sound and ducking down whenever a bird called or winds above disturbed a leaf or twig, sending it rattling toward the ground. He'd been here before—perhaps not this exact spot, but all along this wall—but always with plenty of cover from leaves and bushes turned green in springtime weather. By contrast, the place now seemed far too wide open and dangerous for his tastes. Still, Lyza's confidence slowly won him over, and he found himself less and less concerned as they traveled slowly along. After a while Ithess began to sing cheerfully overhead, and as before, he joined in by humming. Yog, hearing this, shook his head sadly and shuffled ahead, hopping up on stones and fallen logs whenever he could, clearly not fazed in the least by his surroundings.

From his position near the ground, Sithlac had a tough time seeing anything but the brush and snow piles directly in front of him. Noticing Yog's penchant for climbing up on things, he decided to get a better view for himself, so as the group came to a large stone, he scrambled up the side. From here he could see the Man-path much better as it made its way through the forest down below.

Unfortunately, he could also see where it split in two, one section continuing on, while the other joined another huge staircase now plainly visible ahead. Several Men were using this even now, some of them facing directly toward him as they descended from the street high above. As before, they paid the group of Fey no heed, but nonetheless, Sithlac ducked down into a shadowy depression in the stone, while Meathead muttered something from nearby and nestled in among the undergrowth.

"Yep, that's our second challenge, all right," Lyza called out, obviously well aware of the obstacle ahead. "We have to get past that staircase, or go across the path and into the woods further down. Either way we'll be exposed to humans if they pass this way. There's no way underneath, either."

"We could wait until dark," offered Yog. "That'll give us cover."

"Not really," Lyza replied. "See those black towers, with the shiny cap things on top? Well, at night, they turn into great lights, not quite like the Sun but still pretty strong. Not only will we be perfectly visible, our shadows will give us away. We're probably better off now, before it gets too late in the day. Come on, let's get closer."

They pressed on, moving dangerously nearer to the stairs, pausing every time a Man approached—which, while not common, was still way too often for Sithlac's tastes. The closer they got, the more nervous he became. Fortunately, there were plenty of objects nearby to hide behind—mostly stones and logs, but the occasional hardy bush or tall tree that provided plenty of shade. In one case a patch of snow had melted in such a way as to create a kind of natural overhang, and while waiting for a pair of Men to pass, the travelers took the time to quench their thirst with the dripping melt-off just above their heads.

Finally they reached a spot between two large stones where they could see the base of the stairs. Here, where the railing ended, the concrete path sloped down and away, surrounded by trees and densely packed bushes. At a glance, Sithlac supposed he would need a good thirty to forty seconds to dash across the open space. Yog and Lyza would probably be faster, but he had no idea about Meathead. He lumbered along quite slowly, but for all Sithlac knew, the troll might be quicker on his feet than he appeared. Still, it would take only a glance by a previously unnoticed Man to end his travels just as quickly.

As Sithlac wondered about that, Ithess fluttered higher overhead. She zipped partway up the stairs, then toward the path, obviously taking a careful look for Men who might be approaching. For a moment all seemed well, but then she suddenly turned and raced back toward them at high speed.

"Take heed and listen to my song," she insisted in a quick, high-pitched voice, urgently indicating a chunk of fallen tree nearby. "Your refuge here won't last too long. You'd better hide inside that log—some Men are coming, with a dog!"

Morningside Park – Near the 118th Street Stairs

At that they all hurried away from the edge of the path toward the waiting shelter, ducking inside just as a trio of heavily dressed humans came into view. As the zephyr had warned, they did indeed have a dog with them—a large, yellow-haired beast on the end of a very long leash. Unlike the Men, the creature didn't stay on the paved trail but pushed its way into the bushes at every opportunity, sniffing and rooting about with wild abandon.

Yog found a small knothole about two-thirds of the way up the interior of the hollow log and poked his head out for a better view. "You think it'll stick its head all the way in here?" he asked worriedly. "Those Men don't look like they care much what it's doing."

"Possibly," Lyza replied, "but I've got a stink-spell to ward it off—it's like a fresh spraying of skunk, so you'd better prepare yourselves for that."

"Will it be able to sense us?" inquired the worried goblin. "And by us, of course, I mean me, since it's sure to notice you."

"Not sure," Lyza replied with a shrug, not looking all that concerned by the approaching animal, instead poking around deeper inside the half-rotted log. "It's not bound by the Great Bargain, of course, so I'd say so. Dogs certainly have no problem sniffing out elves and trolls if they choose to, but we're not good to eat so they usually just give us a pass."

"I'm not gonna chance it," Yog went on, as if she hadn't spoken. "If it comes this way, I'm sticking myself all the way in the back, so the rest of you watch out."

"I'm sure it'll come," said Lyza, still not terribly worried, "once it has our scent. We'll smell way too strange to pass up. Unless, of course, there's something you can do about that, Ithess?"

The little zephyr fluttered back and forth for a moment, as if considering the suggestion, before finally singing her reply. "I doubt it's possible, this is true, but I'll go try it just for you. The winds are still, and not so near, nor will they listen, this I fear." With that she was gone, zipping out the knothole right past Yog, who ducked down a bit further, keeping an eye on the approaching humans and their dog, who had just passed the crossroads and taken the path toward the stairs.

"They're on their way here," he pointed out. "Ithess is...well, never mind, I lost sight of her. She can be hard to spot, y'know. Wait, I can hear her now, singing...oh, great, and now the dog's headed right for us! I'm outta here."

At that, he dropped to the floor and dashed to the back of the log, pushing his way up into the corner right behind Meathead's neck. The troll, for his part, hadn't said a word since arriving and in fact had collapsed into a half-seated, half-lying position with his hair draped over himself, in a vain attempt to appear as innocuous as possible. Lyza, shaking her head, took up a position in front of the troll, next to a small chunk of half-rotted wood, directly alongside Sithlac, who stared at the round opening at the end of the log with his spear at the ready.

"It's okay, you can go back there too," she told him. "You probably don't want to be here when I let off the stink bomb, anyway."

"No, this is something I must face," Sithlac told her, letting a single eye glance her way while the other remained focused on the entrance. "If I hide and cower at each sign of danger, I will be of little use. Besides, I know it will see me as a rat, not a gremlin, and so perhaps I can scare it off."

"Or get bitten, more likely," she replied somewhat sarcastically, but other than making that remark, she made no other effort to dissuade him. "If that's your plan, just remember not to run. Most dogs don't like a determined opponent, but if you flee, they'll chase you down."

Sithlac nodded, but didn't reply, for now the sounds of an approaching animal could easily be heard outside. There was no sign of Ithess as the dog's shadow fell over the entrance to the log—apparently her efforts to blow away their scent had failed. Sithlac clutched the spear and hunkered down, trying to appear courageous, but inside, he felt only terror. Dogs were immense monstrosities, driven by instinct and hunger, and to defend their human owners at all costs. While foraging during mating-time, he'd seen them here and there within the park, but then, he could simply climb any handy tree or wall to make good his escape. This time, he had no such option.

The dog's nose came into view, sniffing loudly: a great, moist black shape at the tip of a long, hairy face. The dog, a great golden-haired beast, acted as though hunting for food, and now, as it caught sight of the strange creatures inside the log, it froze, lifting a single paw slightly off the ground, ears rising upward at attention. The fearless animal immediately dismissed the crouching elf as unimportant, focusing instead on what it perceived as an enormous rat, fangs bared and hissing.

"What you got there, boy?" a Man's voice boomed from somewhere nearby. "You got a squirrel cornered in there? Let's have a look."

Of course Sithlac couldn't understand the words, but he knew what the human voice had to mean. "The Man comes," he said in a low voice, which sounded like more hissing to the dog. "Hide, and quickly."

"The skunk-spell—" Lyza began, but he just as quickly pushed her aside.

"As a last resort," Sithlac warned. "I will stand firm, and play the bluff. You must allow me this."

"But I—okay, fine, have it your way." She ducked down behind the slab of wood, just behind his feet, and waited, the spell ready upon her lips, but remained silent for the moment.

"Now let's see what you—oh!" A pink, hairless face appeared an instant later, immediately catching sight of Sithlac's hissing rat-form. The startled human instantly jumped back, stumbling, and nearly slipped on a patch of muddy ground.

"What is it?" one of the others, a female, asked worriedly. "What's in there?"

"A rat," the man answered. "Probably sick or something, too. Come on, boy, let's go! We don't want you catching rabies, God forbid."

"Rabies?" another voice went on, as the first Man tugged on the leash, dragging the dog away, whining in disappointment. "Dude, seriously, you know there hasn't been rabies in these parts for like, a decade or more."

"Whatever, I'm not taking any chances. Sheesh, you should've seen that thing! It was seriously pissed off. Got out of there just in time, I'm sure. If either of you two wants to take a look, go right ahead, but keep well clear."

"No thanks, I'll take your word for it. Come on, the game starts in twenty minutes."

Their voices trailed off in the distance. Sithlac, heart pounding, finally let himself relax, the spear tip settling slowly to the ground. "The correct form I did choose, it seems," he muttered after a moment. "Not so sure was I—"

"Nice job, Sithy!" Yog called out, bounding up over the top of the wood slab to pat him on the shoulder. "Didn't think you had it in you. Of course, I know I don't have it in me, that's for sure. I'll be hiding behind you from now on, you can count on that!"

"Yeah, you did good," agreed Meathead, rising and dusting himself off. "You scared 'im off before he saw me, too, so I'm still me, at least for now."

"Yeah, good job, but you didn't have to take that risk," Lyza put in. "The stink spell is pretty effective. If the dog had lunged, I wouldn't have had time to use it, though."

Sithlac sighed, rolling the spear back and forth between his fingers for a moment. "A Man will investigate that which he finds strange," he explained. "This is why we gremlins take only that which will not be missed. A skunk smell without a skunk to cause it might make for curious Men, and that we could not abide. An angry rat, poised to bite, is much more easily understood."

Lyza nodded, but something in her expression suggested she thought there was more to it than that. Rather than press the issue, though, she moved to the end of the log and peered around the edge. "Ithess?" she called out. "You there? We're okay in here, if you were wondering."

The zephyr fluttered up behind her, approaching from the opposite direction, causing Lyza to jump in surprise. "I am here, though not quite all," she sang quietly. "The winds refused to heed my call. It's as I feared, and as I dread, there's nothing more for me ahead."

"Wait, you aren't leaving, are you?" Lyza demanded. "Look, I know you've avoided coming outside for a long time now, but I thought we were making progress—"

"It's not just that, you just don't know," the zephyr interrupted, "it'll be the same each place I go. I understand the why and how—the air itself rejects me now. The trees above will sing its song, but not down here, that would be wrong. The wind blows firm, and all about, but here by me it's all died out."

"What do you—" Lyza began, but as she spoke Ithess rose into the air and circled slowly around the opening beyond the log. Without another word the elf looked out further, at the forest beyond. High above, the branches swayed and turned in the wind, and on the ground, especially on the path, dried leaves swirled about in a sudden gust. Yet, even as Lyza climbed to the top of the log, followed immediately by Sithlac and the others, she saw the truth behind the zephyr's words. Where they stood, the air remained still and silent, even as the bushes not ten feet away whistled in the afternoon breeze. Ithess flew at the center of a pocket of still air, the winds themselves refusing to acknowledge her presence.

"I hadn't noticed," whispered the elf. "This whole time, I didn't know. Even when we went after Bongcor earlier—I didn't see, and I should've, but I was too focused on the chase. Oh, Ithess, I had no idea it was like this! I'm so sorry!"

Sithlac nodded, remembering now how he'd thought, upon his arrival via the exit gate, how the cold didn't feel so bad because of the lack of wind. That wasn't a coincidence after all—the wind just wouldn't blow anywhere near the sad-looking zephyr. *No wonder she stayed inside,* he thought sadly. *Cut off from the very air itself...a wind-spirit with no winds to ride...*

"Wait, so it's not windy around us because of her?" Yog announced, explaining it out loud without the least thought to the zephyr's feelings. "Well, that's great! We don't have to worry about being caught in a blizzard, that's for sure. This is perfect! Come on, let's get moving, there's no Men out there right now."

Lyza turned on him, showing the first anger Sithlac could remember seeing in her, but just before she struck, she caught herself. Gritting her teeth, she shut her eyes and took a deep breath. "I'm going to let that pass because you obviously have no idea," she growled, "but Ithess has been separated from the very thing that makes her what she is. I don't know what happened to her, or what could do this, but it's obviously very painful, and—"

"There's no need, I'll be all right," the zephyr sang sadly. "I know I wouldn't last the night. I'll take my leave and go away—you'll see me not again this day."

"Ithess, no, you can't—we need you," Lyza wailed, reaching out to try to take the zephyr in her hands, but the little creature fluttered away before the half-hearted attempt could succeed. "We don't need winds. We need *you.*"

The zephyr moved slowly upward toward the wall, possibly crying, but it was hard to tell. Sithlac stepped forward, trying to think of something to say, but what? He barely knew this creature, but she must've suffered some kind of trauma in her past—something that wounded her, and left her separated from her people and way of life. *It would be the same for me,* he thought, *if I were banished by the Council. Unable to enter another Tunnel, or talk to another gremlin, ever again...that's what it's like for her, right now.*

He remembered, then, their first encounter. She flew around, whipping up the dust, singing in that strange, entrancing voice, talking about how he could give her something. What was it? Something to do, surely, but she never explained. Something she needed, though. Something only he could provide. That's why she came to help Bongcor when Yog went to find her—why she was here now, presumably, though he couldn't be sure. He could only try.

"Ithess," he called out, "when first we met, you told me what you need was mine to give. The need remains, and can still be fulfilled. Do not fly away, when what you require is just within your grasp. Come with us."

He couldn't see her now, but he felt she must've heard him. There were no more words to be said, though. Instead, he began to hum, as loudly as he could. The others looked at him strangely, but didn't interfere. The humming continued, but she didn't respond or return.

"It was worth a shot," said Yog. "Come on, let's go. There's still no Men around, as near as I can tell."

As they set off again, heading for the crossing, Lyza rubbed her hand across Sithlac's gnarled head. "Thank you for that," she said, withdrawing her fingers just as quickly. "Thanks for trying, at least. You're the strangest gremlin I ever met, but I wouldn't have you any other way."

Morningside Park – 118th Street Path

As before, the group paused at the edge of the concrete walkway, looking carefully in all directions but seeing no Men at all. The wind rustled all around them now, a new sensation considering how calm the air had been for nearly the entire journey. Still, Sithlac hesitated, unsure about taking a long dash across open ground in broad daylight.

"Go," she whispered in his ear. "The others will follow."

He needed no further urging, bounding out of the shadows and into the open, running as fast as he'd ever tried to run before. To his surprise, Yog was there, running alongside and even passing him, laughing all the while. "Too slow, youngster!" he called out, disappearing into the brush on the far side of the path. Sithlac followed him into the gap and slid to a stop, struggling to catch his breath. Gremlins aren't built for speed, and the mad dash took everything he had.

A few seconds later, the lumbering troll crashed into the bushes and stomped to a halt, taking up a sheltered position next to a large, lichen-speckled stone. He seemed not the least bit winded by the effort, but smiled at having completed the task successfully. Lyza followed on his heels, sucking in a couple of deep breaths but otherwise not looking all that tired.

"Didn't think I could still beat you," Yog chuckled, in between a few rasping gasps. "These old bones still have some speed in 'em. Good thing nobody came over the hill just then, that's for sure."

"Oh, we would've known," said Lyza with a smile. "Ithess would've warned us."

"She's gone, though, isn't she?" asked the goblin. "Or, I guess not, or you wouldn't have said that, huh?"

"No, she's watching, from high above, I'm sure," Lyza replied. "Don't look, you fools! She'll return on her own time. Your words did the trick, Sithlac—and that humming of yours. The two of you have a connection, so don't let go of it. I think she's just afraid, that's all."

"Afraid?" asked Yog. "What does a zephyr have to be afraid of?"

"Whatever did this to her," the elf explained. "Look, I've seen zephyrs before. They're hard to spot, but you can pick them out of the winds sometimes. They don't control the air, but they can ask for help from it when they need to. Plus, they can use the wind to get around. They can fly wherever they like, as high and as far as they want. They're free to see the world and all its wonders. I can only imagine what she's seen and where she's been."

"Which makes her fate so terrible," remarked Sithlac. "Such a gift, to have it ripped away...what a torture it must be. For her my heart does ache, oh yes."

"So does mine, my friend, and that's why she can't give up. I hope she stays with us. Wind or no wind, this is where she belongs, not locked up in some dusty tower. Now come on, let's get moving. If we keep on, we might reach the nexus by sunset."

As before, they kept to the shadows, moving under the brush and between rock outcroppings as much as possible. Where snows blocked the way, they moved around, gathering drops of meltwater to quench their thirst. Though he didn't mean to, Sithlac kept glancing skyward, hoping to catch a glimpse of Ithess, to prove she was still with them. Every now and then something would glint or glimmer in the sunbeams poking through the trees, but he couldn't be sure it was her. He hoped so, though. Something about her presence felt strangely reassuring.

They stayed near the wall as long as possible, avoiding the path, which grew uncomfortably close as it meandered through the woods. At one point the wall jutted outward, forming a kind of protrusion into the woods, and it pushed them very close to the trail. On several occasions they had to hide as Men passed by, but managed not to draw any attention their way. In the meantime, the Sun slipped ever lower in the sky, below the level of the wall itself, and soon they found themselves cloaked mostly in darkness. This made the going easier, but Lyza grew more and more nervous as they went along.

Finally she called a halt. "Decision time," she explained. "Just ahead, there's another wall, and it's actually the back of another one of these huge staircases. The path goes right up next to it so there's not a lot of hiding space. We could cross the path here, and go downhill, but that's the tricky part. See, this is right about the middle of the park and that means we're on the border between two of the elf-lands. Soon as we go across the trail, we risk getting spotted by a patrol."

"Is that bad?" asked Yog. "I mean, you're an elf, right? Just tell 'em what we're up to and keep on walking."

"The Birchspear Elves aren't likely to care about me one way or another," she explained, "but the three of you make for very strange company. We should probably get our stories straight right now, before we go any further."

"What's there to get straight?" inquired Meathead, scratching idly at his blocky chin. "We ain't gonna tell 'em the honest truth?"

"Well, let's see…" Lyza said with a sigh, changing the inflection of her voice just so, "Hey, don't mind us, we're just on our way to the nexus in your neighbor's lands, off to see the faerie of Central Park, nothing funny about that at all! You really think they're going to believe us?"

"Well, what choice do we have?" Yog asked derisively. "It's not like any of us have ever been here before."

"Well, I have," Meathead pointed out.

"Other than you," Yog went on. "Okay, fine, most of us haven't, so we have no idea what to say. If you think lying is our best option, well, then, I'm all for it."

Lyza sighed. "It's not that I want to lie, don't get me wrong. I just think we're not a very likely bunch as we are. Let me ask you this: if we did tell them the honest truth, and they didn't believe us, what do you think will happen?"

"I don't know, they'll send us back here? Refuse to let us pass? What?" Yog paced back and forth, fuming. "You don't think they'd kill us, would they? Just for walking through the forest?"

"I doubt they'd go that far, with me here to put in a good word for you. Look at it from their angle for a moment. Right across there, just out of view from us, there's a junction of walking paths, and that's the dividing line between the Birchspear and Sprucebow tribes, who don't like each other much at all. If we tell them we're heading across to the nexus, they might well think we're spies, and yeah, death's one possible penalty for that, around these parts."

"Well, do we have to go that way?" Yog complained. "You said if we stayed on the hillside here, we could get up along the edge of those stairs. Could we just make a dash for the other side, like before?"

"I saw how tired you were last time," she pointed out. "It's about ten times farther. You think you can last that long? I doubt it. Plus, the lights are on now because of the shade. Oh, and this is the middle of the park, like I said, so we probably won't have much time before some Man comes wandering along."

"Well, I'd rather do that than risk getting my throat cut by some stupid elves, no offense," Yog insisted. "Meathead, you said you've been here before. How'd you get through?"

"I just walked," he said with a slow shrug. His voice grew softer as he struggled with the memory. "There were elves all round because...well, it was a...a prisoner exchange."

They waited a moment for him to go on, but he didn't say another word, just shut his eyes and sighed heavily. "Okay, that's new," Lyza muttered, putting her hands on her hips and staring accusingly at the troll. "You were a prisoner? Of the elves? You never told me anything about that!"

"Never seemed important before," Meathead replied with a shrug. "It really ain't now, either, seein' as it was a buncha years ago and that war's long gone. My hair was shorter then, and my skin much darker—they ain't gonna know me now."

"I want to hear that story later," Lyza commented with a very slight tone of frustration in her voice, "but we're wasting time. Tell you what, let's move ahead along the wall, past that next tower, as close as we can get to the stairs. Maybe there's some other way around I don't know about. Who knows, maybe we could climb up and cross the stairs up top, and drop down the other side. That would get us by for sure."

"Sounds good to me," said Yog, raising his voice somewhat. "If *only* we had a *zephyr* around to look for stuff like that, it *sure* would make things easier!"

Lyza smacked him loudly on the back of his head. "Knock it off! If she's there, she'll help us if she can—just don't scare her away! Now come on, and keep quiet. The Spears may have scouts watching this ridge. I doubt it, this time of year, but you never know."

They pressed on, sticking close to the enormous wall, keeping to the brush as best they could. A few scraggly trees gave some cover, but mostly they were forced to dart from shadow to shadow, hiding in the darkened cracks at the bottom of the wall itself. Luckily, the wall was made mostly of thick stone blocks with plenty of gaps between them, making hiding spots easy to find. Meanwhile, the wind grew colder as the afternoon wore on, occasionally cutting through Sithlac's warming spell, and he shuddered more than once, wishing he'd brought heavier clothing.

In due course they came to the next wall protrusion, which actually formed the base of a small plaza overlooking the park high overhead. Moving around this, they found themselves in a cul-de-sac that ended at the curve in the stone staircase winding its way up and to their right. To the left, the wide path cut a swath through the park, with very little in the way of vegetation beyond. If they went that way, the only cover they would have would come from clumps of fallen leaves and here and there a patch of partly melted snow. Sithlac couldn't help but feel they'd walked right into a dead end and would surely have to turn around.

As he considered that, Yog scrambled up onto the wall and peered about. A few Men meandered along the trails, and a pair of joggers passed by after descending the stairs, but no one looked in their direction. "See anything?" Lyza called out. "You might want to stay down here, in the cover."

Sithlac, studying the area, couldn't help but think there was something familiar about it. He followed Yog's lead and climbed up over a few blocks in the wall, trusting in his rat disguise to cover him if any Men glanced his way. The view looked familiar, and he kept going, soon reaching a point about a quarter of the way up. From there he could see that the path looped around, further downhill, and off to the left there was something familiar...an open, oval-shaped area with strange curving structures inside.

"I know this place," he called down to the others, scurrying down the wall as quickly as he could. Gesturing and pointing, he indicated the corner of the stairway high above. "I have seen this place before, from higher above. There, in that very spot, I had my nest, two seasons past."

"You nested here?" Lyza studied the wall carefully. "Up there, on the wall? Just out in the open, with all the Men about?"

"Not the open, no," Sithlac explained. "A gremlin-nest is like a hunter's hole—a pocket just outside the world. They are deep within the walls, between the stones, if you but know to look. Within, we are safe from Man's passing eyes, and I could venture forth at night to forage well."

"Hmm, that's good to know, but I'm not sure it does us any good right now."

"Perhaps it does at that," Sithlac explained. "Climb up now, and hide within, keeping watch for Men, and when a break appears, we are off to the next, upon the other side."

"And climb down at our leisure," she agreed. "Brilliant plan! Now we just have to get up there, which should be fun, but at least there's all kinds of plants and shadows to help out. Come on, let's get started!"

Helixtech Labs –
Animal Storage

For at least an hour, Bongcor worked his way along the edges of his cage, studying the smooth, clear surface carefully, as well as the sealed joints at the edges and corners. Despite Jozan's warnings not to use magic, he risked uttering a few simple chants to test the soundness of the material. Almost immediately he discovered this substance, while thick and clear like similar items he'd encountered before—either in the scrap heaps of his home Tunnel or while hunting with Sithlac— was nothing like ordinary glass. For one thing, his fingertips felt a slight resistance when sliding across, unlike the nearly frictionless surface he'd encountered before. The sound of it, when tapped, came back different as well, and light passing through looked slightly distorted, the colors from beyond somewhat dulled. His testing-spells revealed no weaknesses whatsoever.

Reluctantly, he concluded he couldn't possibly break through and retreated to the corner, where he sullenly gnawed on some of the green leaves the Men left there. They tasted flat and bland, but he ate anyway since he had no other choices. Afterward, he drank his fill from the stagnant pool nearby and shuffled back over toward Jozan.

"Satisfied now?" said the goblin with a long sigh. "No getting out of here, that's for sure."

"I must agree, to my dismay," admitted Bongcor with a heavy sigh. "What will they do with us now?"

"No idea," admitted Jozan. "Yesterday, after I got here, Men came in from time to time and peered inside. Sometimes they pointed some of their strange tools at me, but I don't know why. One of them opened the roof—it lifts up at their command—and held me down with some kind of long stick while another poked me with a spear and drew blood. I thought death was certain, for they could've killed me at their leisure, but apparently that's all they wanted and left me be."

"So, as you say, your invisibility failed you," noted Bongcor sullenly.

Jozan rubbed absently at his shoulder. "Yeah, the one I told you about before was standing there, and another one too—his skin was all wrinkly, so maybe he's diseased, or dried out for some reason...who knows? Anyway, whatever the case, they both had no problem spotting me. Others that come by don't seem to notice me, but these two did. Anyhow, after they left, Telan yelled over to tell me they did the same thing to everyone else here—it must be some kind of ritual they have."

Bongcor nodded slowly. "Then I can expect no less," he commented, his throat-sac deflating almost completely. "If that is the way of things, I shall not resist."

"Good thinking," agreed Jozan. "I hate the idea of doing whatever we're told, or forced to do, but what choice do we have? Besides, if we keep an eye out, maybe we can learn enough about them to figure out some kind of escape plan. It's a shame that sorceress elf just tried to run off on her own—if she'd worked her magic on all our cages, maybe some of us might've gotten away. Too late now, I guess."

"What became of her?" inquired Bongcor curiously.

"After she did that, and the Men recaptured her," said the goblin with a sad shake of his head, "they put her in a much smaller cylinder of glass, and carried her away. I expect if they considered her dangerous, they probably executed her, but don't say that in front of Telan. He's still holding out hope she might yet be alive."

Bongcor nodded. "I shall not mention her again in his presence, oh no," he agreed readily. "Now, what else can you tell me of—"

"Hsst, the Men come!" interrupted Jozan, scrambling away and pointing with his clawed finger. "Remain still, and keep to your disguise."

Bongcor nodded, retreating to the back of the cage, up against the metal back wall. Outside, several Men came into view, one of them pushing an enormous metal structure ahead of him. While that one and another wore simple work overalls, the rest—four in all—sported white lab coats and carried strange devices in their hands. One of them, a male, reached out and tapped on the lid of Bongcor's cage, and the gremlin crouched down nervously, struggling to contain his fear. When he saw the other one's hands, wrinkled with age, he began to quiver and shake, remembering Jozan's frightful tale of his recent wound.

The Man outside rattled something overhead and all at once the ceiling lifted away, swinging back on an unseen hinge. The wrinkled hands moved up there, one holding a long-handled metal device tipped with a clamp, while the other clutched a syringe with a long needle attached. Bongcor's eyes swiveled to the sharp metal tip and he shuddered even more, knowing now what was to come.

Sithlac would not quail in terror, oh no, he insisted to himself. *He would stand and face the danger, and I must strive to do the same. Besides, there is no escape from this place, no alternative but to do as my captors will. I must be strong!*

The clamp came down and he made no attempt to resist. As the thick pads wrapped around his neck and pushed him down, the Man uttered something in his choppy, brutish tongue. "Odd, this one's not fighting," he said, but of course Bongcor couldn't understand.

"Just get the sample so we can get on with it," another remarked impatiently, and the needle pierced the gremlin's skin mere moments later. Bongcor flinched at the pain, but remained steady, surprising himself with his calm reaction, and how the wound only hurt for a moment. When he opened his eyes a few seconds later, he saw the needle and clamp retreating away, the Men apparently satisfied with completing their task, and the lid slammed shut soon after.

"Well done," Jozan's voice called out. "That looked like it barely hurt at all. I should've stayed still like that too! Anyway, they usually leave now, but there's something else going on out there this time. Brace yourself."

Bongcor nodded, feeling slightly dizzy. He had no idea they'd actually drawn blood from his body—he hadn't seen the reddish liquid pooling in the bottom of the syringe, and even if he had, he might not have made the connection. The idea that humans might want his blood never even occurred to him. Instead, he cautiously moved up toward the front of his cage, his vision swimming a bit but slowly recovering, and watched in surprise as the Men outside started loading the enclosures onto the odd metal lattice, one by one.

"Careful with these," said the Man who appeared to be in charge. As he spoke, he pointed at several of the cages, including Bongcor's. "They go to the top floor when you're done delivering the others to the testing labs."

"Sure thing," said another. "The usual drill, then? Leave 'em in the elevator?"

"Yes," the leader replied. "See to it they don't get mixed in with the others. We need each for a special project we're working on."

"Sure, sure. I don't know what you need a rock for, or empty cages, but the cat makes sense, I guess."

The first man smiled. "You only think you see nothing inside," he said in a deliberately ominous voice, "but you see, we think we've discovered the cause of all the rodent problems the city's been having recently—some of the rats have learned how to turn invisible. We're working to figure out how they do it, so we can make them all visible again."

This drew a laugh from the other workers. "Good one, Mr. Spencer," said one, even as he lifted up Bongcor's cage and shoved it on the bottom rack. "Ha-ha, invisible rats, very funny! Come on, guys, let's get these delivered so we can get out of here—weekend shifts are the worst."

Mr. Spencer exchanged a quick grin with the scientist nearby as the workers filed out, rolling the cart full of cages further into the lab. On the bottom rack, Bongcor hastened over to the nearby wall to find Jozan staring back at him, eyes wide with fear.

"Where do they take us now?" asked the gremlin nervously.

"No idea," answered Jozan, shaking all over, "and I don't really want to find out. I'm gonna go shut my eyes, and maybe when we stop moving and I open them, we'll be Outside again."

Bongcor nodded slowly, collapsing down to the floor as though trying to bury himself in the soft sod below. "If only it could be so," he muttered to himself. "If only..."

Morningside Park - 116th Street Stairs (Bottom)

Climbing up proved slow going. They had little trouble securing the rope in a safe spot among the oblong bricks at the ledge high above, but Meathead wasn't exactly a fast climber. Yog and Sithlac even offered to take his backpack up for him, but the troll refused, insisting they'd never be able to move such a load on their own. Though he was probably right, Sithlac still felt obligated to make the offer.

They ascended at the corner, where the staircase section jutted out from the wall and they could find shadows aplenty. Despite the extremely time-consuming effort, they were never in serious danger of being spotted. Trees obscured the few humans passing by below, who were busy with their own errands in any event.

While the troll steadily climbed up one step at a time, Sithlac occupied himself by searching around for nest entrances. Similar to the hunter's holes back in Adams Hall, these resembled nearly invisible windows into a hollow space not quite part of the real world. With a relatively simple chant, he could open up any of these entrances as though lifting a hidden access panel on the wall. The space beyond was about the size of the brick behind it, but hollow and usually filled with dried grass and other materials left over from the previous occupants. In the spring, when the mated gremlin pairs arrived, they would seek out an unoccupied nest along the wall and further west, where the cliffs began. Late arrivals faced the longer journey, although it was said that foraging was easier there. Sithlac didn't know for sure, as he'd never had to go farther than this spot.

Looking down, he remembered the view quite well. With the leaves and ivy cleared by winter's harsh touch, he could see much further now. The roughly oval shape of the playground, filled with odd-shaped structures used almost exclusively by human children, could easily be seen from even this great distance, as well as the road beyond, filled with cars and trucks of all shapes and sizes. Sometimes, when resting during or after a foraging run, he would sit with his eyes facing the other way, at

Morningside Drive, and watch the occasional vehicle rush past—a great shadow in the night, with eyes of pure white fire, and angry red orbs in the back, presumably to discourage pursuit. However, the cars there never seemed all that numerous. Here, watching through the sparse tree cover, he had a much better view. In that distance, they flowed past the lower edge of the park like a great river, seemingly endless in shape and number.

Bongcor was taken away in such as those, Sithlac reminded himself. Even with the clue preserved by Lyza's elven magic, how could he ever possibly locate a single individual vehicle in such a crowd? He could only hope the faeries would have some answer, should they ever find them.

And what if they did? The male was the mate to the one Sithlac aided in the tower, if Lyza had connected all the dots correctly. Once a Man, he clearly chose to accept the Fey transformation, as magic couldn't affect him if he didn't wish it—assuming, of course, the old tales were true. So if he had indeed turned his back on his own kind, what possible reason could he have for helping a gremlin he didn't even know? Why would he even consider such a thing?

Sithlac sighed and shut his eyes. He very well might not—a grim possibility that must be faced, and prepared for. Of course, just below Sithlac on the wall were three others—an elf, a troll, and a goblin, of all things—who had thrown in their lot with him, just to help Bongcor, whom they barely knew. There had even been a zephyr, and might still be, if his earlier words had struck a chord with her. He opened his eyes again and glanced around, studying the sky in two directions at once, hoping to spot the little creature, but saw no sign of her at all.

He let out another sigh. She at least gave aid before, and that's all he could ask. In fact, considering that, he realized he did have one other thing he could try when he finally met the faerie—his assistance to the female, the one named Tillianita. Perhaps, if he mentioned that detail, the male would see fit to respond in kind. In fact, things might not have worked out for the pair, had Sithlac not done as he did. That in and of itself might be enough to sway a reticent faerie, yet something about it felt inappropriate—as though he might be altering a bargain already struck, now completed to the satisfaction of both parties. *I shall try that option if I must,* he decided at length, *though only as a last resort.*

"Okay, he's almost here," Yog's voice called out, referring to Meathead's slow but steady ascent. "You got a place for us? Where is it? I don't see anything."

"Next to me it is," Sithlac responded, pointing at the faintly visible curtain in the air nearby, just above the nearby brick. The rounded stone, rough and scarred from years of weathering, looked otherwise completely ordinary.

"Where? I still don't see it." The goblin pulled himself up almost on top of the entrance, glancing around without noticing the window. "You're not playing a joke on me, are you?"

"Perhaps they appear to gremlins only," Sithlac responded, uttering a chant and lifting up the covering, revealing an oval-shaped cavern beyond. "An answer, then, to the question why the nests are empty when we come. A mystery now explained, oh yes."

Yog stuck his head inside. "Oh, this is great! We could hide in here all night, too. Great fallback position. Smells like something died, though. Nothing did, did it?"

"Not yet checked have I, oh no, but do so if you wish."

Yog started to enter, but just as quickly changed his mind and backed out. "Nah, there might be nasty stuff in there. I'll let Meaty go first. Hey! You two! Over here!"

Sithlac glanced down at the others, and Lyza immediately redirected Meathead toward the opening. Still hanging onto the rope, anchored a couple of rocks overhead, he angled his way over and pulled himself inside the opening, just barely managing to squeeze through. Once within, he dropped to his knees and took a few deep breaths. "Tougher than I thought," he managed. "Guess I'm needin' more exercise!"

"Yep, you should get out more," Lyza agreed, following on his heels. Once inside the hollow area, she uttered a light-spell and glanced around appreciatively. The oval-shaped cavern, smooth-walled and filled with dried grass and dead leaves, seemed filled with floating motes of dust. "Nice place you got here," the elf went on. "So this is a nest, huh? Doesn't look like much, but it feels pretty comfortable. So, how exactly does it work?"

"To what do you refer?" Sithlac responded, fixing an eye on her curiously.

"You know," she answered. "The nesting thing."

"I will explain, oh yes," began Sithlac as he let the window shut behind him. "Each spring, a gremlin-pair will seek a place like this, and spawn a child. The method here, of course, I need describe no further, oh no, but the rest I shall. It is the male's task to bring the grass and nesting-leaves, and other needed things, as the female desires; for it is she who builds the nest itself, for her comfort and the child when it arrives. The male hunts and forages as he must, returning often, for she cannot depart until at least the weaning-day. Once that happens, he is free to return home, and usually he does so at once."

"But not always," Lyza finished for him.

Sithlac nodded slowly, fidgeting a bit, as though now forced to admit something a bit uncomfortable. "Sometimes," he went on, "the male is not yet ready. The child may be in poor health, or the mother weak from indolence. Or...other times...he may become...*attached* to one or another of them, for reasons of his own. In time, he comes to realize this is folly and departs." With that, he sighed softly and let his eyes sink slightly back into his head, despite not really intending to do so.

Lyza nodded, and didn't ask another question right away, perhaps because she was still trying to figure out how to prod Sithlac further without upsetting him. In any event, Yog interrupted, breaking up the conversation entirely. "So, let me get this straight," he said, just barely suppressing a snicker, "you bring your girl here, and she gets to lie around all day and tell you what to do, and you just go out and do it? That's how this works?" He began to laugh. "Oh, that's rich! No wonder you gremlins are always so uptight! You get what, five minutes of fun and then you gotta pay for it for a whole season or more? Oh, ha-ha-ha, that's great! Ha-ha-ha-ha-ha!"

He kept on laughing for a few seconds, opened his eyes to see Sithlac's scowling expression, and started laughing again. "There is nothing whatsoever amusing about it," the gremlin hissed defensively. "She must bear and raise our child, a painful responsibility I am grateful not to have to face. You have not been witness to such things, for if you had, you would find our tasks of equal challenge."

"Oh, ha-ha. Sorry, Sithlac, ol' pal," Yog went on when he finally recovered his breath. "Yeah, thanks for that, best laugh I've had in a long while. Don't worry, I totally believe you're not the one getting shafted here. Totally believe it!"

"Sure you do," Lyza chuckled. "Anyway, fun as this has been, we should probably get a move on. Meaty, you ready to climb some more? Just two bricks up to that ledge, then we can scoot across the top of the stairs when there's a break in traffic. Meaty? You okay?"

She reached out to touch him on the arm, but he didn't respond.

Instead, he kept his head moving back and forth slightly, eyes fixed on the back of the chamber. There, the light from the glowing spot on the wall, where Lyza cast her illumination spell, created a host of wavering shadows, mostly from the spikes of grass and broken leaves piled up in the middle of the room. Immediately, all eyes turned to face that way, seeing nothing but the dimly lit area, where the shadows flickered from side to side as if created by candlelight.

Except the light wasn't moving...and neither were the leaves. "We ain't alone," Meathead whispered quietly. "Somethin's back there."

"Who's there?" Lyza yelled, swiftly drawing her swords. "We don't want any trouble. In fact, we're leaving right now, so we'll just be on our way..."

Her words trailed off as the shadows grew even more animated, dancing about in a flurry. After a moment, a thin, soft voice responded, hissing like an invisible snake hidden deep in the long grass.

"Leaving so soo-o-oooon?" the unseen creature whispered.

"Such tassssty magic," another answered. "Such variety!"

"Ssssstay longer, friendssss," said another—or was it the first? The voices all sounded alike, very low in pitch, like a hollow echo amplified by a broken, raspy speaker. The shadows on the walls began to wave back and forth in the dim light. "We're hunnnnngry."

"Ssssso hungry!"

"Screw this, I'm outta here," Yog barked, pushing past Sithlac toward the exit, but he couldn't seem to find it. He scrambled about, clawing at the stony wall. "Where is it? Open it up! C'mon, let's go!"

Sithlac, who hadn't moved very far from the opening, moved over and tried to chant, but the words wouldn't come. The portal stayed shut, shimmering slightly as though taunting him, but his fingers slipped through it ineffectually. "The spell—I cannot open it," he complained aloud, swinging an eye back toward their unseen foes.

"Yesss, darkling magic," a voice called out. "Again! Try againnnnn!"

"Yesssss, more!" called another.

"The elf hassss magic, too. Much magic. Sssshe made the light."

"Make more, elf. Moooooore!"

"Taste the aurasssss," said another, this time off to the left-hand side. More shadows flickered there, but nothing seemed to be making them. "So many choicessss..."

"What the heck are these things?" demanded Yog, suddenly producing his knife, this time seemingly drawing it from empty air.

"They're seriously freaking me out! Get back, you stupid things! Let us out of here!"

"The portal openssss, as it will, just casssssst your spell and gooooo," came the reply.

"Yes, just casssssst it," another hissed. "Go on, casssssssst...!"

"Draw another weapon, goblinnnn," a third said, this one off to the right. There were at least four of these things, based upon the sounds, but they still had yet to actually see any creatures, just flickering shadows on the walls.

"Don't do it, it's a trap," Lyza countered. "They want us to use our magic. They're devouring it right off of us. Can't you feel it? Our cold-wards—they're fading."

"If we can't open the door, how do we get out?" complained Yog. "After they finish with our magic, what are they going to do to us?"

"Nothing," Lyza explained, standing up straight and putting away her blades. "They have no power, other than to take our *kai*. Actually, I'm pretty sure they're just whisks."

"Our secretsssss!" one complained. "We were having such fun, toooooo..."

"They were sssssssssso scared!" said another. "Did you seeeeeee?"

"The goblin almost made me laughhhhhhh," said a third.

"Not the trollllllll," the fourth one pointed out. "A dead zone 'round himmmmm...."

"And such a sourpusssssss...!"

Sithlac pointed an eye at Lyza. "Whisks I know very little of," he said quietly, keeping his spear at the ready. Other than the fact that they were wind-spirits, kin to zephyrs and mistrals, he knew next to nothing about them. "What more danger do we face?"

"Not much, just the loss of all our *kai*," she replied hastily, before stepping toward the middle of the chamber with hands held up. "Look, I'm sorry we disturbed you," she explained, "but like we tried to explain, we didn't mean to. We're on our way across the park, and this was a convenient place to take a break, that's all. We'll be on our way, if you'll just open up the exit for us."

"No, don't go," one replied. "We're lonelyyyyyy..."

"Ssssssso lonelyyyyy..."

"The whole winter by ourselvesssss…!"

"Awake now. Sssssstay...and talk…we'll let you outttttt..."

"We promisssssssse...."

Lyza sighed, but tried to remain diplomatic. "We can't stay, I'm afraid. We've got to reach the central nexus by dark."

"Ssssso farrrrrrrrr," one of the whisks whispered.

"If only they could flyyyyyy," said another.

"A flying troll, that would be a sighttttt...!"

"Stay with us, and go tomorrowwwwwww..."

"Give us the morning's gift, then you can gooooooooo...!"

Lyza shook her head. "We just don't have that long. Look, if you let us out, right now, I'll personally give you all my magic. I'll sing to you, and you can draw the power as you like."

"Why bargain? We could just take it as we willlllll..."

"So much effort, though...I'm sssssso tiredddddd...!"

"It'll take too long. And she might dieeeeee."

"Then decay in here with us. Ewwwwwwwww...!"

"I say let her tryyyyyy..."

"I say it's a trickkkkk."

"A gift freely given is the tasssssstiest of allllllll..."

They continued to argue for another minute or so. Sithlac, still unable to get the window open, cast an eye in Lyza's direction. In response she moved a hand behind her back and wiggled her fingers in the direction of the exit, while moving her mouth up and down slightly. Sithlac gave a slight nod in response and inflated himself somewhat, indicating he understood her plan—or at least thought he did. She would distract them, and he would get the others out, when they were no longer paying attention to him.

Finally the whisks seemed to come to an agreement. "We agreeeeee," one said, "but make it a storyyyy..."

"A good storyyyyy!"

"*Your* storyyyyy..."

"Yes, why are you hereeeeee?"

"Tell us, and give us all your tasty magicccccc...!"

"All right, all right, but to do that we need music," Lyza remarked, reaching into her pack and withdrawing a small three-stringed instrument, rather like a miniature ukulele carved from a single piece of wood. This was a *timaryn*, a favorite tool of tale-spinners the world over. After a couple of plucks of the strings, to ensure all was well, she began to play, and as she played, she sang.

The story she told was indeed that of their current mission. She began with Sithlac's assisting the faerie and then his budding friendship with Bongcor, taking her time and embellishing details as she went along. In fact, she created a couple of sidebars out of whole cloth, even though she didn't really need to. As she sang, she carefully added magic to the words, so that it steadily flowed out into the cavern—just barely visible, like faint waves of heat rising up on a hot afternoon. The shadowy whisks, drawn to the *kai*, flickered and fluttered in the light, gradually taking form: tiny, black, insect-like motes with gloom-shrouded wings, no bigger than Ithess the zephyr. They were definitely not a physical threat, but that didn't make them any less dangerous.

Sithlac, without realizing it, found himself drawn into Lyza's song. He could see himself now, traveling in the dark tunnels, his allies at his side, searching for his lost friend Bongcor. Trapped here, there would be no end to his quest, but he didn't care, lost in the elven tale. Her magic had enraptured him, just as the faerie's had, all those many days ago. Her methods were the same, but the song was different, and the notes were hers alone. He could almost hear them now, echoing in his head…

He started to hum along with Lyza's tale, not really knowing why, but feeling like doing so was important somehow. The notes floated out into the air, as hers had done, joining the story, but just as quickly flickering away from it. Sithlac turned to follow, to compel them to return, but they had other ideas. *There is another path*, they seemed to say, as he chased after them, toward a distant glow within the maze of endless shadowed corridors, lined with doors to nowhere. *A way out. An exit, right here, before you. Just open the door…this one here will set you free…*

Without hesitation, he opened it, and light streamed in. Sithlac blinked, and his eyes emerged from where they'd withdrawn all the way inside his head. He found himself looking Outside, at the great park beyond, exactly as he'd left it. How much time had passed? He didn't know, but night had not yet come.

"Outta my way!" squealed Yog suddenly, pushing past him onto the slight ledge in the wall beyond. "Come on, get the others and let's go!"

Sithlac shook himself awake and turned around. Lyza continued singing as several (he couldn't tell for sure how many) whisks bobbed up and down around her. He tugged at Meathead's arm and managed to get the troll's attention. Without a word the hulking creature pushed its way through the exit, grabbing hold of the rope Yog had already retrieved for him.

Sithlac began moving toward Lyza, but just as quickly realized he didn't have to, as she'd already started backing up. As she did so, she finished off her story and let the last of her magic flow into the room. Then, with a final strum of the *timaryn*, she held out her hand in farewell, and gave a quick bow before following Sithlac out the door.

"Done alreadyyyy?" one of the whisks complained.

"Such a storyyyy!" another put in. "Well done, elfffff! Your name will soon be whispered on the windsssss...!"

"Don't go!" a third begged. "Tell us anotherrrrr!"

"But how did they open the dooooooor...?" one argued.

"A trick, as I warneddddddd...!"

"Who caresssss...? It was worth it…a feast in every way, it wasssss..."

"Of words, of song, and magic tooooooo..."

"Such magic! Never have we dined so wellllll..."

"Indeeeeeeed," another said, moving toward the wall, even as Lyza made good her escape and the door sealed shut behind her. "One last item for dessert, let's not forgetttttt...!"

The whisks moved to surround Lyza's light-spell, devouring it quickly, and the room descended once more into darkness.

Morningside Park – 116th Street Stairs (Top)

Sithlac, naturally, felt relieved at escaping the nest-hole, but just as quickly found himself overwhelmed by another feeling: *cold*. The whisks had drained his warding spell, and now the bitter wind cut deeply into his barely covered flesh. The others, too, had huddled into the corner, shivering, all but Meathead, who held gamely onto the rope with his feet upon the nearby wall. "Now what?" he asked sullenly. "Them things might be in any of these holes, and we won't get out so easily next time."

"Gotta...get...my ward...up…" mumbled Yog, struggling to cast in the sub-freezing temperature. Nearby, Lyza shuddered and clutched at her cloak, obviously unable to do the same since she'd just sacrificed her entire store of power.

"I knew not of this," Sithlac managed between shivers. "That...such creatures...would occupy our nests…we come here in the winter not at all, so how was I to know?"

"Who cares?" Yog demanded. "Just...find us some warmth…can't concentrate."

"I thought that fancy coat of yours was all you needed," chuckled Meathead, walking his way sideways toward the rest of them. "Hang close, I got yer backs."

With that he began to chant softly. A small piece of stone near his feet started hissing as the flakes of snow still held within its cracks melted away. Within a moment the rock glowed with a faint reddish light, emitting waves of heat that drew them in like moths to a flame. Warming their hands, they gradually grew more comfortable, until at last Yog and Sithlac were able to restore their wards. Lyza, unfortunately, had no such opportunity.

"I need to soak up some *kai*," she said after a moment. "It comes from the Sun, and that means I have to go up top, out of these shadows. Someone go and keep watch, and make sure there's no humans there."

"On it." Yog scurried up before the rest could even think of moving.

In a flash he'd reached the top of the wall. "Looks fine, nobody here. You better hurry, though. Sun's almost behind the towers now."

"If needs we must, our own power we will give," Sithlac told her, even as she started climbing up the taut rope, with Meathead following. "Upon the coming of the night, I can replenish what I need with ease."

"It has to be the Sun's gift," Lyza replied. "I appreciate that, Sithlac, but most elves—well, elves like me, anyway—can't use night-magic. I don't have any problem with those who do, it's just not possible for me. I hope you understand."

"I knew that not at all," he told her honestly, but inwardly he thought there might be more to it than she was saying. Rather than press further, though, he changed the subject. "Those creatures within the nest—the whisks. What are they, truly?"

"Air-spirits, like the zephyrs," she answered, noticeably relieved to be talking about something else. "They like dark places, shady areas, that sort of thing. Some say they're the reason you feel uneasy looking at some spooky dark location, but that's just a myth—or at least I think so, anyway. Usually they play tricks, joke around, and feed off magic. In the spring and summer, they can get their own, but this time of year the Sun grows weaker, and they can't get enough *kai*, so they find some dark, shadowy place and hibernate. I guess that bunch figured your old nesting site was the perfect spot. Of course they'll be long gone before you gremlins show up next season, so don't worry about running into them next time you're out here."

"Fairly noted," agreed Sithlac, feeling a bit more at ease about that particular subject, "but the Sun grows weaker? I knew this not, as well."

"You're going to find there's lots of things out here you don't know, my friend," Lyza pointed out. "You know about cycles, yes? The day and night, the changing of the Moon? The seasons are another cycle, just like that. You see, the Sun has phases, just like the Moon does. It waxes and wanes, you just can't tell because it's so bright. When it's winter, the Sun has waned, so it's like a new Moon. In summer, it waxes full, and is at its strongest."

Sithlac nodded. "Never before have I thought of it that way, yet there is truth within your words." They had by now reached the top edge of the wall, and he swung a single eye toward the distant Sun, visible just above a faraway tower, partly obscured by a few gnarled tree branches clutching at the sky. "I look forward to asking many more questions I as yet know not to ask, and learning much that now I know not at all."

Lyza grinned. "Sometimes I wonder how you get all those words out of that huge mouth of yours without choking. Anyway, quiet now, I've got to soak up some magic. Keep watch in case any Men come by, and see if you can figure out how to get across while you're at it."

Sithlac agreed and took up a position along the edge of the stone wall, where a few dead ivy clusters still provided a little bit of cover. The vertical surface upon which he stood rose quite a few body-lengths over the level of the top step, forming a retaining wall bordering the stone staircase beneath him. From here, he could see the entire open area where the stone stairs descended down and to his left, into the depths of the park. The uncomfortable feeling of exposure, with no cover should any Men look his way, made Sithlac shudder and flatten himself on the irregular rocky surface. He could, of course, retreat back the way he came if needed, but even so, any Man striding past could simply look over and spot him clinging there.

Even worse, the trembling gremlin considered, he had quite the challenge before him. In order to cross the stairs, he would have to descend the wall upon which he stood, dash across the wide landing, and ascend the opposite wall, all with nowhere to hide should any Man happen past. Furthermore, even should he succeed in this task, the others would have to follow. He had little doubt Lyza could accomplish the maneuver with little to no trouble, but Meathead, not the world's best climber, would find the effort daunting.

Sithlac glanced back with one eye, to find the troll ascending slowly but steadily. The other eye pivoted around to follow the Yog's movements. The swiftly scampering goblin, already having clambered down the inside of the retaining wall to the landing, now reached the opposite corner where the stairs ended and a metal fence began, separating the steep drop-off into the park from the edge of Morningside Drive. From his position at ground level, the goblin glanced both directions, hunkering down as a couple of cars rolled past on the road nearby, and finally raised his head to give a hasty thumbs-up.

Taking the initiative, Sithlac went over the top and peered down the stairs. Seeing no Men there, he hastened down the wall and raced across the open landing, toward the stone barrier opposite. Yog, watching intently, kept his thumb in the air as Sithlac ran. From his position, the hurrying gremlin could still see down the stairs well enough to dart sideways should any humans come, and with Yog on watch he felt certain he could get up the farther wall in time to escape their notice. Besides, even if they caught a glimpse of him, they would see only a rat—

Sithlac almost froze in his tracks. *My disguise...!*

He hadn't noticed before, in all the excitement of escaping the whisks, but they must've drained his defensive aura as well as his frostward. That meant any Man who spotted him would see his true form!

He immediately doubled his efforts and leaped onto the far wall, racing up as fast as his suckered fingers could carry him. He could still see no Men upon the stairs, but his right eye swung around and caught sight of Yog, a horrified look on his face, waving back and forth with both hands. In almost that same instant the goblin made a sideways glance and ducked out of sight behind the bricks.

Sithlac barely made it over as a youthful-looking jogger came into view, passing between two parked cars as she crossed Morningside Drive from the general direction of Columbia. Dressed in a purple sweatsuit and hood tied close over her head, she hopped over a patch of snow along the curb and hastened along the sidewalk, absently adjusting an ear bud to keep it from slipping out as she ran. Just as she turned the corner to head down the stairs into the park, she glanced sideways as a dark shape disappeared over the right edge of the wall. For an instant she paused, as though wondering what she just saw, but shook it off and continued past, fortunately not bothering to investigate.

On the other side of the wall, Sithlac hung onto the icy stone with both hands, barely keeping a grip. Along this edge, mostly blocked from the Sun's rays, the snow hadn't completely melted and he found himself slipping downward quickly. Only a fortunate bare spot saved him from losing his tenuous handhold and falling dozens of feet to the distant ground. He clung there, struggling to keep his grip while occasionally slipping downward, for several minutes until Yog's head appeared above. "You okay down there?" the goblin called out. "Need any help? No Men around, at least for now, but they sure can move quick when they want to!"

"I am well," Sithlac replied, wishing he remained close enough that Yog might reach down and help pull him over, "but trapped in this position most surely. To move from here is to lose my grip and fall. The rope would help, oh yes."

"Can't help you there, the troll's still got it," came the reply. "I'll get him moving. Lyza's gonna be a while, I think. Hang on as best you can."

Sithlac grunted in reply and considered his situation more carefully. He had enough dry space to shift his grip without risking a fall, but trying to climb in any direction amid the snow was out of the question. He swiveled his eyes this way and that, looking for options, as his feet shifted around, testing for a gap or crack to slide into. He could hold on for a minute or two, but eventually, his body's weight would be too much, and his arms would give out. The suckers in his fingers weren't meant for long-term endurance tests, unfortunately.

What to do, then? He couldn't expect the rope any time soon. Meathead would have nowhere to hide once he came over the top of the wall, and would have to wait while Yog brought the rope across and repositioned it. Another Man going past would turn him to stone for sure, and in such an exposed location, he might remain like that for quite some time. Sithlac knew he had to get out of this himself, but how?

His right eye found nothing to help, but his left eye swiveled over to face the nearby corner. He'd gone over the top at a place where the stairway platform extended out away from the main wall running alongside Morningside Drive. That wall was too far away to reach, but could he make it with a leap…?

As he considered that, Sithlac finally found a gap in which to place his feet. The crack wasn't wide but it felt stable enough. Kicking out and sweeping from side to side, he cleared the snow and ice from that spot and tested the opening more carefully. Suckers along the bottoms of his toes unfolded, slipping around, and finally found a good purchase at a spot where the lichen hadn't yet taken root. He shifted back and forth, but the suckers didn't quite hold like he'd hoped. If he tried to leap, he'd probably slip, and not make it far enough to grab the wall.

Then he noticed something else. Squinting carefully, he spotted the telltale glimmer of a nest-hole a little further down. Was it close enough to open, and would it contain more whisks, or something worse? He didn't know, but staying here wasn't an option. The foothold bought him a little more time, but not much. If either of his hands gave out, he'd never survive the fall.

Summoning up what little magic he had left, he uttered the chant that unlocked the entrance door. The shining curtain remained closed, but now it rippled back and forth, no longer impeding entry into the hole beyond.

Sithlac took a breath, held it, and let it out slowly, deflating himself as much as he could. Then he rocked back and forth three times, gathering momentum with each swing, and finally launched himself toward the hole. As expected, his feet slipped, sending him tumbling through the air, barely managing to avoid panicking.

Sithlac knew at once he'd miss the hole, but he still had one chance left. Stretching out to his maximum length, he clutched at the edge of the opening with both hands. One slipped free, but the other caught on and held fast. His body swung around, slamming into the wall, drawing a grunt of pain and loosening his hand's grip in the process. This caused him to tumble downward, but as he did, he slapped both hands into the wall, and the suckers on his exposed palms caught hold. Unfortunately, the momentum of his fall carried his body still further, flipping and twisting him around so he wound up upside-down, with his back to the wall and arms sideways, dangling helplessly.

Yog's face appeared overhead a moment later. "Hey, I'll have the rope in—wait, what? How'd you get over there? Stop screwing around, we've got to get Meathead over the top as fast as we can."

"This is not intentional, oh no," complained Sithlac, "nor is it comfortable. A fall from there was certain, but now, I have but moments before—"

At that he finally lost his grip, unable to keep it in that unnatural position. As before, he started falling, but managed to get his hands around and onto the stone surface, slowing him down tremendously. His feet found purchase in the gap between two bricks, and at last he stopped his deadly descent with his right palm, about halfway down the wall. He hung there for several long seconds, catching his breath, before finally shifting to a better position, finally feeling safe.

"As soon as you're through embarrassing yourself," chuckled Yog, "get back up here and secure this rope. I've got to keep an eye out for Men until Lyza's done sunning herself."

He disappeared again and Sithlac began the slow climb upward, this time avoiding the frozen spots as best he could. Up until now he'd had no trouble climbing because the rocks were rough and dry, but here, shaded and coated in ice, the slippery surfaces proved quite treacherous. A few more close calls forced him to take his time, and when he finally reached the top, he could hear Yog grumbling from his position on the other side of the walkway. Lyza's voice followed, unintelligible at this distance, but at least that meant she'd finished gathering *kai*. Sithlac explored the top edge of the stone wall for a bit, located a good protrusion to tie the rope to, and tested it with his own weight. Hopefully it would work for the troll, too, but he couldn't be totally sure.

Lyza appeared on the other side of the staircase as he finished his work, topping the retaining wall opposite and peering around to make sure no Men were about. Now, she too had to navigate the open landing, if she hoped to reach Sithlac's position and then descend behind him into the park. Nervously, and admittedly curious to see how well she might perform this task, the gremlin watched her carefully through his left eye, keeping his right on the still-empty staircase.

After a moment's pause to gather herself, Lyza suddenly jumped straight down to the landing, making no attempt to climb at all, instead making a controlled fall all the way to the surface below. Sithlac got the impression she cast some spell just as she hit the ground, and perhaps with its assistance, she rolled to a halt uninjured. With barely a break in stride, she leaped to her feet, dashed across the opening toward the wall upon which Sithlac stood, yelling for the rope the whole way over.

Sithlac tossed it down there and she immediately climbed swiftly to the top. "Can't do that spell too often," she explained as she caught her breath, "but it's sure handy in a pinch. Hmm, good knot. You were watching, I can tell. See you at the bottom!"

At that she moved straight past the gremlin, rope in hand. Flashing a quick smile, she went over the side and slid rapidly downward toward the park's edge far below, stopping occasionally to change her grip lest the rope's friction destroy her gloves. In less than a minute she reached the distant ground and dropped clear, landing in the patch of snow covering the forest floor. Sithlac watched her dust herself off and wave, then vanish into the shadows of a small evergreen close by.

He turned his attention back to Yog, as well as the barely visible top of Meathead's hairy forehead, poking up over the opposite retaining wall with a comically worried look. Yog pointed a couple of times at the bottom of the stairs, and made a gesture with his fingers in front of his eyes. Sithlac nodded and moved slightly over, taking up a position where he could fully see down the staircase, wishing he still had his disguise spell going. If a Man saw him...but no, best not to think about such things.

From his new position, Sithlac had a clear view of the curving steps, at the moment still empty. He could see a couple of Men down along the path far below, but they were in no hurry and didn't appear to be coming this direction. The nervous gremlin waited a couple of moments in case any more Men might be hidden from view by trees, but none appeared, so he gave a thumbs-up toward Yog and waited, watching both directions simultaneously.

Yog said something, also putting up a thumb, and Meathead came over the top, still looking quite concerned. In great haste he tossed his rope over the side and descended to the landing as quickly as he could, his progress mind-numbingly slow to the onlooking gremlin. As Yog glanced back and forth worriedly, Meathead lumbered across the open area and started up the rope Sithlac had left for him.

As all this had been going on, cars passed by occasionally on Morningside Drive, passing uncomfortably close to the stairs, but so far none had so much as paused as they rumbled down the lane. Now, however, one approached without nearly as much speed, and to everyone's surprise, it pulled into an open slot nearby and came to a halt.

"Oh, crap, move it—quick!" yelled Yog, his panicked voice reaching all the way across the upper platform. As the goblin hurriedly rolled up the rope from his side and scuttled down to the ground, Sithlac took one last look at the stairs, and, seeing no one coming, gave up his position and moved to assist the troll. Meathead, now looking quite terrified, scrambled desperately up the side as Sithlac pulled ineffectually on the rope in a vain attempt to help.

Yog came screaming over the side like a goblin possessed. "Hurry, they're coming!" he squealed, clawing his way past Sithlac and heading down as fast as he could. As though aware he had no chance of reaching the bottom in time, he instead spotted a wide enough crack to duck into and pressed himself inside, obviously intending to rely on his innate ability to become, if not invisible, at least unnoticeable by Men.

The humans came a few moments later, just as Meathead reached the top. Sithlac, moving to head down the wall and stay out of sight, saw the rope come tumbling over as the troll changed its position. Then he heard the voices, coming from very close at hand.

"So then he says, no way am I voting for that guy," a Man said forcefully, the words punctuated by a loud slamming noise. "I'm telling you, if he gets in, it's all over for us working stiffs here in the city. Might as well move back to Staten Island."

"Oh, it's not that bad," said another Man, also slamming his car door. "Mikey needs to get a grip on reality. Besides, the election's not for another week. You got plenty of time to change his mind. Now come on, let's stop with the politics, I wanna enjoy the park for a bit. Peace and quiet, y'know."

"But politics are fun," complained the other, coming around the corner and onto the platform above the stairs. I'm telling you, it's like a soap opera, but nobody knows what's comin' next. Hey, what's that?"

As the Man spoke, Meathead came into view overhead, trying to get into a position where he could descend without accidentally loosening the rope from where it had been tied. At that moment, one of the two humans glanced his way. That gave Sithlac a perfect view as the troll, shutting his eyes as though in defeat, suddenly turned to stone. The change happened in less than a second, as Meathead's living body transformed, the details spreading outward and dissolving like a reflection in the water disturbed by great ripples from below. In a moment, the troll was no longer recognizable as such, but appeared only as a smooth gray rock, with only a few pockmarks and striations where the arms and legs had been.

The Men moved over to the edge. "Huh, I thought this thing was moving for a second, but it's just a rock," the first said, grabbing hold of Meathead and lifting him up, giving him a quick once-over.

"Funny kind of stone, I'd say," commented the other. "Wonder where it came from?"

"Ah, some kid probably pulled it out of the wall. Stupid vandals—if they keep doing that, sooner or later it'll collapse. Oh well, not our problem."

"Hmm," said the other, "look down there. See that? Someone built a snowman."

The second Man glanced down toward the path. Sure enough, in between it and a grove of trees to the right, a half-melted snowman stood watch. "Oh, yeah, not much left though. I bet I know what you're gonna do now, don't I?"

"Yep. Five bucks says I hit it."

"You're on."

Sithlac's heart sank as the Man leaned back and heaved the stone over the side. The distraught gremlin watched in horror as the rock that had been his friend sailed away, struck the snowy ground just to the right of the partly melted figure, and bounced away, leaving circular indentations in the white surface as it disappeared into the brush.

"Ha! Not close enough. You owe me five bucks."

"Yeah, yeah—wait, what the hell? Holy crap!"

At that, the first Man leaned over the side, pointing, his mouth open in surprise. Sithlac had been so focused on watching Meathead's flight that he fixed both eyes on the falling troll, not keeping one of them on the humans. As they, too, watched the rock sailing away, they chanced to lean on the edge of the wall, and now the first had glanced down to spot Sithlac clinging there—unprotected by his customary illusion.

"What the hell is it?" the second man gasped. "Some kind of freaky frog thing?"

"Who knows? Quick, get your phone out!"

Of course, Sithlac couldn't understand a word of their Man-speech, but now that he'd been spotted, he had no choice but to run. He scurried down as fast as he could, angling for the shadows as the humans overhead pointed strange rectangular devices in his direction. Afraid at any moment to be struck by some sort of weapon, he hurried as fast as he could, finally leaping off into the snow at the bottom and dashing out of it as fast as he could, not stopping until he saw Lyza's familiar form waving and pointing toward a pair of stones along the nearby ridge. Darting inside, he squeezed in as far as possible, ignoring Yog's complaints, gasping for breath and shivering all over.

"It'll be okay," Lyza told him. "Luckily for you they didn't have weapons. I don't know what they were doing, but it wasn't an attack. They probably just didn't know what to make of you. We'll stay here until they're gone—I doubt they'll find us this deep inside the rocks."

"Very well," gasped Sithlac, and they did, indeed, wait there for quite a while.

Helixtech Labs – Lower Floors

The Men outside wheeled their cart around the facility for quite some time, obviously in no particular hurry. For the early part of the journey, Bongcor watched carefully from his position just above ankle level. The Men strode along through gleaming hallways similar to, but far cleaner and brighter than, the passageways he remembered from back in Adams Hall. Much of the difference came from the bright lights all around, which all but set the corridors aglow, whereas Sithlac's hunts always took place in comfortable darkness. However, there were other differences, too: floors of shimmering tiles, freshly waxed and polished; the pure whiteness of the paint and trim; the almost clinical sterility of the place. Furthermore, each of the Men that passed nearby wore shoes and clothes that shone nearly as brightly as the rest. Bongcor got the feeling that perhaps he'd never really known what it truly meant to stride through Man's dwellings, for the hunts he'd experienced before now felt like pale shadows of how humans truly lived.

The cart moved steadily through a maze of corridors, occasionally pushing through huge doors to arrive in enormous rooms just as white and clean as the rest of the place. At each such stop the workers outside lifted one or more cages free and set them on a counter or table nearby, all while speaking to other Men towering in close proximity. These errands continued for quite some time and Bongcor quickly lost interest in following along, for each delivery felt like more of the same, and he couldn't possibly keep track of how the great cave outside was organized. He decided after a while that sooner or later he, too, would be hefted onto one of those tables and then he might learn his fate at last.

Ultimately, the two workers finished their deliveries, leaving only the line of five enclosures on the bottom rack as they were. At this point they began chatting loudly between themselves as though excited by something before wheeling the cart into a small room with shiny, reflective walls. They'd already used this chamber twice before, stepping inside and waiting patiently as the doors closed, then opened again to reveal more hallways—or perhaps the same ones, Bongcor couldn't be sure. In the interim he felt a strange sensation in his stomach, as though he felt momentarily nauseous. This seemed familiar, but didn't last long and he couldn't quite place it at the time.

On this occasion, to his surprise, the two Men didn't stay in the room—instead they exited, one of them working with one of his handheld devices, while the doors slid shut. Jozan scuttled over and tapped upon the wall. "They leave us to our fate," he called out. "Where are they sending us now?"

The funny feeling in his stomach returned, even as a faint grinding sound reached Bongcor's ears. "Sending us?" he asked curiously. "What mean you by this?"

"We're moving, can't you tell?" said Jozan. "Didn't you notice before? This room moves—that's why the halls look different when the doors open."

"The room...moves...?" Bongcor stared at him for a moment and then it suddenly clicked. "This is a Hub!" he cried excitedly. "We are inside a Hub!"

The goblin just stared at him in confusion. "What do you mean? What's a Hub?"

"You have seen one not at all, then?" Bongcor shrugged. "In the great Tower of Man where my Tunnel dwells, there is a central structure called the Hub. It rises and descends, up and down, and we can ride upon it. This must be such a thing, as well—I recognize the feeling now, within my gut, as we rise high into the air."

"Yeah, yeah, I get it now," agreed Jozan. "You're right, I think we're going up! Never felt it quite like this before, not being able to see, but yeah, it makes total sense. That must be how Men get around inside all those spires they build."

"And so we learn a thing of Man," Bongcor noted, inflating his throat somewhat with pride. "That is what we should do, Jozan—learn what we can, for if we escape this place, our fellows must know what we know, to better avoid our fate."

"Sure," agreed the goblin, "whatever gets my mind off all this despair in my gut. Uh-oh, we've stopped."

The doors slid open then, and another Man appeared, pulling the cart into a hallway beyond. He wheeled them along through another corridor, but it soon opened into a much larger space, and from their position near the ground, Bongcor saw something up ahead, higher up, that looked like a vast shimmering dome, beneath which a piece of land awaited.

The Man outside bent down, his enormous face smiling at each of the containers in turn. "All right, new arrivals," he said with a smile, "welcome to your new home."

Morningside Park – South of 116th Street

"Tony, come on, seriously, the ground's soaked—my feet are gonna freeze."

His companion ignored him for a moment, pushing his way deeper into the brush, waving his cell phone in front of him. The glowing light coming from its activated flash cast flickering shadows all around, in among the leafless bushes and clumps of stones, but other than a startled squirrel that took off up the nearest tree trunk, nothing else came racing out of hiding.

"I'm telling you, that thing was not normal," said Tony after a moment, trying to step through a particularly dense cluster of branches, the tips of which clutched and clawed at his face as he poked around relentlessly.

"Yeah, yeah, I'm looking at the video I made," said his friend, standing in between a couple of patches of snow, trying to keep from sinking into the moist earth and wetting his feet too badly. "It looks kinda like a frog, but it runs like a rat, and goes down the wall like a lizard."

Tony, apparently ready to give up at last, extracted himself from the ragged bushes and slapped a few sticks and dead leaves off his coat. "So it's a frog-rat-lizard," he remarked, switching off his phone's flashlight and flipping through his own hastily taken photos. "A frograzard— sounds like one of those Pokey-whatevers my kids are always yammering on about trying to catch."

"Yeah, I guess," came the reply. "This is no game, though. We both know what we saw."

"Morty," sighed Phil, "why do you think I've been trying to run it down over here? Nobody's gonna believe a few shaky pics. It's like that Loch Ness Monster photo, you know? The thing was a toy submarine all along."

"Yeah, yeah, I know," agreed Morty with a shrug, "but you've been looking for fifteen minutes already and it's probably long gone. Plus it's almost sundown and there's no way you're finding it in the dark. Let's jog, already, before my toes freeze solid."

"Fine, fine, but before we do that, share that over to me. Come on, do it, I've got an idea."

Morty shrugged and held his phone up to his friend's, pushing a few buttons until he got the two to sync up. Tony smiled and nodded as his device beeped a moment later. "Okay, that's got it. Now hang on a sec, I'm gonna mail a sample over to someone who might want to take a closer look at it. You never know."

"What? Who are you talking about?"

"Someone who pays good money for stuff like this, my friend," said a smiling Tony, finishing off the message and hitting the Send button. "In fact, from what I hear, he'll believe just about anything."

Citizen's Reporter – Offices

Travis Hellerman unzipped his heavy coat as he made his way through the main entrance, passing by the receptionist's desk in the process. As usual, the insufferably cheerful Grace Lillian awaited him, perking up as he drew near, hopping to her feet and eagerly handing over a small stack of messages written on yellow Post-It notes.

"What's this?" asked the reporter, setting down his briefcase to collect the unusually thick stack of references. "Something new and different, I hope?"

The smiling Grace just shook her head. "Nope, just more of the same. Funny music in Central Park. Squirrels moving like they're choreographed. Flowers blooming right while people are watching. Oh, and a guy walking around with birds on his shoulder. The usual stuff."

Travis sighed. "They're just jerking me around now," he muttered, shaking his head and rubbing absently at his sore nose, which still hurt almost a month after getting punched in the face outside his own office. "They're taunting me."

"What's that?" Grace inquired, not quite hearing his low-volume mumblings. "Sorry, sir, I didn't—"

"It's not important," said Travis gruffly, flipping through the notes in haste. "The guy with the birds—did he match the profile of Dave Thompson, by any chance?"

"Not really, more like the other one—Kyle what's-his-name. Is this some kind of prank I should know about?"

"Probably," replied the reporter, "but keep collecting the reports. If they're trying to get a rise out of me, it's not going to work, and sooner or later they'll make a mistake. I don't suppose there's anything in here that doesn't have to do with Central Park?"

Grace shrugged. "Well, something came onto the email account with pictures of some kind of weird frog-thing running down the wall in Morningside Park, but it looked pretty fake to me. It just came in like ten minutes ago, so you won't have to scroll far. Might be worth a closer look, though."

"Okay, I'll see what's up," said Travis, brightening up at the prospect of something new that didn't involve potential faerie activity in Midtown. "Thanks, Grace. I'll take a look, then stick around for a couple more hours polishing up my main article."

"That's good because Dean said if you go home without finishing, it better be because you coughed up a lung."

"Yeah, yeah," chuckled Travis. "Tell him not to worry, it'll be in his email box by seven. Let me know if anything else interesting happens."

"I always do," agreed Grace, sitting back down at her desk, whereupon she set immediately to going over the next batch of incoming messages. Travis, meanwhile, removed his coat, laid it over his arm, and collected his briefcase with some difficulty. Then he made his way to his office, carefully holding onto all the Post-Its, waving like little flags in the air as he shuffled steadily along.

Once inside his private space, he tossed the stack down disdainfully and plopped into his chair, frowning at the slight joint pain that ached every time he got into or out of his seat. He felt older every day, it seemed, and recent events only made things worse, forcing him into long hours in the park that left his feet sore and muscles throbbing. He reached into his desk for some Tylenol, but shook off the impulse and leaned back instead, taking a few deep breaths and willing away the pain.

Just about a month ago, he had the story of a lifetime stolen from him, and now he couldn't let it go. He'd found a faerie—an actual, live one, not just grainy photos or shaking video—and brought her to his office, where he had her safely locked away, or so he thought. Somehow, despite everything, her human friends, Dave Thompson and Kyle Morris, tracked her down and rescued her, fleeing into Central Park and eluding pursuit. During the chase, Travis had his nose broken by a lucky punch, and while the injury had mostly healed, it still felt sore all the time, especially in the cold. He rubbed the bridge absently, feeling the kink underneath the cartilage that would likely be with him for the rest of his life, scowling at the thought of it.

Since the escape, Travis lost all track of Dave Thompson, who apparently vanished off the face of the Earth. He never returned to Columbia University, apparently, and nobody had seen him since. Kyle Morris, on the other hand, went back and got to work almost immediately helping clear out Dave's dorm, apparently not the least bit concerned by his lifelong friend's disappearance. With some detective work, Travis managed to locate Dave's mother in Albany, but she refused all phone calls and interview requests, wanting nothing whatsoever to do with any reporters. After the third such attempt, Travis found himself in possession of a crisply folded cease and desist letter, topped with a threateningly delivered cover page on the letterhead of one of New York's top law firms, so he grudgingly dropped that angle. Still, he did what he could to keep an eye on the other one, Kyle, without being too obvious about it.

In the past few weeks, Kyle made regular trips to Central Park, where he went on long walks alone, and occasionally sat for short periods feeding pigeons, watching football on one mobile device or another, or just relaxing in the chilly winter air. Travis himself did the surveillance on more than one occasion, but usually relied on office interns looking to make an extra buck or two on the side. Kyle never did anything unusual, unless you count talking to yourself as strange—which Kyle did frequently, even looking around from time to time as if speaking to an invisible friend.

Travis had a pretty good idea what his quarry was up to, but somehow the faerie remained out of sight, even to cameras and passersby. Nobody ever seemed to notice anything unusual, but Kyle managed to have long conversations with empty air, and unless he'd set up some sort of long-term unending prank, he had to be talking to the faerie. Yet Travis knew if he confronted the annoying college student about it, he'd just button up and refuse to say a word.

So Travis just continued his surveillance, knowing one day, sooner or later, one of them would make a mistake, and he could take advantage of it. His last article, with the photos he'd taken of the tiny winged woman, received quite a bit of acclaim, though as usual his audience wanted more. If he could catch the little creature again, and prove to the world this wasn't just another batch of tabloid nonsense, his life would be complete.

Not now, though. Things like this had to simmer for a while, bubbling on the back burner, until they were ready. In the meantime, he had another article to finish, and a few more leads to look into. He decided to start with the latter, scrolling down through his messages until he came to the one about the strange frog-rat-lizard in Morningside Park.

He studied the images for a while, as well as the choppy video, and had to admit there might be something to them. The pictures didn't have the usual Photoshop telltales, and the videos looked remarkably seamless. The email said there was more, as well, but he'd have to inquire—which meant the owner expected to be paid. Travis nodded to himself, accepting this as a matter of standard procedure, and typed out a quick reply, sending it on its way.

"Monster in Morningside," he muttered to himself, imagining the article title already, the wrinkled corners of his mouth turning up into a smile.

Morningside Park – South of 116th Street

"I think they're gone," said Yog, poking his head back into the hollow space under the rocks. "They were standing around yammering for a bit, then they put those box things away and took off running. Yep, there they go, down around the path, like they forgot about us already."

"What is it with humans and running?" wondered Lyza, shaking her head as she stepped out into the evening gloom. With dusk fallen, the lamps overhead provided a pale, unnatural glow, making the darkening park look like a shadowy, indistinct version of itself. "They do that all the time, you know. Running back and forth, on the paths, not really going anywhere. You think it's some kind of punishment?"

"Maybe they just do it for fun," suggested Yog with a shrug. "Who knows why Men do the stuff they do? Anyway, let's go find Stony, before he turns back to normal and wonders where we disappeared to."

Lyza nodded. "More than likely he'll be stuck that way a bit longer, especially as long as those Men were looking around out there, but you could be right. Come on out of there, Sithlac—you're the one who saw where he went."

"Could you not track him?" inquired the gremlin, quivering a bit as he emerged into the open, still not quite recovered from the terrifying encounter fifteen minutes before. In all his wanderings through Adams Hall, and in the Outside during mating-time, he'd never once had a human look directly at him before. Something about being seen by one just made his blood turn cold and his whole body shake and shudder.

"Sure, I could," Lyza responded with a smile, "but that might take a while, so why don't you just take the lead?"

Sithlac nodded uncomfortably and started forward, holding Bongcor's spear before him as though it would be of any use whatsoever should the Men return. He plodded along slowly, bypassing one of the tufts of half-melted snow, paying no attention to the squishing of his feet on the moist earth. With his frost-ward renewed, he didn't feel the least bit physically cold, but the ever-present fear left him chilled nonetheless.

After a few minutes they left the open ground and came to a carpet of crunchy snow, through which several human footprints could be seen—leftovers from the joggers' wanderings as they tried tracking him down earlier. Beyond these, several upturned spots marked the places where Meathead's rocky form bounced along, heading gradually downhill. At the sight of this track, Lyza frowned and put up a hand, causing the others to stop at once.

"What?" demanded Yog. "You see something?"

"No, not yet," replied the elf, "but this is the edge of Sprucebow territory. I was hoping to stay along the edge of the park, and work our way around to the nexus, but it looks like Meaty bounced right through that plan. Stay on alert—this particular tribe won't be too happy if they catch intruders on their lands. If we do meet them, just let me do the talking, okay? I'm at least known to them, so I might be able to get us through."

"Okay, sure," agreed Yog, "but I could really use the Moon right about now—getting low on *kai* here. Stupid whisks."

"Not for a while yet," explained Lyza. "It has to top the rise first. Can't you darklings just soak it up out of the night air?"

"Should we stay quiet and calm, oh yes, this can be done," answered Sithlac, "but a slow process it is. In such a place, wrapped in worry and fear, it is possible not at all."

Lyza nodded. "All the more reason to stay quiet and look as non-threatening as possible. Yog, I know how much you like disappearing when trouble shows up, but don't even try that with these forest elves. By the time we see them, they'll already have spotters watching you. Try vanishing and you'll find yourself full of arrows. Just stay close, keep your weapons down and let me talk us out of it."

"Okay, okay," agreed the goblin morosely, "but I'm quicker than you think. They try anything and I'm gone."

"The blow will come without warning," she hissed, continuing to press on across the soft blanket of snow. "Now, quiet! There, look, see that? Meaty bounced here, and here, but now it's not holes, but a track. He must've started rolling, which means he's not far off. Yep, there, I think I see him—aww, how pretty, he's all wrapped up in white! Come on!"

They hurried forward, and came upon what looked like a boulder coated in snow, some of it already melting away. Lyza strapped her bow over her shoulder and started wiping the icy coating off, while Sithlac used his spear to accomplish much the same thing. Meanwhile Yog moved around back, clambered up on some withered ivy, and swung over to land atop the rock with a flourish. He kicked the snow away and sat down in satisfaction. "There, now I'm like a troll-hat!" he chuckled aloud. "Say, can he see us like this? Does he know we're here?"

"From what he's told me, yes, in a way," explained Lyza, "but it's more like a dream, if that makes any sense. When he comes back to normal, he'll remember we were here with him—so don't do what you're thinking of, if you know what's good for you!"

"Oh, you wound me, friend elf!" laughed Yog from atop the rocky troll, feigning a sudden embarrassment. "It does sound like a really gobliny thing to do, though, doesn't it?" He patted the stone below him with both hands. "Don't worry, bud, I'm not gonna deface you—not gonna risk never getting any more of your soup, that's for sure! In fact, I'll—"

"Hssst!" Lyza interrupted, raising a hand and glancing around at the shadowy brush all around. Meathead's flight, and subsequent rolling, brought him to the edge of a dense pack of undergrowth, near a partly decayed log coated in snow. The elf-girl glanced to and fro, her eyes wide as she peered into the shadows, before finally hopping up onto the log and raising a single arm skyward. Meanwhile, the others went completely silent, standing in place as though paralyzed.

"I am Lyza Sparrow-wind," she called out into the gloom, "tale-spinner and seeker of news and knowledge. My companions and I seek no trouble within these lands, only safe passage as we search for a lost friend."

Yog, still perched on Meathead's stony figure, exchanged worried glances with Sithlac, the latter rotating a single eye toward the goblin momentarily while the other peered into the darkness. The gremlin felt his fear abating, much to his surprise, for the thought of dealing with elves didn't worry him nearly as much as the gigantic Men. For a few moments, though, he saw and heard nothing, wondering if perhaps he should risk a sight-enhancing chant—but before he could utter a single syllable, a tall shape stepped out from the shadows alongside the fallen log, emerging as though from nowhere.

The elf, a male, wore a full-length brown and green coverall festooned with small twigs, clumps of mud, and here and there a speckle of partly melted snow. As he emerged, he reached up and removed a leather helmet, revealing a thin, angular face with pointed chin and ears, but a tiny nose that looked far too small to be useful. He glanced momentarily up at Lyza, then turned his gaze to Sithlac and Yog, who obeyed orders and remained still, keeping their weapons lowered and trying very hard not to appear threatening.

"Well met, Lyza," the elf called out, "and your songs are most welcome here, in ordinary times, but pray tell, what twist of fate brings you here in the company of a goblin, a gremlin, and a troll?" He flashed a quick glance at the partly defrosted rock nearby.

"Galisan Badger-hunter," replied Lyza, quickly dropping back down to ground level, "it's good to see you again. Still captain of the outer ring, I see. I thought perhaps to find you here."

"Your charming words won't work this time, Lyza," the guardsman responded, his hands moving threateningly toward twin weapons sheathed at his sides. Atop the stone, Yog glanced furtively about, but stopped at the barest glance from his companions. "As you must surely know, we are once again at war with the Birchspears, and we have no tolerance for spies."

"We knew not of this development, I assure you," responded Lyza, her voice sounding forceful and self-assured, but the others caught the vaguest sense of concern in her words. With as much confidence as she could muster, she turned to her companions. "This is Sithlac, a gremlin dwelling in one of Man's great towers. He witnessed one of his fellows captured and taken away by Men. We seek to pass through these woods in order to track him down, and learn the nature of Man's plans for him."

Galisan shook his head, and made a couple of gestures with his hands. Sithlac, remaining still, picked out brief hints of motion nearby, his eyes independently flicking toward the cause. He saw no one, but here and there a piece of vegetation twitched in the shadows, or a patch of snow showed a disturbance that wasn't there moments ago. He got the sense that more than just a couple of other elves were out there, moving to surround the little group. All at once he understood completely why Lyza insisted on doing the talking, for with a single gesture the captain of the guard could bring the gremlin's quest to a swift and brutal end.

"There are no Men here, save those upon the paths, as they always are, and likely always will be," said the elven patrolman firmly. "By what logic do you reason to track a missing gremlin through our territory in pursuit of such?"

Lyza nodded slowly. "It is a tale better served by song," she noted succinctly, "but I sense you have little patience this night. Suffice to say we seek the faeries of the Greater Park, and intend to transit there using the Waterfall Nexus—thence not to trouble you again."

"How the faeries could assist, I can but only imagine," replied Galisan, looking no less relaxed with this utterance, "but you're quite right—I have no interest in hearing your song. Explain to me why you pass this way, when you know full well you could avoid our borders should you so choose."

Lyza sighed, patting at the rocky body of the troll by her side. "As should be obvious, we came hither not by choice," she explained. "As we attempted to bypass your lands, we were seen by Men. One of them used my poor companion here as—well, as the ammunition in a game of target practice, is the best way to put it. Upon his return to his true form, we'll exit back the way we came, and give your lands a wide berth—on this you have my word."

Galisan nodded, frowning slightly—the first emotion he'd shown during the conversation. He looked around at the others, focusing his gaze on each, before returning once more to Lyza. "I know from experience your word is your bond," he said sadly, "but I'm afraid this is beyond my control. I have orders, you see—orders not to permit any intrusion."

Lyza shut her eyes momentarily, before fixing them once again on his. "Galisan, I've visited your camps on many occasions," she told him firmly. "I've traded news and songs for many seasons, in times of war and of peace. I've always obeyed your rules and kept your secrets—you know this to be true."

"That may be so," said the guardsman, "but I can't disobey my—"

"What we're doing here is greater than your current troubles," Lyza interrupted, starting to grow a bit desperate now. "In case I didn't make our predicament clear, Sithlac's friend was kidnapped by Men. Do you understand what that means? The Men set a trap designed specifically to capture and abduct the Fey. That means they've found a way to break through our defenses—the Great Bargain is at risk! What happens if humans come back here, able to see us clearly, immune to elven magic, and armed with nets and cages? What good is your tribal animosity then? You have to let us pass, Galisan. We've got to get to the bottom of this.

Why else would I travel with such as these? This danger affects all Fey—forestals, darklings, windshears—everyone. You shouldn't be threatening to stop us—you should be begging to join us! Help us, Galisan, I beg you, or everything we know could be lost!"

The elven captain sighed and lowered his head. For a brief moment he remained silent, as though gravely considering her words and then he pulled his camouflage helmet back on, tugging it into place with a flourish. "Your words are compelling, Lyza Sparrow-wind," he said, stepping back toward the log, "and rest assured I'll report your sad tale to my superiors, but this is where we part ways. If it makes you feel any better, I'll miss your songs most greatly. Farewell."

"No, please—!" begged Lyza, taking a step forward, but as she did, Galisan made a quick motion with his hand. Instantly, several other figures stepped into view, surrounding the group, each pointing a well-made bow at its target. As one they drew back to fire, following their orders implicitly, but even as they did the air all around suddenly erupted.

With all the talking going on, Sithlac hadn't noticed the way the winds nearby came to a halt, plunging the little group into an area of unusual calm. Now, in the blink of an eye, all of that changed, a swirling gust rising up out of nowhere, spinning and howling as though a storm descended out of the clear night sky. The elves nonetheless loosed their arrows, but the whirlwind swept the projectiles away before they could strike home, sending them spinning out of control into the darkness.

"What foul magic is this?" gasped Galisan, grabbing hold of a chunk of wood protruding from the log by his side. "You dare seize hold of the very winds themselves? I should think you not so foolish, Lyza—you know where such a thing must lead!"

As he shouted out those words, Yog dropped off the troll's stone shoulder all the way down to the ground, landing next to the surprised Sithlac. They, as well as Lyza, stood amid the eye of the storm, their clothing barely waving in the breeze, while beyond, the elven soldiers struggled to keep their feet. "It was not I who loosed this maelstrom," the tale-spinner insisted, "nor either of these others."

Galisan reached for his blades, leaning forward into the gale. "Then who—?" he began, but just as quickly got his answer.

Above the others, a tiny figure descended, flickering and glowing in the darkness, flitting back and forth like an angry hornet. "I'm the cause, as you can see," shrieked a furious Ithess. "There's no doubt you should fear me! I call the winds to save these four, and seal my doom forevermore! Now go, be quick, if you're to live—I have no patience left to give!"

Galisan, scowling under his hooded helm, started to draw his weapons, but as he did Ithess rose up higher, her frail little figure gesturing outward with both hands. The gale winds increased still further, knocking down most of the others, the captain holding steady only by pressing himself up against the nearby log. As the winds whipped about him, flaying away most of the leaves and twigs from his carefully designed camouflage, he at last gave up, giving a "retreat" gesture to his patrol team. At this the others scrambled away, taking their bows with them as they scrambled into the darkness.

After a few moments Ithess lowered her hands and descended into Lyza's waiting palm. She settled there, breathing heavily, as the storm gradually faded. Before anyone could say a word of thanks, though, an odd cracking sound echoed out of the gloom nearby, and the stony figure of Meathead began to move. Within moments he'd returned to his normal form, unfolding like a man rising to his feet after lying for hours in the fetal position.

"Ah, good ta be back," rumbled the troll, stretching and yawning as though having awoken from a long nap, "and I ain't avoidin' givin' thanks where it's due, but maybe we oughta move off, afore them elves come back?"

"They won't return," said Lyza sadly, cradling the tiny zephyr in her hands. "Even now they're racing for their shelters—they know what comes next."

"What?" demanded Yog. "The whole lot of us telling Ithess here how amazing that was? Because wow, for such a little critter, you sure are a force for reckoning!"

"For these others I cannot speak," added Sithlac, "but you certainly saved me, for I possess no skills to save myself just now. For this I am in your debt."

Ithess rose up into the air, shaking off a momentary bout of weakness after what must've been a significant effort on her part. "I'm glad to help, you owe me none," she sang quietly, "but my ordeal has just begun. I'm not allowed out here, you see, but quiet stillness wasn't me. The need was great, I had to act, and now I'm through and that's a fact. Concern you not about my fate, better now and not too late. I've had my fun these last few days, but now it's time that we part ways."

Sithlac just stared at her, both eyes fixed on the tiny zephyr. "I understand not at all," he told her. "Whatever concerns you, let us help—"

"You mustn't stay, it's time to go," Ithess insisted. "This I always had to know. She comes for me, and I'll not run—I always knew my day was done. You'd better go, and please don't stay; just know now it's best this way. I really hope you find your friend—but now, for me, this is the end. Remember when you sing your song: stay true to you, you can't go wrong."

At that she flew up to Sithlac and caressed his face with both hands, causing him to shudder involuntarily, completely at a loss for words. As Meathead shuffled uncomfortably behind them, Lyza reached up to wipe away a tear, glancing suddenly off to the side as a distinct, distant howl echoed through the trees.

"What is she singing about now?" demanded Yog. "What does she mean, her day is done? And what's that awful noise?"

"She broke the rules," Lyza replied sadly. "Now she has to pay the price—and that sound you're hearing is the enforcer, coming to collect."

"What enforcer?" Yog asked nervously, even as Meathead, the hulking brute whose strength dwarfed them all, looked skyward and cringed in obvious fear. Something that could terrify a troll must be dangerous indeed. The goblin, sensing the shifting mood, produced his dagger from its hidden sheath as though preparing to fight.

"Something we don't have a chance of defeating, if that's what you're intending," Lyza insisted. "Our best chance now is to make for the nexus, and fast."

"Why?" Yog went on, crouching and hissing in defiance. "What is it? What's coming?"

Lyza didn't answer right away, instead turning toward the rapidly growing wailing noise approaching from the east. The howling whipped up the wind, rattling the trees, sending snow whirling everywhere in the fading twilight. Even the humans on the paths took notice, retreating from the area in sudden haste, either fleeing the park or desperately seeking shelter as best they could. As the noise grew in strength, drawing ever closer, Lyza finally turned to the others, her next words barely above a whisper.

"It's a banshee."

Helixtech Labs – Top Floor

Bongcor watched, crouching down low, as the Men outside rolled the cart up to the edge of the immense central platform. He no longer felt merely afraid, but completely numb with dread, aware that at any moment his life might come to a sudden end at the hands of these cruel, uncaring giants. His eyes flicked this way and that, seeing their legs moving back and forth as they walked, carrying him to some unknown fate. Ahead, high above, he could just see the edge of the glass dome atop the huge table, and somehow he knew that's where they intended to put him.

A few moments later, after more guttural chanting from outside, one of the Men started lifting the cages off the bottom shelf, saving Bongcor for last. Each of the small enclosures moved rapidly up and out of sight, while the Men did something up top that concluded with a loud scraping sound and a few harsh clatters. Bongcor shivered, yet to his surprise he felt his terror fading, for he now no longer expected death to come. The Men wanted him for something else, some other purpose entirely, and killing him was not their plan. Were it so, they would've put him down much sooner, of that he felt quite sure.

As a result of this revelation, when the hands reached down to collect him, he almost felt relieved. Instead of cowering as before, he lifted himself up, peering out to see what lay ahead. He saw through the glass a great domed enclosure, looking much like a piece of open land in the park, although seeing as he'd never been beyond the walls of Adams Hall, he didn't make the connection. The grass, sparse bushes, and transplanted tree stump he saw registered in his mind as something natural from Outside, but he knew little else of such things.

Instead, he found his attention captured by the other Fey within—two elves and a goblin, staring back at him from the shadow of a large, leafy plant. He caught a glimpse of them only for a moment before the Man nearby rotated the cage so the metal door faced a panel set into the dome. He slid both apertures open and then rapped on the walls with a stick, pointing at the exit.

Suddenly Jozan appeared in the square opening beyond, apparently having already been released from his own confines. "Come on out," he said urgently. "If you don't, they'll drag you out like they did to Telan. He still looks pretty stunned, too."

Bongcor nodded and partially stood, then remembered he was supposed to be in his cat disguise and moved forward on all fours. The Man outside grunted something and smiled, obviously pleased to not have to use force to extract the gremlin from his cage. As soon as Bongcor cleared the opening, the observer slid the panel shut, clamped it down with a latch, and retreated, taking the glass-walled enclosure with him.

The new arrival watched with one eye as the Man outside turned to two others and began a noisy conversation. Bongcor's other eye swung over to regard Jozan, and the shaken-looking elf behind him, leaning up against a large, roughly square-shaped stone. From behind that, another goblin peeked out, his eyes huge and fairly shining with terror, before suddenly darting off and disappearing into the bushes.

After a moment Bongcor's roving eye fell once more upon the three Fey partially concealed under the great leaves of the unusual plant a short distance away. As he fixed his gaze on them, the two elves stepped forward while the goblin stayed behind. The elves, both males, wore crude clothing sewn together out of dried bark and animal fur. One, slightly taller and thinner, covered his upper arms with some sort of black, shiny material that turned out to be fitted pieces of thick insect shells, put to use as armor of a sort. In one hand he carried a short-hafted club tipped with a barbed spine or stinger, perhaps from a dangerous insect. The other one, with noticeably darker clothing, wore a large belt upon which hung a short sword made of sharpened metal. Though armed, they didn't approach in a threatening manner and Bongcor felt no concern at all as they moved closer.

"Hail to our new fellow prisoners," said the one with the club. "I am Nolzun, formerly of the Greenbriar tribe, and this is Tomluk of the Turtleshells. Behind me lurks Tox of the Deepwound enclave, but he's a bit skittish around newcomers. The rest are too tired or bored to come greet you, so it falls to us to welcome you to your new home, such as it is."

Bongcor started to reply, but before he could, the injured elf struggled to his feet and forced himself forward. "I am Telan of the Rimefire elves," he said, still somewhat wobbly. "Your people and mine are sworn enemies."

As he spoke those words Bongcor took note of the youthful elf's attire, which, unlike the others, looked more like a uniform: strips of carefully sewn together cloth, with dyed stripes of green and brown up and down his back, and tall boots made of cured animal skins. At his side hung a long dagger similar to that carried by Tomluk, and his broad shoulders supported a shortbow and quiver, yet he made no move to draw any of these weapons—wisely so, perhaps, considering his current condition and the fact that he was outnumbered two to one.

"That may be so," replied Tomluk with a casual shrug, "but in case you didn't notice, we're not in our home territory any more. This is neutral ground, and we must work together if we wish to face our current enemy." He pointed at the Men outside, now peering through the grass and watching the little assembly with curiosity. One of them held a small notepad and stood stock still, while the other two chatted openly between themselves.

"Our old animosities serve no purpose here," agreed Nolzun. "Living under the Dome, we are all on the same side. Therefore, we ask that you honor this truce for as long as you remain within. No violence is permitted here—not just by us, but by them as well. Should you cause trouble, you'll be removed, to face whatever punishment the Men see fit to impose upon you."

Telan nodded at that, shaking his head and rubbing his temples vigorously. "Good, I was hoping for something like this. Upon seeing this place, a part of me thought perhaps we were expected to do battle for the entertainment of those monsters out there. You have my word I'll observe this truce as you say, but now I must ask—are there any other elves here? I seek my charge and consort, Lady Sellyn, Princess of the Rimefire tribe, who attempted to escape not four dawnings past and was taken away by Men."

The two elves exchanged glances. "Your consort, is she?" asked Tomluk. "You have the look of a soldier, not of royalty."

Telan sighed, clenching his fingers together and frowning as though trying to contain his emotions. "She is—we had a—ugh, this is harder than I thought," he complained. "The circumstances no longer matter, I suppose, trapped as we are within this place. She and I first met when I was assigned to her as a bodyguard. We—well, I fought well to defend her during an ambush, and she rewarded me with—oh, never mind about the details." He flushed somewhat at the memory.

"We all have stories," Nolzun pointed out. "You'll hear ours in time, as well, but do go on."

"We were in love," said Telan with a sad sigh, "but kept this fact well hidden, denying the truth even to ourselves. When we were captured by the Men, we thought our lives short, and confessed all to each other. We took our private vows, then, in Gaia's name, and are betrothed; thus it is I can call her my consort for now, although I doubt this will be looked upon well should we somehow return home. I wish only to be with her, above all else, and protect her from further harm, so if you know of her whereabouts, please, I beg you, tell me now."

Nolzun shook his head. "I don't know if she's the one you speak of," he explained, pointing out into the vast space beyond the Dome, "but we saw an elf-maid brought in some days ago, trapped within a smaller cage and quite alone. She was placed there, in a special compartment amid the strange structures the Men have built to aid them in their terrible work. Since then we haven't seen her, but the Man who works in that part of the great chamber spends a great deal of time there—your consort is most likely alive, but I dare not think of what she must be going through."

Telan moved over to the edge of the Dome and put his hands on the wall, peering through. The huge open space beyond, lit by strange artificial lamps, seemed filled with shadows and strange, sharply angled structures. He shook his head and shut his eyes. "I must find her," he said in a low voice. "I must save her, and flee this place somehow."

"There's no way out—believe me, we've tried," explained Tomluk. "No spells can pierce this strange, clear material that surrounds us, and even the trolls lack the strength to move those doorways aside. Even if we did escape, we don't know where we are, or how to get back home. You'll come to realize that, in time, but for now, we leave you to your grief. Now what of you, goblin and gremlin? Who are you and how came you here?"

"I am Jozan, of the Dark Oak enclave," said the goblin in a friendly tone. "Nice meeting you. They grabbed me when I went to check out the funny-looking box that wasn't there when I passed by that spot earlier."

"Bongcor am I, of the Morningside Tunnel," the gremlin answered. "I too explored a strange structure, in the same place as Jozan, yet a single moonrise apart. Unlike him, I had friends observe my capture, and thus, I have some hope of rescue."

The two elves exchanged glances. "Not likely, unless your friends can move through Man-lands unimpeded," said Tomluk. "Might as well forget that possibility. Let me explain what's going on here, in case you haven't figured it out. These Men know who and what we are—not by name, obviously, as they can't speak to us, but they can see our true forms, no matter what spells we weave to hide ourselves. As you look out there, you can see several different Men, including that scary-looking female who stares at us endlessly while only barely moving. Each of them has their own tasks and they perform them with ruthless precision."

"What tasks?" asked Jozan worriedly.

"They change details with each rising of the Sun, or so it seems," answered Nolzun grimly, "but they test us with their hands and tools. They make us do things, and cause pain when we refuse. They watch us work our spells and charms with great intensity, and work sometimes to repeat our words and gestures—never with any success, of course, for what Man can do Fey magic? Yet we have come to believe that this must be their true goal—to find a way to command the magic that is denied them, by learning our ways and methods."

"Then we must not assist," Bongcor replied immediately. "We must not allow Man to command that which is ours alone!"

"That's easy for you to say now," replied Nolzun with a faint shudder, "but not so when you're clamped on a slab of wood while sharp tools caress your flesh."

Bongcor cringed at those words, while Jozan just shook his head sadly. "Men already own the world," he said, scowling. "What do they need our magic for? What good would it do them to possess even more power than they already have?"

"We have no idea," Tomluk answered, "but you might find comfort in knowing that so far, they haven't succeeded. I think that's why they're so interested in his consort, though."

At that, Telan perked up again and regarded the speaker with a grim scowl. "What do you mean by that?" he demanded.

"I know of your Princess Sellyn," replied Tomluk, giving a casual shrug. "Like the members of our own royal family, she wields great power, is that not so? One such as she would be a great help to their wicked plans."

"All the more reason I must find and free her," complained Telan, staring back out through the thick glass. "I don't know if you can hear me, my love," he whispered, "but I'm coming for you, somehow—this I swear!"

Tomluk rolled his eyes at that. "I felt as he did when I first arrived, twenty-two dawnings ago," he explained. "I stood with my hands upon this unbreakable surface and swore I would escape. I needed five more dawns to realize the futility of such a vow and rescind it. Now I seek only to survive and hope that one day the Men realize the folly of their task and set us free, or slay us and end our misery at last. The sooner you accept your place here, and embrace the same conclusion, the better off you'll be."

Bongcor bobbed his head up and down. "I speak not of how I might feel in future-times unknown," he noted, "but I as yet refuse to give up hope. I will do as the Men require, but as I am but a lesser gremlin, lacking in any true abilities or skills, I feel I will be of no use to them. Now I must inquire, do other gremlins dwell within this place?"

"There are two," said Nolzun sadly, "but unlike you, they've surrendered all hope, and mostly sleep within small dens beyond the further stump. We also have three other goblins besides Tox back there, but they couldn't be bothered to come meet you. The others you can meet on your own, when they choose to come out, probably in the morning."

"Oh, that's another thing you need to keep in mind around here," put in Tomluk. "We're all stuck together under this Dome, and so there's not a lot of places we can go to be alone, except that which you make for yourself. You can dig out a burrow or make a shelter out of whatever you like—branches, leaves, or anything else you find that someone isn't using. The only thing we ask is that you respect the domain of others here. Don't go poking into any holes or camps without permission and don't touch anyone else, or wake them, unless you've got their word that it's okay. Got that?"

The newcomers nodded, and as they did, Nolzun pointed upward, toward the distant ceiling. Far above, beyond the top of the curving glass, they could see what looked like flat panels, the faint lights of stars just barely glimmering in the dark. "High up there," said the elf, "way above the top of the Dome, there are openings to the sky—covered in more of this unbreakable *rinitani*, no doubt, but it lets in the light of the Sun and the Moon, so you can take as much *kai* as you wish. Oh, and the Men are fully aware we use that light to power our magic—if you try to rebel against their wishes by keeping in the shadows and not restocking, they'll punish you until you comply."

"Good to know," said Jozan with a snort. "We are naught but slaves to them—playthings forced to dance upon command. A terrible fate, indeed."

"Yes, well, we'll leave you to contemplate that as you like," went on Nolzun, brushing off those words as unimportant, or perhaps something he already knew quite well and thus deserved no further comment. "With the setting of the Sun, we choose to retire for the night. Feel free to wander about and explore, but as my companion said, don't go poking into anybody's lair. When you see a spot you think might be a good place to claim for yourself, just go for it—nobody's going to stop you, and once you're settled in, that'll be your place from that point on."

"Oh, and if you see any others, feel free to say hello," Tomluk continued. "Once the Men leave for the night, which they will soon enough, the trolls will awaken and they might feel like chatting. Most of the others like to keep to themselves, though, so don't get too pushy. If they don't want to talk, leave them be. This whole thing will be more bearable if we don't get on each other's nerves."

At that, Nolzun gave a protracted yawn. "Okay, that's it for me," he told the others. "Time to get some sleep. Good luck, and well met."

He and the other elf sauntered off, and as they did, Telan hesitated momentarily before following close behind. He started to ask another question, but the trio quickly moved out of earshot. Jozan looked up at Bongcor and gave a quick shrug, and as he did the other goblin, who so far had barely moved, suddenly approached.

"S-sorry I didn't c-come up s-sooner," he squeaked in a thin, nervous voice. "Th-those elves are s-so big, and—and I didn't w-want to be rude. M-my name's Tox."

"Jozan," came the swift reply, "and this is Bongcor."

"It—it's nice to m-meet you both," the little figure twittered, keeping his gaze fixed on Jozan. "Th-there are other goblins here, as the t-tall one said. W-we have a c-communal hole, and you are—are w-welcome to join us. G-goblins only, I fear...so sorry, friend g-gremlin, but w-we cannot share our space with you."

Bongcor nodded. "I understand most surely, oh yes I do indeed," he replied without a hint of disappointment, for he'd expected no less—he knew full well the gregarious nature of goblins, and had no interest in staying close by a large number of them. "Solitude is my preference, so worry not at all. I shall seek a place to be alone."

"Thanks, Bongcor," replied Jozan, reaching up to pat him gently on the arm. "Keep hoping, too. Maybe your friends will come."

"I hope so, well and truly," he replied with a nod, but he let his throat deflate completely nonetheless.

Morningside Park – Sprucebow Border

Sithlac just stared at Lyza for a moment, one eye fixed on the elf while the other flitted back and forth between her and Ithess. He knew very little of banshees—terrible creatures loosed in the heart of the fiercest storms, or so he'd been told. He considered them on par with demons: dangerous monsters best avoided at all costs. Why one would be here, now, menacing a tiny zephyr and her companions, he couldn't even fathom.

Ithess, for her part, just nodded sadly. "It's true, I really must admit—but that's not the heart of it," she told them urgently. "I've not the time to say it all, lest my doom besets you all. Suffice to say it's what I've earned, because of who and what I've spurned. Please don't try to resist her...let me face my own sister."

"Your sister?" Lyza just gawked at her. "You—I knew you must've done something terrible to be cut off from the air, but—you never told me..."

Ithess hung her head. "She sought to bend the winds just so," said the zephyr, her voice getting more difficult to hear over the approaching tempest. "I never should've let her go. The power claimed her then, you see, and now this time she comes for me."

"I have no idea what's going on right now," Yog interjected, "but judging by the way the trees are swaying, we really oughta leave if we're gonna."

"Yeah, I gotta agree with the pipsqueak," huffed Meathead, looking very nervous and worried. "A banshee's wrath ain't nothin' to take lightly. Come on, climb aboard," he insisted, putting down a hand before Yog. "You were comfy sittin' on me before, now you can hang on while I run us outta here."

While the goblin climbed aboard, quickly scuttling up onto the troll's shoulder, Sithlac moved to follow, but found himself hesitating. Lyza, for her part, whispered something else to the forlorn-looking zephyr, who floated in the air, already looking defeated. *Something about this doesn't feel right*, the gremlin considered, and even though he knew he should start hurrying away, his feet didn't want to move.

"Come on," urged Lyza, putting a hand on his shoulder. "She sacrificed herself to save us. We can't let that be in vain."

"I understand this not at all," muttered Sithlac, still unable to take his left eye off the hovering zephyr in the clearing. "For what transgression has she been sentenced to death?"

"She took control of the wind," answered Lyza sadly, even as Ithess shut her eyes and rose higher into the air. "Zephyrs aren't supposed to do that—nobody is."

"But she controls the wind at her whim," complained Sithlac.

"They can move still air about, as they choose," said Lyza, "and ask the winds for help, in time of need—but the air is a force of nature, like the earth and fire. No Fey dares take direct control. I think that's what her sister must've done—anyway, we don't have time to argue about it. Come on, unless you want the banshee's wrath to fall upon you, too."

Sithlac looked up at Lyza, twisting both eyes to meet the elf-girl's much smaller ones. He struggled with himself for a moment, even as a faint melody echoed through his head, along with Ithess's words from mere moments ago.

Remember when you sing your song: stay true to you, you can't go wrong...

"Depart if you must," said the gremlin, shuddering slightly as the howling wind grew ever louder. "I wish you well, but I will stand with her, as best I can." He hefted up his spear, wishing he felt even close to as confident as his words made him sound.

"This is madness," insisted Lyza. "You'll die for no reason—"

"Ithess risked all to come with us," Sithlac snapped back. "She knows most of us barely at all, yet chose to do what must be done, to protect her friends. I can do no less."

Lyza glanced away, toward the barely visible silhouettes of Meathead and Yog, about to make their way into the nearby thicket. For an instant she started to join them, but just as quickly came up short, drawing her bow in a single quick motion. "For someone so new to the concept of friendship," muttered the elf, "you seem to have it all figured out, don't you? Very well, gremlin, I'll stand my ground—perhaps one day a tale-spinner will tell our story, too." She patted him on the back before turning to face the approaching storm.

"Please, you really must not fight," called out Ithess, her thin voice barely audible now over the roaring winds. "You'll perish here, and that's not right."

"Ithess," said Lyza firmly, "we all decided to come on this journey together. Sithlac and I won't leave you now, and whatever happens, don't give up. Together we might have a chance."

"Yeah, together," a deep voice rumbled from behind them, as Meathead tromped back into the clearing, clutching a gnarled chunk of wood half again his height, trailing thick clumps of earth in its wake—obviously something he'd just ripped out of the ground. "Not sure what we're gonna do, but we're gonna try, ain't that right, tiny?"

From his shoulder, the head of Yog popped up barely into view. "Yeah, yeah, whatever; I should've been dead four seasons ago anyway," muttered the goblin. "This is a pretty good way to go out, I guess. What a bunch of idiots we are—but I wouldn't have it any other way. Bring it on, you stupid banshee!"

"You're about to get your wish," Lyza replied, pointing at a dark cloud coalescing amid the trees overhead. The winds swirled and a thunderous roar split the air, whereupon a spinning mass of vapor descended toward the little group, wrapped around a core of whirling energy. As they watched, steeling themselves and fighting the overwhelming urge to flee, an angry female face took form within the miasma overhead.

"Sister mine, how long I've waited," screamed the wind in a cruel, taunting voice. "The hate I hold has not abated! Join me as you should've done...I promise we'll have lots of fun!"

A fiendish cackle followed, and the spinning winds whipped around the group, pelting them with dried leaves, clumps of snow, and other debris. In response, Meathead stepped forward, raising his arms and wrapping himself as best he could over the top of Sithlac and Lyza, turning himself into shelter of a sort. Simultaneously, Yog burrowed into the troll's pack, disappearing from sight.

Lyza hefted up her bow, swiftly drawing an arrow and pointing it at the mass of crackling energy. "Leave her," she hissed. "She's under our protection. I don't know or care what history you have—she did what she had to do to save our lives."

The creature overhead spun and swirled about, forcing Lyza to turn and try to hold her aim, despite the winds whipping at her from all directions. "Foolish elf, you can't hit me," laughed the storm, "How can you, if you cannot see?"

At that the cloud expanded, descending over the top of the clearing, completely blotting out the view in a spinning vortex of dust and debris. Sithlac squeezed his eyes nearly shut, stepped forward, and waved his spear around, struggling to come up with a way to fight something like this. In the gloom he caught sight of a small figure floating in the air, inside a bubble of calm, and he moved a few steps forward to find himself in safety, with Ithess bobbing up and down just over his head. Her tiny hands covered her face as she wept.

"We stand with you," Sithlac told her. "What know you of this creature? How can such a one be defeated?"

"You should've run and let me be," wailed the distraught zephyr, "now no safety can I see. She'll make me join her, this I know...you really dare not let me go. There's one way still to stop all this—strike me down and she'll desist."

Sithlac just stared at her, understanding at once what the little creature meant. As their eyes met he realized what must've happened, sometime in the distant past—her sister went too far, abusing her power over the winds, and became corrupted, turning into the banshee they now faced. Now, having committed the same baleful act, Ithess would likewise be transformed, and forever lost—unless Sithlac acted now to put a stop to it. He knew then exactly what she intended, and even as one of his eyes flicked out to his spear, he knew just as surely he could never follow through.

"I must find another way, oh yes," he muttered, turning his attention back to the battle. Outside, still sheathed in winds, the banshee bobbed up and down, back and forth amid her roiling clouds, not giving the others any kind of target. Meathead swung several times with his broken tree limb, while Lyza fired arrow after arrow into the bright core of the storm. Likewise, Yog occasionally popped out of his hiding place to throw something in the same direction, but none of these attacks had any discernible effect.

After another failed bowshot, Lyza lowered her weapon and muttered to herself, "Let's try something else." Then she raised a hand and began a chant, pointing in the general direction of the vortex before her. In response, Meathead also paused his swings, and started to hum loudly, in time with her casting. Almost immediately, the air began to slow, the spinning ball of light at the center gradually coming to a halt.

"So now the spells have joined the tale," wailed the storm. "Too bad they're all doomed to fail. Go on and try, if needs you must—it's fun to see them turn to dust."

"Go...now..." muttered Lyza through gritted teeth, obviously struggling to keep her spell focused. "Can't...hold her...long..."

Sithlac saw at once what she intended and rushed forward, out of the calm space by Meathead's feet. Instantly he felt the pounding of the winds on his face as he passed through Ithess's protective bubble. Obviously the banshee intended to smash through the defensive aura, and by the looks of things that would come very soon. Sithlac pressed forward into the maelstrom, holding Bongcor's spear with both hands, approaching the vortex one step at a time, struggling to spot the creature he knew had to be somewhere within...

He kept his left eye fixed on his target, but the other one flicked to the side as he spotted Yog also moving forward, low to the ground with a dagger clutched in his withered hands. The goblin's wrinkled face looked oddly warped by the force of the winds assaulting him, but he pressed on. Meanwhile, Lyza's chant repeated, the words somehow penetrating the storm, and the resistance faltered momentarily, giving Sithlac the chance to move a few steps closer. Yog almost simultaneously gave a shout of triumph and pushed rapidly ahead, lunging with his weapon and plunging it right into the middle of the vortex. For an instant Sithlac caught sight of his friend's toothy grin, before suddenly the little creature spun about, emitted a shrill cry of despair, and flew away into the darkness.

The winds redoubled then, pushing Sithlac back, driving him into the ground to roll back up against the troll's thick legs. Lyza gave a choking cough and fell backward, saved from falling only by the giant creature's meaty paw. A moment later Yog crawled out of the brush to lay gasping by the troll's right foot.

"Tried," mumbled Lyza. "Too strong...she's just...playing with us..."

The vortex rose over them, flowing in dark reds and pinks, the female face returning with a taunting leer. "You're fun, I truly must admit," laughed the banshee, "yet really don't know when to quit. Now sister dear, it's time we fly...for them, though, well, it's time to die."

The winds accelerated, closing in, wrapping the little group in a tempest unlike anything they'd yet encountered. Sithlac, Lyza, and Yog collapsed into a heap, huddled under the kneeling form of Meathead, even as flying sticks and pebbles bounced off his sturdy form. Just ahead of them all, now enclosed in a tiny ball of calm air, the miniature figure of Ithess hovered in place, wiping tears from her eyes as she sang one last time.

"No truer friends could I have had," she told them, the words just audible over the din, "still with me through the good and bad. I wish we had more time, but no...this is it, it's time to go. Although my heart must turn to frost, I weep for kinship that I've lost."

At that she shut her eyes and went silent, the only sound now the ferocious howling and bitter laughter from their foe. Sithlac, driven to his knees by the force of the winds, saw his end approaching and shut his eyes, knowing he'd made the right choice...and yet regretting how he'd now never get the chance to help find Bongcor.

Bongcor...the first friend he'd ever had...the only one back home he'd ever really considered as anyone other than just another gremlin. Someone he'd taken under his wing, taught how to face his fears, and worked alongside to achieve a greatness neither one of them ever could've found on their own. Someone who showed him that he didn't have to live a solitary life, that interacting and teaming with others had a greater meaning than he'd ever imagined.

In those last fleeting moments Sithlac thought back to how it all began. On the hunt, as always, until he met a sad, lonely faerie, singing in the dark...wishing only to be free...and he helped her, for reasons he still didn't quite understand. In the process something unlocked within him, leading him to befriend Bongcor, and these others...

And it all began with a song.

The song...!

He felt it welling up within him, as it had on several other occasions, like a light shining in the darkness. Sithlac heard the music, as he had that dark night long ago, and found himself humming along, the pleasant noise growing steadily louder. Almost unconsciously he opened his mouth, raising his voice, and through a dry, parched throat the song burst forth, a sound no gremlin could ever hope to make—yet still it found its way out nonetheless, pushing back against the wind, driving back the gusts, causing the banshee at last to quell its horrid laughter.

"What is this you dare now try?" shrieked the creature, its whirling core turning red with anger. "I'm tired of this, why won't you die?"

The ghostly face twisted up into a demonic sneer as the wind spun and swirled, but Sithlac didn't falter, holding his mouth open as the impossible song poured out into the rushing storm. Nearby, while most of his companions just stared at the gremlin in varying degrees of confusion and awe, Ithess suddenly darted up before them. "Quick, he's found a way to win!" she sang excitedly. "To help him now, you must join in!"

At that she turned about to face the banshee and lifted her own voice, doing her best to echo Sithlac's refrain. As she did this, the storm slowed its whirling, the lights dimming somewhat in the vortex. Bolstered by this, Ithess rose higher into the air, her bubble of calm air swiftly expanding wide enough to encompass the entire group.

Lyza, nodding in understanding, dropped her bow and reached for her backpack, drawing out her timaryn and adding its stringed notes to the song. Her voice joined in a moment later, aided by loud humming from Meathead, who simply stood there, his eyes shut with a wide smile plastered across his face. At his feet, Yog shook his head, mumbled something like "Goblins really shouldn't sing," and then started to do so anyway. At any other time the grating voice might've caused the others to cringe and cover their ears, but now, it meshed seamlessly with the rest, creating an almost visible wave of pure musical energy spreading outward all around.

Outside the bubble, the storm slowly collapsed in on itself. The banshee's face, screaming and spitting in frustration, gradually receded inward until only a small whirling cluster of dust remained. The air grew still, the leaves and other debris gradually settling down as the trees and bushes grew once again silent.

"No, it cannot end this way," whined the defeated banshee, the voice now sounding very faint and pitiful. "Please, don't do this, I can't stay…"

Ithess fluttered forward as the last of the winds died down, leaving behind only a tiny figure, ephemeral and smoky, in a vaguely zephyr-like shape. Sithlac and the others let their song fade out, and he felt the unnatural magic leave him at last, now naught but a memory. Tillianita gave him a gift, though he didn't understand its nature until now, and perhaps he never would—but he made good use of it in the end; that much he knew.

"Nassai, I'm sorry, this I'll say," said Ithess sadly, reaching out as if to take her sister's hands, but encountered only wisps of formless vapor. "I wish it hadn't gone this way. I really should've stopped you then, and now it's just what could've been."

The banshee before them began to spread out on the air, gradually becoming more hazy and indistinct. She looked up at her sister sadly, then gave a bright, hopeful smile. Her voice came only faintly, just barely audible, but they all heard it nonetheless.

"Don't mourn me now, you did what's right," said Nassai, her last words drifting away with the faint evening breeze. "You truly saved me here this night. Now I've but one...last gift...to give. All...you've...done...I do...forgive..."

The banshee's arms reached out to enfold her sister and then the smoky figure dispersed into the air, vanishing as though she'd never been.

Morningside Park – South of 116th Street

The forest returned to normal as the winds settled down. The rustling of branches overhead resumed their normal cadence, and a few night bird calls floated in from somewhere far away. The clattering and rumbling from the cars on the street drifted up from the road running by the park, the noises so ubiquitous none of the five companions even noticed their presence.

As Nassai vanished, Ithess collapsed into Lyza's hand, folding up into a tiny ball with her wings folded back behind her. "Poor little thing," said the elf, reaching down to collect her fallen bow from the ground by her feet. "We should move, before the patrol comes back—whatever damage that windstorm caused might get blamed on us. Come on."

She pushed past the others, heading out of the clearing, but found the going more difficult this time. The storm had thrown great drifts of snow and leaves up against the brushline, forcing her to poke and prod to find a safe way through. As she caught sight of a possible passage, Meathead came up and yanked the branches away with a quick motion of his enormous paws. This caused a shower of flakes to burst outward, covering everyone in a blanket of white.

"Nice job," muttered Yog, looking uncharacteristically downcast as he scuttled forward, into the opening the troll created. "Someone gonna tell me what that was all about just now, or do I have to guess?"

Lyza followed close behind the goblin, making sure Sithlac had room to keep up before answering. "Zephyrs are normally free spirits," she explained quietly, cupping the distraught Ithess carefully as she wound her way through the twisted undergrowth. "Depending on their role in things, they might have an occasional duty to perform, but mostly they do as they will—sailing on the winds, seeing the world, unfettered by the need to stay on the ground. Despite all that, they can't control the air directly, any more than you or I could use magic to move the earth, or summon fire to do our bidding. However, while you or I simply couldn't do something like that, no matter how much we tried, the power to tame the winds rests within each zephyr—a temptation they dare not indulge, lest it corrupt them as it did Ithess's sister."

"So you knew this all?" inquired Sithlac, trailing close behind the others, with Meathead pushing through right behind him. "A truth you dared not speak till now?"

"I suspected something similar, yes," answered Lyza carefully. "Ithess never told me directly, but I had an idea of what must've happened. I won't ask her for the details now, either. When she's ready, she'll explain, but I don't think she was directly responsible for her sister's predicament. She probably witnessed it, though, and that's why she's been hiding all this time, staying away from the outdoors, where she belongs. She knew her sister would come for her, consumed by hatred for everything she knew before she changed."

As Lyza spoke, she managed to push her way through the last of the tangled brush, emerging into another clear space, where drifts of snow now coated the surface of one of the running paths along the edge of the park. Just on the edge of their vision to the right, the track forked in two directions, one going further uphill, while the other descended into the deeper woods. Overhead, a single lamp glowed brightly, the light reflecting off the whiteness everywhere, making the whole area look nearly as bright as the dawn. Sithlac blinked at the sight of it, momentarily confused, before his eyes adjusted to the unusual glow.

The elf came to a halt and Ithess rose out of her palm, her butterfly-like wings fluttering rapidly to dislodge a few pesky flakes of snow. "What she says is mostly true," sang the little creature, miniature tears glistening on her cheeks. "She's not the sister that I knew. We joked and sang and loved to fly...it's such a shame she had to die."

"She died a long time ago," said Lyza in a quiet, calming voice. "What was left of her was caught in that terrible form, but no longer. Her trapped soul is free now—and so are you, by the way. No more hiding, Ithess! You can fly again, and go back to riding the winds, like you used to do. That's what Nassai would've wanted."

Ithess shook her head. "It's not that simple, so you see," she pointed out, rising up into the air, which remained completely calm around her. "The air no longer will help me. What we did, we did as one, and now my power's all but done. Nassai did not work alone—I helped, and now I must atone."

She dropped back down into Lyza's hand and curled back up, apparently done with the conversation. Sithlac tried to think of something else to say, but couldn't find the words—the zephyr appeared inconsolable, so instead he let her be. "Friend elf," he said, deftly changing the subject, "are we yet away from the patrol? Or should we make further haste?"

"This path junction marks their southern boundary," explained Lyza. "Meathead should recognize this spot, hmm?" She looked up at the troll expectantly.

"Yeah, yeah, it's my tribe's homeland thataway," he said, lifting an arm to point across the path to the right, toward the rocky ridge they'd been following since leaving the huge stone staircase behind. "I gots no interest in goin' home just now, though, and they ain't gonna want to see me anyways. We go across here, and through that way, but it's Dog Land—neutral territory, if you dare."

"Dog Land?" asked Yog nervously, twisting his knife back and forth in his hands.

"The place we need to reach isn't much farther," said Lyza, "but for whatever reason, the Men like to bring their dogs here, sometimes letting them run loose. I doubt there'll be too many around after that storm we just went through, but you can't be sure. I know a few hiding spots, but keep your eyes open for places to duck into if a dog shows up—and if all else fails, climb something and take cover. Now come on, there's no Men about just now—the sudden wind probably sent them all running for shelter, but they'll be back soon enough with it gone calm."

With that she jogged boldly ahead, uttering a faint chant that allowed her to dash easily across the snow without sinking in too badly. Sithlac dropped down on all fours to make the passage, hopping more than running, while Yog simply scrambled up onto Meathead's back. The troll, for his part, strode boldly forward, humming to himself, and the snow parted before him, as though avoiding his approach. As he reached the other side of the path, he hummed a bit louder, and the drifts behind him folded up once more, leaving no trace they'd crossed this way.

"Nicely done," said Lyza with a smile. "Now come on, the pond's not much farther."

Citizen's Reporter – Travis Hellerman's Office

"Hey, big guy, you might wanna take a look at the trending feeds..."

Travis Hellerman glanced up from his final editing pass to regard Grace as though she'd interrupted a meeting with the pope. "What is it now?" he demanded gruffly. "More squirrels gone wild?"

"No, this is Morningside Park again," chirped the endlessly happy secretary, not the least bit concerned by his caustic attitude, which she'd long ago learned to safely ignore. "Some kinda freak storm just blew through. There's all kinds of chatter about it. Just thought it might be worth looking into since you had that other thing going on there."

"Yeah, yeah, thanks for the update," groused the irritable reporter. "I'm almost done with this article, then I'll have a look."

"Sure thing. Heading out for a bit, you want anything?"

"Nah, I'm almost done for the day. I've got leftovers in the fridge at home, anyway. Thanks, though."

"Anytime."

As Grace swept back down the hall, intent on taking her dinner break, Travis went back to his computer. For a moment he felt tempted to go look at the feeds, but managed to stay focused on his editing, which only had a few more paragraphs to go. He finished up a few minutes later, slapped the file into an email, and sent it on its way before finally turning his attention to social media.

Sure enough, as Grace explained, there'd been some kind of weird weather phenomenon just after sunset in the park. He easily found several grainy shaky-cam videos, as well as a few injury reports, but nothing serious. Some called it just a freak windstorm, while others described at as nothing less than a winter tornado—the truth, as usual, would probably be somewhere in the middle. Travis occupied himself for a bit checking weather reports, but found nothing official, either in the forecasts or in any actual news footage.

The suspicious part of him wondered if this had anything to do with the strange creature sighting he'd been told about earlier—but that didn't seem to connect with the weather effect, which appeared centered on an area of the park somewhat further south. Travis wasn't about to call it a coincidence just yet, but as near as he could tell, the two events had no common ground.

Something strange is going on, he thought, drumming his fingers on the desk next to his keyboard. *There's a story here somewhere, and I'm going to find it. Just not tonight.*

With a few practiced keystrokes he set up a couple of filters to watch for anything else involving frog creatures, unusual weather, or any other weird reports involving Morningside Park. Then, switching the computer into hibernation, he gathered up his coat and briefcase and left for the day.

Morningside Park – Dog Run

The little group forged ahead through the undergrowth, avoiding the well-lit paths, which they could still see on occasion. For the first ten minutes or so, the trails remained deserted, but after a while the Men reappeared, walking or jogging along as they saw fit. Their guttural voices carried easily through the cool night air, and more than once Lyza called a halt while the group hastened to take cover in a wood-hollow or cluster of fallen branches. The few dogs they saw remained leashed, fortunately, for which Sithlac found himself immensely grateful.

After a while Ithess emerged from her malaise and took off, flying overhead enough to get a better view, occasionally calling out warnings or subtly altering their course. Lyza knew the way, however, and they made good speed, soon catching sight of the pond glittering and gleaming in the artificial lights surrounding it. They made their way over several small ravines before finally topping a rise to look down on the water from above. They stood atop a high cliff made of layers of rock, surrounded by thick clumps of trees and brush. Down below, the outer edges of the pond had frozen, leaving only small patches in the middle that hadn't quite gone solid. Quite a number of Men moved about on the paths beyond, chattering noisily and occasionally pointing strange objects out at the icy water.

"Surely you don't want us to go down there, do you?" demanded Yog nervously. "There's no way they can miss spotting us—it's almost like they're looking at us right now."

"Relax, they're just enjoying the view," said Lyza with a shrug. "Didn't you ever wonder: If the Men were capable of building their great towers wherever they wanted, why they didn't bother doing the same thing to this place?"

"Not really," Yog replied with a shrug. "Never been out here, so didn't know about it anyway until now."

"The simple beauty of it," commented Sithlac, "is more than they could bear to destroy."

"Exactly," Lyza replied, clapping her hands together. "That's exactly it. From this angle you can't see, but the Moon's up, and from their point of view, it probably looks spectacular, hanging out over the pond like that."

"The Moon?" inquired Yog eagerly. "Where is it? I gotta soak up some magic. Can I climb for it?"

"Yes, but be safe. You too, Sithlac—go get your fill. You might need it later."

Nodding, the gremlin followed Yog up one of trees that still had enough foliage to cover their ascent from prying human eyes. As they neared the top, they caught the glimmer of moonlight peeking through and Sithlac stopped at once, clinging to the branches with his feet while he threw his arms wide, soaking in the energy with abandon. Back home, he only rarely had the pleasure of absorbing night-magic directly from the Moon—usually he'd collect his share from the communal rations each evening, offered by collectors down on the commons. On occasion, if on a particularly time-consuming hunt, he might soak up some *dinathi-kai* through a handy window, but otherwise, the only time he ever faced the Moon directly was during mating season, when his mind was usually elsewhere.

Yog, slightly overhead, cackled with glee as he swiftly collected what he needed, quickly scurrying back down past his fellow darkling on his way back down. "Ohh, that feels so much better! Ready to take on those nasty elves now, that's for sure. Come on, slowpoke, let's get moving!"

Sithlac shut his arms and took a deep breath, mentally checking over his spells, ensuring the frost-ward and disguise were in full force. Then he followed Yog down, one eye catching sight of moonlight glinting off Ithess's wings as she descended close by. As he reached the lowest branches, Sithlac caught her singsong warning just in time.

"You shouldn't linger on this shelf," she called out hastily, "for now there comes another elf."

At that, Ithess darted away, disappearing in moments into a tuft of leaves nearby. Lyza looked up and caught sight of Sithlac and Yog emerging from the tree overhead. "You heard the zephyr, we'd better move. Stay close to the edge, and follow me—the nexus isn't far. We can easily—"

"Lyza!" a voice called out, coming up from behind them, back the way they came. "Please, I would speak with you! I mean no harm to you or your companions."

"Galisan," muttered Lyza angrily, recognizing the speaker at once. "If this is some trick—!"

They could see him now, running headlong through the brush, making no effort to hide himself this time. Although they couldn't spot anyone else nearby, the rest of his patrol couldn't possibly approach at the same speed without giving themselves away. "No trick," he yelled back. "I'm alone. I ordered my team to stay behind, so the risk would be mine to bear."

"Risk? What risk?" Lyza aimed an arrow at him, and he came up short, just beyond the edge of the brush. "You certainly didn't seem to care about risks a short while ago."

"That's because I had no idea you wielded such power," came the awestruck reply. Galisan steadied himself, slowly catching his breath, obviously having run hard to catch up to them. "After what you just did, my fellows consider themselves lucky we escaped your presence with our lives. To think you could survive an attack by a banshee—surely the battle will make a tale-song for the ages!"

"Not right now," insisted Lyza impatiently. "Like I tried to explain, we're on a mission, and we're not going to let you stop us."

"I wouldn't dream of it," Galisan insisted. "I just wanted to know— that story you told, of Men capturing Fey—is it true? If so, I want to help."

"You want to join us?" Lyza looked at him doubtfully, but she let her bow drop just slightly nonetheless. "You really think we'll trust you, after you tried to have us all killed?"

"No, no, I can't join you, much as I wish I could," explained the captain. "And please accept my apologies for that misguided act. I really did have explicit orders that I dared not disobey. Of course, your actions have rendered those somewhat moot." He glanced back behind himself, as though wary of someone watching.

Lyza put her arrow back in its quiver and lowered her bow. "Are you out here on your own, then? Not on official business?"

"No, this is just me. I'm not a captain of the guard right now, just helping a fellow elf in need. You've used the Waterfall Nexus before, I trust?" Seeing Lyza's nod, he continued quickly. "But you've never activated it yourself, have you?"

"No, but I'm familiar with—"

"If you don't have someone opening the portal for you," said Galisan quickly, "you need to utter the words with perfect clarity. One slip and you could wind up Gaia knows where. Let me anchor you, Lyza—that doesn't even come close to making up for what I tried to do, of course, but it's a start."

She glanced around at the others. Sithlac hopped forward, both eyes fixed on the elven guardsman, trying to decide what to say. He didn't know much about portals or anchors, but something in Galisan's voice made him feel at ease. "Though I have little reason to trust such as you," he said eventually, "I feel somehow that it's all right to do so."

The captain regarded him with a somewhat befuddled expression. "I've not had occasion to meet many gremlins," he remarked, "but you seem quite altogether unlike any other I've known."

"Yes, this I've heard quite often of late," commented Sithlac with a casual shrug. "I have neither the time nor the interest to explain, oh no. I wish only to find the faeries and then, should all go as hoped, locate my friend and return home at last."

"If you succeed," said Galisan, "I want to hear all about it, so send Lyza back with the tale. You have my word I'll grant you all safe passage next time—it's the least I can do."

Morningside Park – Above the Waterfall

Having accepted Galisan's offer of aid, the little group, now six strong, proceeded along the top of the cliff, carefully picking their way through the rocks and scrubby growths. Although a human might have great difficulty moving across such uneven, ragged terrain, for the Fey it proved a fairly straightforward, if somewhat ponderous, undertaking. The trees remained thick overhead, and although they could see plenty of Men along the path across the pond far below, they felt totally safe and covered the entire time.

At length they reached the nexus, which they felt rather than saw. The energy emanating from the focal point caused the air to become thicker, as though partly solidified into a kind of bubble against which they found themselves inexorably pushing. Even Ithess, normally unaffected by changes in the air, found the going difficult. They stopped as Galisan put up a hand, chanting a few words of power, and the nexus appeared before them, a spinning whorl of white sparks dancing in the shadows ahead.

"You can't see it from here," said Lyza, her face lit up with the reflected sparkles, "but just below us, coming out through the cliff itself, there's sometimes a waterfall. Right now it's probably frozen, but it's still quite entrancing. The Men preserved it for its beauty, but they had no idea they also preserved this, too. Lucky for us."

"We're supposed to step into that?" complained Yog. "While he's the one controlling it? Yeah, why am I suddenly not so keen on this idea?"

"It'll be fine, pipsqueak," grumbled the troll, reaching down to pluck the goblin off the ground and deposit him on his back. "Sithy trusts 'im, so should we. Seems to me he's got a way of knowin', y'know?"

"Not really," groused Yog, "but whatever. Anything bad happens, I'm blaming you!"

Meathead's rumbling laugh echoed off the rocks nearby. Galisan simply shook his head, marveling at the interplay between the others.

"I really must hear this tale of yours when you return," he said to Lyza. "How such a strange quintet as you came to join together will make quite the story, indeed. Now attend me as I open the nexus, and when you're ready, step through as one."

"I'll return, and tell you all, you can be sure of that," agreed Lyza, gathering up the others nearby. "Now follow me through, and don't hesitate, or you'll be left behind. This should only take a few moments. Oh, and thank you, Galisan—you're right, it'll be a whole lot easier with you assisting."

"Like I said, it's the least I can do." He flashed her a quick smile, which she returned, and Sithlac's dual eyes caught both of their unusual expressions simultaneously. Before he could consider what he'd seen, though, Lyza began to sing an elven spell, which Galisan echoed almost immediately. Within moments they all felt the pressure in the air lessen and then fade entirely.

As Lyza sang, Sithlac shut his eyes almost completely, caught up in the spell as he had been on other occasions before. This time, though, he could feel what she intended—to travel somewhere beyond this park. After a moment, he found he could see a place, an opening between several great trees, looking up at a smooth slope of bare stone topped by a square structure obviously put there by Men. The image in his mind looked like summer, for all the trees were green, the skies blue and flecked with clouds, with a strange pennant fluttering in the breeze above the out-of-place square building. Something about it looked familiar, in a way, though Sithlac knew he'd never seen the place before.

He felt a tug and opened his eyes, to find Lyza starting forward, her hand caught in his tunic, almost dragging him ahead. Meathead also ambled forward, Yog perched on his back, and in between them all came Ithess, zipping ahead to reach the nexus first. She vanished and then so too did Lyza and the troll. Without the slightest hint of fear, Sithlac followed, disappearing into the portal an instant later, and for the first time in his life, he left Morningside Heights behind.

Central Park – North Woods Nexus

The light from the nexus faded and Sithlac opened his eyes, swiveling them back and forth to take in his surroundings. He and his companions now stood amid three huge tree trunks stretching up into the clear night sky, the view obscured only by a few scraggly twigs from the sparse brush surrounding them. The cluster of trees stood adjacent to a huge rocky outcrop rising high overhead, while in the other direction, the ground also rose steadily up a surface of smooth, slick-looking stone. The valley they were in looked well-trod, and Sithlac felt a momentary surge of fear as he realized he stood among what must be thousands of footprints made by Men.

Nearby, Lyza clambered atop a large stone, peering each direction along the dirt path, staring into the darkness and listening. Though the sounds of distant vehicles penetrated the forest, rushing by on their endless travels through the city, the five new arrivals heard nothing else save an occasional night bird's call. No Men spoke, and no sounds of giants crashing through the forest reached their ears.

"I think we're safe for now," the elf called out after a moment. "This trail isn't often used after dark. The Men prefer more solid footing and better light."

Sithlac relaxed a bit, stepping up onto the rock to get a better look around. Yog did the same, by climbing up onto Meathead's broad shoulders, where he looked quite comfortable—a far cry from how fearful he'd been of the troll upon their first meeting. Meanwhile, Ithess took flight, ascending and disappearing into the darkness. Sithlac could still hear her buzzing about, though, in testimony to how much quieter this area seemed. Back in Morningside Park, the din from the nearby streets seemed all but overwhelming by comparison.

In darkness, Sithlac could see well enough, but only for short distances, so he couldn't see all the way up the smooth stone slope, but he felt he knew what must await atop that rise. "In a flash before we came, I saw a place," he said quietly, almost afraid to raise his voice in such placid surroundings. "A square dwelling of Man, high above this hill."

Lyza nodded. "To use the nexus I had to summon a mental image," she explained. "Obviously it must've carried over—you all probably caught a glimpse of it. The building's up there, and if you look close you can see a square shape blotting out the stars. The humans call it the Blockhouse. I have no idea what it's for, but it's more of a ruin than anything else. In the daytime, you'll find Men coming up and down this trail quite frequently to visit. They have a ritual where they stand in front of it, and smile, while they point little boxes at each other, but I don't know what that means."

"Sacred it must be," suggested Sithlac. "A place of pilgrimage, perhaps, but for us, best avoided, oh yes."

"Yeah, I don't wanna go up there," complained Yog. "All this wandering has me pretty exhausted. We gonna rest anytime soon?"

Lyza narrowed her eyes in his direction. "I thought you darklings were mostly nocturnal," she commented. "The Moon's not even over the rise yet and you're already talking about making camp?"

"Hey, I'm old, don't forget," Yog pointed out. "I need my beauty sleep. Plus, I'm pretty sure you and Meaty here aren't night critters, and neither are faeries—so how are we supposed to find them if they're in bed already?"

"Not to mention the owls," noted Meathead. "Probably won't bother us with me along, but who knows, they might like a tasty goblin for a snack."

"Okay, seriously, let's find a hole to crawl into now," insisted Yog, peering around nervously at the dark sky overhead, cowering as though expecting a huge bird to swoop down in silence at any second.

"Very well, and we don't even know where to start looking for these faeries, don't forget," noted Lyza with a shrug. "We talked about this earlier, but nobody ever had any good ideas on what to do about that, other than send Ithess out to search—but at her size she'd take days to cover even a small fraction of this park."

At the sound of her name, the zephyr dropped back down from overhead. "I'll try, if that's what I must do," she remarked in a slow sing-song, clearly worn out from the day's events, "but nothing more tonight—I'm through."

Noting Yog's use of the troll as a perch, Ithess seized the idea and fluttered down onto Sithlac's shoulder. One of his eyes swiveled around to look at her, and she smiled at it before huddling into the folds of his tunic, looking quite ready to pass out at any moment.

The gremlin smiled slightly at her choice of his thick neck as a resting-spot and swung his other eye to regard Lyza. "There will be no need to search, this I have realized," he noted cryptically. "We need find only a place to wait, a noteworthy place, and she will come to us."

The elf just stared at him doubtfully, while Yog gave a clipped laugh. "Really? You can summon faeries now? You sure sang like one earlier, that's for sure."

"Her song it was," admitted Sithlac freely. "A gift to me, now spent, and well indeed, oh yes, leaving behind only the memory of how and whence it came—and therein lies our answer. Thought I have, at length, upon my first meeting with the faerie, and what she did and said; and now, the memory clear, I remember all."

Lyza nodded. "What did she say, then, that could let you call her forth? Some secret spell or a twist of magic?"

"No, oh no, nothing so complex," replied Sithlac, his head bobbing up and down, as he savored the revelation to come. "When we met, she begged for aid, to be set free from her captor's lair. I could not do such a thing, this you know, but even if I had, with her wing broken, where did she have to flee, but out into the cruel world of Man? Yet she said to me these words, she did: '*Please, Sithlac, help me from this place—a bird will heed my call, and carry me home, this I know.*'"

At that, Meathead gave a low groan and nodded, the sudden shift causing Yog to scramble to keep his footing. "Yeah, sure, that's the way," he said approvingly. "Shoulda thoughta that, but then, I ain't seen faeries in so long, I forgot what they can do."

"So she calls a bird, so what?" demanded Yog. "What does that have to do with anything?"

"Everything, don't you see?" Lyza laughed. "He's right, I didn't even consider that, but then, I've never met a faerie at all. I'm surprised you have, Meaty, but then, you're a whole lot older than me. Good call, Sithlac— that's the perfect plan, and even better, it won't really work until morning, so we can find shelter for the night and get started with the dawn."

"Still not getting it," muttered Yog. "You all wanna fill in a poor, sleepy goblin or do I gotta come down and bang it out of your fool heads?"

Lyza smiled up at him. "Faeries are caretakers of nature," she told him patiently. "One of the things they do is make sure the animals and birds are all ready for winter. To do things like that, they have to talk to them. It's not the same as how we talk—mostly it's just basic ideas and urgings—but they can communicate well enough, or so I'm told."

"Still lost," muttered the goblin. "How does faeries talking to birds have anything to do with anything?"

"It's your idea," said Lyza, turning back to Sithlac. "Go ahead, tell him."

The gremlin nodded, puffing up his throat a bit with pride at having come up with this plan entirely on his own. "We need not seek her out at all, oh no," he said succinctly. "The birds of this place will find her for us."

Central Park – North Woods Trails

The ridge where they arrived turned out to be the back of a large outcropping of exposed rock, behind which the hillside dropped away, leading into thicker brush and snow-topped stones. Lyza led the group down into the undergrowth, pointing out the tracks of mice and other creatures, and a larger trail most likely made by raccoons. Of the other travelers, only Ithess had ever seen a raccoon, but Lyza's bombastic description made the beast sound immense and terrifying. Even worse, such creatures liked the nighttime as well, so they'd be out hunting right now. Another reason to find shelter at once, or so everyone agreed.

After more descending they came upon a thick tree branch fallen across a quartet of large stones jutting up from the middle of a flat piece of ground. The broken chunk of wood lay at a sharp angle, creating a cavity beneath, wide enough for all of them to fit inside. Ithess flew up to check the surrounding area while Sithlac and Yog took a closer look at the interior, finding little more than a few old spiderwebs easily cleared out by Bongcor's spear. Meathead only barely fit, but after a few minutes of digging, he hollowed out a wide enough space to make himself comfortable in the back end of the makeshift cave.

By the time Ithess returned, reporting no sign of any trails or other worrisome artifacts of Man, they'd carved out a reasonable shelter for the night. The troll lumbered out to search a bit further and soon returned with a great chunk of tree bark, which made a good cover for the entrance. With their dwelling thus prepared, he removed his pack and set about fixing a simple meal for everyone, regretting only that their current situation precluded any means of actually cooking a proper dinner. Nobody seemed to mind, just happy to fill their bellies after their long journey.

Yog fell asleep almost before finishing, and Ithess politely declined any food at all before succumbing as well. Meathead managed to put his pack in order before also collapsing into sleep, his low rumbling snores soon joining Yog's higher-pitched ones. That left Lyza and Sithlac as the only ones awake.

"I can stay on watch until the Moon's all the way up, if you'd like to nap," she said amiably. "I'm used to long days when I'm on the road."

"This is my hunting-time," explained Sithlac. "While I slept little this day, I am as yet not tired enough for bed."

"Okay, then I'll take my sleep shift now, and when you're ready, just wake me up. Before I shut my eyes, though, explain to me how you did that thing with the song earlier. I've never heard anything like that from a gremlin."

"When the faerie I did meet," explained Sithlac, "she begged me for aid, as I did say before. Her freedom was not mine to give, but a deal was struck: I would carry her from her perch to safer ground, and she would sing her song to me."

"So that's what it was," replied Lyza, nodding. "A faerie song. I bet you didn't think she'd take you literally, did you?"

"This I do admit, oh yes, for I wished naught but to hear her voice once more, so pleasing to the ears of such as I, living where no such sounds are made! Yet ever since, I've heard that song repeat, deep within myself, and now I know the why of it. She did give her song to me, exactly as she said she would, oh yes she did indeed."

"So you really had no idea that's what happened?"

"Oh no, never had I thought such a thing possible," replied the gremlin, shuddering a bit at the thought. "And it is well that I did not, lest I would try to remove it, and thus be denied the means of our escape this day. Yet now it's gone, and while I hear its echoes still, no more power does it have."

Lyza nodded again. "Let me ask you this, friend gremlin," she said somewhat worriedly, "do you think that's the reason you...well, I'm not sure how to put this, but...well, the reason you're so different than your fellows? Do you think that song changed you somehow, and that maybe without it you'll change back?"

"Possible this is indeed, oh yes," he replied somewhat disdainfully, "and yet, I hope not, for if changed I am, I like what I've become. In many ways, more difficult it is, for sure, but had I the choice to make, I would go back not at all."

"Good, I'm glad to hear you say that," Lyza commented with a smile, "because I like you, too, exactly as you are. If you feel yourself slipping, just hum that song to yourself again and remember who you are right now. If you need any help, don't hesitate to ask, either. That's what friends are for, after all. Now I'm going to get some sleep, and let me know when you're ready to change watch. Goodnight, Sithlac."

"Goodnight to you, friend elf," he replied as she stretched out upon the ground nearby, huddling up against Meathead's bulk. She shut her eyes, and perhaps fell asleep soon after, but if so, Sithlac couldn't tell. She didn't snore like the others, nor did her breathing appear to change.

For a while, he sat there twisting Bongcor's spear back and forth in his hands, thinking about her words, the faerie song, and how things had so quickly changed. Just a few moonrises ago, he would've never imagined being in a place like this, nor would he have wanted to be here at all. Yet now everything felt natural and right, like this is where he belonged.

"On the morrow, Bongcor," he whispered quietly to himself, running one hand gently up and down the smooth metal pole before him, "we come to seek you out, oh yes...and find you we shall, of this I am sure."

To Be Continued

in

*The Djinn of the
Upper East Side*

Available Spring 2022 from

Tanstaafl Press

Other Works Published by TANSTAAFL Press

Novels by Bruce Graw

Demon Holiday

Torval, Demon Third Class, Layer Four Hundred Twelve of the Eighth Circle of Hell, has been in the business of chastising sinners longer than he can remember. Delivering punishment is the only job he's ever known—the only job he's ever wanted. After Torval witnesses something unexpected, his demonic Overseer demands that he take time off to resolve this personal crisis. And so, Torval, the demon, finds himself sent on vacation . . .to Earth, the proving ground of souls!

Demon Ascendant

Torval, Demon Third Class, Layer Four Hundred Twelve of the Eighth Circle of Hell, on vacation to Earth has managed to find another demon, dated a woman and inadvertently explored some of the sins of humankind: greed, gluttony, and lust. Through all this, his biggest struggle involves deciding if he wants his holiday to end or to continue forever.

Lady Hornet

Elizabeth Fontaine is a lonely, ordinary young woman in a world where superheroes struggle daily against evil. To fill the empty void within her soul, she becomes a hero fangirl, following every super's event, subscribing to multiple fanzines, and never missing the daily superhero talk shows... until one day, fate grants her the opportunity to leave behind her boring, dreary life and become what she's always dreamed of...a superheroine!

Elizabeth learns the hard way the meaning of the phrase, "Caveat Emptor!"—let the buyer beware!

The Faerie of Central Park

The last of her kind in New York City, Tillianita tends the land and beasts as best she can, reluctantly obeying her departed father's warning to avoid humans at all costs. A freak accident casts her out of the relative safety of Central Park. Lost and alone with a broken wing, she wonders if she'll ever see her home again.

On his own for the first time in his life, college freshman Dave Thompson isn't sure he'll ever fit in. When he stumbles upon an extremely realistic fairy doll, he thinks perhaps it might make a good present for a future date until he discovers that it's not a doll at all. His find turns not only his life upside down but also expands his narrow view of the world.

Novels by Tom Gondolfi

An Eighty Percent Solution – CorpGov Chronicles: Book One

In a world where corporations suborn governments as a part of good business practice and unregistered humans can be killed without penalty, Tony Sammis, a midlevel corporate functionary, finds himself unwittingly a pawn in a guerilla war between a powerful cabal of business leaders and an elusive but deadly underground movement. His final solution to the biological terror unleashed mirrors Tony's own twisted sense of justice.

Thinking Outside the Box – CorpGov Chronicles: Book Two

Winning one war doesn't seem to be enough. Tony Sammis and the Green Action Militia are once again thrust into the center of a conflict that will change the lives of everyone in the solar system. This time they are allies with the fledgling CorpGov and even the United States government against the ravages of the corrupt Metropolitan Police force. The GAM and their allies are fighting a losing war with few soldiers and even fewer weapons. Behind the scenes, a humble and unsuspected power block lurks with its own axe to grind.

Self-interest, romance, freedom, and a lust for power simmer together in this chaotic soup of tension, intrigue, assassination, and war.

The Bleeding Edge – CorpGov Chronicles: Book Three

Tony Sammis and Nanogate lead a patchwork alliance that includes the nascent CorpGov, Green Action Militia, the president of the United States, the Pacific Northwest Mob, most of the megacorps and the United Brotherhood of Bodyguards. The war the CorpGov alliance knows they can't win has begun, but they are no longer fighting to win. Tony and Nanogate know they may not survive, but they intend to deliver the most grievous wounds they can. The most dangerous animal is one with no hope.

Window of Opportunity – CorpGov Chronicles: Book Four

Window of Opportunity offers short stories from the CorpGov Chronicles universe. They give backstories of familiar characters, provide foreshadowing for upcoming novels, and paint color onto what makes the CorpGov universe unique. "Life Cycle" fills in some background on how a young Christine becomes the sociopath that we know and love. A corporate sponsored final solution to an ongoing brush war in South America can be found in "Lose-Lose.""Come to Jesus Moment" tells us more about Michael Beckman-Ford (son of Nanogate) and how he finally makes his first mark on the world. Interpol uncovers prophetic corruption in the church in "Pain Point" and continues into the story "Kick into the Long Grass." Grandma Ice must deal with a hate crime against her family in "Cradle to Grave.""Negative Growth" shows the impact of overpopulation on something as normal as the birth of a child. One man's unique solution to a corporation changing its retirement criteria is investigated in "Exit Strategy." And MANY more! Twenty-eight tales of the trials, victories, and failures in the dark future.

Toy Wars

Flung to a remote world, a semi-sentient group of robotic mining factories arrive with their programming hashed. They can only create animated toys instead of normal mining and fighting machines. One of these factories, pushed to the edge of extinction by the fratricidal conflict, attempts a desperate gamble. Infusing one of its toys with the power of sentience begins the quest of a 2-meter-tall purple teddy bear and his pink polka-dotted elephant companion. They must cross an alien world to find and enlist the aid of mortal enemies to end the genocide before Toy Wars claims their family—all while asking the immortal question, "Why am I?"

Toy Reservations

For years the living toys of Rigel-3 live in the peace that their president for life, Don Quixote, fought so hard to achieve. Their former masters, the Factories, watch on in silence as President Quixote leads his people through many of the growing pains of a new society. On the anniversary of their tenth year of peace, the exiled and mentally unbalanced Isp returns at the head of a massive new Army of the Humans. He openly announces his intent to replace President Quixote's democracy with a theocracy, either peacefully or by force.

Wayward School

After a media blitz that surpassed the Rodney King riots, the Patty Hearst trial and the acquittal of OJ Simpson combined, Elizabeth sits on Alcatraz' high-tech, death row awaiting execution at the age of thirty. A Catholic priest convinces Elizabeth to tell her story as a warning to other young women who might find themselves in similar circumstances. Elizabeth shares how as a teen she is barely tolerated in an abusive family. When the private shame of her rape becomes an unwanted pregnancy, her father coldly sends her away to a school for wayward girls. At the School Elizabeth trades her naiveté for a home and family of sorts. Out of her unique position and her nightmarish start to adulthood Elizabeth goes on to save tens of thousands of lives, for which a jury of her peers condemns her to die.

Anthologies by TANSTAAFL Press

Witches, Warriors, and Wyverns
Enter the Apocalypse
Enter the Aftermath
Enter the Rebirth

www.ingramcontent.com/pod-product-compliance
Lightning Source LLC
Chambersburg PA
CBHW051334020726
47501CB00007B/2080